HANNAH FRASER'S
Autumn

HANNAH FRASER'S AUTUMN

The following is a work of fiction. All names, characters, places, and incidents are the product of the author's imagination. Any resemblance to persons, living or dead, is entirely coincidental.

ISBN: 979-8-9918823-3-0 (paperback)
ISBN: 979-8-9918823-2-3 (hardcover)

LCCN: 2025919698

Cover design by Alt19 Creative.

Printed in the United States of America.

First printing, 2025.

Sunny Day Press
Kalamazoo, Michigan

www.ursiengebretsen.com

HANNAH FRASER'S

Autumn

URSI ENGEBRETSEN

ALSO BY URSI ENGEBRETSEN

Summer at Fraser's Mill

For Cili, the best of sisters

Table of Contents

Hannah's Bank Account

"Your payment method was declined."

Hannah Fraser stared at the words on the card reader's screen. There must be something wrong with it.

"Try it again?" The platinum-haired mall cashier gestured with sparkly fingernails.

Hannah reinserted her debit card and waited for it to authorize. Hopefully she'd gotten everything at this store that she'd need for her "fall styles" video. Should she have gotten crew socks? Supposedly everyone was wearing them these days. Well, she wouldn't show her footwear in the video.

"Your payment method was declined."

Oh, no. Something must be wrong with her bank account. Maybe her card was locked. Maybe somebody had stolen her card number and used it to make fraudulent purchases. Hannah took a deep breath. Speakers in the ceiling above her blared pop music from about a decade ago.

"Do you have another payment method?" The cashier tapped her nails on the counter. A throat-clearing noise behind Hannah told her other customers were waiting.

$157 for the clothes she needed to buy. Hannah didn't carry that kind of cash. Her only cash right now was a two-dollar bill she couldn't bring herself to spend. But she did have a credit card.

"I've got another card," Hannah said. She wrestled with her wallet. The credit card ought to be in here under all these coffee shop loyalty cards.

Where was it? Hannah pulled out the whole stack of cards and sorted through them. Nothing. No credit card. Oh, no.

"Found it?" The cashier's voice seemed to come from a distance.

"No." Hannah thumbed through the stack one more time. Where was that card? It had to be there.

It wasn't. Hannah shoved everything back into her wallet, straightened herself to her full height of five foot six—plus three-inch heels—and faced the cashier. "I'm sorry," she said. "I can't find it. I'll have to look for it at home."

The cashier nodded, her expression telling Hannah she saw this kind of thing every day. How was this happening to Hannah? She'd always pitied people who had to put things back because they couldn't afford them. The cashier probably thought Hannah was an irresponsible person who went shopping when she was flat broke.

"Want me to hold the things for you?" the cashier asked.

"Sure," Hannah said. "Thanks. I'll be back."

The cashier whisked Hannah's bag behind the counter. Hannah stepped aside and let the next person in line go past.

What a waste. A fifty-minute drive to Traverse City's mall—not even a big mall like she was used to—and she couldn't buy anything. She'd better check her bank account. Hannah walked out of the store, head held high.

In the middle of the mall, near the food court, Hannah sat on a bench to check her mobile banking app.

$0.67. Sixty-seven cents. Hannah's stomach dropped. Where had all her money gone? She was never out of money. She had heard of lots of people getting their card number stolen. Maybe some thief was having a good time in Florida buying jewelry with her money.

But her account history only held familiar-looking purchases. Fraser's Mill gas station. Gas was sure high these days. Some online purchase, $148. It must have been that cream-colored coat she saw in an ad and couldn't resist. Groceries. New shoes. Restaurants in Cadillac. Movie streaming services. Student loan payment. Phone bill. Fee from her gym in Chicago. She couldn't cancel it unless she showed up at the gym in person. On and on, down the list, the truth sank in: she had spent all her money.

A panicked feeling gripped Hannah in the middle of her chest. This couldn't be happening to her. She had always had enough money to pay for the things she needed. Stuck in Fraser's Mill for the summer with nothing to do, she'd spent more online than usual. Her monthly trust fund payment must be used up, as well as the revenue from her video channel. What would her parents say if they learned she had run herself out of money?

And she still didn't know where her credit card was. Maybe it was at home. She should go look for it. There was no point hanging around the mall—she couldn't buy anything. She'd planned to have lunch at a restaurant, but now she'd have to go home hungry. Good thing her car already had enough gas.

Hannah sighed and headed for the mall exit. This whole thing was annoying, frustrating, and totally humiliating.

She could hear Dad's voice. "I've decided to give each of you children a monthly trust fund payment so you can afford to do things that interest you—like volunteering or travel or creative projects—without worrying too much about money. But I expect each of you to use your payments wisely."

Quite a few things on Hannah's bank statement wouldn't match up with Dad's idea of wise spending. The last thing she wanted to do was ask her parents for money. Her siblings probably never had that problem. They were all doing well for themselves. Hannah didn't want to be that one kid who couldn't make it and had to be bailed out by her family.

She could make it until the next month's trust fund payment—about a week away at the beginning of September—if she used her credit card to buy everything and paid it off when the trust fund money came in. That is, if she could find the card. Either way, she also needed a way to make more money so this didn't happen again. If she wasn't making enough with her video channel to supplement her trust fund, she might have to go back to some random job—at least until her channel's revenue improved. This wasn't what she wanted, so many years after graduating college. She'd said she was going to succeed as an influencer, and she was going to do it, even if it wasn't easy.

Hannah's Town

During the fifty-minute drive back to town, Hannah had time to mull things over. It was a warm day in late August, and she was grateful for her car's air conditioning. At least, even though she had missed lunch and had to leave all her shopping bags at the mall, she wouldn't arrive home all hot and sweaty.

If she could call the log house in the tiny town of Fraser's Mill home. Despite spending the whole summer there, Hannah still didn't feel like she belonged. Home was Chicago, and Hannah couldn't wait to get back there.

Earlier in the year, it had seemed like a great idea to spend the summer in a small town. Fraser's Mill was important to Hannah's family. Her grandfather, Theodore Fraser, had built the water-powered sawmill that started the town in 1952. Theodore had also built a log house on the river. Now he and Grandma were retired in Florida, and they had sold the house to Hannah's parents. This summer, since Hannah's parents were traveling a lot, they had told Hannah she could stay in the Fraser's Mill house if she wanted.

She had jumped at the chance. How many twenty-seven-year-olds got the opportunity to stay in a riverfront log house for a whole summer for free? It would be the best vacation ever, and she could get a lot of content for her channel.

Now August was ending, and Hannah was vacationed out. She'd done everything there was to do in this little town in the first few weeks.

The road wound past farms and through pine forests, past Interlochen State Park, between lakes, and through more trees. It was amazing how long she could drive and be in the middle of nowhere the whole time.

At last the woods gave way to Fraser's Mill. The first structures in town, coming from the north, were the buildings that belonged to the lumber mill, housing the more modern sawing equipment and the office. The original water-powered mill, which was still running, was on the river.

Next door to the mill, right on the water, was the log house Theodore Fraser had built. It was a large house, big enough that in the old days Hannah's grandparents had invited the whole town to their house for parties. It had a living room with a twenty-foot ceiling stretching all the way up to the loft, a partial second story. A deck out back, outside a walk-out basement, looked over the water. A tennis court sat to the left of the house.

In that big house, Hannah rattled around by herself like a solitary penny, but she got to stay there for free, which was a definite benefit. And she liked tennis, when she had someone to play with. Currently, she didn't.

Back in Chicago, Hannah hadn't lacked for friends and family and tennis partners. She hadn't realized how exciting her life was until she'd traded it for the boring peacefulness of rural Michigan. But there wasn't anyone in Fraser's Mill that she was close enough with to invite over.

Hannah parked in the driveway and struggled with the unwieldy front door lock. Inside, she kicked off her high-heeled sandals, tossed her sunglasses on the entryway bench, and headed upstairs. That credit card had to be here somewhere, unless it had been stolen.

Where had she last seen it? She racked her brain. The last time she remembered using it was in April, when she had flown cross-country and rented a car for her friend Becca's wedding. Had she used it after that?

She wouldn't have put the card down someplace random. It wasn't in her purse. Maybe it was in a different purse. Or her backpack.

After a frantic rummage, Hannah finally turned up the missing card. It was in an outer pocket of one of her old purses. She must have put it back there in a hurry instead of in her wallet. Good thing she'd brought that purse with her, even though her sister had laughed at her for packing half her bedroom. Thank goodness, she could access money now. Dad still wouldn't be happy. He had strong feelings about racking up credit card debt. But she wouldn't spend any more than necessary, and her trust fund money would come in on the first of September. Dad had told her to put a small charge on the card every month and pay it off promptly to build credit, but she kept forgetting to do it. She'd barely used the card at all, even though she'd had it for years.

Wait a minute. That card must be really old. What was its expiration date? She flipped it over. Oh, no. It expired in July.

They must have sent a replacement in the mail. Her parents had been forwarding any important mail that came for her while she was in Fraser's Mill, but maybe this one had slipped through the cracks. Hannah pulled out her phone and called her mom.

She reached voicemail. Mom must be busy. It was Saturday, after all. Maybe she was having lunch with friends. Hannah left a message, asking whether a replacement credit card had arrived for her earlier in the summer.

Should she call Dad too? No, he was probably on the golf course and wouldn't answer anyway. Besides, it felt easier to ask Mom about this. It was too late today for her parents to send the card in the mail, and in fact, there was no way they could mail it before Monday. Hannah would have to get along without it until then. Maybe the store wouldn't hold her saved items that long, but she could find the same things if necessary.

In the meantime, she needed to focus on a way to make money. She should make her video for this week, hopefully one good enough to get a lot of views.

Hannah had been running a video channel for three years. Every Tuesday she uploaded a new video. In Fraser's Mill, she'd been doing a series titled "Summer in Small-Town Michigan." She had given a tour of her family's sawmill; she had gone fishing for the first time; she had interviewed Doc Johnson, the young town doctor; and she had covered the town's Fourth of July.

At this point she was almost out of creative video ideas. Not much went on in Fraser's Mill at any given time. The next big thing was the town's fall festival. By that time, the beginning of October, Hannah would be back in Chicago.

Hannah started putting back all the things she'd flung around the room looking for her credit card. What a mess!

What video could she make, now that she couldn't make the video about this fall's clothing styles? She lived next door to Elaine, the town librarian. Maybe she could do a video tour of the library. No, the library closed early on Saturdays.

Maybe her sister-in-law Christine would have ideas. Christine was married to Hannah's oldest brother Steve. Steve and Christine lived forty-five minutes from Fraser's Mill with their four-year-old daughter, Evelyn, and their one-year-old son, Noah. Steve was the boss at the lumber mill, having taken over from Dad. Christine stayed home with the kids. She had gone to beauty school before she met Steve, and she still styled hair occasionally for weddings and special events. She also kept up with a lot of homemaker video channels.

Hannah called Christine.

"Hannah! What's up?" Christine asked.

"Hey, Christine," Hannah said. "I wondered if you would give me a little advice. I'm trying to come up with an idea for this week's video for my channel, and I'm stumped."

"Hmm," Christine said. "Have you done a tour of the sawmill yet? I don't think Steve would mind, as long as you're not underfoot when they're busy."

"I already did that one," Hannah said.

"You could review a restaurant," Christine said.

"I did that too. There's only one restaurant in town."

Christine laughed. "I forgot Fraser's Mill is so tiny. I can see why you're stumped for ideas. You could drive out to the lake and do a beach video."

"I've done so many beach videos in Chicago, my viewers are probably sick of them," Hannah said.

"Well, I'm out of ideas. Have you tried looking online for inspiration?"

Hannah sighed. "I guess I'll do that."

"I hope you find something. I'd better get off—Evelyn wants me to braid her hair."

"Oh, sure," Hannah said. "Thanks, Christine. Bye."

As she hung up, Hannah got an idea. Christine was a fantastic hairstylist. Why not go out to Christine's and shoot a hairstyle video?

Hannah called back.

"Christine," she said breathlessly, "sorry to bother you again, but I've got an idea. Would you be willing to do a hairstyle video tutorial for my channel?"

"Video tutorial?" Christine asked. "I don't know, Hannah. I don't like being on camera."

"We don't have to show your face," Hannah said. "We can set up the camera so the viewers only see your hands doing the hairstyle. You must know dozens of good styles."

Christine hesitated.

"I'll make it up to you," Hannah said. "I'll trade you free

babysitting. You and Steve can have a nice date night, any time you pick, and I'll watch Evelyn and Noah."

"Steve and I haven't been on a date in a while," Christine said. "All right, I'll do it. When? Today?"

"Sure, if you're available," Hannah said. "What are you up to now?"

"I'll be at home all afternoon. Steve's working overtime at the mill. He won't be home till late."

"Perfect," Hannah said.

∽∾∿∽∾∿∽

Hannah knocked at Steve and Christine's door. She had been going to ring the doorbell, but she didn't want to wake baby Noah if he was napping.

Steve and Christine lived in a comfortable two-story house not far from Lake Cadillac. It was a long commute back and forth to Steve's work in Fraser's Mill, but the couple preferred that to living in such a small town. Christine had a lot of mom friends in Cadillac, so there were plenty of kids for little Evelyn to play with. Shopping and dining were also more convenient in the city. Compared to Chicago, though, Cadillac was nothing.

Christine answered the door. "Come on in, Hannah."

Hannah's sister-in-law was a cheerful woman with chestnut hair, brown eyes, and dimples in her cheeks. She often wore red lipstick, even when—like today—she was casually dressed in jeans and a striped T-shirt. The bold red suited her. Hannah tended toward more neutral tones herself.

"Aunt Hannah!" Evelyn appeared, flinging herself at her

aunt. "Yay!"

Christine laughed. "She's hoping you'll play dolls with her when you're done filming. She keeps telling me about the story you made up for her dolls the last time you watched her."

Hannah tousled Evelyn's blonde curls. "I'd love to play dolls," she said. "Right after we finish."

"I braided her hair, but she took the braids right back out." Christine shook her head, smiling. "She doesn't like the feel of them. So, Hannah, what do you want me to do with your hair?"

"I'm not sure. I don't know how to do anything with it."

Christine shook her head. "It's not too hard to learn," she said. "All right, then. Let's do something easy, so you can do it yourself after you watch the video. I'll try a few different kinds of half-ups."

The video process went swiftly. Christine wasn't used to making videos, but she was good at explaining things. As she deftly twisted Hannah's straight honey-brown hair into different styles, she broke down the process into steps that didn't sound too hard.

"What do you think?" Christine asked, when the last style was finished and the camera was off.

Hannah turned her head this way and that, surveying Christine's work. "I like it. You're right. I ought to do more with my hair. Thanks a lot, Christine. I think this will be a nice change of pace for my channel."

"Stay for dinner?" Christine asked. "Steve says not to wait for him. He doesn't get off till seven."

In the excitement of the video-making, Hannah had forgotten

her missed lunch. "I'd love to. I'm starving."

Christine laughed. "Did you skip lunch again?"

"Not on purpose," Hannah said. "I kind of forgot."

Christine shook her head. "You'd better eat a snack. We're having Crock-Pot beef and gravy over noodles, and I haven't started the noodles yet."

"I want a snack too." Evelyn appeared in the doorway, now wearing a pink cape and a plastic tiara.

Hannah laughed. "Aunt Hannah will find you a snack, princess. Then we can play dolls before dinner."

৶৶৶৶৶৶

Hannah really had been hungry. Over beef with noodles and Christine's excellent kale salad, the miserable tension of the long day finally began to evaporate.

"Christine, can I tell you something?" she said, clearing bright fiesta-colored plates off the table after dinner. "I don't really want to tell it around the family."

She hadn't come out here planning to tell Christine about her money troubles, but she had to talk to somebody. She wouldn't make a big deal out of it, though.

Christine put her head on one side. "Is this about a guy? Have you found the other half of your 'power couple'?" Her eyes were teasing, but kind.

Hannah raised her eyebrows. "You think I'm going to find the other half of my power couple in Fraser's Mill?"

"I thought there was somebody. Didn't you say something about some guy you were playing tennis with?" Christine

13

loaded silverware into the dishwasher.

Of course Christine remembered. Ever since she and Steve had gotten married, she'd been on a mission to find a man for her sister-in-law. She'd never suggested a guy that Hannah would dream of dating, but she was persistent—coming up with everybody from the "cute pizza delivery guy" to the "local butcher, who was such a nice uncle to his little nieces."

Hannah pushed her hair back. "Oh, him. That didn't come to anything. He's dating somebody else. Where do you keep your broom?" She opened a closet door. A bag of chips fell down on her head. There was the broom, next to some pantry shelves.

"Oh," Christine said. "I'm sorry. Do you want to talk about it?"

Hannah shook her head. "Not right now. It was a while ago. I've been trying not to think too much about it."

A handsome face with laughing blue eyes flickered in Hannah's memory. Doc Johnson wasn't easy to forget.

Early in the summer, Doc had unknowingly swept Hannah off her feet. In a tiny town like Fraser's Mill, Hannah never expected to meet a guy that interested her, until she met this young, handsome doctor at a parish picnic. He had just taken over the town's medical practice from his uncle.

Doc was friendly, funny, and well-educated. When he smiled, his face crinkled in a way that made Hannah's heart race. He intrigued her in a way the farm and mill boys of Fraser's Mill didn't have a chance of doing. He and Hannah hit it off right away—or so she thought. In the beginning of the summer, Doc took it upon himself to show Hannah around town. He'd been there since January, so he knew more people and was involved in town activities. He learned Hannah liked tennis, so they played quite a few matches on her home tennis court. He convinced her to sing in the choir for the noon Latin Mass at St. Anthony's. He went with her to town events where she otherwise would have known no one. It had been so much fun, hanging out with him.

And then Grace Murray came to town to work in her parents' grocery store, and Doc fell hard for her. His feelings for Grace were obvious from the first day he told Hannah about this new girl in town who mistook him for a car thief. It became increasingly obvious that Hannah was never getting out of the friend zone. Then, a number of weeks ago, she'd heard that Doc and Grace were officially dating.

Doc wasn't easy to forget, but talking about it wouldn't make things any better.

Christine's face was sympathetic. "Aw, Hannah. There's got to be somebody around here for you. Maybe Steve knows a good guy at the mill. There's this dispatcher, Jack, I think his name is—"

"I'm done with Fraser's Mill guys." Hannah swept vigorously. How could any of the guys around here compare with Doc? She'd never find someone else that impressive in Fraser's Mill.

"Anyway, it wasn't about guys," she said. "It's about money. Which is why I don't want it told all around. I'm gonna be okay, and I don't want people telling Dad I'm not financially responsible. I mean, I don't think he would be mad if he heard, but he'd be disappointed in me, and I don't want that."

"What happened?" Christine asked.

Hannah filled her in on the shopping trip, the empty bank account, and the expired credit card.

"So now I have to wait to learn if the new credit card's at home," she said. "And I won't have any actual money until my trust fund comes in on the first. I already got this month's payment from my channel, and I guess I used it up."

"Are you going to be okay for the next few days?" Christine asked. "Do you have enough groceries? Can I lend you anything?"

It was nice of Christine, but it would get around to the family and make her look bad. Hannah shook her head. "No, thanks," she said. "I got myself into this mess, and I can get myself out of it. It's only until Thursday."

"But what if you need gas or something?"

"I won't drive anywhere," Hannah said. "I'll find things to do in Fraser's Mill. And I've got food left in the pantry. It won't be great, but I'll make it through."

Christine shook her head. "I don't know. I don't like the idea of you being stuck without any money at all. I know what Steve would say."

"Yeah, me too," Hannah exclaimed. "He'd say, 'Hannah, you ought to get a job.' He'd give me the whole big-brother lecture about being responsible. And he'd tell Dad about the whole thing, and there'd be an uproar."

Christine shook her head. "Steve wouldn't do that. I mean, he'd probably suggest getting a job other than your video channel, but I don't think he would tell your dad."

Christine must see Steve through rose-colored glasses. Growing up, Hannah had often been the recipient of Steve's big-brother lectures, and she didn't want another one.

Hannah swept even more vigorously. "I'll be fine. Don't worry about me. I was just venting, that's all. I've been stewing about it all afternoon, and I had to tell somebody."

"You're sure you won't let me help you?" Christine asked.

"Positive," Hannah said. "Thanks anyway."

Diner Food and Disappointment

It was a good thing Hannah had a video to edit, because the next few days, cooped up at home without money, felt like the longest days of her life. She hadn't realized how often she drove out of town or how much she went shopping. She couldn't even rent movies online.

Mom had found her new credit card in a stack of mail and sent it to her. It was supposed to come on Wednesday, the day before Hannah's September trust fund money would come in.

On Tuesday, after getting her video finished and posted, Hannah found herself at loose ends. She might as well clean her room. She'd been putting it off, and now she had no excuse.

While sorting through old mail, shredding things she didn't need, Hannah found a birthday card her grandparents had sent her earlier this summer. Inside the card, U.S. Grant's face looked up at her—a fifty-dollar bill. She'd already sent a thank-you note, but had forgotten to put the money in her wallet.

Hooray for her grandparents! Good thing she'd forgotten about that birthday money. Now she could buy something.

Hannah would be responsible with the money. But she was sick of eating at home. She put twenty dollars in her gas tank, bought fifteen dollars' worth of groceries at Murray's Grocery (just the basics—chicken, salad stuff, yogurt, and brown rice), and saved fifteen dollars for Chuck's Diner, which was the only restaurant in town if you didn't count the tavern.

The diner sat in the center of town, right down the street from Hannah's house and the sawmill. Usually she would drive there, but today she decided to save gas by walking. It was a nice evening, anyway. And although Fraser's Mill was a dull little town in the middle of nowhere, Hannah had to admit it was a pretty town with a lot of nice trees.

Chuck's Diner was almost as old as the town. It had been started by the husband of Hannah's next-door neighbor, Elaine Keller. Now the diner was run by Charlie, the couple's grandson. It served American food along with some German and Italian family specialties. Hannah was usually health-conscious, but she'd been trying to use up the same enormous bag of kale for the last few days. The idea of old-fashioned comfort food made her mouth water. Maybe she'd get the meatloaf.

She walked in, looked around, and wished she hadn't. At the farthest booth of the restaurant, by the window, sat a couple Hannah knew: Doc Johnson and Grace Murray. Hannah hastily turned away.

It wasn't like Doc and Hannah had dated. He'd never told

Hannah he liked her. He had never asked her on a date. He used the word "friend" more than Hannah would have liked. But the two of them had always seemed to have such a good time together.

Then Grace had come to town, and the next thing Hannah knew, she had lost the one real friend she'd made in Fraser's Mill. Doc wasn't unfriendly to her by any means, but she felt awkward talking to him now that he was in a relationship. Hannah and Grace didn't really click. And besides, Hannah would rather die than go around as their third wheel.

Hannah didn't want to get a booth now. Doc and Grace seemed absorbed in conversation, but they'd be sure to notice her eventually. They might feel obliged to say hi. She'd better get takeout.

Here came Charlie to take her order. Thank goodness.

"Could I please get the meatloaf to go?" Hannah asked.

Charlie nodded. "Just a minute."

Hannah sat at the end of the bar, head bent over her phone. With any luck, Doc and Grace wouldn't notice her. The diner was busy this time of day, and if Doc or Grace did look over, Hannah might look like any random brown-haired woman.

Someone tapped her on the shoulder. It was an older woman she didn't recognize, wearing a blue tracksuit.

"Are you Hannah?" the woman asked. "I'm Barb. I've seen you around town quite a bit this summer. I know your grandparents."

"It's nice to meet you," Hannah said.

Barb nimbly climbed onto the barstool next to Hannah. "You're always by yourself," she said. "A while ago I kept seeing you with Doc Johnson. That's okay. Sometimes it takes people a while to figure out what they're looking for. You just need to find a nice guy who's right for you."

Hannah sat back, rubbing her neck. Who was this lady, and why was she cross-examining Hannah about her love life?

"Thanks," Hannah said. "I'm okay on my own right now."

Barb shook her head. "I could introduce you to this sweet guy who rents my basement," she said. "He's single. Do you think you'd be interested in going out to get coffee with him, if I gave him your information?"

Hannah was being asked on a date, vicariously, by a guy's landlady?

"Thanks, but I'm doing okay," she said. "I've got family close by. I'm running a video channel. And I babysit my niece and nephew. I'm not lonely."

Barb pursed her mouth dubiously. "Let me know if you change your mind." She disappeared, leaving Hannah alone at the bar.

"Hannah," Charlie said from behind the counter. "You got the meatloaf, right? It's been sitting here a couple minutes."

She'd been distracted from watching for her food. Hannah paid and turned to go—just as Doc and Grace approached the counter. That woman had held her up at the worst time. Well, she hadn't studied acting for nothing.

Hannah put on the friendliest smile she could muster. "Hey."

"Hey, Hannah." Doc's cheery face showed no hint of awkwardness. "How are you doing?"

"Fabulous," Hannah said. "How are you two?"

"Wonderful," Doc said.

"Great," Grace said. She smiled, but if Hannah wasn't imagining things, she did look a little awkward.

"Well"—Hannah held up her box of meatloaf—"I'd better get home before this gets cold."

"Sure. See you around, Hannah," Doc said easily, and turned to the counter to pay.

Hannah nodded at the couple and started for home, head held high, walking as fast as she could walk and still look dignified. One did not sprint through the streets of a small town clutching a box of meatloaf.

Only a few more weeks, and she would be home in Chicago. She wouldn't run into Doc and Grace everywhere.

Of course, it would be better to get over Doc. It wasn't like she was sitting around mooning over him. But she had enjoyed his friendship and his company. And the bitter disappointment that he wasn't interested in her still stung.

✤

When she got home, Hannah was determined to blast the whole thing out of her head. She put on the Beach Boys at high volume, danced around the kitchen as she set the table (food tasted better on a real plate than on a Styrofoam tray), and turned on the living room TV.

She was sitting down to enjoy her meatloaf and watching Superman rescue Lois Lane for the hundredth time when the doorbell rang.

It was Elaine, her next-door neighbor. Elaine was a wiry, energetic woman Hannah could hardly believe was in her late seventies. She ran the town library, even though she was retired, because she loved being around books.

"I hope I'm not bothering you," Elaine said. "I have a favor to ask. Would you help me move a bookcase from my car to my basement?"

"Sure! How big is it?" Hannah asked.

"Oh, not too big," Elaine said. "But I thought I'd better not do it myself. If I fell on those hard stairs of mine, I probably couldn't get back up them to call for help."

"I'll get my shoes." Hannah left the meatloaf and followed Elaine to her yellow bungalow.

The bookcase was small and fairly light. Hannah was able to get it out of the car easily. Getting it down Elaine's narrow basement stairs was another thing. Elaine stood at the top of the stairs giving instructions while Hannah struggled to bring the bookcase down in one piece.

At the bottom of the stairs, Hannah massaged her aching arms. She needed to go to the gym more when she got back to Chicago. Fraser's Mill had a small gym in a church basement, but it was too stuffy for Hannah's liking.

"Thank you so much." Elaine showed Hannah a spot for the bookcase along her basement wall. "Stay for dinner? I'm late starting it, but I'll whip up something in a jiffy."

"Oh, thanks," Hannah said, "but I actually got meatloaf from the diner."

Elaine smiled. "Did you know that meatloaf at the diner is my mother's recipe? When Chuck and I started the diner, I convinced her to write it down and figure out the amounts for me. She never measured anything, herself."

"Wow," Hannah said. "That's really cool."

"So you're all alone in that big house," Elaine said. "How do you like it?"

"Well," Hannah said, "it's been interesting. It was cool living in my grandparents' house for a while. But I'll be glad to get back to Chicago. A lot of my plans for this summer didn't pan out, and I'm kind of at loose ends now."

"What are you doing these days?" Elaine asked. "You run a video channel, don't you?"

Hannah nodded. "I can always think of video ideas back home. But I've run out of ideas for small-town summer videos. So lately I've just been planning for all the things I can do with my channel when I get back."

She expected Elaine to ask whether she was looking for a job. Most people did. Nobody seemed to understand that running a video channel was a job.

To be fair, with the kind of money she was currently making, it didn't seem like much of one.

"It's a good thing to have plans." Elaine began putting books on the shelves. "Although many times, I've found the things we plan for ourselves don't end up nearly as interesting as the things we're really meant to do."

Hannah grabbed a stack of books, sitting on the floor to help.

"Thank you," Elaine said. "Tell me about your video channel. What are you planning to do with it?"

"Well," Hannah said, "the thing about having an online persona is that you can use your influence to help people. You can raise money and awareness for important causes. I guess that's my real goal. It's fun making videos and getting comments, but at the end of the day, I want to affect people's lives positively."

Elaine nodded. "For sure," she said. "I've heard about your parents' philanthropy."

"Yeah." Hannah sat back on her heels. "The thing is, I feel like I'm expected to follow in their footsteps—owning companies and such. I mean, I don't think my parents expect that, but everybody else does. So when I tell people I'm an influencer, they always look at me funny. I know I can make this channel big, but it's not there yet."

"In my experience," Elaine said, "everything worth doing takes some time to get off the ground."

"See, that's what people don't understand," Hannah said. "I want to grow my video channel until it's a self-sustaining job and I'm not depending on my trust fund money. I can't do that here, but I could in Chicago, especially if I collaborate with some better-known influencers. I don't want my channel to be a side thing. I want to go big with it so I can use it to make a difference."

Elaine's face was thoughtful. "There's a lot of pressure nowadays to 'go big.' But I think the people making the biggest impact in this world aren't the superstars, but just ordinary people doing what they can to help others in their own little way."

"Ah." That probably satisfied lots of people, but it wasn't enough for Hannah. An ordinary life in a little town, puttering around doing good deeds, was okay if you couldn't do anything bigger. But if you could—why waste the opportunity to make that larger impact on the world?

She wasn't about to argue with Elaine, though.

"Do you want to stay in Chicago?" Elaine asked. "That's home, right? What's your home like?"

"Yeah," Hannah said. "I know there's a lot of crime in Chicago, but there's a lot of cool stuff too—arts and culture—and I grew up there, so I'm used to it. It would be nice to have my own place sometime, but with the housing market the way it is, it works better right now for me to live with my parents. It's a big house, and everybody's traveling so much, I'm not in anybody's way."

Why was she feeling defensive? Elaine wasn't grilling her. But she could imagine what a lot of people would think if they heard she still lived with her parents. There was a stigma about it, like there was about not having a "real job."

Elaine nodded. "That's what everyone did in the old days," she said. "Young women lived at home until they got married. There's no point in moving out just to move out. I think this idea of independence leads a lot of young people to spend too much money just to live in lonely apartments by themselves."

That was all very well for Elaine to say, but back in her day people usually got married in their late teens or early twenties. It was harder being in your late twenties, still living at home. But— as Hannah had found this summer—it was lonely living alone.

Hannah put the last book stack on the shelves. "I wouldn't want to live with my parents forever. But it works for now."

Elaine got up slowly, dusting off her hands. "I won't be nosy and ask if you've found a good man yet," she said. "I'll let you go home and eat your dinner. That meatloaf is better heated up in the oven. But don't put the Styrofoam in the oven. Heat it up on a baking sheet."

Her eyes twinkled. She'd been so kind this evening, and Hannah warmed to her. "Thanks, Elaine," she said. "I'll make sure to do that."

"Do you want any pudding?" Elaine asked. "I made bread pudding for my grandkids, and I've got some left. I put leftover cinnamon rolls into it. A little more exciting than the regular kind."

If Elaine made it, it must be good. "I'd love some," Hannah said.

Elaine led the way into a sunny kitchen, partly painted yellow, partly papered with vintage flowered wallpaper. "Charlie always offers to redo my kitchen. But I like the wallpaper. My husband and I hung it up together when we moved in here. Anything else would feel soulless." She pulled a covered dish out of the refrigerator. "Let me get you a plate. You don't mind returning it? I'm out of paper plates."

"No problem," Hannah said. "Thanks, Elaine."

The golden-brown bread pudding was covered in a creamy sauce. Elaine cut a generous piece. "Now, you heat that up too," she said. "Charlie eats it cold, and it drives me wild. That boy's worked in the diner too long. He's used to eating fast, standing up."

Hannah laughed. "I'll heat it up, I promise."

Elaine handed her the plate. "Thank you for the help."

"Thanks for the pudding." Hannah started for the door, then stopped. "And thanks for not asking me about finding a good man. It's not as simple as people seem to think."

Elaine smiled. "Don't I know it," she said. "Have a good evening, Hannah."

The Bombshell

On Wednesday, the day her credit card was supposed to arrive, it took all Hannah's willpower not to check the mailbox every ten minutes. Funny how desperate she felt about having some spending money. To distract herself, Hannah decided to explore the boathouse. Although she had been on the property all summer, Hannah hadn't gone into the boathouse yet. Grandpa had built it halfway down the hill between the house and the river. It didn't have any boats at the moment—only a rowboat next to the dock—but it had been a storage space for many years, and maybe it had interesting things for a video. It took a long time to find the right key on the huge bunch Dad had given her.

She went in, camera in hand in case she found anything video-worthy. A musty smell hit her. The place was full of the sort of junk she pretty much expected—life jackets, paddles, tackle boxes, Rubbermaid totes, and lawn equipment. At some point Hannah's grandparents must have started using it as a shed.

Hannah pried off the lid of a Rubbermaid tote. If her grandmother's old hip boots were somewhere around, they could come in handy for exploring and making videos. But there were no boots in this tote. Instead, it was full of letters, yellow with age.

What in the world? It must have been put here by mistake instead of in the garage. Hannah dragged the tote outside for a better look.

The first letter was addressed to her grandmother in sprawling cursive. This probably shouldn't be shared with the internet. Maybe Hannah shouldn't open it. It wasn't addressed to her. On the other hand, if it was private, why would it be out in the boathouse with a bunch of junk? What the heck. Hannah opened the letter.

It was a single page, signed "Yours, Teed" at the bottom. A letter from Grandpa. Ooh, maybe it was a cute love letter.

"My dearest Laura," the letter read, "I'm calling you on the telephone tonight, so by the time you get this there probably won't be anything new in it, but there's nothing like a real letter when you're missing somebody. It's been good so far at the lumber expo. We've met a lot of potential customers. I'm really proud of Paul this weekend."

Paul was Hannah's dad. Grandpa must have taken him to the logging expo. So this wasn't a love letter. Bummer. Well, what had she expected from old letters in the boathouse, anyway? Hannah read on.

"For a nineteen-year-old, he has an incredible head for business," the letter continued. "I can't think of anyone better to run the company when I retire. He told me last night he wants to expand to multiple sawmills. I suppose it's some harebrained scheme, but that shows me he's got the Fraser initiative.

"The mail's about to go, so I'll sign off. I miss you and the children. Give them all a hug and kiss from me."

Hannah folded up the letter. Grandpa was so proud of Dad. And Dad had gone on to do far more than work in the sawmill. He had carefully invested the mill's money and bought more sawmills. Fraser's Water-Powered Sawmill was now one among four that the company owned, scattered throughout the Midwest. The Fraser initiative—whatever that was—had done great things for Dad.

But it was a lot to live up to. Dad and his success cast a big shadow. Hannah was almost twenty-eight years old, and what did she have? A business degree from a private Catholic college, classes in music and acting and dance (none of which she was currently doing, unless singing in the church choir counted), and a video channel that didn't make enough money to support her. She was living mostly on her trust fund money.

Hannah's siblings didn't seem to have trouble being successful. Steve managed the Fraser's Mill sawmill, and he was married with a family. Bella, the sister below him, was a journalist whose pieces often made their way to the bigger conservative news outlets. She was married too. Kenneth, the brother above Hannah, was studying dentistry. But Hannah hadn't done anything useful yet.

It wasn't like her parents were pressuring her to do anything big. They loved her, and they'd supported her in what she wanted to do. But she couldn't help feeling like she must be a disappointment.

She was going to do something useful. No matter what uninformed people thought about her video channel, she could make it a success. She just needed to go back to Chicago, work hard, and make it big. And once she found a competent, eligible man who impressed her, they could be a power couple together. Unfortunately, Mr. Right seemed hard to find.

Enough letters. Hannah returned the tote to the boathouse and sorted through some of the other things. She quickly gave up on finding anything there for a video. The boathouse would make a nice shed, if someone cleaned it out. Hannah wouldn't be here long enough to need a shed, though.

She was on her way back to the house when her phone dinged. It was a message from Bella.

"Did you hear Mom and Dad are going to Europe???" the message read. "Dad has a business opportunity over there, and they decided to go for it. They'll be there for six months!"

"No!" Hannah replied. "Did they decide this today?"

"I guess they've been thinking about it for a while," Bella replied. "They told Steve, because he'll have more responsibilities while Dad's gone. Steve told me."

Why did everybody know about this but Hannah?

"Nobody told me. I guess I'll ask Mom and Dad about it later."

Hannah stuck her phone in her shorts pocket and checked the mail again. Nothing. The mail must be slow getting to this end of town. Fraser's Mill probably had only one mailman.

Bella's news was unexpected. With her parents in Europe,

Hannah would have the Chicago house to herself. That would be strange, especially around Thanksgiving and Christmas. The house would be big and empty. Maybe Hannah's siblings would come to Chicago so she wouldn't have to spend the holidays by herself. Of course, maybe Steve and Christine would prefer to host, but Hannah couldn't imagine anything duller than spending Christmas in small-town Michigan.

Maybe she could host some Christmas parties for friends. Her parents wouldn't object to her having a few quiet, well-behaved people over. Like a real Julia Child, she could learn to make fancy appetizers and beef wellington. Hannah didn't particularly like beef wellington, but it looked so impressive. She did like cooking and trying new recipes. She'd buy a new dress—cream-colored—and curl her hair and set the table with Mom's best china. Of course, she'd have to pay for all that food. It could be pricy.

⚬⚬⚬⚬⚬

The mail finally arrived. Hannah snatched the letter out of the box, called the number to activate her credit card, and whisked into the car to drive to Traverse City. She was going to buy the clothes she couldn't buy on Saturday. Then she would treat herself to dinner out. She could pay off the credit card after her trust fund money came in tomorrow.

Two hours later, as Hannah perusued a restaurant menu with her laptop next to her, trying to look like a businesswoman who ate dinner alone not because she was single but because she was working, her phone buzzed.

It was Mom.

Should she answer the phone in the restaurant? She didn't want to bother people. Well, she wouldn't be louder than the people talking at the other tables. Hannah picked up. "Hi, Mom."

"Hannah! I thought you weren't going to pick up," Mom said. "How are you?"

"Doing all right," Hannah said. "My credit card came in the mail today."

"Oh, good," Mom said. "I hope you haven't been having trouble without it."

Hannah didn't need to worry Mom with the saga of the empty bank account. After all, she'd have money in the account tomorrow. And she hadn't had any real trouble, just a few boring days. "Oh, I'm fine," she said. "Bella told me you and Dad are going to go to Europe! What's up with that?"

"That's what I called about. Your father has a business associate in Berlin—his name is Hans Brandt—who offered to do a six-month house swap."

"A six-month what?"

"House swap. You know your dad's been working remotely. Hans and his family want to see the United States. He agreed to pay our airfare to and from Berlin and let us stay in his house—it's a beautiful house—while his family stays in our house in Chicago."

Wait a minute. Strangers were going to stay in Hannah's parents' house? For six months?

"What?" Hannah exclaimed. "I'm coming back to Chicago at the end of the month. This is going to be super awkward for me, Mom. I mean, I don't want to be inhospitable, but I've never entertained a bunch of guests like that, and definitely not by myself."

"Oh, sweetie, we weren't thinking you would have to entertain the Brandts," Mom said. "We were thinking you might like to stay in Fraser's Mill while they're at our house. That way they can have the Chicago house to themselves — like an AirBnB. Since you can do your video channel from anywhere, we thought you'd appreciate staying in the log house a while longer."

Oh, no. Mom had this all wrong.

"Actually, Mom," Hannah said, "I was really looking forward to going back to Chicago. Fraser's Mill is so small. There's never anything going on here, and I've completely run out of ideas for videos. I've been counting the days until I get back."

"Really?" Mom said. "I thought you'd love the idea. Fraser's Mill is such a nice place, and you're close to Steve and Christine."

How had Mom thought she would love the idea? Hannah felt like she'd complained to everyone in the world about Fraser's Mill. Everyone, apparently, except her parents.

"This is difficult," Mom said. "You really can't stand to stay there? I'm not trying to force you to stay, but we've never had an opportunity like this house swap."

When Mom put it like that, what could Hannah say? It was her parents' house. And they had never toured Europe before. This would be wonderful for them.

"I don't want to stay in Fraser's Mill," Hannah said. "But it's okay. This is probably a sign I should get my own place. You and Dad can do the house swap, and I'll find someplace else to live close by."

"Are you sure?" Mom asked. "Your father and I aren't trying

to kick you out of your home."

"I'm sure," Hannah said. "You and Dad ought to be able to go to Europe. I'll be fine. I keep thinking I need to get better at adulting, anyway."

"Adulting?" Mom asked. "All that talk about adulting is overrated. I feel terrible that you feel stuck in Fraser's Mill. I'll talk to your father and see if we can help you find someplace in Chicago. And I'd better mail you some cold-weather clothes in the meantime."

"Thanks, Mom," Hannah said. "I'll text you a list of clothes. But hopefully I won't be here for long. I'll figure something out. Maybe one of my friends back home is looking for a roommate."

"As long as you're sure. I'm not happy about this whole situation. You won't argue me out of trying to fix it."

"Thanks, Mom. I appreciate it. I'll be totally fine, I promise."

Hannah sank down in her chair, elbows resting on the table. Now what? She would have to message the girls she knew in Chicago and see if anybody wanted a roommate. She could split the rent, and she wouldn't be there alone. It would be a good experience.

She'd better pray about this though. It was a lot of news to take in all at once, and a bit of heavenly assistance would be most welcome.

For Rent in the Windy City

Back in Fraser's Mill, Hannah messaged her Chicago friends. There had to be somebody she could stay with while her parents were in Europe. It was hard to figure out how to write the message. She had to phrase it as an attractive offer. It was an attractive offer. She was offering her company—she was good company, right?—and her fair share of the rent (which hopefully wouldn't be too much, because her trust fund money barely supported her already). Who wouldn't want to take her up on that?

Lots of people, apparently. It took frustratingly long for anyone to respond, besides one friend who would have loved the idea if she wasn't moving to Carson City. Hannah could room with her in Carson City if she wanted. Hannah thanked her but declined. She wasn't about to run off to Nevada.

At sunset, as Hannah sat on the dock writing a plan for her next video, she got a text from Christine. "Hey, Hannah! Is it too early to call in that babysitting favor? Steve's having a rough week, and I thought we could go out for dinner tomorrow. I'd pick Friday, but it's a steakhouse, so I'd want to eat meat, and I hate having to do an alternate Friday penance."

"Sure, no problem," Hannah responded. "I'm free all evening. What time do you want?"

"How about five-thirty?"

∾∾∾∾∾

At five-twenty-five on Thursday, Hannah rang Steve and Christine's doorbell.

"I'll get it," a voice called from inside. Steve opened the door in his work clothes. Must be running late getting ready.

"You're early, Han," he said. "Come in. Make yourself at home. Don't step on the Legos."

He disappeared, and Hannah came in. The living room looked like a Lego bomb had exploded. Weren't those things choke-size? They should be put away before Noah got them. Hannah found the Lego bin in the corner and began scooping the little bricks into it.

"Hannah? Are you here?" Christine came around a corner. "Ouch! Stupid Legos." She hopped on one foot.

Hannah laughed. "Steve should have warned you too," she said. "Where are the kids?"

"Upstairs. Evelyn wanted to play dress-up, and Steve's changing Noah's diaper. He just got back. Work got out late."

Christine, in a navy dress with pearls and curled hair, looked nearly ready to leave.

Hannah finished putting away the Legos. "Chris, is it okay if Evelyn and I rummage through your costume stuff? She wanted to do it last time, and I didn't know if it was okay, so I didn't let her."

"Oh, that's fine. It's just old theatre stuff." Christine sat on the couch. "I can't tell you how grateful I am that you're here. I've been on my feet all day, and all I want is a nice evening so Steve and I can decompress."

"No problem at all," Hannah said. "I love watching the kids. It's the best part about being an aunt."

"They're really gonna miss you when you go back to Chicago," Christine said. "How long are you here?"

"Actually, that's complicated." Hannah got up. "You heard about Mom and Dad's house swap, didn't you? How they're trading houses with a family from Berlin for six months?"

Recognition dawned on Christine's face. "Oh, I didn't think of how that would affect you. What are you going to do? You're not going to Europe too, are you?"

"No, but I'm not staying in our Chicago house, either." Hannah sank down on the couch next to Christine. "I'll have to find somewhere else to go. I've messaged some of my Chicago friends in case any of them need a roommate."

"Wow," Christine said. "I hope you find somebody."

"Me too," Hannah said. "Mom thought I could just stay in Fraser's Mill for all that time. I can't do that, Christine. You know how Fraser's Mill is. There's no content for my videos. I won't make any progress toward my goals. And there's nobody to hang out with."

"You have us." Christine pressed Hannah's arm.

Hannah sighed. "Thanks, Christine, but I really need friends too and not just family."

"I could introduce you to some of my friends," Christine said.

Hannah made a face. "Remember when I came to your party last month? All those moms spent the entire time talking about their kids. As much as I love kids, I really didn't feel like I fit in with the group."

Christine laughed. "I can see that. Well, we'll enjoy the rest of your time here. I hope you find a good roommate."

"Christine?" Steve's voice called. He came in, baby Noah on his arm. "Wow. You look great."

"Are you ever getting in the shower?" Christine asked.

"I'm going, I'm going." Steve deposited Noah on the floor. "Everything's taking longer today than expected. It took an extra half-hour at the end of work to fix the mess Faye made with those invoices." He rushed away, taking the stairs two at a time by the sound of it.

"That's the office administrator," Christine explained. "She was supposed to be really good with computers, and she is, but she's no good at answering phones and doing paperwork. Steve would have let her go a while ago, but he doesn't have anybody to fill the job."

In ten minutes Steve was back, wearing a suit, his wet blond hair sticking up wildly. "Let's get out of here before they give away our reservation," he told Christine. "Good luck with the kids, Han. Evelyn stomped on a crayon box upstairs. There're crayon shavings all ground into that white rug."

Christine groaned. "Don't worry about that too much, Hannah. Steve said I was crazy to buy a white rug. I guess he was right."

"I'm always right," Steve said. "Let's go. Hannah's watched the kids before. She doesn't need half an hour of instructions."

"Make sure the food gets stored in the fridge after dinner," Christine said. "And we always close the blinds when it gets dark. I don't want the whole street looking into the house."

"Nobody's going to take their clothes off in front of the windows." Steve handed Christine her purse. "Who do you think is going to look in? Burglars? Come on. I'm gonna start the car."

They lived in a nice area. In Chicago, much as Hannah liked it, burglars were a real possibility.

Babysitting Evelyn and Noah was always a workout and a good time. After an evening racing around, playing dress-up with Evelyn, watching Noah happily mash banana on his high chair tray, answering a million "why" questions, and working on the smashed crayon shavings (that rug would probably never be the same), Hannah settled down on the couch with both kids and a stack of picture books. Hannah read *The Tale of Samuel Whiskers* (Evelyn sure picked the scary stories) while Noah fell asleep, snuggled against her.

In the middle of babysitting, Hannah got a message from Abby Hartman, a Chicago friend.

"I got your message about looking for an apartment," Abby's message said. "A friend of mine is looking for another roommate. Her name's Tori Novak. Want me to send her your information?"

Hannah closed the message. She wouldn't reply yet, not before she thought about it a little. Besides, she had a babysitting job to do.

Steve and Christine got back late but in a good mood. Hannah hadn't managed to get Evelyn to bed—she was still dancing around playing with dolls after being put in bed repeatedly—but Noah was sound asleep.

"Thanks so much, Hannah." Christine kicked her high heels off and sank into a kitchen chair. "We had a great time. We talked about your housing problem, too. If you can't find a place in Chicago, you can always stay with us."

Much as she loved her family, Hannah had the feeling she might not get along so well with Steve and Christine if they lived in the same house. Besides, she was an adult. She didn't need her more-successful family members bailing her out—she needed to stand on her own feet. "Thanks," she said. "But my friend knows a girl in Chicago who's looking for a roommate. I'm going to talk to her. In any case, I'll find something."

In her car in Steve and Christine's driveway, Hannah opened Abby's message again, mulling over how to answer. She'd been hoping to stay with somebody she knew. But if this turned out to be her only opportunity, she probably shouldn't pass it up.

"Sure, go ahead and share my info," she responded to the message. "Thanks a lot."

❧❦❧

It was time for Hannah to make that long-delayed video about this year's fall styles.

Grandpa's log house made an excellent background for videos, she had to admit. In Chicago, her indoor videos were usually against a dull white wall or her bookcase. Here, the walls were made of logs; sunlight from the window provided natural lighting (supplemented by a large ring light). It was best in the evening, in the golden hour.

This year's fall styles were new to Hannah. She wasn't sure she would wear the clothes after making the video; everything was tailored toward Generation Z these days, and she felt silly wearing high-waisted, wide-leg jeans and chunky white sneakers. It made her feel like a teenager. But a lot of her viewers were Gen Z, and a number had asked her to review this fall's styles. It was funny how much the comments section dictated her channel's content. She wasn't always sure that following their advice made her channel better.

The hairstyle video with Christine had gotten a decent number of views, but not much more than usual. If she wanted to bring in more revenue, she had to do something bigger. Hopefully this fall she could partner with other content creators back in Chicago. It was fun making videos with someone else, and that was a good way to get discovered by more people. In the meantime, she'd do the best she could. Maybe she'd reach out to some people before she got back to town, just to start planning.

In green pen, she revised the script she'd written a couple days ago for the style video. The original script was in pink pen. Color-coding made her happy. Then she put on a cheery expression and started filming. It wasn't really talking to a camera in an empty room. She was talking to her followers, the people who were interested in her updates and her thoughts on random topics. It wasn't the same as talking to real-life friends, but it was something.

The video finished, she went down to make dinner. The refrigerator was as bare as store shelves after Black Friday. She'd eaten all her leftovers. There was a block of Parmesan cheese, a carton with two eggs, a bread heel, a few condiments, and half an inch of milk at the bottom of the jug. The crisper held the remains of a bag of kale, wilted beyond recognition.

Unless she wanted to make an open-faced egg salad sandwich with the bread heel, she'd better go to the store. Murray's Grocery closed in half an hour. It was wild to live in a town where the only grocery store closed at seven. If you were too late, you had to go to the gas station or the dollar store, neither of which had anything Hannah wanted.

Murray's Grocery was a family business owned by Ben and Liz Murray, and this summer they had announced their daughter — Grace — would take over when they retired.

That made the store a likely place to run into Grace and Doc together. Hannah steeled herself and walked through the door, the bell jingling. Grace was at the cash register, helping a customer. Doc wasn't in sight.

Hannah got a bagged salad and a bag of frozen salmon (the store didn't carry fresh fish). She added a half-gallon of milk, frozen strawberries, bananas, and whole-wheat bread, then approached the checkout.

"Hey, Hannah." Grace smiled cheerily. "Long time no see! How are you doing?"

"Good," Hannah said, hoping she looked friendly. "How are you?"

"Great! Hey, we missed you at choir practice on Wednesday."

Last Wednesday she'd learned about the house swap. "Oh, whoopsie," Hannah said. "I went into town, and I totally forgot it was Wednesday. Did practice go all right?"

"It went okay. The sopranos were pretty quiet though." Grace leaned forward. "That reminds me. I had an idea. We should get the choir ladies together sometime this fall for a fancy tea. Tea and scones and cucumber sandwiches and things like that. I was thinking maybe you, Alex, and I could organize it."

Alex Martin was one of the altos from the choir. She and Grace had been close friends since childhood. There was no way they needed a third person to organize this. Three was a crowd. Plus the whole thing with Doc was too recent. Hannah would rather stay lonely than hang out with his girlfriend.

"Thanks," Hannah said. "That sounds really nice, but I'll be back in Chicago soon, and I have a million things to do before I leave. I hope it goes well."

"We'll miss you," Grace said.

They wouldn't miss her. They hardly knew her. Grace was just being polite.

"Thanks," Hannah said. "How much do I owe you?"

As she drove off, Doc was approaching the store, whistling. Good thing Hannah hadn't come five minutes later.

⁂

That evening, Hannah got a message request from Tori Novak — the girl who needed a roommate.

"Hi, Hannah," the message said, "Abby Hartman said you were looking to share an apartment in Chicago. I'm about to go to work, but thought maybe we could chat over text and see if we'd be well-suited to be roommates."

That sounded good. Hannah wasn't eager to sign up to room with a total stranger. "Sounds great," she responded. "Thank you!"

Tori asked a barrage of questions. She wanted to know about Hannah's personality, interests, and living habits. Tori herself had a fast-paced job managing a coffee shop and liked art and theatre.

"I love theatre!" Hannah replied. "I was in a few musicals in high school and some Gilbert and Sullivan in college."

"Wow!" Tori said. "Are you planning to do any acting when you come back to Chicago?"

"Maybe—that sounds fun," Hannah said. "I have a video channel that keeps me pretty busy at the moment. I'm trying to work on growing the channel."

"That sounds fun," Tori said. "I'd be interested to see some of your videos."

"I'll send you a link," Hannah promised. "It's not been really exciting lately, because I've been in a small town all summer, but I'll be able to do more when I get back." She sent Tori the link.

"Thanks," Tori replied. "So what do you do for a living?"

Hannah hated the question. But if anybody could understand her life as a content creator, it would be another artsy post-college girl. She explained about the videos and her plans for expanding the channel to be a self-sustaining venture.

"So what are you doing in the meantime?" Tori asked. "Do you have another job?"

Great, now Hannah would have to tell her about the trust fund. Tori would probably think she was some entitled rich kid. It was so hard to explain these things to somebody who didn't know the whole picture. She had to rephrase the paragraph four times before sending it.

Radio silence from Tori. Maybe she'd gotten called away. Lots of people took a while to answer messages, especially on a work day. But it made Hannah nervous. To avoid thinking about it, she washed the dishes.

She'd taken a shower, blow-dried her hair, and caught up on her social media, when she got another message from Tori.

"Sorry for the late response — I was really busy," the message read. "Thanks so much for chatting! I've been thinking about it, and I realized we probably wouldn't be a good fit as roommates. But thanks for reaching out! I hope you find someplace good."

Hannah had to read the message twice before it could sink in. Why didn't Tori think they'd be good roommates? Was it the trust fund? Or had she watched Hannah's videos and disliked them? Did Hannah give off red flags?

What should she say?

It was ridiculous to feel upset. Somebody not wanting to be your roommate didn't mean they thought you were horrible. There were plenty of great people Hannah wouldn't want to room with. This rejection didn't say anything about Hannah as a person. But it felt awful. What was so wrong with her? Why didn't Tori want anything to do with her after hearing about the trust fund and maybe watching her videos?

Hannah began a message. "Hey, thanks for letting me know.

I was wondering why it was that you thought we wouldn't be a good fit?"

She stared at the message, finger hovering over the "send" button.

No. She wouldn't ask. Hannah threw the phone across the room and flung herself facedown on her bed.

The Offer

After the interaction with Tori, Hannah felt shy about searching outside her own friend circle for a place to stay. At least her friends liked her. Unfortunately, no one seemed to need a roommate. Maybe something would turn up soon.

It was Labor Day weekend. Fraser's Mill had a spontaneous cookout and dance in the park. Hannah elected not to go. She didn't want to hang out with the townspeople, and she didn't have anyone to dance with. Instead, she drove to her favorite restaurant in Cadillac, bringing her laptop. She'd find somewhere to stay in Chicago if it was the last thing she did.

Over a quinoa and greens power bowl, Hannah looked at apartment options. She didn't want to get anything in a dangerous area. Thankfully, nowadays you could read reviews for apartments and neighborhoods online.

But Hannah couldn't find any place decent under two thousand dollars a month. She couldn't afford that on her own.

Unless she got another job, a "real" job. Even then, two thousand a month was steep.

The whole thing was so frustrating. Why hadn't her parents asked her earlier about the house swap? Why had they assumed she wanted to stay in Fraser's Mill, where she had nothing to do and nobody to talk to? Why couldn't the German family have stayed someplace else?

Maybe Mom could help with thinking up some option Hannah hadn't considered. Hannah paid her bill, went out to her car, and called Mom.

No answer. Hannah's parents were probably eating dinner. Hannah sent a text instead.

"Hi, Mom," it read, "I'd like some advice. I can't find anybody who's looking for a roommate in Chicago, and I can't afford to pay rent for a single apartment. Do you have ideas for someplace I could stay?"

Her phone dinged, but it wasn't Mom. It was her friend Abby.

"I heard things didn't work out for you and Tori to be roommates," Abby's message said. "I'm sorry about that!"

"Thanks for the suggestion, anyway," Hannah replied, with a smile emoji.

Was it too petty to ask if Abby knew why Tori didn't want to be roommates? Maybe it was better not to ask. But then she'd wonder.

"By the way," Hannah wrote, "do you know why Tori decided we wouldn't be a good fit?"

"I'm not sure," Abby said. "She said she needed a roommate with more 'shared life experience.'"

So Tori probably didn't like that Hannah had no real job

experience and lived off a trust fund from her parents. It sounded so bad, Hannah didn't know that she blamed her.

She would have to do something. Maybe she should get a real job. But she couldn't think of anything she wanted to do besides making videos.

Maybe some video company was hiring. She could do freelance work, or take wedding videos. It wasn't wedding season, but she could advertise on her channel. There had to be something she could do without putting her goals aside.

⋘⋙

Her mom called back later that evening.

"Hi, Hannah," Mom said. "Sorry I missed your call. We were at dinner. But your father and I talked about your problem on the way home."

"Mom, I'm striking out with everything I try. What can I do?" Hannah asked. "None of my friends are looking for a roommate. I talked to a friend of a friend who was looking, but she decided she wasn't interested in rooming with me. And I can't afford a place by myself with the money I'm making from my channel right now."

"Somebody didn't want to room with you?" Mom asked. "Who wouldn't? What's not to like about you?"

Hannah sighed. "She said we didn't have enough 'shared life experience.' I think she got the impression I was a spoiled rich kid who didn't work."

"Nonsense," Mom said. "Your father and I don't spoil our children. You do good work with that video channel—you just don't have much exposure yet. That will come."

"Well, in the meantime, I think it's keeping me from getting any roommates." Hannah sank farther into the living room couch. "Mom, what should I do?"

"Your father and I both think it would be best if you stay in Fraser's Mill."

Hannah groaned.

"Hear me out," Mom said. "I know Fraser's Mill isn't that exciting. But you can stay in the house for free. Steve and Christine are close, and you can see Evelyn and Noah. And it's only six months. You'll be back before you know it."

"Mom—"

"I know it's not what you want, and I'm sorry about that. We don't have the disposable cash to pay six months of rent for you in Chicago right now, and—"

"Oh, Mom, I wasn't trying to get you and Dad to pay my rent," Hannah said. "I'm an adult. I'll pay my own rent. But I can't afford to rent a whole apartment on just my channel's income. That's the problem. Maybe I could get a job as a wedding photographer or something."

"Well, I don't know much about photography jobs. I think you'd be good, if you wanted to do that. But any business will take a while to get going. Until you can afford an apartment, you still have the Fraser's Mill house."

"I'll go stir crazy if I live here. There's nothing to do. I don't have any friends in town. Steve and Christine are busy, and I don't want to bug them by coming over all the time. I really, really don't want to live here."

There was a long silence.

"I don't know what to tell you," Mom said at last, in a firm tone. "I'm sorry this had to happen. But you're not that badly off. You've got a nice place you can stay for free—on the water, too, which is hard to get. It's a pretty little town, and I know there are nice people there. I'm sorry you're bored, but you'll just have to find things to do. You're a smart girl. You can think of something. Fraser's Mill is a nice place, and I think you can learn to appreciate it."

Hannah knew Mom's attitude—it took no argument.

"All right, Mom," she said. "I guess I'll keep trying to figure something out. I do appreciate you and Dad letting me stay here, and I understand it's the best you can do. Thanks anyway."

"We love you, Hannah."

"I know."

Off the phone, Hannah rubbed her forehead. What could she possibly do, stuck in Fraser's Mill? That made finding jobs so much harder. They wouldn't be hiring wedding photographers, or anybody with Hannah's skill set, for that matter.

❧❧❧❧❧

The next day was Sunday, and after an interior battle with herself, Hannah decided to sing in the choir instead of sitting in the pew.

If there was one good thing about Fraser's Mill, it was singing with the parish choir at St. Anthony's. Hannah had sung in her college choir, and she loved it—the more challenging, the better. Maybe she should have gone into music, but she'd rather make videos than compete in the music industry.

For the last few weeks, however, the choir had felt awkward. Grace and Doc both sang. Before Grace came to town, Hannah had sat next to Doc in the choir loft. They had shared many a choir-practice joke. But now Hannah sat on the other side of the sopranos. Everyone must know why she had moved, but at this point, she didn't care.

She had thought of quitting the choir. But people would think she had left because of Doc and Grace, which would be true. Also, the other ladies would hound her to rejoin. As tireless parish volunteers, they meant well, but they could be pushy. Sometimes it was easier to just do the thing they wanted instead of getting nagged about it.

Today, Hannah was determined to pray the Mass and stop stewing over her problems. It was easier said than done—her mind kept wandering.

Those people down below in the church would be her neighbors for the next six months if she was stuck in Fraser's Mill. There was that lady—Barb?—who'd tried to set Hannah up with her tenant, wearing bright purple with her hair in a kerchief. But not everybody down below was elderly. Young families crowded the pews, and there were some young people by themselves. If Hannah made some friends, staying here wouldn't be so bad.

Up to this point, Hannah had been too focused on Doc to make a lot of friends. Maybe there would be a church social or something soon. But the problem was, even if she met people, it might be hard to connect with them. What would she have in common with these small-town inhabitants?

Today's opening hymn was "Jerusalem, My Happy Home," an old American piece.

Jerusalem, my happy home,

When shall I come to thee?

When shall my sorrows have an end?

Thy joys, when shall I see?

Hannah dwelt on how the Israelites felt about being exiled from Jerusalem, and she couldn't help but feel similar (at least a little) about being exiled from Chicago. But the hymn was really about the heavenly Jerusalem. And Hannah knew she ought to pray about her problems instead of worrying about them.

"Dear Jesus," she prayed, "please help me figure out a way to get home!"

On Labor Day, Steve invited Hannah to Sleeping Bear Dunes with his family. Probably Christine's idea. Steve didn't invite Hannah to many things.

Hannah packed snacks and water bottles—Christine was bringing lunch—and drove to the dunes. It was a balmy day in the 70s, perfect for the dune climb. Hannah had been there once as a kid, but didn't remember much. She had spent her time at the bottom of the dunes, playing in the sand around a half-buried tree. She'd heard the dunes were shifting toward the parking lot, so maybe the tree was completely covered now.

She was early, and Steve's family was late. The parking lot was jammed, and the closest big dune crawled with tourists who looked the size of ants in the distance. Maybe it was a bad idea to come on Labor Day. It was like going to the beach on a summer weekend in Chicago.

Finally Steve's truck pulled up. Steve hopped out and unfastened the kids' carseats. "Hey, Hannah," he called. "Sorry, we got held up."

"That's all right," Hannah called, and got out the snacks and water bottles.

Evelyn raced over to her. "Aunt Hannah!"

Hannah caught her in a hug. "Hi, Evelyn! Are you ready to climb the dunes?"

Evelyn nodded vigorously. She wore a pink plaid dress, oversized pink sunglasses, and pink tennis shoes. "Mommy said I could go all the way up to the top."

Hannah squinted at the first big dune. Surely that's what Christine meant. Nobody would take a four-year-old over more than one dune—the walk back was too long.

Christine came up with Noah, and Steve followed, beach blankets over his shoulders and a cooler in his arms. "Come on, girls. I can't hold this stuff all day. Where do you want to go?"

Christine appraised the area. "Let's go over there." She motioned to the left. "By the trees. We can put down the stuff in the shade, and I can stay there with Noah while you guys go up the dune."

"Sounds good. Come on!" Steve led the way across the short, wiry grass toward the bottom of the dune.

Christine said she didn't care about climbing. She was happy to watch the stuff and stay with Noah, who kept trying to eat sand.

Steve and Hannah took off their shoes and went up the dune, Evelyn skipping ahead.

"Look how fast I can go," Evelyn shouted. "Race you to the top, Daddy."

"You're on, Evie." Steve winked at Hannah. "One—two—three—go!"

Evelyn took off. Steve waited a full five seconds before slowly loping after his daughter.

It was a longer climb than Hannah remembered. Funny how climbing a sand hill sucked your energy away—sliding back every step, she struggled to make headway.

Steve caught up with Evelyn as they reached the top. "You win," he proclaimed, swinging his daughter around before collapsing, laughing, on the sand. "Look at that view!"

Hannah turned. Beyond the parking lot shone the blue of a distant lake. In the other direction, there were dunes and more dunes. If you kept hiking, you'd end up at Lake Michigan. Hannah didn't plan to do that, at least not this time, but the view was video-worthy.

"Daddy, I forgot my bucket and shovel at the bottom," Evelyn wailed. "I was gonna build a sand castle."

Steve sighed, hauling himself to his feet. "I'll get it. Be right back."

He took off down the dune at a run. If he wasn't careful, he'd fall on his face.

While Steve was gone, Hannah convinced Evelyn to pose for pictures, some with the dunes in the background and some with the blue sky and the lake. The lighting was harsh today, the sky cloudless, but Christine and Steve would appreciate the photos. People were in the background of a lot of them, but Hannah could photoshop them out.

Steve returned with the bucket and shovel, faster than Hannah would have thought possible. "I'm beat," he announced. "Here you go, Evie."

"Yay, Daddy!" Evelyn hugged him and began digging in the sand. "I'm gonna make a castle with a moat."

"That's nice." Steve lay down. "Have fun. I'm gonna lie here until I get my strength back. Your old Dad"—he was thirty-five—"isn't up to this kind of exertion on his day off."

"It's a good day off, though, right?" Hannah asked.

"Oh, yeah."

Hannah couldn't tell if Steve's eyes were closed behind his sunglasses, but she wouldn't be surprised if they were.

"It's been a week," Steve said. "I fired Faye."

"Is she the one you were having trouble with last time?"

"Yeah. I couldn't stand her in the office anymore. I put out a notice that we're hiring, but I don't know what to do now. I'm doing paperwork and answering the phones myself, until I can find somebody. Can't give it to the dispatcher. He's too busy. Nobody else knows about mill office work."

"That's too bad," Hannah said. "I hope you find somebody."

"The whole thing is a headache," Steve said. "And I hate doing paperwork. I'd rather be on the green chain than do paperwork. I need someone, fast."

Hannah had heard about the green chain, one of the toughest jobs usually given to sawmill newbies. Steve must really hate paperwork.

Wait a minute. Was he hinting for Hannah to take the job? No, he wouldn't want his kid sister working under him. Besides, Steve knew Dad didn't expect all his kids to work in the mill. Hannah wouldn't even mention it.

They stayed at the top of the dune long enough for Evelyn to build her castle. Hannah helped while Steve lay there, presumably napping.

Hannah surveyed the castle. "I wish we had some water for the moat, but we don't want to use up all the water bottles."

"How about one bottle?" Evelyn suggested.

"Fine, one."

The one bottle didn't do much, but Evelyn clapped her hands. "Can you take a picture of it?" she asked Hannah.

"Totally."

Steve rolled to a sitting position. "Are you ladies ready to go back down?" he asked. "I think it's lunchtime."

They went down the dune—it was actually easier to run than walk down—and found Christine and Noah by the trees. The little tree from Hannah's childhood had disappeared under the sand.

Christine was reading a romance novel. Despite missing the dune climb, she looked blissful. "Back already?"

"Lunchtime," Steve announced, kissing his wife in public and taking the book from her. "You're on page fifty-six. Come on, let's put out the food."

"Mommy, I made a sand castle," Evelyn shouted. "Aunt Hannah, show her the pictures!"

They had pepperoni sandwiches with cheese, mayonnaise,

and mustard, Steve's creation. Christine had peanut butter and jelly. "We never ate pepperoni sandwiches when I was growing up," she said. "It must be a Fraser thing."

"It definitely is a Fraser thing," Hannah said. "Mom always said it wasn't the healthiest sandwich, but it was Dad's favorite."

"Speaking of your parents," Christine said, "what's going on with the apartment hunt?"

Hannah groaned. "I've got nothing." She told Steve and Christine about her experience with Tori.

Steve whistled. "That's tough. What are you gonna do?"

"I don't know," Hannah said. "If I stay in Fraser's Mill, I'll be bored out of my mind. I think I've videotaped everything in town by now."

"The offer still stands to stay with us," Christine said. "We'd love to have you."

Hannah shook her head. "Thanks," she said. "But we'd probably drive each other nuts. Besides, there's not much more to do in Cadillac than in Fraser's Mill."

❧❧❧

That evening, back home, Hannah's phone rang. It was Dad. "Hello, sweetheart," he said. "Your mother and I have been thinking about your problem. And Steve filled me in on your financial difficulties."

Of course Christine had told Steve about that, but there had been no need to tell Dad. Was there no secrecy in this family?

"Oh, Dad, I didn't want to bother you with that," Hannah said. "I've got a plan. I'm going to be a lot more careful with my money, and I'm working on expanding my video channel. I'll be totally fine."

"That's one idea," Dad said, "but I think I've got a better one. I know you're bored in Fraser's Mill. What if you had something to do? What if you worked at the mill as office administrator?"

"What?" Hannah sat down at the kitchen island. "Work at the mill? Dad, you said—"

"I know, I know. I don't expect all you kids to work at the mill. You ought to find your own paths in life. But this would be temporary. And here's why I think it's a good idea."

"I'm listening." The sinking feeling in Hannah's stomach said otherwise, though.

"The Brandts will have the house for six months. Let's say you stay in Fraser's Mill for six months, doing your video channel. You'll be bored out of your mind. But if you get a job, you'll be out of your financial jam and keep busy at the same time. It's only six months. Think of it as a summer job, just a little longer."

That was a fair point. Hannah had worked summer jobs in college. It wasn't like she'd be committing to a career at the mill.

"The office administrator job is right up your alley," Dad said. "It's just computer work and invoices and answering phones and greeting people. You have that business degree. And we need somebody at the mill pronto. If you fill the gap temporarily, you'll save Steve a headache and give us time to find another replacement."

How bad could it be? It was true it would solve her boredom problem while also making money, and office work would be easy enough. Dad always had a way of making things sound really convincing. The sinking feeling was going away.

"That does sound like a pretty good idea, actually," Hannah said. "I've got a question though. Did Steve put you up to this?"

"No. I haven't run the idea by Steve, but I'm sure he'd be thrilled."

"Okay." The job sounded good, but it would be smart to take time to think over any negatives. "Can I call you back later tonight? I want to mull this over before making a final decision."

"All right. We're home all evening, planning our trip. Your mother says hi."

"Thanks, Dad. Tell her hi from me."

Hannah needed to brainstorm. She found a notebook and a pink pen and sat on the dock. Coral and peach clouds streaked the evening sky over the water, and a breeze ruffled the trees. It was chillier than it had been earlier. She went back for a sweater.

In the notebook, Hannah made a list of pros and cons of the mill job.

Pros: Good source of money. Probably one of the better jobs in Fraser's Mill. Something to do for the next six months. Next door to her house. Something to tell people when they asked what she did for work. A way to help the family business. Proof for her family that she did know how to work a regular job, even if she preferred making videos.

Cons: Stuck in Fraser's Mill. (Not much way to avoid that, unless she paid a ton of money to stay in Chicago by herself.) Not much free time. Getting up early. Having her brother as her boss.

Hannah looked at the list again, then called Dad.

"Hey, Dad, I think you're right. I'll take the job."

Office Administration

As it turned out, Steve wasn't happy Dad had offered Hannah the job without consulting him. Hannah learned that from her sister Bella.

"Steve was steamed," Bella told Hannah over the phone. "He said he's in charge of hiring and firing. But Dad asked him if he'd rather hire you to fill in or keep answering the phone himself. So Steve said he'll give it a try."

Hannah groaned. "If Steve's mad at me right from the beginning, this won't go well."

"Oh, I'm sure Steve will be grateful to have you," Bella said. "He hates answering phones. And doing paperwork. And if he bosses you around, you can tell Dad."

"I think I can get along with my siblings without having to run to Dad," Hannah said. "But how did you hear about this? Steve hasn't talked to me at all!"

"I called Mom about something else, and she told me."

The family grapevine worked better for the older members of the family. Hannah was always out of the loop. "Thanks, Bella. Did you hear when I'm supposed to start?"

"No. You think you'll start tomorrow?"

"Tomorrow? I hope not," Hannah said. "Nobody told me, and it's late already. I guess I'll text Steve."

She sent Steve a message and went to take her shower. When she came back, Steve had replied.

"You can start tomorrow. Eight AM. See you then."

Eight AM. Ugh. The cons on Hannah's pro and con list were already happening. She'd have to change to an earlier schedule, and from the tone of his short text, Steve didn't sound enthusiastic to have her working for him. At least the mill was next door.

◈◈◈◈◈

Bright and early, and only a little groggy, Hannah arrived at the mill. The place was bigger than she remembered, and the amount of drying lumber—neatly stacked in covered areas—was staggering. Maybe it seemed more intimidating because she was working here now. Hannah walked toward the largest building, which housed the main sawmill equipment, and went through the door marked "Office."

The sawmill's office was a large room with a reception counter and two desks covered in papers. One, judging from the family photos, was Steve's. At the other desk, a dark-haired guy was on the phone. Hannah's desk must be behind the reception counter.

What should she do? Should she go behind the counter and

set things up?

Steve rushed in, right as she approached the counter. He was wearing a hard hat. Things must be busy already, and it wasn't even eight AM.

"There you are," he said. "Good. I've got time to show you around."

On the tour, Hannah learned that the office administrator did a lot of things besides answering the phone. Hannah's duties included printing invoices, greeting truck drivers, keeping track of customers in a client database, selling lumber to walk-in customers, scheduling lumber deliveries, keeping the business website updated, and maintaining the inventory.

How she was supposed to do all those things at once, Steve didn't say. It was becoming clearer why the previous office administrator had struggled.

"I don't expect you to do everything on the first day." Steve must have noticed Hannah looking overwhelmed. "Mostly, I need somebody to answer the phone. You can figure out the other things as you go. If anybody calls to schedule a lumber delivery, you'll need to coordinate with Jack there. He's the dispatcher. He sends out the truckers, and he knows how much they can handle per day."

Steve disappeared, leaving Hannah alone at the desk. Her hands were oddly shaky. There were so many things to do. She was going to mess up and be worse than the woman who got fired. Steve would be livid.

The phone rang.

Hannah took a deep breath and answered it. "Fraser's Mill

Lumber. This is Hannah. How may I help you?"

"Hi," a guy's voice said. "This is Bob Lynde. I ordered a shipment of lumber from you, and it was supposed to get here tomorrow, but I learned I need it now. I'm out by Traverse City. Can you move the shipment up to today?"

That sounded like a question for the dispatcher. "Please hold a minute, and I'll check." Hannah pushed a button—hopefully the right button—to put the call on hold and went to the other desk.

The dispatcher was a broad-shouldered guy, solidly built, with tousled black hair and glasses. He was also on the phone again, staying so busy that Hannah hadn't even gotten a chance to introduce herself. Right then he was talking to a truck driver who had apparently broken down with an important load of lumber due this afternoon.

It was taking a while. The guy Hannah had put on hold was probably tired of waiting. She was just standing there, probably looking stupid. When would the dispatcher ever get off the phone?

"Yeah, go check and call me back," he finally said, and hung up.

He got to his feet and held out his hand to Hannah. Farm boy, by the looks of his clothes. He wore a denim shirt, the sleeves rolled up, tucked into blue jeans. A textbook example of the kind of guy you met in Fraser's Mill.

"Hi! I'm Jack Rogers."

This wasn't a time for social pleasantries. "Nice to meet you. I've got a guy on hold who was supposed to have a load of lumber delivered tomorrow. He wants it changed to today. He's out by Traverse City."

Jack shook his head. "Can't do it. The schedule's full and one of the guys is broken down. I can't spare anybody. Please tell the customer we're sorry, but it's gonna have to be tomorrow."

"Okay." Hannah raced back to her desk. "Are you there?" she said into the phone.

"I'm here. What took so long? Can you get me the lumber today?"

"I'm very sorry," Hannah said, "but the schedule's full, and one of the trucks has broken down. We can't do it any earlier than tomorrow."

The customer swore. "I gotta have it today, or it's no good. I'll have to find someplace else that can deliver it. Cancel my order, will you?"

He hung up.

That wasn't good. Steve wouldn't be happy that his customers were canceling orders. Maybe there was something else Hannah could have done. She didn't know. She'd better figure out how to cancel the order.

It took forever to figure out the system before Hannah successfully canceled it. Wow, that was a lot of money. So far, Hannah's phone-answering had lost the mill five grand in sales. Why couldn't Jack have worked it into the schedule? There had to be some way they could have gotten that guy his lumber today. Hannah didn't look forward to telling Steve.

Hannah glared across at Jack, but he was on the phone again. Those trucks must get on the road early. Only eight in the morning, and the mill was already in high gear.

Steve had said there were invoices that needed printing. She'd better figure that out. She hoped he would train her more soon, because she didn't know anything about most of the supposed office administrator jobs.

"Hey," a voice said, and she looked up to see Jack at her desk. "What happened with that order?"

"The customer canceled it." Hannah folded her arms. "I wish you could have fit it in somehow. Now we're out five grand. If Steve gets mad at me, that's not fair. It's your truck schedule. It's not my fault."

He didn't look particularly taken aback. "It's not anybody's fault. These things happen. Steve won't be mad."

He sounded like a farmer saying "these things happen" after his crops were flattened by a hailstorm. Hannah wasn't used to approaching problems with that attitude. She preferred a solution-based approach.

"There ought to be a better way to run this," Hannah said. "Maybe have some orders with a flexible delivery window so you can move them around. You wouldn't lose so many customers that way."

"We have flexible delivery windows," Jack said. "But we're short-handed today. There's only so much you can do."

The phone rang, cutting Jack off, and Hannah answered it. It was a potential customer, asking if the mill still sold pre-cut fence pickets and if he could order enough for a half-acre lot.

Steve hadn't said anything about pre-cut fence pickets. Hannah looked around the office frantically, but she didn't see anything about it. "I'll go ask," she told the person on the phone. "Please hold."

Jack still stood there. "Problem?" he asked.

What was he still doing here? This wasn't a dispatching

problem, it was an inventory problem. She didn't have time to talk to him while a customer waited on the phone.

"I've got a question for Steve," Hannah said. "Do you know where he is?"

"In the mill. Is there anything I can—"

"No, I'm fine, thanks." Hannah headed for the door into the mill.

A big sign on the door read Danger: Hard Hat Required. Where were the hard hats? Hannah looked around wildly. She spotted one on a filing cabinet in the corner. She shoved it on and went into the mill.

The saws were loud, tearing through logs at an alarming rate. The workers must wear earplugs. Hannah could just feel her ears getting damaged. Plugging them tightly with her fingers, she dodged other employees coming through and looked for Steve. She found him all the way on the other side, talking to one of the workers.

She waited. Why did it take so long to talk to anybody around here?

Finally Steve turned to her. "What?" he shouted over the noise.

"A guy on the phone is asking if we sell pre-cut fence pickets," Hannah yelled back, "and if there's enough for a half-acre lot."

"Didn't you see our inventory list? We've got tons of those."

Maybe he'd showed her the list, in the few minutes that he "trained" her, but she didn't remember. It had to be on the desk or the computer. She could find it.

Hannah raced to her desk and picked up her phone. "Hello,

are you still there?—Yes, we have pre-cut fence pickets. How many feet do you want?"

She successfully navigated the phone order, emailed the customer an invoice, and printed it. Thank goodness, she had done one thing right.

A shadow fell across her desk. Jack leaned on the counter.

"Everything go okay with Steve?"

Now he was just being nosy. Hannah had things to do. "Yes." She turned back to her computer. "Everything's straightened out, and I'm good. Thank you though."

She didn't want to be rude to her new coworker, but she didn't want him or anybody else to get the idea she was here to hang around and not take work seriously. Steve would be disgusted. Plus, part of Hannah's reason for being here was to prove she could do a real job. She didn't need Jack to hover.

Jack hesitated. "Well, if you need anything else, I'm right over here." He went back to his desk, where he doubtless had his own work to do.

Meanwhile, where was that inventory list Steve had mentioned? It wasn't on the desk. She searched "inventory" on her computer and a spreadsheet came up. Oh, she did vaguely remember Steve showing that to her.

It shouldn't take long to learn the ins and outs of this busines. And with the mill being so busy, the work day would fly by, right? As long as she didn't make any horrendous mistakes— and as long as Steve thought she was capable—she could stick it out for six months. Or until she got enough money to rent her own place in Chicago.

Hannah looked at the clock. Eight forty-five AM. Gross. She dropped her head down onto her desk. This would be a long day.

Jack

After what felt like a hundred-year morning, Hannah was more than ready for lunchtime. Though she had forgotten to bring lunch and heard the break wasn't quite long enough to leave and come back. Besides, Steve might be annoyed if she left. Thankfully, she'd heard there was a vending machine in the break room.

At least she hadn't lost any more customers. She had experienced a printer paper jam, mixed up some invoices, and gone into the mill three more times to ask Steve obvious questions, but she hadn't done anything catastrophic.

Grubby mill workers with steel-toed boots were eating lunch in the break room. Some tables were empty. Good, Hannah could sit alone and check social media while she ate. Not that she'd have much to eat. The vending machine was discouragingly low on nutritious food.

Between candy bars and cookies, Hannah went with cookies.

She'd better pack lunch tomorrow. She would have skipped lunch today, but she hadn't eaten much breakfast, and the rest of the work day was long.

Someone came up next to her as she punched in the numbers on the vending machine. "Forgot your lunch?"

It was Jack, with a lunchbox slung over his shoulder and a book in his hand. Was he being helpful or patronizing?

"Yeah." Hannah fished her package of cookies out of the bottom slot. "It's all right. I'll have a big dinner later."

"Do you want a ham sandwich?" he asked. "I've got extra."

Hannah shook her head. "Thanks anyway. I'm fine."

She headed over to an empty table across the room, near the window.

"Want some company?" Jack asked at her elbow.

She didn't have the mental energy to make small talk with coworkers right now. "No, thanks," Hannah said. "I've got things I have to do."

"Oh." His face sobered. "All right." He sat down at the next empty table. When Hannah glanced over a minute later, he was eating and reading his book.

Maybe that had been too rude of Hannah. She'd brushed Jack off more than once now. She just—she didn't know. Now she felt uncomfortable inside. Jack's face hadn't looked the happiest.

More guys filtered in for lunch. "Who's the new girl?" one guy asked loudly.

A minute later, two men approached Hannah. "Mind if we sit here?" A tall guy with a buzz cut grinned at her in a way she didn't quite like. Without waiting for Hannah's answer, he swung out a chair and sat next to her, plunking down a large, grubby lunchbox. "What's your name? I'm Drew. You just start work here?"

The other guy, short and stocky, sat down on the other side of her.

Hannah sat up straighter. She had just told Jack she had things to do. Now she was stuck with these two guys. And she ought to be polite. "Um," she said.

"What's your name?" Drew asked again.

"Hannah. I'm the new office administrator."

"I thought you were gonna work on the green chain." The shorter guy guffawed. "I'm Spencer. You wanna go for drinks with us tonight? We're gonna go to Cadillac, hit up a couple pubs."

These were just coworkers. They were probably fine. They probably weren't hitting on her. But that didn't sound like Hannah's scene. "Uh, thanks," Hannah said. "I have to do a bunch of stuff tonight. And I've got to get up early."

"You gotta do a bunch of stuff on Tuesday night?" Drew shook his head. "You oughtta relax. This place sucks the life outta you. Might as well enjoy your time off work. We'll show you the best bars."

"No, thanks," Hannah said.

"What's the matter?" Spencer grinned. "We don't bite."

People only said that if they thought you were scared of them. Hannah wasn't scared of these guys. She just didn't feel like hanging out with them.

Hannah caught Jack's eye from across her table. He was watching the conversation, still holding his book. He looked ready to spring up to help a damsel in distress. She wasn't in distress. But she'd rather have sat with him than with these guys.

"You live around here?" Drew asked.

"Not too far," Hannah said.

"Yeah? I live out by Cadillac. Throw parties sometimes. You oughtta come."

"Thanks." Hannah rose. At this point, she just wanted to get back to her desk for the rest of the break. She had finished her cookies. There was no reason to stay.

"Where you going?" Spencer asked. "Want some candy? I've got Mike & Ike's." He reached into his lunchbox.

"I've gotta get back to work."

"Sure you don't wanna come with us tonight?" Drew asked.

"No, thank you." Hannah shoved her phone into her pocket and walked away, throwing her cookie wrapper in the trash as she passed.

Back in the office, she sank into her desk chair. If it was allowed, she might start eating lunch at her desk to avoid dealing with the guys from the mill. Now she could check social media before lunch was over.

Before the afternoon started, Hannah discovered one other woman in this sea of men. The woman walked into the office from the parking lot, on her way to the break room, but stopped when she saw Hannah. She was around forty, with blonde hair pulled back in a tight ponytail, jeans and a T-shirt, and a fluorescent safety vest.

"Howdy," she said. "You must be the new office manager. I'm Sarah." She held out her hand.

Hannah shook it. "I'm Hannah. Steve's sister."

"Uh-huh." Sarah surveyed her. "How are you holding up?"

"Okay," Hannah said. "Mostly. I've made a bunch of mistakes, but I don't think Steve's about to fire me."

Sarah laughed. "Gotta keep on his good side, even if you are his sister. How're you getting along with the crew? Boys in the break room bother you any?"

"They seemed a little excited to see somebody new." That was probably all it was, right?

Sarah nodded knowingly. "They pay me no mind since my husband's an operator. But Faye—the last girl—used to complain the guys were bugging her. When she started dating Chad West, one of the forklift drivers, the rest of the guys settled down. Chad was mad when Faye got fired. Said he'd quit, but he didn't. Well, I gotta eat before lunch is over. Good to meet you, Hannah." She disappeared into the break room.

As lunch finished, Jack reappeared with his book, stopping in front of Hannah's desk. "How's it going?"

Although Jack had been part of losing that five-thousand-dollar order earlier, lunchtime had shown that his behavior was, comparatively, better than some of the other mill workers. And since Hannah would have to work with him regularly, it made no sense to be unfriendly. Jack probably already thought her unfriendly already. Yet here he was, giving her another chance.

"It's going all right," Hannah said. "There's still a lot I don't know, but I think I can make it through the day."

He nodded. "It's a lot to learn all at once. I heard you're Steve's sister."

"Yeah. Hannah."

"Nice to meet you, Hannah." Jack smiled. "New in town?"

"I'm from Chicago. But our grandpa built the mill, and I've been staying in his old house over the summer. Kind of a vacation place."

"How do you like Fraser's Mill?"

Hannah shook her head. "It's not really my speed. But I don't have a place to live in Chicago right now, so I'm working this job for six months. As soon as that's done, I'm moving back."

"The city must be exciting," Jack said. "Not that I would really know. I grew up on a farm down the road."

Hannah's analysis of him as a farm boy had been correct. He seemed like the quintessential Fraser's Mill guy—mild, relaxed, content. How could people be content in such an insignificant town? But—as a high-strung person herself—she appreciated his relaxed attitude. Honestly, it reminded her a little of Doc's attitude toward being a doctor.

Of course, there was a world of difference between Doc and Jack. Doc was an impressive, charming guy who would have done well anywhere and just happened to want to live here. She'd long given up on finding somebody else in Fraser's Mill who compared to Doc.

Jack's desk phone rang. He dashed to answer it, and just then Steve came to show Hannah how to add people to the client database.

Five PM rolled around, and Hannah prepared to leave. It hadn't been such a bad day. She had to deal with cranky customers, piles of paperwork, and a lot of racing back and forth with questions. But at least she was totally done at five.

She was starving, after her lunch of cookies, and too exhausted to cook something elaborate. The diner it would be.

This time Grace and Doc weren't there, thank goodness. Alex was at the front counter talking to Charlie. Town gossip said they were dating. Hannah ordered a burger and fries. She wasn't a fry person but was too hungry to care. She got a fruit smoothie too. The diner had recently started making those, which Hannah appreciated. She wasn't a milkshake person. Who wanted melted ice cream drunk through a straw?

Maybe when she got the hang of this job, she'd have things together enough to cook her own food regularly again. Being stressed at work and eating dinner out every night wasn't Hannah's idea of living. Of course, her real idea of living was being an influencer back in Chicago, with a solid enough channel that she didn't have to supplement her income with another job, and finally meeting her Mr. Right. But that would come in time. Hopefully. Based on the guys at the sawmill, she definitely wasn't going to meet Mr. Right around here.

The Sawmill

The next morning, a ringing tune woke Hannah. She groggily reached for her cell phone on the bedside table.

"Hannah, where the heck are you?" Steve's voice over the phone jolted her wide awake. "You're half an hour late. Don't tell me you're still in bed."

Hannah whisked out of bed. "I'm not," she said. "I'm so sorry, Steve. My alarm didn't go off. I don't know what happened. I'll be right over."

She checked her phone. No alarm. She must have forgotten to set it.

No time to plan an outfit. Hannah threw on a black tee and the same jeans and sandals she'd worn yesterday, gave her face, teeth, and hair a lick and a promise, and rushed out the door. She'd better drive, because there was no time to walk.

Whoops, she didn't have her keys. She rushed back, nearly tripping in her high-heeled sandals, and found a locked door.

She had fastened the spring lock behind her. Oh, no! Panic rose in her chest.

She'd deal with being locked out of the house later. Right now she had to run to work.

She rushed into the mill, hot and out of breath, to find Steve talking on the office phone. Her phone.

"Thanks, talk to you soon." Steve slammed down the receiver. He turned to Hannah.

"I know you've never had a job like this before," he said, in a tone that Hannah had particularly disliked when they were younger, "so maybe you don't understand that we take punctuality seriously around here. I expect you here at eight sharp."

The "or else" was heavily implied in Steve's voice.

"Steve, I didn't do it on purpose. I thought I set my alarm. But nothing went off."

"You forgot to set it," Steve said. "You might as well set one right now for Monday to Friday. It'll go off every day and you won't have to think about it. Now get to work. I'm wasting my time doing your job."

He stalked off. Hannah sat down, trying to compose herself. It would be okay. She wouldn't let it happen again, and Steve would get over it. Having her here was better than having nobody. It was his own choice to fire that previous office administrator.

"Are you okay?" Jack, wearing all denim again, appeared at her desk. Great, he'd heard the whole thing.

"I'm fine," Hannah said. "Just a rough morning. You probably heard Steve." She'd resolved to be nicer to Jack, but she wasn't in the mood for friendly chit-chat. "I need to get to my work."

He held up his hands, stepping backwards. "Okay, okay, I'm going."

Being late was only the first curveball of the day. When Hannah went to print invoices, the printer was out of toner. Where did they keep the new toner? She looked in all the drawers and boxes she could find. She'd have to ask Steve, and he was already mad.

There was nothing else to do. Hannah jammed on a hard hat and went into the mill, plugging her ears. Where was Steve?

Nowhere, apparently. She went all the way around the mill. Maybe he was outside. Hannah went out a side door. A number of men were out there driving forklifts and loading lumber. No Steve. She ventured around to the front, where guys were loading a truck. No Steve.

Maybe he was in one of the other buildings. It wasn't an emergency. She could wait until Steve got back.

She returned to her desk and found the phone ringing. It was a guy complaining that the load of lumber he'd received was missing some of the order. Hannah promised she'd get it set right ASAP.

"You'd better," the customer said gruffly. "Call me back."

What should she do? Where was Steve when Hannah needed him? It wasn't fair to train somebody only partway and leave them in charge of a whole office. She didn't know where to find the mistake. Faye had probably handled it, and unfortunately Hannah couldn't ask her.

Hannah started with looking up the customer's order. The invoice didn't match up with what the guy said he had gotten.

Should they send the lumber he claimed was missing? What if he was lying to get extra free lumber? Hannah groaned.

"Can I help?" Jack appeared over the desk again. Didn't he have truck drivers to talk to?

"No," Hannah said. This wasn't an issue for dispatching. "I'm just miserable. But I'll figure it out."

"I couldn't help overhearing your phone call," Jack said. "Why don't you give me the invoice number—"

"Oh, go away." Hannah made a shooing motion toward him. His suggestions were the last thing she wanted. Sure, he meant well. But at this point, Hannah didn't even care. "I've only been here a little over a day, I keep getting chewed out by my brother, I forgot my lunch again, and I don't need some goody-two-shoes farm kid in a Canadian tuxedo telling me how to do my job!"

Jack put his hands on his hips. "What am I supposed to do? Sit and watch you be miserable over here?"

"Yes," Hannah said. "I don't need your help. I took this job, it's my job, and I'm gonna do it."

"All right then." Jack shook his head. "Just trying to be helpful, Hannah." He turned on his heel and left.

Hannah laid her head on her arms. Why did she take this stupid job? There was nothing she could do about the toner or the messed-up order until she found Steve.

The phone rang again. Some guy wanted a lumber quote. Hannah managed to find the correct spreadsheet and work out the price. That was one thing she did know how to do.

Finally Steve came back, fractionally less cranky than earlier.

He'd been in the old water-powered mill, supervising the repair of a broken part. Hannah asked about the toner and the missing lumber.

"There's another spreadsheet with the links to buy office supplies," Steve said. "You use the company card. I'll get it to you. And talk to Jack about the missing lumber. He'll look up what truck it was on and talk to the guys who loaded it. They're required to do load checks and take photos. We'll see if there was a mistake or if this guy's trying to scam us." He disappeared into the mill.

Great. After yelling at Jack, Hannah needed his help after all.

Slowly, she approached him and waited until he got off a phone call.

He leaned back in his chair, looking up at her.

"Jack," Hannah said, "I suppose you heard Steve. Would you—"

She choked a little on the words "help me." It was exactly what he had offered.

"Yeah?" If he had heard Steve, he wasn't letting on.

"This guy says his order is missing lumber. Steve said you would know who packed the load."

"Uh-huh." Jack was still waiting, the suggestion of a smile on his face.

Hannah sighed. He was going to make her ask this outright, wasn't he? "Would you please help me figure this out?"

Jack sat upright at once. "Of course."

He helped Hannah get to the bottom of the issue. There had been two loads of the same kind of wood, and the order numbers had gotten switched. They would have to send the customer his missing lumber.

"Is it always like this around here?" Hannah asked Jack, as they came back from interviewing the guys in the lot. "Customers canceling orders, trucks breaking down, and wrong shipments being shipped?" When Dad and Steve talked about the mill, it never sounded so chaotic.

"Not always," Jack said. "It's just a coincidence, having all those things happen this week. It'll get better."

Hannah hoped so.

When lunchtime rolled around, Hannah used the vending machine again. She really needed to remember lunch tomorrow.

"Uh-uh," a voice said behind her. Of course it was Jack. "You're having too bad a day to eat vending machine candy."

"I'm not eating candy. I'm eating cookies." Hannah inserted her card in the machine and made her selection.

Jack picked up the cookie package before she could. "Protein: zero grams. This is all fat and sugar. I'll make you a deal, Hannah. You give me one of those cookies, and I'll trade you a sandwich. I've got an extra."

Of course he did. He must have been a Boy Scout. "Always prepared" could have been written on his forehead.

"Fine," Hannah said.

Jack smiled. "That's better."

He led the way to an empty table near the window, plunking down his lunchbox and book alongside the cookie package. "Ham on white or ham on rye? I've got both."

He launched into a silent meal prayer, making the sign of the cross. After her own prayer, Hannah asked, "Are you Catholic?"

He nodded, his mouth already full.

"Do you go to St. Anthony's?"

He swallowed. "Yes. Do you?"

"Yes. I sing in the noon choir."

"Aha," he said. "Then we've probably seen each other before. I go to the noon too. The choir sounds great."

"Thanks," Hannah said. "I don't remember seeing you before."

It wasn't like Hannah stared down from the choir loft every Sunday trying to identify the parishioners by the backs of their heads. She didn't usually hang out and talk with people after Mass either. By the time she had said her prayers after Mass and put her books away, she was ready to go home.

She started on Jack's extra sandwich. Surprisingly, the ham wasn't thin lunchmeat, but thick irregular slices. He must have cut it by hand. The bread—she had taken the white bread, thinking that if Jack had brought rye he probably liked rye—was crusty and also hand-sliced. Not what she would have expected from a workman's lunch. Jack must know something about food.

"So tell me," Jack said, "what do you do when you're not working in the sawmill? What's your job in Chicago?"

After Hannah's experience with Tori, she was extra reluctant to tell people what she tried to do for a living. But why should she care about what this farm boy thought of her?

"I have a video channel," she started her spiel. "I'm trying to grow the channel until I can make a living from it. But I'm stuck in Fraser's Mill because my parents did a house swap with a family in Berlin. I can't stay at their house, and I can't find any girls in Chicago who want me as a roommate."

She must sound inane and breathless.

Jack was listening seriously. "I've heard some people make a good living that way. Do you like it? Making videos, I mean?"

That was unexpected. Usually people were curious how much money her channel made, if they were interested at all. Nobody asked if she liked it.

"Most of the time," Hannah said. "I usually have fun making content. But I've been running out of things to videotape in Fraser's Mill."

Jack nodded. "I don't watch a lot of videos, but it seems to me you could do some nature videos with the local wildlife. There's always something interesting there."

That sounded too boring for Hannah's viewers, but she didn't mention it. "Thanks," she said.

Someone approached the table. It was Drew from yesterday. Hannah groaned interiorly.

"Hey, Hannah." He swung out the chair next to Hannah, between her and Jack. "We missed you last night." He turned to Jack. "What are you doing here? Shouldn't you be in a corner reading a book?" He sniggered.

Jack didn't react. "Hey, Drew."

Drew turned back to Hannah. "You're gonna hang out with him? Mr. Goody Two-Shoes?"

Hannah had called Jack a goody two-shoes herself, but it sounded different when Drew said it. "Excuse me, Drew," she said in her iciest tone, "Jack shared his lunch with me, because I came in late and didn't have a chance to bring mine."

"Oh! Should have asked me. I've got tons." Drew opened his lunchbox. "I've even got ice cream. It's not too melted." He pulled out a squishy-looking carton of mint chip, setting it in front of Hannah.

Jack raised his eyebrows, but didn't say anything.

"I've got a spoon somewhere." Drew opened an exterior pocket of his lunchbox that seemed mostly full of nails and screws and dirty napkins.

Was there no way to get out of this situation?

"No thank you, Drew," Hannah said. "I've had plenty to eat. I—"

"Was just going back to the office," Jack said. "I'm gonna show Hannah some dispatching things."

Thank goodness. "Yes," Hannah exclaimed. "Come on, Jack." She got up and nearly fled to the office, Jack following.

"Hey," Drew called. "I just sat down, and you're gonna leave?"

In the office, Hannah sank down at her desk. "Thanks, Jack."

He laughed. "Sorry, but your face when he plunked down that ice cream was priceless."

Hannah had to laugh with him. "Oh my goodness! I didn't know what to say when he dragged out that squishy carton and started looking for a spoon."

"Just a regular lunch break at the mill." There was mischief in Jack's smile.

"In that case I may keep on eating lunch at my desk."

"Yeah, it's a little less like the Wild West. Those guys aren't bad, but they're probably not the crowd you're used to."

Hannah smiled, shaking her head. "Nothing around here is what I'm used to."

"That's fair." Jack's brown eyes rested on her.

Hannah's gaze moved to her computer. "Are you really going to show me some dispatching things?"

"Sure. We have to coordinate your customers with my truckers. You might as well know a little about how dispatching works."

It really wasn't bad, working with Jack.

A Trip to Doc's

Hannah got home to find herself still locked out of the house. She'd forgotten about that. Sitting on the front porch, she called Dad.

Dad didn't know. He said Hannah should call her grandparents—if there was a spare key, they'd know where it was. Incidentally, he had heard about Hannah coming late for work. Hannah groaned. Of course Steve had told on her. Whatever Christine might say, Steve did tell his parents everything.

She called her grandparents and found that there was, in fact, another key. Grandma used to lock herself out often. The other key was behind the house, inside one of the deck chair cushions. "Don't forget to put it back," Grandpa said.

"Thanks, Grandpa, I won't."

"I hear you're working at the sawmill," Grandpa said. "How do you like it?"

Hannah hesitated. Apart from various mishaps, it hadn't

been too bad. "It's—definitely more interesting than I thought it would be."

Grandpa chuckled. "Most jobs are. I'm glad you're giving it a try. I'm proud of you."

Hopefully Grandpa wouldn't be too disappointed when Hannah quit and went back to Chicago. When she made it big with her video channel, he'd be proud of her for sure.

❧❦❧

Hungry after her long day—despite Jack kindly sharing his lunch—Hannah looked through the fridge and pantry. Just odds and ends. She'd better get something for dinner. And she needed something for lunch tomorrow.

There was nothing for it but to go to the grocery store. She may as well pick up enough to get by for a week or two. No need to shop every couple of days and dread running into a certain couple every time.

She poked her head in the door of Murray's Grocery, a bell jingling above her head. Was Doc there hanging out with Grace? No, Grace's dad was at the counter. The coast was clear. Now for her groceries. Hannah began perusing the dinner options. The store had a large display of local produce, lots of fall fruits and vegetables. They even had chestnuts in the shell. Someday she'd like to learn how to roast chestnuts, but it was too late for that tonight. The last time she and her brother Kenneth had attempted that, the shells (and the hard papery layer underneath) had been so hard to peel off that they'd given up.

She was picking out sweet potatoes when someone spoke behind her.

"Hannah?"

Hannah turned around to find Jack, smiling down at her. He was still wearing the denim outfit from earlier, and his hair was tousled.

"Jack!" she said. "Hi."

"I thought that was you," Jack said. "How's it going?"

"Oh, good, good," Hannah said. "I'm just getting some groceries."

"Me too." He smiled.

"I'm going to pack my own lunch tomorrow," Hannah told him. "So you won't need to rescue me from eating vending machine cookies."

Jack laughed. "Glad to hear it. Although, if you forget your lunch again, I'm always happy to share. Really, Hannah."

That was kind. "Well, thank you." Hannah tucked a strand of hair behind her ear. "That was a good sandwich. But I definitely intend to bring lunch from now on."

Jack's eyes crinkled behind his glasses. "I take it you're not going to pack any mint chip soup?"

Hannah burst out laughing. "Mint chip soup! I'm never going to live that down, am I?"

"Not if I have anything to do with it." Jack grinned.

Hannah shook her head at him, smiling in spite of herself.

"Well," he said, rousing himself, "I won't keep you. I'm just grabbing a few things before my shift starts. Have a good evening, Hannah. I'll see you tomorrow—bright and early!"

Hannah laughed. "A little too bright and early for me. But I'll be there."

He smiled. "I feel that. See you, Hannah."

He headed for the dairy section, leaving Hannah looking after him. What did he mean about grabbing a few things before his shift started? They didn't work again until tomorrow. Did Jack have a second job?

Well, no need to stand around wondering about Jack. Hannah still hadn't gotten her groceries, and her precious free time was slipping away.

⁙

Hannah started her third day of work in a better frame of mind. Her alarm went off without an issue, and she had packed her lunch, a chicken Caesar salad, right after getting home from the store. She had forgotten about choir practice last night, but the choir could hardly expect her to sing when she'd just started a new job. It felt like a different world than Hannah had lived in a couple days ago.

The morning went well, which was a relief. Steve showed Hannah a few things, Jack showed her others, and altogether she felt she was getting a handle on her job.

Right before lunch, Hannah noticed an invoice on her desk that ought to have been taken out to the guys in the yard. She grabbed the invoice and ran outside, leaving the door open behind her.

A few steps later, her high-heeled sandal caught in a hole. She tripped, and her ankle turned under her. She cried out, landing hard on her side.

So much pain. Hannah lay on the ground, trying to take deep

breaths. Maybe her ankle was broken. She didn't know what a broken bone felt like. Did it crunch? She might have felt a crunch when she fell.

Running footsteps approached on the gravel, and someone bent over her. "Hannah! Hannah! Are you okay?" It was Jack, his face concerned.

"I twisted my ankle." Hannah gasped as she tried to move it. "I don't know if it's broken."

"Does anything else hurt?"

It was hard to think about anything except the ankle. One of Hannah's elbows had gotten scrubbed when she fell, but at least she hadn't skinned her hands or knees.

"Can you sit up?" Jack gave Hannah his hand.

She sat up and evaluated the ankle. "Ow." It hurt terribly. There was no way she would try walking on it.

"You'd better get that sandal off." Jack reached for her foot, but stopped. "May I?"

Hannah nodded, her teeth clenched. She was trying not to cry. Jack unbuckled the sandal and slid it off, his hands gentle, trying not to jar her ankle again.

"The ankle's swollen, but it doesn't look misshapen," Jack said. "Could be a good sign. Does it hurt when I press here?"

Hannah gasped. "Ow."

"How about here?"

"Ow." Tears flowed down her face.

"Hmm. It could be broken, or it could be a sprain. Let's get you inside."

He crouched down. Before Hannah had a chance to protest,

he scooped her up in his solid arms in a seemingly effortless motion and carried her toward the building. He set her carefully on her desk chair and grabbed his own chair to put under her foot. He found an ice pack somewhere, wrapped it in paper towels, and placed it over her ankle.

"How are you doing?" His eyes, behind his glasses, showed concern.

"It hurts a lot."

"I'm gonna call Doc," Jack said. "You'd better get it checked out."

Doc? No. That would be so awkward. Hannah had never seen Doc professionally, and she didn't intend to start now.

"No," she said. "It's probably just sprained. I don't need to go anywhere."

"Nonsense," Jack said. "You won't pay a dime. It happened on company time. And if it's broken, you don't want to wait to get it checked."

He picked up his phone and dialed. "Nobody's answering. I'll just take you over there."

Hannah groaned. Nobody listened to her. And her ankle throbbed miserably. Maybe it was broken. She wiped her eyes.

She probably wouldn't have tripped and fallen if she hadn't been wearing high heels. People had told her she would trip in those sandals, and she hadn't listened. She didn't feel like getting a scolding for that on top of being injured. Better take the other sandal off. Hannah flung it under her desk.

"What's going on?" Steve appeared. "Hannah, what happened to you?"

"I stepped in a hole and fell and hurt my ankle."

"Oh, no." Steve surveyed the ankle. "That looks pretty swollen. You'd better get over to Doc's."

"I told Jack, I don't need to go anywhere. I don't think it's broken."

"If you don't get it checked out, the company could be liable," Steve said. "You're going. Jack will take you. It's almost lunchtime anyway."

"I can bring you right over, Hannah," Jack called from across the room. "Steve, I might not get back by one. I'm gonna forward my calls to my cell."

"Sounds good. Feel better, Hannah. I hope it's not broken." Steve vanished into the mill.

She had no choice now. Hannah began to stand up.

"What are you doing?" Jack demanded. "You can't walk on that ankle. I'll carry you out to the car."

"You'll do no such thing," Hannah said. "I can hop."

"Uh-huh." Jack sounded dubious. "Then I'm following you."

Hannah hopped to the door, lost her balance, clutched wildly at the doorframe, and found a strong arm steadying her.

"You still want to hop out there? Barefoot?" Jack asked.

Hannah looked at the gravel parking lot. It looked painful. Great. It was one of those I-told-you-so moments.

"Okay, fine," she said. "You can carry me. But only because it would be miserable to hop on the gravel."

"Of course." His eyes were innocent, but his tone betokened amusement. "At your service, ma'am," he said, and swept her off her feet.

Literally.

Why hadn't Steve helped Hannah to her car? Why had he left her to be a damsel in distress for Mr. Football Player Farm Boy to rescue?

He held her like she weighed nothing. It was ridiculous, being carried bridal style by a random coworker—incidentally, a coworker whose arm and chest muscles were incredibly solid. What in the world did Jack do for his workouts?

Jack deposited her in the passenger seat of her car and put the driver's seat all the way back before getting in.

"I'm not that short," Hannah said.

He shook his head. "I'm not saying a word."

Doc's office, on the lower floor of his house in town, looked crowded. Cars were parked in his driveway and on the road.

"We'll be here all day," Hannah said. "Come on, let's go back. I don't think my ankle's broken."

Jack shook his head. "Boss's orders. What are you gonna do about it?" His tone was amused again.

"Jack Rogers, you are the most aggravating man," Hannah said, but she unbuckled her seatbelt. "Fine. Let's go in. You are not carrying me." The last thing she wanted was Doc and the Fraser's Mill people seeing that. What on earth would they think?

She hopped to the door, Jack shadowing her.

Doc's waiting room was full. Hannah had been in there a few times before, when she and Doc used to hang out. She had done a video interview in his exam room. But she had never been there as a patient. This was so embarrassing. She sank down in a folding chair, the injured ankle stretched in front of her.

"You all right? I've got to take a phone call," Jack said.

"I'll live."

Jack vanished. Of course he would get a call and leave her with a bunch of sick people and Doc.

The door of Doc's exam room opened, and an elderly woman with a walker came out. "Ed?" Doc called, and a guy with a bandaged hand—didn't he own the gas station?—got up.

Doc looked around the room. "Hannah? What are you doing here?" He came by her chair, stooping to see her ankle. "What happened?" He sounded concerned, but businesslike.

It felt weird. Back when she was hoping to date Doc, Hannah had told herself she would never come to him as a patient. Now he was dating someone else, and Hannah was an ordinary patient like any other.

"I stepped in a hole and rolled my ankle," Hannah said. "I don't think it's broken, but my brother's making me get it checked out."

"Ah, I see." Doc straightened up to his full height. Hannah had to crane her neck to look at him. "I'll check it out. You'll have to wait a bit, but I'll get to you as soon as I can."

Jack had returned by the time Doc called Hannah's name. She let him support her as she hopped into the exam room. Better than letting Doc help her.

She sat on the exam table, and Doc, blue-gloved and official, examined her ankle, pressing it in different areas and asking whether it hurt. It hurt a lot.

"As far as I can tell," Doc said at last, "you just sprained it. Let me wrap it, and I'll give you crutches to borrow. You could get it X-rayed at the hospital, but I don't think it's necessary."

He took off his gloves. "An over-the-counter pain reliever will probably help."

"Thanks," Hannah said.

He raised his eyebrows. "I told you you were gonna trip someday with those high-heeled shoes."

How did he know she had been wearing high-heeled shoes? Hannah did remember him saying something like that, early in the summer. Grace probably never wore high heels. Grace probably followed every health and safety regulation Doc gave her. Well, Hannah liked high heels. It wasn't her fault there was a hole in the parking lot. Anybody could trip stepping in a hole.

Doc pulled out a pair of crutches. "Have you ever been on crutches before?"

Hannah shook her head.

"Then be careful. I'll lend these to you. Get your boyfriend to help you to the car."

He thought Jack was her boyfriend? Ugh. He had probably been sizing them up as a couple when Jack helped her hobble into the room. If Hannah did go out with anybody, she wanted it to be someone impressive. Someone she could proudly introduce to Doc.

"He's not my boyfriend. He's a coworker."

"Coworker? Did you get a job in town?"

Doc didn't know about the mill job. Word must not have spread around town. Considering the Fraser's Mill town gossip, that was surprising.

"The sawmill," Hannah said. "Office administrator."

Doc whistled. "Wow. So you aren't going back to Chicago?"

Hannah shook her head. "I'm stuck here for six months. Long story."

"Good, then we'll see you around town." Doc smiled.

"We" — that meant him and Grace. Hannah had to go.

"Thanks, Doc." Hannah crutched her way to the door as Doc held it open.

"See you, Hannah."

"See you."

Jack was in the waiting room, taking another call, but he got off the phone to help Hannah and her crutches into the car.

On the way back he was unusually quiet and thoughtful. For someone so mild-mannered, Jack usually talked a good deal.

They were almost at the mill when he spoke. "Hannah, if your ankle isn't too bad this evening, would you go to dinner with me?"

Oh. She hadn't expected that. Although, thinking back, it made sense. All the attention he paid her — sharing his food, hanging around her desk, talking to her at the grocery store, helping with her injured ankle — must stem from interest in her. That wasn't what she was looking for. Besides, they'd just known each other a couple days. It was time to nip that in the bud.

Hannah shook her head. "Thanks anyway, Jack. But I don't date coworkers. Besides, I'm far too busy to go out with anybody right now."

His face was serious. "I see."

Silence ensued. Jack pulled into the mill parking lot. Wasn't he going to say anything?

"I wonder how Steve did with my job this afternoon,"

Hannah said hurriedly. "Maybe he'll appreciate me more now. I don't know what he thought he was going to do after he fired that last lady."

She kept up a stream of one-sided conversation as Jack helped her across the parking lot until she was safely ensconced behind her desk. Jack went back to his own desk, and—having missed lunch—Hannah worked her way through a salad while answering the phone and printing invoices. She was so busy she almost didn't notice her ankle.

When she glanced over, Jack seemed glum. Hannah hadn't wanted to hurt his feelings. But he didn't interest her romantically. He was friendly and kind, and it was nice working with him. But Hannah knew what kind of guy she wanted to date. And Jack—a farm boy, content to live in a little town—wasn't that kind of guy. Hannah needed somebody who fit into her life, the other impressive half of her "power couple." Jack was sweet, and he was strong—she hadn't forgotten how effortlessly he'd picked her up—but he wasn't Hannah's type. How in the world had Doc thought they were dating?

Demise of a Cell Phone

It was maddening, being on crutches. Steve found out about Hannah's high-heeled shoes and loudly told her he had a dress code which specifically didn't allow high heels. The mill workers wore steel-toed boots and Jack wore tennis shoes, so the rule was clearly made for Hannah.

When Saturday rolled around, Hannah had never been so glad to have a day off. She hadn't even worked a full week at the mill, but it felt like she had been there her whole life. She would relax all day and maybe shoot a video. She didn't have anything yet for next Tuesday, and if she didn't put videos out on time, her viewership would wane.

She was sitting on the dock behind the log house, admiring the sunlight on the river, when a video idea came to her. She'd done a fishing video before, but that was focused on fishing (and she hadn't caught much, anyway). She could do a video of the river itself. It wasn't big, but the scenery was pretty. She could set it to nice music.

Last time Hannah had taken the rowboat, but she'd recently discovered a kayak in the garage. It might be fun to take the kayak. She was still supposed to be careful of her injured ankle, but kayaking kept your feet elevated, right?

Should she use her camera for the video? After some internal debate, she took her phone instead. There were too many ways to damage a camera—water, sand, blowing debris—and she shouldn't risk it.

It was surprisingly hard to get the kayak on the water without putting weight on her bad ankle. Oh well, Doc hadn't said exactly how long she had to stay off the ankle. It would probably be fine.

It was a perfect September day. The sky was a rich blue, scattered with cumulus clouds. Hannah pushed off and paddled away from the shore, heading downstream. It was too early for the leaves to turn colors, but the greens and flowers of late summer were nice too.

The real problem was paddling while videotaping. It was a small sit-on-top kayak, and Hannah had to rest the paddle across her lap whenever she held up her phone. She was afraid she'd knock it into the water. This was really a job for two people, one to paddle and one to videotape. Maybe she should have asked somebody to help her. Earlier in the summer, Doc probably would have done it. She pushed aside the thought of Doc sitting opposite her, rowing and making jokes.

There was a beautiful bit ahead, near a bank where rays of sunlight fell through the trees into the water. Hannah approached slowly so the kayak wouldn't drift too much. Was that a turtle on a log? She laid the paddle across her knees and pulled out her phone.

Oh, a message from Christine. She might as well read it. Hannah clicked into the message, squinting at the screen in the outdoor glare.

"Hey, Hannah, Steve and I were wondering if you want to come for dinner tomorrow. I want to hear about your first week at work."

Hopefully Steve wouldn't come up with any new reasons to be irritated with her before tomorrow. The last time he had seen her—on Friday—he had told her to go home and rest her foot over the weekend. There wasn't any overtime this week. Sometimes, Hannah had heard, everyone had to come in on Saturday. She was lucky it hadn't happened her first week.

"Sure, I'd love to," Hannah replied to Christine. "See you tomorrow!"

A crash in the brush startled her, making her jump. The paddle on her lap tilted and slid into the water. She lunged to catch it. Oh, no. Her stomach dropped. She was going over.

The shock of cold water hit hard, and she gasped, trying to orient herself, held upright by her life jacket. She was next to the kayak. She had dropped her phone. The water was dark and murky, and she didn't see the phone anywhere. Panic hit worse than the cold water—how could she lose her phone?

There was the paddle, floating away. Hannah swam over and grabbed it, then returned to the kayak. She flipped it over. If she tried to get in, she'd probably tip it again. Did real kayakers know how to get back in from the water? Probably. Her best chance was to swim to shore, pushing the kayak along.

The nearest shore was too thickly wooded to beach the kayak, so it took a while for Hannah's plan to work. Coming onshore, drenched, the wind bit through her. It was gonna be a cold time getting home. Hannah got into the kayak and started paddling back.

Why had she been so stupid? Why had she brought her phone with her, in her hand, and managed to capsize the kayak? She had so much stuff on that phone. She didn't even want to think about all the things she didn't have backed up. A ton of B-roll footage and notes for her channel—including some financial records—and a million photos and screencaps and things she'd downloaded because she wanted to save them. Hannah groaned.

She should have brought somebody else with her. If she'd asked Jack, he'd probably have been enthusiastic. He was probably great at boats—he'd never talked about boating, but he seemed like that kind of guy. But she'd just turned down a date with him a couple days ago, and asking would have felt awkward.

How was there so much wind out here? It wasn't a cold day. But the sun seemed to make no difference to someone who was soaking wet.

It seemed an eternity before Hannah beached the kayak and trailed soggily into her house. She was putting too much weight on the sprained ankle. It was beginning to ache. And the ankle wrap from Doc was sopping and would be hard to get off.

After a warm shower, blow-drying her hair, and re-wrapping her injured ankle with a pair of stockings while the real ankle wrap dried, Hannah sat in the living room with her laptop. She needed to see how much data she had lost on her phone.

According to the internet, her photos and contacts were backed up. But everything else was gone.

It was a blow. She'd have to take so much footage over again, and she'd never remember the other things she'd saved on the phone. So many missing messages and notes. Why hadn't she backed that stuff up? She wanted to cry.

Pull yourself together, Hannah. Crying wouldn't fix this. There was no getting the data back. Hannah remembered vaguely where she had been, but the river was too murky and deep to find anything. All she could do was replace the phone. The same model was still available online.

Hannah groaned at the price. That would make a dent in her salary. Maybe she'd better find it used.

After a little searching she was proud of herself when she bought a used phone, over fifty dollars cheaper than the new one. It would take a few days to ship, but she could make do. She'd use her laptop for internet in the house, and she could get a cheap flip phone from the gas station to make emergency phone calls. Things would be okay. It would do her good to have a tech vacation. She tended to be glued to her smartphone too much. She'd just have to make this week's video on her computer.

☙❧❧❧☙

It was annoying not having her phone. Hannah kept going to check social media and remembering she only had a flip phone. Whatever did people do before smartphones? They must have had to write a lot of things down. Hannah shuddered to think what would happen if all technology suddenly disappeared.

After the hard work week, the sprained ankle, and the kayak incident, it was pleasant to go to Steve and Christine's. Even though Steve was her boss.

"So how do you like your job?" Christine asked, serving Hannah a generous portion of her favorite asparagus and tomato salad.

Hannah looked at Steve, who was eating potatoes with gusto and entertaining Noah. "Do you want the real version, or the I'm-in-front-of-my-boss version?"

Christine laughed. "Fair point," she said. "Well, Steve has been having a much easier time with you there. Trying to run the front desk himself was crazy. I tell him he needs to hire more supervisors, but he says there's a lot of things he has to oversee himself."

"Steve never did like to delegate," Hannah said.

"That's because when I delegate, things go badly," Steve protested through his potatoes. "There's no point in delegating when you can do it better yourself."

"Darling," Christine said, "I have Evelyn help me with folding the laundry — even though it doesn't come out like mine and takes far longer — because she needs to learn that skill. Someday she'll do it better than I do. It's probably the same way for adults."

"That's different," Steve said. "When you teach your kids things, you hope some of it will stick. These guys at the mill — you tell them something and five days later they're doing it the same stupid way they were before."

It was funny how Steve was the opposite of Dad. Dad

liked to delegate. He checked in on the family's four sawmills occasionally, leading from a distance. Hannah doubted that many of the sawmill workers had even met Dad. There was a pretty high turnover among the workers, mostly because the job involved so much manual labor.

Christine shook her head at Steve. "You'll run yourself ragged," she said, but her voice was affectionate. "Hannah, I still want to hear about your week."

"Well, I learned pretty quickly not to eat lunch in the break room," Hannah said. "It's like the Wild West in there. There's one other woman — her name's Sarah, and she's married to one of the operators — but I haven't seen her much since the first day. She must be busy."

"Have you had any trouble with the guys?" Christine asked. "That would be strange being the only single girl there."

"There were a couple guys who were badgering me to go out for drinks with them, offering me melted ice cream, stuff like that," Hannah said. "The second time it happened, the dispatcher came up with an excuse for us to go back to the office. I'm gonna eat my meals at my desk from now on."

"It shouldn't be a problem, Chris," Steve assured Christine. "Some of the guys are pretty rough, but we don't have any real bad eggs."

"Good." Christine looked relieved.

"Besides, Jack can keep looking out for her," Steve said. "That guy was born to be a bodyguard. Or play football."

"Ah, so Jack's the dispatcher you mentioned who helped you out. What do you think of him?" Christine's expression was knowing. Oh no, she was probably trying to matchmake.

"He's all right," Hannah said. "A farm boy with his nose in a book. I hope it won't be awkward working with him—he asked me out yesterday, and I turned him down."

"Ooh!" Steve grinned at Hannah.

Hannah stuck out her tongue. Steve always teased her about guys.

Christine had been bustling around, but now she sat at the table. "He's interested in you?"

Hannah groaned. "Yeah. I guess I should have figured that out from the start. But I thought he was just friendly. He's not my type, Christine. He's so—mild. And he's a goody two-shoes. He grew up on a farm, and he does nothing but read books and do his job. We have completely different lives. The only things we have in common are working at the mill and going to St. Anthony's."

"Maybe a mild farm boy would be a good change of pace for you," Christine said. "Opposites attract, so they say."

Hannah sipped her water. "Look, it's not like the idea didn't cross my mind. I've been around him enough. He literally picked me up and carried me to my car when I sprained my ankle."

"He carried you?" Christine's eyes gleamed. "How have I not heard this story yet?"

Steve must not have bothered to mention Hannah's ankle. Hannah filled Christine in.

"Wow." Christine sat back. "That was super nice of him. You're sure you're not interested? He sounds like a real catch."

Hannah groaned. "The whole thing was so embarrassing. I felt like a damsel in distress. And just because somebody happens to have some good qualities doesn't mean he's a match for me. I'm not looking for a farm boy, Christine. I don't want to stay in Fraser's Mill, planting radishes. I need to find somebody who fits with my life in Chicago. The whole power couple thing. You know."

"All right, all right," Christine said. "You don't have to convince me. Maybe you should get together with one of the guys from your college."

"Nobody gets together with college classmates this long afterwards," Hannah said. "There are lots of young single Catholics in Chicago. I'd rather find somebody there."

Evelyn piped up, mid-dessert. "Aunt Hannah, will you play hide-and-seek with me after dinner?"

Hannah brought herself back to the four-year-old world with a start. "Totally."

Much better to entertain her niece than talk about her nonexistent love life.

Someone to Watch Over Me

It was late when Hannah left. She had played many rounds of hide-and-seek with Evelyn and tried to teach Noah pat-a-cake. Christine said he was a little young for it.

Finally Steve reminded Hannah she had work in the morning. "At least you don't have a forty-five minute commute," he said. "You can roll out of bed and go in."

Hannah made a face. "I also have to put on semi-clean clothes and pack a lunch. Okay, I'm going." She gave hugs all round and departed.

The road from Cadillac to Fraser's Mill was dark and lonely, winding through virgin forest. Hannah wasn't used to going this way in the dark, only during the daytime—it seemed unfamiliar and gloomy. It would be a good place to hit a deer, too. This was deer season. Hannah put on her brights and watched the road. She only had to dim the lights for oncoming traffic one or two times.

Wait. Her dashboard was glowing with strange lights, and

the car slowed to a crawl. Oh, no. Hannah's hands tightened on the wheel. What was going on?

Hannah pulled over. She didn't know what the warning lights meant, but it didn't look good. She sniffed. No strange smells. Maybe the car had stalled. She tried to start it again. Nothing.

She'd better call somebody. Steve would know what to do. Hannah went for her phone and came up with the flip phone. Good thing she had bought it. Her hands were shaking.

She flipped the phone open, but the screen was black. Hannah pressed the power button, to no avail. Oh, no. She had forgotten to charge it.

There was still juice in the car battery, even if the car wouldn't start, so she could charge it enough to call someone. Hannah fished out the charger cable she kept in the console. In the dark car, it wouldn't plug in. She opened her door to look at it in the overhead light. Her charger was USB-C, compatible with her smartphone, but apparently not compatible with this.

Great. She was stranded in the middle of nowhere with a broken-down car and a dead phone.

Hannah began to cry, her face in her hands, sobs shaking her. How had she been so stupid? Why did these things happen to her all the time in Fraser's Mill? Stuff like this never happened back home.

Finally she blew her nose and wiped her eyes. Crying wouldn't get her anywhere. Maybe she could learn something from the engine. Hannah popped the hood and got out, leaving the car lights on. It was dark under the hood, and she had no idea what to look for. There wasn't any steam. The car had turned off for no apparent reason.

It wasn't the battery, because the lights worked. It wasn't the radiator. Might as well give the car one more try. Without much hope, Hannah tried starting it again.

To her surprise, the car roared to life. Thank goodness. She didn't know what was wrong, but maybe she could limp it back to Fraser's Mill.

She had only gone about another mile when the car shut off again. She coasted to a stop at the side of the road. Now she was in a long straight stretch, with uninhabited woods on either side.

Don't panic, Hannah. It would be okay. She waited a few minutes and tried again.

Nothing. It didn't even sound like the car was trying to start. Those warning lights were as unintelligible as ever.

Maybe the car manual would help. Hannah fished in the glovebox and pulled out the manual, scattering insurance and registration papers all over the car. She'd pick them up later.

Hannah turned on the dome light, using still more car battery — yikes — and looked up warning lights in the car manual. It wasn't much help. Apparently the car shut off automatically if there was something wrong with the engine or the powertrain. Hannah didn't know what a powertrain was.

She was too far from Fraser's Mill to walk, and she wasn't going to walk by herself in the dark anyway. This was a dangerous situation for a young lady. It was the kind of thing Mom always worried about. This was why Hannah had bought that stupid flip phone — it was supposed to help in emergencies.

There was nothing to do but wait here and flag down passing

cars for help. At least whoever came by would probably be harmless. People didn't get mugged in rural northern Michigan, did they?

Hannah rocked back and forth, arms wrapped around her, as she watched the road. Lots of tourists traveled this way—it was the same road that went from 131 to Traverse City.

Lights were approaching, and her heart leaped. Better catch the driver's attention. Hannah got out of her car, carefully staying off the road—her cream-colored outfit should be fairly visible—and waved wildly.

The car sped past. Was it possible the driver hadn't seen her? Maybe he or she didn't feel safe stopping, or didn't care if someone was stranded.

Hannah got back in the car with a sigh, adrenaline still pumping from the hope that had arisen when she saw the lights. If worst came to worst, Steve would come by in the morning, and he'd recognize Hannah's car. Hannah didn't even want to think about being out here all night. She'd do a rotten job at work tomorrow. But if she took a day off, Steve would have to man the office.

Hannah folded her arms, hugging herself. Why hadn't she brought a jacket? She closed her eyes. "Jesus, please—send help!"

Finally another car approached, and lights began flashing red and blue. The police. Oh, thank goodness, she was as good as rescued. She could explain the situation to the officer.

Hannah turned on the dome light. It was good if the police could see how many people were in the car and what was going on. Hannah didn't want to alarm anybody.

The police car parked across the road from her. Footsteps crunched across gravel, and Hannah rolled down her window. Thankfully that still worked.

"Ma'am, are you okay?" a male voice said, and a young dark-haired officer appeared next to the window. His tone changed abruptly. "Hannah?"

Hannah blinked, staring at the officer. It couldn't be. This guy didn't wear glasses. But she knew him. "Jack?"

He nodded. "Uh-huh."

"You didn't tell me you were a policeman." Hannah raised her eyebrows. So that was why Jack was in such good shape. And must have been what he had meant when he mentioned getting groceries before his shift.

"Volunteer deputy sheriff," Jack said. "I help out when they need it. Speaking of which, you look like you could use some help. Car break down?"

Hannah nodded. For some reason—maybe from all the stress and adrenaline—her eyes were tearing up again. This was ridiculous. She was stranded in the middle of nowhere, and who should show up but her ever-present coworker, who happened to be a deputy sheriff. "The engine shut off," she said. "I got it started once but then it stopped again. My phone's dead."

His eyes looked concerned. "Okay. Why don't you wait with me in the police car. I'll call you a tow truck."

Hannah nodded. "Do you need my license and registration?"

"Yes. We always ask for that."

"Uh." Hannah looked at the papers scattered all over the car. "I've got the registration and proof of insurance, but they're mixed in with all these expired ones from the glovebox. Is it okay if I dive on the floor for them?"

He smiled. "Sure. But for your own ease of access, you might want to organize your papers later."

Of course he would say that. Hannah dived toward the floor and scrabbled among the papers. Last year's insurance. Old registration. Where were the current papers? It took an age to find them, with Jack waiting patiently at the window. When Hannah finally sat back up, she had been upside down so long her head swam.

"Thanks," Jack said simply. "Come with me."

Hannah had never sat in a police car before. In the front seat, she didn't feel like a criminal. Jack called for a tow truck. He had already told his dispatcher about the incident over the radio.

He was all business and efficiency as he talked to the car insurance people. Hannah took a sidelong glance at him. Hard to believe her mild, bookworm coworker was also a deputy sheriff in a brown-and-black uniform and a badge. That was pretty impressive, actually. She barely recognized him as the mild farm boy she'd met in the mill office. Although—no. He was still the same farm boy, even in a police uniform.

His head turned, and she looked away.

"The tow truck should be here in about forty-five minutes," he said. "We'll wait here, unless I get other instructions."

"Thanks."

Hannah wanted to say how grateful she was for the rescue, but after having just refused a date with him, she felt awkward. For the rest of their work week, he had been quiet and only interacted with her when necessary. He probably didn't want anything to do with her. This was just part of his deputy sheriff duties.

All that came out of her mouth was, "You're not wearing your glasses."

"Contacts," he explained. "I wear them for sports and when I'm on duty. It's easy to get your glasses knocked off."

"Oh, I see."

He turned toward her. "Were you on your way somewhere important? Can I take you somewhere after this?"

She shook her head. "I was just going home. I had dinner with Steve's family."

He nodded. "It's nice to have family nearby. I had Sunday dinner with my family before I went on duty."

"On the farm?" Hannah could just see Jack in a barnyard surrounded by cows, pigs, and chickens. "How many are there in your family?"

"Nine, counting my parents," Jack said. "Five sisters and a brother. I'm the oldest."

"What made you decide to work in the sawmill instead of on the farm?"

Maybe she shouldn't have asked that. It probably sounded like he should have stayed on the farm to help his family.

"I've got three cousins working on the farm, besides my family," Jack said. "I came back from college and my dad didn't need me. The mill needed a dispatcher, and I'm pretty good with maps and routes, so I applied there."

"And you drive around at night rescuing people who are stranded by the side of the road," Hannah said. "Thanks, by the way."

He smiled. "Glad to help."

Maybe he wasn't mad at Hannah for refusing the date, after all. Working with him might be more comfortable now.

The tow truck finally arrived, and Hannah rode back with Jack, feeling a little like she was on a police ride-along. It was after midnight. She'd be groggy at work tomorrow. How did Jack do it, taking night shifts before a long day working at the mill?

She'd underestimated him. He wasn't just a goody two-shoes who worked in dispatching and sat around reading. He must really care about the people here, working a second job to help protect them. It was good knowing there were people like him keeping the community safe.

Complaints and Tea

Monday morning hit like a ton of bricks. Hannah's flip phone went off at seven AM, and she had to fumble for thirty seconds before figuring out how to silence the alarm. Stupid flip phone.

Somehow she strained her sprained ankle again. She'd tried to baby it after her couple days on crutches, but with all her weekend activities, it had been hard to rest. She turned on her light and blinked miserably in the brightness. Why did people have to get up before sunrise for work?

In the bathroom, Hannah peered at the dark circles under her eyes. She splashed cold water on her face. That was supposed to help with dark circles.

Who cared, anyway? She wasn't trying to impress anybody at the sawmill. She'd been dressing more casually than usual—jeans and T-shirts—because what did it matter, here?

She still hadn't made a video for this week, and she needed to put one out tomorrow, unless she was going to make an apology video for being late. Other channels had done that, and it could work as long as your reason was interesting. She could always tell about her sawmill work or the sprained ankle or the kayak incident. Too bad she didn't have video footage from any of those things.

Maybe she could come up with an idea during lunch.

She took so long getting ready she almost made herself late. Since her car was in the shop, she had to walk to work. She half walked, half ran, mindful of her ankle. At least she wasn't wearing heels. The chunky white Gen Z sneakers she'd bought were pretty comfortable.

Jack was already there, on the phone, when she got in. The dark circles under his eyes matched Hannah's. He must have been up late on that police shift.

Around ten AM, Jack had to help the guys in the lot. While he was out, a truck arrived. Hannah went out to meet the driver. Part of her job was greeting truck drivers and making sure everyone was on the same page.

This truck driver was a thin man who looked like he didn't know how to smile. "I'm coming in to fill my water bottle," he said.

"Sure, no problem." Hannah led the way. "How was your drive?"

"It could have been worse," the driver said. "No thanks to that idiot dispatcher. He sent me on the world's worst route. All hills and potholes. The man doesn't know a thing about driving a truck."

"Hey." How could this guy badmouth Jack like that? "That's my coworker you're talking about. He's a good dispatcher. If he sent you on a route with hills and potholes, that must have been the only one."

"Ha," the truck driver said. "That's your opinion. That guy's a—"

"And besides that," Hannah cut in, "do you know what he was out doing last night? Volunteering as a deputy sheriff, making sure people were safe, including me when I got stranded by the side of the road with a dead phone. Then he got up for work this morning, even though he'd been up all night. I'm not going to stand here and let you call him names."

The man threw up his hands. "Chill, lady," he said. "I didn't know he was a friend of yours. Just let me fill my water bottle. I've gotta get back on the road."

He went out, and Hannah went for a drink of water, her face flushed. It wasn't usual for her to get worked up like that about an offhand comment. But how dare that guy? He didn't know anything about Jack and all the hard work he did.

At noon, Hannah was starting her lunch—not a great lunch, because she'd been running late—when Jack came up. "Hi," he said.

"Jack, you look terrible. You look like you haven't slept in three days. Do you do this every weekend?"

He smiled. "No. Last night the regular deputy was out sick."

"Oh, I see."

Jack turned serious, a warm expression in his brown eyes. "I heard you defended me to some truck driver."

"Oh." Hannah's face warmed. Somebody must have overheard her. "It was nothing."

Jack shook his head. "I appreciate it." He cleared his throat, raising an eyebrow. "What are you eating? Is that plain lettuce?"

Hannah raised her eyebrows too. "I was running late. It's not my whole lunch. I have a tuna packet."

Jack laughed. "All right, all right. If you want a sandwich, you know where to find one."

He went for his lunch, and Hannah opened the lackluster tuna packet. She wasn't going to mooch off Jack's lunch today. He could probably use the extra food after being up so late.

It really wasn't a big deal, her defending Jack to the truck driver. People deserved somebody to stand up for them. She'd have done that for anyone.

❦

Before dinner, Hannah went grocery shopping. She was already running low on everything. Good thing Murray's Grocery was within walking distance, because her car was still in the shop.

Grace Murray was manning the register. Doc wasn't around. Hannah picked out her groceries at leisure—this place didn't have a lot of variety, but at least they had local organic produce. Maybe Jack's family sold produce to the store. She didn't know what kind of farm they had.

At the checkout counter, Grace hailed her. "Jim told me you're staying in Fraser's Mill for the next few months."

Hannah winced interiorly. Grace usually called Doc Jim, which made sense, since she was his girlfriend and it was his name. But since everyone else in town called him Doc, it felt like Grace was rubbing it in by calling him that.

"Yeah," Hannah said. "I'm working at the sawmill." She

120

explained about the house swap.

At least Grace wouldn't think badly of her for living with her parents. Grace also lived with her parents in a house next to the grocery store. It was just the current fad for young people to move out on their own. Dad said in many cases it was a waste of money. That made sense to Hannah, but it was hard to explain to other people.

"How do you like working at the mill?" Grace asked.

"Oh, it's okay. The work's complicated, but I think I'm getting the hang of it. And it's okay having my brother as my boss."

Grace nodded. "Probably a lot like me having my dad as my boss."

As Hannah left, Grace called after her. "Hey, Hannah!"

Hannah stopped. Had she forgotten to pay or something? No, she remembered putting her card in the card reader.

"Since you'll be here," Grace said, "would you be interested in helping with the choir ladies' tea? It won't be a big time commitment. I thought it would be nice if you and I and Alex did it together."

Afterwards, Hannah never knew why she said what she did. Maybe it was because she'd been around so many men lately. Maybe it was because she appreciated Grace reaching out, even when Hannah hadn't been that friendly.

"Sure," Hannah said. "I'll join you."

Grace smiled. "Thanks, Hannah. It'll be a lot of fun."

Hopefully it would be fun. Hannah really did need to make friends while she was stuck here in Fraser's Mill. And Grace was clearly making an effort to be kind. Helping with the choir tea seemed like a good decision.

When Grace started a project, she got going quickly. As Hannah was frantically piecing together her Tuesday video on Monday night, trying to think of the funniest way to present her recent misadventures, Grace sent her a text.

"Hey, Hannah! Would you be available after Wednesday choir practice to come over to my house and plan for the tea? I'll provide snacks."

Was Hannah crazy to get involved in this? Maybe, but if she went to choir practice (and she should, or Mary Jane would think she was slacking for missing so many times), what was a little time afterwards?

"Sure," Hannah replied.

Accordingly, after Wednesday choir practice, Hannah walked to the Murrays' house with Grace and Alex. She had her car back—she couldn't make heads or tails of Ed's explanation of what had been wrong with it—but the other girls were walking, so she joined them.

Grace and Alex were both talking about the upcoming fall festival, since their families' businesses would both have booths there. They weren't trying to leave Hannah out, but she didn't know what was so funny about the pie competition or how some people cheated in the largest vegetable contest. Close friends like Grace and Alex just had a lot of inside jokes.

Hopefully there would be some way for Hannah to fit into the conversation. Otherwise, what was she doing here? So far, it only made her realize she didn't have any friends—even in

Chicago—that were as close as these two were.

"Hannah," Grace said, "are you coming to the festival?"

"I don't know. What is it, anyway? Is it like a county fair?"

"Kind of." Alex twisted her long chestnut hair and secured it flawlessly with a hair clip without looking. "But without any animals. There are rides, but the mayor gets worried that they'll break and somebody will get hurt, so he always supervises the setup like crazy."

"Jim says the mayor cares a lot about health and safety," Grace said. "He appreciates it."

"Anyway," Alex said, "the festival is mostly a place to showcase cooking and gardening and crafts and stuff. And sell things. And play games. The sheriff's gonna be in the dunk tank."

Grace laughed. "You know you've got a peaceful town when the sheriff volunteers to let people throw things at him."

The festival did sound fun. No reason for Hannah not to go, even if she didn't have any crafts or things to sell. She could do a video for her channel.

At the Murrays' house, the girls said hello to Grace's parents, who were doing a project on the porch. They went into the spacious kitchen, where Grace pulled out a jar of oatmeal raisin cookies.

"We can have tea." Grace twisted her blonde curls into a bun, securing it with a pencil, before heating some water. "I'll get a notebook, and we can brainstorm."

Over oolong tea (which Alex said was supposed to be drunk plain, but Grace scoffed at that and added milk and sugar liberally), they talked about the tea party. It would be in the church basement at the end of September. Hannah drank her tea (with milk and sugar) and listened.

Alex had decorating ideas, things like flower centerpieces in mason jars—that sounded charming in a rustic way. She often decorated their family's pole barn for parties, but they couldn't use the barn for the tea party, because her brother Sam was using it for a building project. Whatever he was making had fresh paint, and he didn't want to leave it outdoors to get rained on. Hannah nodded in sympathy for Alex's original plan not working, but completely agreed that the weather here was erratic.

Grace was most interested in the food. She had plans for cucumber sandwiches and scones. She would make gluten-free versions of both things for Alex, who couldn't have gluten. "What other things should we eat?" she asked.

Hannah always had ideas about food. She hadn't had time to cook much lately, but she had thoughts. She hoped Grace and Alex didn't shoot them down.

"You know those French macarons?" Hannah asked. "I've never made them myself, but this little tea shop I like in Chicago sells them, and they're the best."

Alex bounced in her chair. "I've seen those, but I've never tried them. I like that idea. I think the ladies would be excited."

Oh, good. Hannah smiled.

"I still don't know what those are," Grace said. "Let me look them up."

She pulled up a picture: many different-colored macarons, artfully arranged on beautiful china, surrounded by doilies.

"Wow," Grace said. "That's a great idea."

It was what Hannah had hoped for—the girls actually liked

her idea. "They're sold in some grocery stores. But those kinds probably aren't as good. I heard they're hard to make, but if we practice, I thought maybe we could make them ourselves."

"I'm not the world's most precise baker," Grace admitted, "but I'd love to try it. We could practice them together."

"We can give the worst ones to the guys," Alex said. "Charlie will eat anything."

Grace laughed. "So will Jim."

Hannah didn't have a special guy to eat her food failures. Sure, Steve would eat anything, but he was just her brother, and Christine cooked for him all the time.

Looking over, Grace stopped laughing. Had Hannah's feelings shown on her face? Did Grace know she was still disappointed about Doc? It took a while to get over a guy.

"Thanks so much, Hannah," Grace said. "This is gonna be great. I'm glad you're doing it with us."

"Three makes a better team than two," Alex said. "That way you have a tie breaker."

"Speaking of tie breakers," Grace raised her eyebrows, "Hannah puts milk and sugar in her tea too."

"You ladies don't know how to appreciate real tea." Alex lifted her pinky, sipping her plain oolong.

Hannah laughed. "I keep expecting it to be coffee."

"Coffee?" Alex scrunched her nose. "You can be buddies with Grace. She's the coffee queen—a big snob, too."

"I am not," Grace said. "I just use a French press. It's quick, it's convenient, it makes good coffee, and it doesn't take up as much room as a coffeemaker."

It was late when Hannah said she needed to leave. Grace offered to drive her. "I don't like walking that far in the dark by myself," she said. "Alex, why don't you come with us, and I'll drop you at the farm."

They dropped Hannah at her house, and she waved at them as she went in.

It had been a surprisingly nice time. There hadn't been too much talk about Doc, and they hadn't made her feel like a third wheel friend. They also hadn't quizzed her about being single, the way a lot of people did.

Hannah actually found herself looking forward to making macarons with the girls. It was the first time, since hanging out with Doc, she'd been excited for a Fraser's Mill event. But she still wished she had her own Mr. Right to eat her failed cookie attempts.

That Match Made in Heaven

Saturday morning rolled around, and after getting up late (she deserved to sleep in after her long work week) and making herself a spinach, feta, and tomato omelet, Hannah made a decision. She was sick of everyone here in Fraser's Mill dating and flirting and baking cookies for guys, while she stayed single. She wasn't returning to Chicago until the spring, but there was no reason she couldn't meet somebody in the Chicago area before then. There were bound to be plenty of young, accomplished, Catholic guys in Chicago. And surely some of them had online dating profiles.

Even though she was online a lot, Hannah had never tried online dating. She had always had the idea that the kind of people who joined online dating sites were desperate people who couldn't find somebody in real life. The impressive guys could find women in person. And Hannah wanted an impressive guy.

But statistics showed that nowadays, the internet was the

most common place to meet. And since Hannah was stuck in Fraser's Mill with no dating prospects, she might as well set up a profile. Hannah took a deep breath and looked up Catholic dating sites.

Wow, a lot of people didn't seem to know how to take a good profile picture. A grainy selfie with sunglasses, taken from below? Really? Come to think of it, though, Hannah could probably use a photo shoot before setting up a profile herself. Despite making videos all the time, she didn't have a lot of photos of herself, and from what she read, it was important to have recent, flattering pictures on your dating profile. Maybe Christine would help her.

Without further ado, she messaged Christine about it. "Nothing too official," Hannah explained. "I just want a few nice snapshots for my profile."

Christine messaged back, interested. She'd never tried online dating. She and Steve had met in college. She hoped Hannah was doing okay and wasn't getting desperate.

"No, I'm not desperate," Hannah replied. "I just think it might be good to meet some Catholic guys from Chicago before I go back there. Lots of people meet online."

Time was ticking, even in Fraser's Mill. She might as well get ahead of the game.

Christine agreed to take the photos, if Hannah came over for dinner. She didn't think Hannah's car would break down two weeks in a row.

That afternoon, Hannah was at Grace's house, trying to figure out how to make macarons with Grace and Alex. Baking supplies and ingredients were everywhere. All three girls had their hair tied back and aprons on. "We look like a culinary school," Grace said.

"I just hope these things turn out." Hannah pulled out the bag of almond flour.

"It shouldn't be too bad." Alex was reading the recipe. "It's a kind of meringue. I've made plenty of meringue pies. You just have to bake these the right amount. The main thing is to not burn them."

"I don't know," Grace said, looking over Alex's shoulder. "This looks tricky. Look at all those steps. You have to mix everything a specific amount so it has the right amount of air in the batter, and then put the batter in a piping bag—that's always a mess. And—after you've piped the circles onto the baking sheet, you have to let them rest for half an hour."

Hopefully the other girls didn't regret getting mixed up with this, and it would end up being fun despite the challenge.

At least, with three people, it didn't take as long as Hannah feared. The batter was soon made and piped into circles. While they waited for the batter to rest, the girls worked through other details of the tea—china, dress code, and menu. Hannah was surprised to learn that "high tea" was more casual than "tea." She would have expected it to be the other way around.

Bluegrass music started playing from somewhere, and Alex jumped up. "That's my phone." She dug through her purse on the kitchen counter. "Sorry, when I'm on the farm I leave the ringtone on, or I miss all my calls."

"No problem," Grace and Hannah said at the same time.

Alex found the phone just as it stopped ringing. "Oh, it's Charlie."

"Why don't you call him back?" Grace said. "Hannah and I can keep an eye on the macarons."

"Thanks." Alex stepped into the next room. "Hey, Charlie. What's up?"

At the kitchen table, Grace smiled. "Those two are cute. It took a push to get them together, though. Not that I'm trying to take credit for it. But I did suggest Alex could bake Charlie some cookies."

"Aha," Hannah said. "There seem to be a lot of matchmakers in Fraser's Mill."

Grace laughed. "I guess there are."

"They're very determined. The other week at the diner, a woman tried to match me up with a guy who rents her basement." Hannah tucked back a strand of hair that was escaping from her ponytail. "But I'm not looking for somebody from Fraser's Mill. I'm going back to Chicago in the spring, anyway."

Grace nodded. "I've heard long-distance relationships can be tough."

Not to mention that there wasn't anybody in Fraser's Mill for Hannah, but Hannah didn't need to get into that.

"I thought I'd try online dating," she said, "and maybe find somebody back in Chicago before I go back there. Have you ever tried it? Online dating, I mean?"

Grace shook her head. "I kept thinking I would when I was in California. But I was so busy, I never ended up creating a profile. And then I met Jim. But I've heard a lot of people find a good match online. Alex's brother, Sam, met his girlfriend that way. I hope it works well for you."

Hannah smiled. "Thanks."

It was actually comfortable talking with Grace. It wasn't awkward, the way Hannah had feared. And the look on Grace's face seemed sincere, like she actually cared about Hannah finding somebody.

Alex returned, dropping into her seat. "Sorry," she said. "Charlie wanted to know what I'm doing this evening. I think we're picking apples."

"No problem," Grace said. "We're just waiting for the macarons to rest, anyway."

Finally the waiting time was over and the macarons were in the oven, a second sheet of circles waiting for the test batch to be done. The girls soon found that burning the macarons was not the only possible problem. The first batch came out of the oven with all the tops cracked.

"Rats," Grace said. "What did we do wrong?"

"Let's look," Hannah said. "I'll troubleshoot online. I thought they cracked when there were air bubbles. We were so careful to make sure there weren't any air bubbles."

"I'm gonna try one," Alex said. "Since they're gluten-free, anyway." She loosened one from the pan. "Ouch. Hot." She bit into it, breathing in deeply. "It's good," she said with her mouth full. "Just cracked. Let's make filling for these and give them to people who don't care about the looks."

Hannah read on her phone. "It says there are a number of reasons they could crack. Either we didn't rest them long enough, the egg whites weren't stiff peaks, or the oven was too hot. Grace, does your oven run hot?"

"Maybe," Grace said. "Things usually get done early. We could try turning it down twenty-five degrees."

They waited with bated breath as the second batch came out. Hannah carefully touched the top of one of the macarons. "Yeah, they're done."

"Wow," Grace said. "They look great."

"They really do," Hannah said. Lovely light pink cookies with gently ruffled edges—feet, they were called—and not a cracked shell in sight.

"Wonderful." Alex clasped her hands dramatically. "Let's fill them."

It was fun, hanging out with these girls. Hannah ought to spend more time with them.

✺✺✺

On Sunday, after Mass, Hannah looked through her closet. What should she wear for her photo shoot with Christine? She decided on a breezy white floral dress (it was after Labor Day, but she was a firm believer in wearing white all year round) with flat sandals that wouldn't reinjure her ankle. She brushed her straight brown hair a hundred strokes. It was too bad she couldn't do much with her hair, but she would be wearing sunglasses on top of her head anyway. In case it got cold, she brought a jacket.

Christine suggested a park along the beach at Lake Cadillac for Hannah's photos. The day was sunny, reaching the golden hour, with mellow light on the water. Hannah breathed in the fresh air deeply as she and Christine walked out to the lake.

"So," Christine asked, "what sort of vibe are you going for? Are we going with businesswoman Hannah, or content creator Hannah, or something else?"

"Uh, how about living-her-best-life Hannah?"

Christine raised an eyebrow. "Aren't you always complaining you aren't living your best life? How you can't do anything big here in Fraser's Mill?"

Hannah sighed. "I know, I know. But I'm living my best life as well as possible under the circumstances. And it'll be even better if I can find a guy who's right for me."

"Ah." Christine's eyes were understanding. "That makes sense. I know you've been frustrated with the dating options in Fraser's Mill."

Hannah nodded. "I always feel like I'm the only single girl around. And I want to find somebody who's actually right for me. I'm not going to bump into him walking down the street. But maybe I'll find him online."

"Well, I'm happy to help. And I'll pray that you find your Mr. Right. If you don't mind my asking, what kind of guy do you think is actually right for you?"

That wasn't hard to describe. Hannah had thought about it a lot. "Well, you know about my 'power couple' idea," she said. "Somebody impressive, who wants to do big things. Somebody I'm proud to be with. Somebody who interests me."

Christine's mouth quirked. "I can see why you're not having a lot of success in Fraser's Mill."

Hannah grinned wryly. "That's why we're out here

taking photos."

Christine pressed the power button on her camera. "In that case, we'd better get started while the light's still good."

When both Christine and Hannah were satisfied with the variety of photos, they packed up to go home.

"I'll look through and pick out some good ones," Christine said. "I should be able to get them back to you by tomorrow evening."

"Really?" Hannah asked. "Wow. How do you manage being so efficient? You have Evelyn and Noah and everything else around the house!"

Christine smiled. "Mom superpowers," she said. "And it won't take me too long to go through these. You're a photogenic subject, and you know how to pose. The guys online will take one look at them and faint right over."

Hannah laughed. "Hopefully not," she said. "They can't message me if they've fainted."

∞∾∾∾∞

"Late night last night?"

It was Tuesday morning. Hannah raised a groggy face from her desk. Jack was standing there, his arms folded. "Oh, hi," Hannah said.

"You look like you could use about a month of sleep," Jack said. "Want some coffee? I just made it."

How did he have time to work dispatching and also make coffee for the office? "Sure," Hannah said. "Thanks."

It was a good thing work was slow this morning, because Hannah couldn't keep her eyes open. She'd set up her dating profile the evening before, staying up far too late. There were so many forms to fill out, and it was difficult to try to encapsulate her entire personality in the profile.

Hannah didn't want to seem silly or unprofessional, but she didn't want to seem boring either. And although her biggest passion was video making, she didn't want to give enough information that strangers could stalk her video channel. She had put her location as Chicago, with a note that she was away from the city but was coming back in six months. That way Chicago guys were more likely to be interested.

She laid her head on her desk. Napping at her desk was unprofessional, but hopefully Steve wouldn't come in.

She was roused by a touch on her shoulder. "Hannah," Jack's voice said, as if from a great distance.

She shook herself. "Oh, thanks."

He handed her a steaming cup. "Here you go. I brought cream and sugar."

Hannah put in plenty of both. She expected Jack to make a snide comment. Most of the men she knew drank their coffee black.

Jack didn't say anything about the coffee. He leaned against Hannah's desk instead, half sitting on it. "You sure you're okay? Maybe Steve could spare you for a few hours while you get some sleep."

Hannah shook her head. "I'll be fine." She took a sip of the coffee. It was surprisingly good for sawmill office coffee. "It was my own fault, staying up late. It was stupid of me."

He smiled. "Happens to the best of us."

His phone rang, and he answered it. Hannah drank her

coffee and tried to stay awake.

At lunch, she ate a pre-bagged salad and logged into the dating website. Since last night, she had received several messages.

Oh, no. They were all generic messages, things like "Hello" and "You have a beautiful smile" and "Hey how was your weekend." Nobody seemed to use any punctuation these days. Hannah glanced at the profiles of the guys who had messaged her. One of the guys wasn't even in the U.S. One's profile said he wanted to get married but didn't want kids. What was the point of that? Hannah didn't want to go out with any of these guys. None of them were from Chicago, either.

She had a definite idea of the kind of guy she was looking for. He had to be educated and interesting, outgoing and driven, sharing at least some of Hannah's interests and understanding of her world. He would mesh well with Hannah's family. He would impress her. And he certainly wouldn't send low-effort messages like "Hey how was your weekend."

Hannah hid all the message threads. She couldn't expect Mr. Right to message her on the first day. Maybe Mr. Right was at work this morning and hadn't checked the dating site. Maybe she'd stumble across him herself, browsing profiles. Things that were worth finding usually took time to find.

Chicken Soup for the Co-Worker

Midway through the week, Jack didn't come in to work. Did he have the day off? Maybe he was late. He'd always been punctual before, so that was weird.

Steve came in, looking harassed. "Jack's sick," he said. "He came in, but he looked so bad I sent him home. I'll have to do dispatching today. Don't expect me to help you with anything—I'm up to here with work." He motioned to a spot far above his head.

"Sure, Steve, I'll do my best."

"Thanks." Steve sank down in Jack's chair. "Hope I'm not gonna pick up a bunch of germs from using Jack's stuff. Christine's got an immune system of iron, but Evelyn catches everything. Maybe I should feed her more vitamins."

The phone rang, and he answered it. "This is Steve. I know. Jack's out sick. You're gonna have to talk to me."

How sick must Jack be? He was good at powering through exhaustion, like a mill shift after a police shift. He must be really bad for Steve to send him home. Maybe somebody should check on him.

Taped by Hannah's desk was a list of phone numbers. One said: "Jack Rogers, cell." It wouldn't hurt to text and see if Jack was okay. If he was asleep, he just wouldn't respond.

"Hey, Jack, this is Hannah Fraser," Hannah wrote. "I heard you were sick. I hope you're doing OK now!"

When he finally answered, his message was laconic. "Thanks! I'm making it through."

That sounded suspicious to Hannah. "Making it through" could be "I'm basically dying." Somebody ought to do something for Jack. As far as she understood, he lived in town. Maybe he didn't have anything good to eat while he recovered. If he was sick, he probably hadn't been cooking.

When she got out of work, maybe she could bring him something. Maybe some hot chicken soup. The diner had chicken soup, homemade, and Hannah had heard people rave about it.

Hannah texted Jack again. "Hey, after work can I bring you some chicken soup from the diner? I've heard it's really good."

Jack's reply sounded sheepish. "Hannah, you don't have to bring me anything. Steve sent me home because he thought I looked sick, and he didn't want germs. But I'll be all right. I can heat up a can of soup myself."

"Canned soup is just salt and preservatives," Hannah replied. "I'm bringing it."

"Okay, fine," Jack replied. "You're the stubbornest woman I know."

Hannah smiled. Of course Jack would say that. But he was

stubborn about sharing his food when she forgot her lunch. She was going to be stubborn about this.

"Great!" Hannah messaged. "I'll bring it over after work. What's your address?"

∽∽∽∽∽

Jack lived in the walkout basement of a house, about halfway between the mill and the center of town. If you could say a town as small as Fraser's Mill had a center. Clutching the bag with the chicken soup, Hannah knocked on the house's door. Her hands were sweating. Hopefully this wasn't weird. She didn't know who else lived in the house where Jack rented.

A woman in her seventies or thereabouts with gray hair in a bun, wearing a purple tracksuit, opened the door. Wait a minute. It was Barb, who had tried to set her up with her renter. Wait another minute. Barb had been trying to set Hannah up with Jack? That was before she'd met Jack. Hannah felt her cheeks redden.

"Well, hello, Hannah," Barb said. "Long time no see! Jack said you'd be coming. He lives right through here. It's so sweet of you to visit him."

She didn't hint about Hannah and Jack dating, thank goodness. She just led the way to a basement door and opened it. Jack's apartment didn't have a locking door?

Hannah looked down the wooden stairway — the kind with spaces between the steps, so you felt like you might fall through. At least it didn't look like a dark, creepy basement. She could see a counter and a window with yellow curtains. Should she call for Jack, or go down, or what?

She was spared doing any of these things, because Barb shouted down the stairs. "Jack, your visitor's here."

"Would you please ask her to come down?" Jack's voice sounded sick.

"Sure, I'll come down." Hannah went down the steps, watching her feet carefully. How people had managed in the old days with primitive staircases, she'd never know.

She found a cheerful apartment, cut in half by the staircase. Large windows looked out onto a sunny backyard. One side of the basement was part living area, part kitchen, with a door at the end that probably went into a bedroom. The other side was a laundry room with a furnace and water heater. And there was Jack, pulling wet laundry out of a washer.

"Jack Rogers, what on earth are you doing?" Hannah asked. "I thought you were sick. Shouldn't you be in bed or something?"

He looked sheepish. "I forgot to do my laundry." His m's and n's sounded stuffed up. Yes, he was clearly sick. His face was a grayish color, and he moved in a lethargic manner.

"I brought you soup." Hannah held out the bag.

"Thanks a lot, Hannah. You didn't need to." Jack set the bag on a counter. "I want you to know I appreciate it."

"No problem at all," Hannah said. "It wasn't far."

"Thanks, anyway." Jack smiled. He had a dimple to the left of his mouth that Hannah hadn't noticed before.

"You're welcome." Hannah tucked her hair behind her ear. Now what?

Jack turned back to his laundry, pulled out a brown button-up shirt, and shook it. That must be part of his sheriff's uniform.

"So how did work go?" Jack asked. He pinned the shirt to a clothesline that went across that end of the basement. A clothesline?

"It went all right," Hannah said. "Jack, what on earth are you doing? Don't you have a dryer?"

He shrugged. "Barb doesn't have a dryer. She says hanging up clothes was good enough for everybody in the old days."

Hannah shook her head. She had a laundry rack for special care items, but the idea of hanging up everything—even towels—was crazy. Those denim shirts and jeans of Jack's must be so stiff and crunchy when he took them off the line.

"Let me do that," Hannah told Jack. "You eat your soup. I'll hang up the laundry. You shouldn't be doing chores when you're sick."

Jacks' ears were turning red. "Don't worry about it."

"Nonsense." Hannah went past him and took a pair of jeans from the basket. "You get out of here. Eat your soup."

Jack threw up his hands. "All right, all right. My mother taught me to do my own laundry, you know."

He disappeared to the other half of the basement, and Hannah hung his shirts, pants, and towels on the line. Jack's clothes took up a lot more space than her clothes ever did. Funny how much bigger men were than women.

When she finished, she went to find him. Jack was at the kitchen counter, pouring chicken soup into a bowl.

"All finished," Hannah announced.

"Thank you." Jack turned to her. "I appreciate it, Hannah. You really went out of your way for me."

"That's what coworkers are for," Hannah said. "After all,

you've shared your lunch with me. And you took me to the doctor when I sprained my ankle. And you rescued me when my car broke down. The least I could do is bring you some soup."

"You're a kind person, Hannah." Jack smiled. "Do you want a cup of tea? You'll have to get it yourself so you don't catch my cold, but the tea's in that cupboard, and the mugs are in that one. There's hot water in the kettle."

He probably wanted company. Hannah didn't want to leave him alone. "Tea would be great. Thank you."

She found the tea—Jack had chai and oolong—and made herself a cup of chai. Jack sat at one side of a small round table with his soup, and Hannah sat opposite him and waited for her tea to steep. The evening sunlight, through a sliding door, fell on the table in just the right way to look aesthetic without getting in anyone's eyes.

Jack's apartment was cozy—a little tight, but what could you expect from a basement apartment? Rag rugs scattered over the cement floor warmed up the room. The aesthetic, rustic with bright pops of color, was good. The wall on the far side of the basement—the side that didn't have any windows because it went into the hill—was totally lined with books. Lots of history, but some fiction, too. A bin of sports equipment, including a tennis racket, stood in a corner. So Jack played tennis! It might be fun to play with him sometime, if it didn't remind her too much of playing tennis with Doc.

"So what are you up to this evening?" Jack asked. He tried the soup. "Mm, this is good."

"Oh, good," Hannah said. She sipped her own tea. It was

strong enough now, and she took out the tea bag. "It's choir practice night. And then I'm trying to plan next week's video. I want to start early because I had to throw last week's together last-minute." She told the story of the flipped kayak and the dropped phone.

"Wow," Jack said. "That must have been a rough afternoon." Across the small table, his face was sympathetic. They were close together—if Hannah moved her foot, she would accidentally kick him.

Hannah nodded. "I got a flip phone after that," she said. "That's why my phone was dead that time my car broke down. The car charger only worked with my smartphone."

Jack shook his head. "You've had an interesting life lately."

Hannah laughed. "Tell me about it," she said. "Just as I think I'm going back to Chicago, I'm stuck here in Fraser's Mill. I take a job at a sawmill with crazy coworkers who moonlight as deputy sheriffs. Then I sprain my ankle, I fall in the river and lose my phone, my car breaks down, and now I'm sitting in a basement drinking tea."

"Crazy coworkers?" Jack raised an eyebrow. "You were the one who fell in the water and sprained the ankle and got in a car breakdown, all on your own."

"Fine, maybe we're both crazy," Hannah said. "Deal?"

Jack held out his hand, then retracted it. "Germs," he said. "Deal."

Hannah gave him an air handshake. "Deal."

Jack ate a spoon of his soup. "What you need is somebody else to row the boat."

"What?"

"That river video. You need somebody else to row while you hold the camera. That way you won't drop your paddle. When I'm not sick anymore, why don't I help you get a few video clips?"

"Really?" That was the most supportive anybody had been yet for Hannah's video channel. People often asked about her channel, and sometimes they'd help if she asked, but they didn't usually volunteer without prompting. "That would be fantastic," she exclaimed. "I'd love it. Just let me know when you're available."

Jack nodded. "I'll check my schedule, and we can work out a day."

Hannah smiled at him. "Thank you, Jack. You're the best."

His eyes were cheery behind his glasses. "Anytime."

He still sounded sick. "We'll have to wait until you're better," Hannah said. "I don't want you coughing and sneezing all the way down the river."

Jack laughed, which turned into a cough. "Don't you mute the audio? Nobody will be able to tell."

"Not on your life." Hannah shook her finger at him. "You're going to stay right here and get better."

The Elusive Mr. Right

Back at the log house, Hannah had a long evening, mostly spent on her dating site. She had filled out her profile as well as she knew how and spent time carefully browsing profiles. She used filters to weed out non-practicing Catholics, guys who were too old or too young, guys that lived too far away, guys that weren't free to marry in the Church, or guys on the opposite side of the political spectrum. She sent carefully-crafted messages to a few men. It didn't seem like chasing men when you were on a dating site. Besides, it couldn't be worse than Hannah's behavior toward Doc earlier in the summer.

Two things frustrated Hannah about online dating. First, most of her messages were ignored. A number of the men she'd contacted had viewed Hannah's profile and chosen not to respond. This was their prerogative—they probably didn't think they would be a good match—but it felt humiliating to have someone look at her profile and decide not to answer her.

The second problem was that the guys who did message didn't interest her. She sent polite messages back, wishing the guys the best but explaining they wouldn't be a good fit. Was there no way to find someone interesting who would also message back?

She'd have to keep looking. Rome wasn't built in a day, and she couldn't meet every eligible guy on the site immediately.

Jack returned to work the next day, still showing cold symptoms but insisting he was well enough to work. Steve didn't grumble too much. He had had his fill of doing Jack's job.

It was lunchtime, and Jack and Hannah were discussing the relative merits of tennis and football, when the door opened and three young girls came in.

Jack, who was sitting on the edge of Hannah's desk, looked up. "Now what are you three doing here?" he asked, in a tone that told Hannah that these girls were his siblings.

They looked like Jack. They had the same dark hair and almond-shaped brown eyes. The oldest must be sixteen or seventeen. The other two were probably around fourteen and twelve. All three wore hoodies, jean skirts, and boots.

"Mom said you were sick," the oldest girl said. She held up a basket, covered with a red-and-white checked cloth. "Chicken soup. Mom says to heat it up before you eat it. Also she says to tell you to wear warmer socks."

Jack laughed. "It's too hot for warmer socks." He got off Hannah's desk. "My sisters," he told her unnecessarily. "Mary, Martha, and Zita. Girls, this is Hannah."

"Nice to meet you," the three girls chorused politely.

"Nice to meet you," Hannah replied.

"The three youngest girls," Jack explained. "Triple trouble. We call them the Three Musketeers."

Hannah could tell by the affection in his voice that he rather enjoyed the triple trouble.

Jack turned to his sisters. "You girls came all the way out here to give me soup and tell me to dress warmly?"

"Not exactly," the oldest girl—Mary—said. "Dad went to help Mr. Martin repair his barn. It'll be several hours, and he said we could bum around in town. He said when you got off work, maybe you'd show us around."

It would be fun to have younger siblings to show around town. Hannah was the youngest child, and the siblings above her—Bella and Kenneth—had hung out more with each other than with her.

The three girls looked hopeful. Jack let out a mock groan. "You know I don't get out until five, right? What are you going to do until then?"

"Window shopping," the second girl, Martha, said promptly. "And there's the ice cream shop and the park. And the library. We've got tons to do."

Jack shook his head. "Isn't it a school day?"

"We finished all our school at ten o'clock," Mary said. "We came up with the idea of going with Dad last night, and before bed we all did as much of today's school as we could."

"It was a secret mission," the youngest girl, Zita, said. "We didn't tell Felicity or Agnes. We thought they would want to come and then we wouldn't all fit in the truck. And they went to town last time."

"I see how it is," Jack said. "Sneaking around, begging to go into town, counting on your older brother to entertain you." He shook his head. "I'll take you around after work. Be careful and don't get into trouble. And don't run in the road."

"We're not five years old." Zita pouted. "We'll be careful."

They whisked out of the office, leaving the basket on Hannah's desk.

Jack shook his head, smiling. "I guess my mom heard I was sick." He looked in the basket. A jar of soup was surrounded by thickly sliced bread (homemade sourdough), throat coat tea, and a small glass container of butter.

Never having met Jack's mom, Hannah was beginning to get an idea of her: kindly, generous, and stubborn. A lot like her son, in fact.

"How are you going to entertain three girls all evening when you're sick?" Hannah asked.

"We'll have dinner at the diner and watch a movie at my apartment." Jack looked at her. "Want to come along? It'll be entertaining."

It sounded better than being alone all evening, working on videos or scrolling through endless dating profiles. "You know what," Hannah said, "I think I will."

❧❧❧

At five PM on the dot, Mary, Martha, and Zita Rogers appeared again.

"Ready?" Jack asked, grabbing his lunchbox and book.

"Hannah's coming with us."

"Are you Jack's new girlfriend?" Zita piped up.

"Oh, no, we're not—" Hannah began.

"Not dating." Jack shook his head. "We're coworkers."

"Uh-huh." Zita's tone told Hannah she didn't believe it. Hannah had better be careful not to give Jack's sisters the wrong impression about the two of them.

Jack waved a hand in his sisters' direction. "Everybody get in the truck. We're going to the diner."

"Shotgun," Zita shouted once they made it outside, and the three girls ran to Jack's truck, slapping the passenger door at almost the same time.

"I touched it first," Mary shouted.

"No, you didn't," Zita shouted.

"Ladies, ladies," Jack called. "You three all get in the back. Hannah's riding shotgun."

"Aw, Jack," Mary grumbled, but all three got in the back. Hannah swung herself into the passenger seat. Jack got in, and they were off.

Hopefully Hannah riding in the front seat didn't make her and Jack seem like an item. She'd never been in his truck before. It was clean, recently vacuumed by the looks of it, and smelled fresh—she couldn't place the smell, but she associated it with Jack. Maybe it was his deodorant.

It was prime time for dinner, and the diner parking lot was full. "We might have a wait," Jack said. He held the door for his sisters and Hannah, following Hannah inside.

The diner bustled with talking and clanking silverware.

Charlie led their party to a round booth in the far corner, with windows on both sides. "I'll put a chair on the other side of the booth so you all fit." Hannah slid into the booth, while Mary and Martha slid in after her.

"I'll take the chair," Zita said loudly. "Jack, you can sit on that side." She waved Jack to the booth, on Hannah's other side. Zita's strategy was obvious. But wild horses wouldn't drag Hannah to mention it.

"All right." Jack slid in next to Hannah, keeping a gentlemanly gap between them. "Just don't tip the chair backwards and fall over, like you did at Sunday dinner."

Zita stuck out her tongue at him.

The table conversation was noisy. All three girls wanted to tell Jack about recent farm adventures. There had been a huge wasp nest on the barn, and their three boy cousins had gotten rid of it in the dead of night. Martha had started a pumpkin for the fall festival, but somehow it had gotten a huge rotten hole in it and now she might have to do a craft instead. Zita was writing a book about a family going down the Oregon Trail. It was impressive how many projects these girls had.

Jack listened to the girls, gave comments and ideas, and used half a box of Kleenex blowing his nose. That man needed to get home and rest.

Charlie took their orders. The Rogers girls ordered burgers and fries, Jack ordered steak and potatoes, and Hannah ordered a chicken Caesar salad.

They were eating when someone walked by. "Hey, Hannah," a guy's voice said. "How's the ankle?" It was Doc. He was dressed nicely — probably having dinner with Grace.

"Oh," Hannah said, "hi, Doc. My ankle's a lot better."

"Good." Doc's face crinkled in a grin. He turned to Jack. "Jack."

"Doc." Jack smiled, shaking hands with him.

Doc strolled away and sat down in a booth across the diner. Caught up in her own table's conversations, Hannah hadn't noticed Grace sitting there. Doc said something, and Grace looked in Hannah's direction. They were talking about her, no doubt. Maybe Doc still thought Hannah and Jack were dating. He'd seen them together twice now, after all.

Why did Hannah care if Doc thought she was dating? It didn't make any difference.

Jack's sisters ate their burgers and fries with impressive appetites. They must get plenty of exercise on the farm. While they ate, they regaled Jack with more stories. They asked Hannah a lot of questions: how long she'd been working at the mill, if she knew about beef cows, if she baked pies, if she had any siblings their ages, and if she played the violin.

Jack went off to get a Kleenex, and Hannah was left with his sisters.

"Jack's old girlfriend played the violin," Zita said, leaning forward confidentially. "But she broke up with him and went to play in some orchestra in New York."

"Ah," Hannah said. Interesting — information about Jack's love life before she had known him. What kind of woman had the previous girlfriend been? She wasn't going to ask.

"You're not going to New York, are you?" Zita asked Hannah.

Hannah shook her head. "No. But I am moving back to

Chicago in the spring."

Zita pouted. "That's basically the ends of the earth."

"Good thing you're not Jack's girlfriend, then." Martha evaluated Hannah, her head on one side.

Hannah laughed awkwardly. "Yeah, good thing, right?"

Hannah considered Jack a good friend now, and they didn't need to remember the time Jack had asked her out. Little sisters must be natural matchmakers. Hannah wouldn't know—she didn't have younger sisters.

Jack reappeared, clearing his throat. "I think it's time to go watch that show. Come on, Musketeers, finish your dinner."

Charlie came with the check, and Hannah asked him to split it—she was paying for herself. Jack paid for his sisters.

They piled into the truck and went to Jack's apartment, where there wasn't much room to watch movies on his small couch. Zita and Martha said they preferred sitting on the floor, so Jack found them blankets and pillows.

Mary plunked herself down on one end of the couch. "I'm sitting here," she announced.

That left Jack and Hannah next to each other. Had Mary done that on purpose? She looked like butter wouldn't melt in her mouth.

Hannah sat down in the middle, and Jack joined her on the other side. Like a gentleman, he left space between them—but only about an inch, which was much less than the roomy diner booth allowed. If Hannah moved at all, she would touch him. She folded her arms, watching the video screen. Jack's body heat, emanating through his henley, warmed her right side.

Funny how men were so much warmer than women. Hannah was usually freezing.

They watched an old western with cowboys and bank robbers. A visiting young lady, obsessed with dime novels, wanted to find adventure in the Wild West she had read about. Comedy ensued when the young lady developed a crush on the ranch foreman and he had to figure out what to do about it. Jack's sisters kept up a running commentary — the episode was an old favorite of their family.

Between the humor of the episode and the girls' running commentary, Hannah hadn't laughed so much in a long time. Wiping her eyes, she straightened up. Uh-oh. She'd been leaning against Jack's shoulder. How had that happened?

She stole a glance at Jack, but his face, fixed on the movie screen, was unreadable. Was that the ghost of a smile? Maybe he was just enjoying the episode.

They had just finished when Barb called down the stairs. "Jack, your dad's here to pick up the girls."

They trooped upstairs to Barb's tidy kitchen.

Jack's father was at the door, keys in hand. He was a tall, sandy-haired man, strongly built, wearing a plaid shirt and jeans. Jack and the girls must get their dark coloring from their mother.

"You girls ready to go?" Jack's father asked. "Hello, son. Feeling any better?"

"Better than yesterday," Jack said. He hugged his father and turned to Hannah. "Dad, this is —"

"Hannah?" Jack's dad held out a hand to Hannah, his smile warm. "Pete Rogers. Nice to meet you. My son's talked a lot about you."

Jack looked embarrassed. What kinds of things did he say about Hannah?

"Nice to meet you." Hannah shook Pete's hand. "How did the barn work go?"

"One more day, and we'll be done," Pete said. "Did the girls behave themselves?"

"As well as you can expect from these hooligans," Jack said. "Have you had dinner? Mom sent me a basket of food."

Pete shook his head. "Your mother's waiting with dinner for me. We'd better get back before everything's dried out. Come on, girls."

They trooped out. "Say hi to Mom for me," Jack called after them. He turned to Hannah. "I'll take you home."

They got back in Jack's truck and started for Hannah's house.

It had been such a nice evening, even if Jack's sisters were incorrigible matchmakers. Hopefully Jack didn't think Hannah leaning on his shoulder during the show had been on purpose. But when he spoke, it was simply friendly.

"Thanks a lot for joining me and the girls tonight," Jack said, his face open and serious. "They all had a blast. I hope you had a good time."

"It was great," Hannah said. "I can understand why you guys call them the Three Musketeers, though. I can imagine them getting into all kinds of mischief."

"Every day." Jack laughed, pulling into Hannah's driveway. The laugh turned into a cough.

"You get that cold under control," Hannah warned him, and

jumped down from the truck. "See you tomorrow."

"Thanks for coming along."

"I had fun," Hannah said. "Your sisters are really something."

"Yeah." He grinned. "I bet you were a lot like that as a teenager. More sophisticated, of course." His eyes were teasing.

"Of course," Hannah said promptly. "See you tomorrow, Jack."

❧∾⦿∾❧

Before bed, Hannah checked the dating site again. She might as well do a quick search for Chicagoans. There had to be somebody interesting—Chicago was a huge city.

So many profiles, and so little possibility with most of them. Hannah was tired of reading profiles with terrible grammar and punctuation, profiles of guys who only went to Mass once a month, and profiles where the guy's only interest was watching sports.

Three more messages, and then I'm done for the night. This had to be the worst way to find a man.

In the bottom-left corner of Hannah's screen, her eyes caught on the profile of a dark-haired guy with a stubble beard, wearing a suit. His name was Blake, and he was from Chicago. Hannah clicked on the profile.

Blake's bio was well-written and entertaining, and his interests were varied. He had been involved in moviemaking, app development, and beer-brewing; he attended an Ivy League college; he had traveled in Europe and Asia. His photos showed him on beaches, in mountains, and in a couple Chicago spots Hannah recognized. He was good looking in a movie-star way.

Here, maybe, was somebody intriguing. Hannah thought for

a minute and sent him a message: "Hi! I saw you're interested in moviemaking. What's your favorite kind of movie project to work on?"

Not too deep, but a good icebreaker, she hoped.

That was enough of the dating site for tonight. She didn't want to spend her whole night browsing—best to sign off on a good note. This guy Blake seemed impressive. Maybe he was the guy Hannah had been looking for. A girl could hope.

On the River

Hannah checked the dating site assiduously, but Blake from Chicago hadn't seen her message or profile yet. Maybe he wasn't on the site much. Maybe he was seeing somebody else. Well, she shouldn't fret. Blake seemed interesting, but he wasn't the only guy on the site.

That Friday evening, as Hannah was checking the dating site in the office after work, Jack appeared at her desk, leaning on the counter.

"Tomorrow's the day," he said.

"The day for what?" Hannah asked, tabbing out of the dating site in case Jack came around the desk. She wasn't embarrassed about online dating, but she didn't want Jack to think she was desperate to find a man.

"If you're not otherwise engaged," Jack said, "we ought to shoot that river video."

"I thought you were still sick."

"Not that sick. It's not cold, and I'm not gonna fall in." He grinned. "You have a rowboat, right?"

"Yes," Hannah said. "Sure, Jack. That'd be great. Thanks. When do you want to do it?"

"How about after lunch tomorrow? One-thirty at your place?"

"Sure. One-thirty."

The next day, after sleeping in—the exhaustion of working always hit once the weekend started—Hannah got everything ready for the video. She brought her new phone. If she stupidly dropped the phone again, it would still be better than dropping her expensive DSLR camera.

At one-thirty precisely, the doorbell rang. Jack stood on the porch, wearing a T-shirt and cargo shorts with a baseball cap. He wasn't wearing glasses—he must have contacts in.

"Ready?" he asked.

"Totally."

They went out in the rowboat, Jack rowing with practiced strokes, Hannah clutching her phone tightly. She wasn't dropping it this time.

"Where did you learn how to row?" Hannah asked.

"My parents' farm backs up to the river," Jack said. "We had a rowboat too. It got too full of holes to keep patching it, so we got rid of it."

They went downstream, toward the place Hannah had found before. The sun was bright, and the glare on her phone screen made things tricky, but with Jack rowing it was easier to keep the camera steady and take videos of the scenery. She was planning on a nature video with music, maybe some voice-over narration.

"There's a turtle." Jack motioned with his head.

"Where?"

"Your four o'clock."

Hannah looked in time to see a turtle slide off a log, disappearing underwater.

"Shucks," Jack said. "Maybe we'll see another one."

Water bugs hovered, and mosquitoes swooped. Hannah tried to wave the latter away.

"You think this is bad, you should come here earlier in the summer," Jack said, as Hannah slapped ineffectively at a mosquito that had already eaten and left. "Around the Fourth of July, if we've had a lot of rain, they come in clouds."

"I was here for the Fourth, but I'm glad I wasn't out on the water then," Hannah said. "We don't have nearly so many mosquitoes in Chicago."

"I guess they don't live so well on concrete."

"We have trees in Chicago," Hannah protested.

Jack grinned. "Not this many, you don't."

It took a while, but Hannah finally got enough footage for her video. "I guess we should head back."

Jack turned the rowboat around. They went upstream, the bright sun making Hannah squint.

When she got home, she'd have the rest of the afternoon and evening alone at the log house. She'd make dinner and work on the video. But the rest of the day was empty. And then she had all of Sunday after church. Of course she could catch up on social media, and look more on the dating site, but the weekend ahead seemed to stretch interminably.

"Penny for your thoughts." Jack was watching Hannah.

"Oh, sorry." Hannah shook herself. "I guess I'm not very good company right now. I was just working through some things in my head."

"Ah." Jack nodded sagely. "Hey, want to go a little farther? I want to show you something."

"What is it?" The only place past Hannah's house was the sawmill, and after that you were out of town.

"You'll see," Jack said.

He continued to be mysterious as they passed Hannah's house, the mill, and a thick pine wood that cast deep shade on the water.

The woods thinned, deciduous trees replacing the pines. Where in the world was Jack taking her? They were going to get eaten alive by mosquitoes.

"Is this another scenic spot?" Hannah asked. "I think we have enough footage for the video."

"Nope. It's something else." Jack steered toward the shore at a place where the ground sloped to meet the river. He beached the boat, jumped out, and helped Hannah get out without dropping her phone or stepping in the water.

"Follow me." Jack led the way into the woods.

Hannah followed. "We're not trespassing on somebody's property, are we?"

Jack shook his head. "This is the back of my parents' property."

"Ah." That made more sense. Jack wasn't taking her to his

parents' house, though, was he?

He stopped at a large oak tree. In the tree was a treehouse with a ladder, an open doorway, and two windows.

"Dad and I built this when I was twelve," Jack said. "I've tried to remember to replace boards on it as they wear out."

"That's impressive," Hannah said. "What's the sign?" She pointed to a faded sign by the doorway.

Jack laughed. "It used to say 'No Girls Allowed.' I was trying to keep out my sisters. But they came anyway. Wanna come up?"

"Sure."

Hannah ascended the ladder, strips of board fastened onto the tree, hoping fervently that nothing would come loose. It was funny how much strength it took to climb a vertical ladder, like those rock climbing walls some gyms had.

Finally she pulled herself over the edge of the treehouse. She sat on the floor, getting her breath back.

Jack swung himself up easily, trusting his weight to the boards. He sat down in the cabin doorway, his legs over the edge.

"Look at that view."

Hannah joined him in the doorway. It was a tighter fit than she had thought—her shoulder was against Jack's. He did have broad shoulders.

From the treehouse, there was a view of the path they'd come up through the woods and a glimpse of the river, like looking down a tunnel. The dark green foliage of September rustled in the wind. Poplar leaves shivered. By the water, white-trunked birches contrasted with the other trees.

"Wow," Hannah said.

"I would always come up here to read and think about life," Jack said. "I still do when I have a problem to work out. It's funny, but I think more easily up here. If you've got anything on your mind, this is the place to sort it out."

Hannah could just imagine younger Jack, sitting here with a book, planning his future. Did he already see his life as a dispatcher and a deputy sheriff? Probably not. When Hannah was young, she had always wanted to be a ballerina or a movie star or a singer. She hadn't dreamed of working in a sawmill office. Probably nobody did.

"It looks like a good place to think," Hannah said.

"One of the best," Jack said. "And in case you're thinking I was a miserable loner, my friends and I also used this place as a high school clubhouse."

"I thought you were homeschooled."

"I was, but we had a homeschool co-op in Cadillac. We'd drive out once a week and have classes with our friends. My younger siblings still do it. You weren't homeschooled, were you?"

"No, I went to private Catholic school."

"So you know how to stand in a straight line." Jack's eyes twinkled, so Hannah knew he was kidding.

"Unlike you homeschoolers," she retorted. "So did you do any extracurricular activities?"

"We had field trips and dances sometimes."

"Homeschoolers have dances?" Hannah slapped ineffectively at a mosquito. At least there weren't as many here as there had been by the water.

"Mostly barn dances. It wasn't just a homeschool thing, the town had dances too. They still do. Have you been to any of those?"

"I went to one." It had been earlier in the summer. Hannah and Doc had both gone—not together, although at the time she'd still hoped Doc might be interested in her. On that occasion he'd asked Grace Murray to dance. Hannah looked back on that dance as the beginning of the end of her hopes toward Doc.

"You didn't have a good time?" Jack asked.

Hannah shook her head.

He watched her keenly, his face serious. "You ought to try it again. I know it's not like Chicago. You probably have formal dances with people in ballgowns and tuxedos."

"I can't imagine a formal dance in Fraser's Mill," Hannah said. "I can't see you in a tuxedo."

"Really." He grinned. "There's probably a tux rental somewhere around here. I could get one for the next barn dance."

Hannah laughed. "Better warn your date, or she'll come in a flowered dress and cowboy boots."

"That goes great with a tuxedo." There was that dimple to the left of Jack's mouth.

It was surprising that a guy like Jack was still single. There had to be some nice girl in town for him. Somebody quiet and demure, who liked barn dances and sewing bees (did they have sewing bees anymore? It seemed exactly like the kind of thing they would have in Fraser's Mill).

A dead sensation had settled in Hannah's right leg. "Ouch," she said. "My leg."

"You okay?" Jack asked.

"Yeah, my right leg's asleep."

"Must be from sitting on the edge of the treehouse." Jack got up.

Hannah scooted backward, struggling to get to her feet. Jack offered a hand and pulled her up.

"Thanks." Hannah hopped on the leg that was asleep, pins and needles shooting up and down. "I'll be okay."

Her leg finally back to normal, she stopped hopping.

"Are you all right now?" Jack was looking down at her, his head almost touching the treehouse ceiling.

"Yeah."

So close together in the small space, Hannah was suddenly aware of how well-built Jack was and how brown his eyes were. The hint of a smile played at the corner of his mouth. She found herself drawing closer to him, as though magnetized.

What was she doing? Why was her heart pounding? Must be from all that hopping up and down.

"Uh," Hannah said, "maybe the rowboat's getting stolen. We'd better get back."

Jack let out his breath in a laugh. "Of course. I'll go first. If you fall, I'll catch you."

Hannah laughed too. "I'm not gonna fall."

"If you drop your phone, we'll have to take that footage all over again," Jack warned her. He started down the ladder.

"Nice try, Rogers. It's already backed up in the cloud."

Her heart rate was still elevated. What was going on? For a breath, she'd felt something strange—about Jack—that felt a lot like the way she used to feel about Doc. That was ridiculous.

They were just getting to be better friends, that was all. Hannah needed to find her Mr. Right in Chicago. Maybe that Blake guy would see her message soon.

Tea, Cookies, and Basketball

October was under way, and Fraser's Mill was preparing for the fall festival while Hannah, Grace, and Alex were busy with the much-anticipated choir ladies' tea.

The tea was on a Saturday afternoon. That left all morning for the girls to get ready at Grace's house.

Up early, Hannah debated what to wear. A tea party called for pastels. Hannah liked pastels, especially white, but she didn't know that a white summer dress was the best for an October tea party. Today was chilly.

She picked a light pink dress with black dots and put it in her backpack. She wasn't getting dressed for the tea yet—they had a lot of cooking and decorating first.

At Grace's house, Hannah started on the macarons. Grace was making scones, which should be out before the macarons needed the oven, and Alex was cutting up cucumbers, lamenting that this was not cucumber season and these cucumbers had been in cold storage for months.

"Alex, we can't eat seasonal fruits and vegetables all year long," Grace said. "This is Michigan. What are we supposed to do all winter?"

"Move to Florida." Alex elbowed Grace in the side. Grace laughed, going to wash her hands.

All three girls wore aprons over old clothes. Alex had a kerchief around her head—to keep flour out of her hair, she said.

Hannah beat egg whites with cream of tartar and caster sugar, stopping every few seconds to check if the mixture had reached stiff peaks. It was taking a while.

"Hey, Grace," Alex called over the sound of the mixer. "Charlie wants to know if there's basketball tonight. Do you know?"

"I don't," Grace called back. "Jim says they keep being short on people. Hard to play basketball with four or five guys."

Hannah checked the egg whites again. Still not stiff peaks.

"Where are they going to find more guys?" Alex asked. "Has Doc asked around?"

Wait a minute. Hannah knew somebody athletic.

"Maybe Jack Rogers would be interested," Hannah said.

The other girls turned. "Who?" Grace asked.

"Jack Rogers. The mill dispatcher. He goes to St. Anthony's."

"Is that the guy you were at the diner with?" Grace looked intrigued. "Jim said he brought you into the office when you sprained your ankle."

Hannah shook her head. "I know what you're thinking. We're just coworkers. But he seems pretty athletic."

"Ooh!" Alex raised her eyebrows. "I know who you're

talking about. The oldest Rogers boy. They've got a farm north of town. I know the girls a little. I don't really know Jack—we didn't hang out with the same people growing up—but he's good looking, isn't he?"

Grace grinned. "Very. I say this impartially."

Alex bounced on her toes. "Hannah, we should totally set you up with him!"

It was nice of them, but Hannah shook her head. "No, no. He and I would be totally wrong for each other. Besides, I'm hoping to find somebody in Chicago on that dating site."

Alex put her head on one side. "Methinks the lady doth protest too much. Maybe you could bake him cookies."

Hannah laughed. "No cookies!" she said. "I don't feel that way about him. We just work together. We get along pretty well. But we're just friends. Nothing romantic. I just thought, if the guys want another basketball player, he would be a good person to ask. I can give you his number for Doc—I don't think he'd mind."

Grace didn't seem convinced about Hannah and Jack just being friends, but she nodded. "I'll tell Jim. Alex, would you reach me a knife? I need to score the scones."

It was nice, hanging out with Grace and Alex, even if they teased her. It was too bad they were almost done with the tea party stuff. Maybe there would be other opportunities to hang out this fall.

ᕫᕬᕫᕬᕫᕬ

The tea party was a cheery affair. The girls had decorated the church basement with flowers and crepe paper streamers. There wasn't much you could do to beautify an old basement, but at least it was a walk-out with natural light coming through the windows. The tea tables, with their china and flowers, and the big food table were lovely.

Hannah took some pictures. She wasn't going to make this a video—since it was a private event—but she wanted to be able to look back and remember how pretty everything had been.

The choir women all came, except one alto who was sick. Nearly everyone wore flowered dresses. Two ladies had big straw hats with flowers.

Hannah was beginning to wonder if they had made too much food. Besides the girls' cucumber sandwiches, scones, and macarons, the other ladies brought tea cake (made by a young alto who wanted to be a professional baker), mini quiches, several kinds of cookies, bacon-wrapped dates, and lemonade.

"Go sit down, Hannah," Grace commanded, filling a china teapot from an electric kettle. "You've done enough already."

"Sure, Grace—thanks."

She didn't know most of the choir ladies well. But there was Elaine, sitting with choir director Mary Jane. Hannah should get to know Elaine better—they were neighbors, after all.

"May I sit with you?" Hannah stopped at Elaine's table.

"Of course," Elaine said at once. "You may be sorry you did," she added, as Hannah sat down. "If you don't want to talk about philosophy, and politics, and the state of the world, this isn't the table for you."

Hannah smiled. "That sounds great."

Elaine patted her hand. "I'm glad you're doing more town

activities. I didn't see you much for a while."

Hannah really had become a hermit after Doc and Grace started dating. Most people probably hadn't noticed. Elaine must be observant.

"I've been getting to know some of the other girls," Hannah said. "And I'm going to try to make it to more choir practices. Sorry, Mary Jane."

The cheerful, curly-haired choir director smiled. "That's all right," she said. "I know things come up. But it's good to have you back. The soprano section isn't the same without you."

"Thanks." Hannah took a bite of her macaron. Oh, these had turned out well. It practically melted in her mouth.

It was nice to be appreciated. It was too bad the choir would be minus a soprano when Hannah went back to Chicago. But maybe they'd find somebody else.

Mary Jane and Elaine were discussing a fall pro-life campaign. There was a lot more going on at St. Anthony's than just the choir. It impressed Hannah how busy these ladies were in such a small town. The activities they had going on probably rivaled the number of things Hannah did in Chicago.

The bacon-wrapped dates were savory and sweet, the mini quiches were delectable, and the tea cake was light and fluffy with tangy jam. Fraser's Mill people could really cook.

Everyone agreed the tea was a success. It wasn't the Ritz Hotel with a fancy Edwardian-era tea, but this was a country town, after all.

"So, what did you think?" Grace asked Hannah, as the girls carried boxes to Grace's car at the end. "Was it worth all the fuss?"

"Totally," Hannah said. "It was a lot of fun. Thanks for letting me help out."

Grace smiled. "We couldn't have done it without you."

"We definitely couldn't." Alex set a box in the car with a thump and then frantically checked to make sure the china hadn't broken. "You ought to do more things with us, Hannah."

"Hey, Alex, did you ask your parents about the dance?" Grace had swung herself up to sit on the edge of the open hatchback of her car, boxes filling the space behind her.

"They liked the idea," Alex said. "Sam says he'll help. He doesn't know about decorating, but he's a good gofer. And Charlie's doing the food."

"What's all this about?" Hannah asked.

"I'm having an All Hallowed Eve party and dance at the farm," Alex said. "You should come. It'll be fun. We're inviting the whole town. Anybody who comes should wear a costume, unless they hate wearing costumes, of course."

Hannah didn't have any costumes here, but maybe she could borrow something from Christine. And she'd show Jack she wasn't afraid to give Fraser's Mill dances another try.

"I'd love to," Hannah said. "It sounds like fun."

"Yay!" Alex bounced on her toes. "It oughtta be a good time. I'm going as Arwen. I'm trying to get Charlie to be Aragorn. He says if he gets to wear a sword and doesn't have to wear a wig, he might do it."

A notification sound dinged somewhere among the boxes, and Grace rummaged for her phone. "It's Jim."

Of course it was.

"Alex, Jim says to tell Charlie—if you see him—they're playing basketball tonight," Grace said. "His phone's turned off. And Hannah, he says thanks for suggesting Jack. Jack's gonna play with them tonight."

Hannah nodded. "No problem."

◦◦◦◦◦◦

"You should enter a competition at the fall festival," Jack told Hannah at her desk on Friday. Lunch together had become a routine. Jack had started saving his reading time for later and bringing his chair and lunchbox to Hannah's desk.

According to Jack, his family was preparing to have their largest farm stand ever this year. His sisters were entering all kinds of food and craft competitions.

"What competition would I enter?" Hannah asked him. "I don't make jams and jellies and preserves like all these Fraser's Mill people. I don't know how to use a pressure cooker. I'd burn myself, and you'd have to take me to Doc's again."

Jack grinned. "How about baking? They have contests for pies and cakes and cookies. I've heard your baking is fantastic."

"How did you hear about my baking?" Hannah asked with her mouth full. News traveled fast in Fraser's Mill.

"At basketball. Doc and Charlie said your macarons were terrific." Jack bit into a tuna sandwich on sourdough toast. How he managed to make these fancy lunches before coming to work, Hannah would never understand.

She shook her head. "Doc and Charlie don't know what they're talking about. Besides, those macarons took forever and

172

required three of us to make."

"Okay, okay," Jack said. "I thought you might feel more at home in Fraser's Mill if you were part of the goings-on."

"I think just going to the fall festival will be fine," Hannah said. "For that matter, what are you doing for the festival? I don't see you making jams and jellies and preserves."

Jack laughed. "I'll be on duty. Sheriff Hank needs extra help, with all the out-of-towners that always come."

"Do you think there'll be trouble?"

"No, I'll probably be telling people not to park in front of driveways and pointing out the bathrooms. But that's part of the job too."

"Not all heroes wear capes," Hannah said. "It makes people feel safe to have a police presence."

Jack looked thoughtful. "Unfortunately, not everybody thinks that, these days. I'm glad they do in Fraser's Mill."

"I can't imagine a criminal in Fraser's Mill at all," Hannah said. "But I appreciate the extra safety. If you're going to be on duty at the festival, maybe you'd better be a police presence at the Martins' Halloween dance, too."

"Hannah, are you asking me to the dance?" Jack's eyes twinkled dangerously.

"No!" Hannah sputtered. "I was just thinking, since the whole town's going to be there wearing costumes—"

The corner of Jack's mouth twitched. "Whatever you say, Hannah." He got up. "I should get back to work. Glad you took my advice about the dance."

He went off to his desk, leaving Hannah looking after him.

Jack affected her strangely lately. She wasn't sure what to make of it. But she certainly hadn't been asking him to the dance. The idea!

An Evening at the Log House

That afternoon, Hannah's desk phone rang. When she answered, Mom's voice came over the line.

"Hi, Hannah. How's your day going?"

"Mom," Hannah exclaimed. "How did you get my work number?"

Mom laughed. "The office has had the same number since the nineties."

"What's going on?" Hannah asked.

"It's getting late in the year, and the dock has to come in. Our normal guy we hire to get it done has a bad back. Could you scout around and find somebody willing to take in the dock? We'll pay whatever seems reasonable. And we've got a floating log to float the sections to shore, so whoever does it won't have to get completely frozen and miserable."

That sounded better than wading around taking out the dock. The air was distinctly chilly these days, and Hannah hated to imagine how cold the water must be.

"Just one person?" Hannah asked.

"One or two," Mom said. "It's not as heavy as a wooden dock. It gets stored in the boathouse. And don't even think of trying to do it yourself."

"Don't worry, Mom," Hannah said. "Just thinking of going in that water makes me shiver. I'll see if I can find somebody. You don't think Steve would do it?"

"I already asked him. He's too busy this week."

"Okay. I'll try to find somebody else."

Across the room, Jack was on the phone with some cranky person. Jack was tall and strong and knew about farm work. Maybe he would take in a dock.

When Jack was off the phone, Hannah approached his desk. He was sitting with his chair tilted backward so he'd tip over if he wasn't careful.

He raised his eyebrows. "Hannah?"

"Uh, Jack, I have a question for you."

"Yes?" He waited, fingertips together.

"My parents are trying to find someone who would be willing to take in our dock," Hannah said. "You don't have to say yes—it's totally fine if you don't want to do it, I wouldn't—but if you did want to help, my parents will pay whatever seems fair."

Jack's brow furrowed.

"It's an aluminum dock," Hannah added hastily. "And we've got a floating log to bring the sections in. So you wouldn't have to get completely soaked and miserable."

He probably thought she was just asking him because

she had nobody else. She was a damsel in distress, as usual. "Don't feel like I'm pressuring you," Hannah added. "I can ask somebody else who—"

"I'll do it."

"What?"

"I'll do it." Jack righted his chair. "On one condition."

"Great." Hannah blinked. "Wait, what condition?"

"You help me out," Jack said. "I'll take it apart. You can hand me tools and help put things away. We can split the payment."

Jack didn't know her lack of skills. "I don't know the first thing about putting away docks. Do you?"

"No, but I can figure it out," Jack said. "It'll be fun."

"You think the strangest things are fun," Hannah said. "Sure, fine. When do you want to do it?"

Jack grinned. "How about tonight?"

"Tonight?" He was proactive. Hannah fumbled for words, trying to sort out her thoughts. What did she have going on tonight?

He raised an eyebrow. "Busy tonight? Big video interview? Date with the CEO of the biggest company in Chicago?"

As if. That guy Blake had viewed her profile, but never replied to her message. Hannah's dating life was stagnant. "No," Hannah said. "I don't have plans. I'll help you."

⚛

After work, Jack came over. By this time, Hannah had watched several videos for taking down docks. The whole thing looked impossibly difficult. At least they didn't have to wade in the water. She had found the floating log and the tools in the boathouse.

Jack had read about taking down docks in his down time at work this afternoon. He didn't need to watch any of the videos, he said. Good thing he knew what to do. Hannah never liked assembling and disassembling things. She stood around in the cold wind—grateful for her warm clothes—and waited for Jack to give her tasks.

Jack wore a henley and jeans, and his sleeves were pushed up. He said he wasn't cold. How men could go around in the freezing wind and unscrew bolts and things and stay warm, Hannah didn't know.

They stacked the dock sections in the boathouse, the nearest sections on top. That way, installation in the spring wouldn't be too bad.

"There." Jack dusted off his hands as Hannah locked the boathouse. "Now we know how to do it next time."

"Shall I tell my parents you're our new permanent dock guy?" Hannah asked. "You'll have to get a new partner, though. I'll be in Chicago."

Jack nodded. "Right."

He started toward the front yard. Hannah followed him, hugging herself for protection against the wind. All she wanted was a cup of cocoa. And some company.

"Hey, Jack," she called. "Would you like some cocoa?"

He turned. "What?"

"Cocoa," Hannah said. "I don't know about you, but I'm freezing."

Jack smiled. "Then let's get you some cocoa."

It was getting dark. Inside, Hannah turned on the lights and rummaged in the cupboard to find cocoa mix packets. Jack, who had never been in Hannah's house before, walked around the living room, looking at the log walls and the fireplace.

"Do you ever light a fire in here?" he called to Hannah.

"No," Hannah called. "I don't know how to light a fire. And it was hot all summer. My grandparents never did it when we were younger because they were afraid somebody would get hurt." She poured milk into a saucepan to heat on the stove. Some people made cocoa with water. Hannah believed that if you were going to have something as rich and sugary as cocoa, you ought to make it properly.

"That's a shame," Jack called. "This is a nice old fireplace." His voice turned echoey. "Looks like the chimney's clear."

Hannah came out of the kitchen to find him on his hands and knees, looking up the chimney. "You look like you're waiting for Santa Claus."

Jack emerged from the fireplace laughing. "Well, I tried to be a good boy this year," he said. "You've got a woodpile out front, don't you? What if I make a fire?"

"Go for it. I'll finish making the cocoa."

Hannah came in with the cocoa on a tray and found several logs blazing on the hearth. Of course Jack was adept at making fires. "We have bonfires all the time back home," he explained.

"Is there anything you don't know how to do?" Hannah asked.

"I'm not so good at flying," Jack said. "Let's bring this couch over by the fireplace."

They sat on either end of the couch, the tray with the cocoa mugs on the cushion between them.

"Do you want whipped cream or anything?" Hannah asked. "I think I have heavy cream."

Jack took a sip of his cocoa. "No, this is perfect."

"Thanks." Hannah took her own cocoa, stretching her feet toward the fire. "This is the life."

Jack chuckled. "Warmer than taking in a dock," he said. "I saw you got your video finished."

"Oh, yes, I posted it on Tuesday," Hannah said. "You watch my videos?"

"I do now," Jack said. "You did a good job. I liked how you did the voiceover with the sounds of the river and the wildlife. You could make nature documentaries." He grinned. "I can just hear your voice narrating the life cycle of the water bug."

"Thanks?" Hannah laughed. "Water bugs aren't really my thing."

Jack turned toward her, his arm along the back of the couch. "What is your thing?" he asked. "You make lots of different videos—interviews, tutorials, shopping—is there one kind in particular you really want to do?"

Hannah sipped her cocoa. "I've often asked myself that question. I feel like there ought to be some particular thing I focus on. I want to use my channel someday to make a difference to somebody—to help people—but I've got to grow it first."

"You mean, like raising awareness for causes?"

"Maybe." Hannah sipped her cocoa. "I've seen lots of channels raise awareness for different causes. Pro-life things, political things—they're all really important. I don't feel like I've really found my niche yet. I'm not sure which people I could make a difference for. I mean, I'm more of a lifestyle videographer. My channel is mostly snapshots in the life of Hannah."

"Reality TV, five minutes at a time?"

Hannah started to glare, but Jack didn't seem to be making fun of her. "I guess it is sort of like reality TV," she said. "Except reality TV is manipulated in a way that isn't really 'real.' I don't think the people's lives are really like that. Not that I watch reality TV—I've just heard about it. But I try to be authentic about the way I'm presenting myself. And I don't put my whole life on there for the world to see."

Jack nodded. "You seem pretty private about your personal life in your videos."

"People speculate about me in the comment section anyway. They don't need more fodder for gossip." Hannah laughed. "I can't post a video that has a guy in it without the comments blowing up about whether I'm dating him."

That had happened when Hannah posted her interview with Doc, and, later, with the Fourth of July video Doc had helped her make. She doubted Doc watched her channel, but she'd been embarrassed when it turned out Doc was interested in Grace instead. Hannah didn't like rewatching those videos.

Jack smiled. "People like making matches. And you're an eligible match."

That was what Hannah had been trying to get Doc to see all summer, but he hadn't seen it. "Thanks," Hannah said. "Personally, I think people are nosy and want to find out all about their neighbors."

"Barb—my landlady—does know a lot about me that I didn't exactly tell her." Jack grinned.

Somehow, that wasn't surprising. Hannah herself had only heard snippets about Jack's personal life. How he had hung out with a different circle than Alex growing up. How his ex-girlfriend played the violin. It would be nice to get to know the man behind the glasses.

"What kind of deep, dark secrets does Jack Rogers have?" Hannah gave Jack a scrutinizing look. "Let me guess. You're an ex-con who changed his identity and moved here from California. Or a secret agent. Or Superman—that seems most likely."

Behind his glasses, Jack's eyes gleamed. "Oh, really. Let me guess. You've never seen me and Superman in the same place."

"Nope. Let me see you without your glasses again."

Jack laughed.

His phone rang, and he put down the mug and slapped his pockets. He frowned when he looked at the screen. "Oops, I gotta take this."

Hannah poked the fire and tried not to listen to Jack's call. He appeared to be talking to the sheriff.

He stood up once he was off the phone. "I've got to go. There's a fight at the tavern and the sheriff's out on the other side of the county. Thanks a lot for the cocoa."

He vanished into the night, and Hannah looked out to watch his truck zoom off. He'd had to leave so soon, and he hadn't finished his cocoa. The life of a volunteer deputy sheriff wasn't dull, that was for sure.

The Admirer

It was a dull afternoon at the sawmill. Hannah had so little to do that she was planning next week's video. On the other hand, Jack was on the phone with a constant string of disgruntled truck drivers. Between calls, he was running around in the yard, supervising lumber loading. How did he keep his cool, with all his busyness and the crankiness of the guys on the phone?

"If something doesn't happen soon around here," Hannah called to Jack, "I'll ask Steve for the rest of the day off."

"You'll ask Steve?" Jack looked up, his phone still held to his ear. "Have you been drinking wishful-thinking juice, Hannah?"

Hannah laughed. Then her phone rang, so she had to scramble to answer it.

It was a woman. She had recently moved to Fraser's Mill and wanted to build a shed. She was handy with tools, which she knew was surprising, but some women liked to do yard projects. When the shed was finished she might want to put a privacy fence around her yard, but she wasn't sure. In any case, she wanted to know if the mill sold certain specific sizes of lumber.

"She ought to go to Menard's instead," Hannah grumbled, her phone muted, as she looked up the lumber the woman wanted. "What does she think this place is? We don't have every possible size of lumber."

Jack laughed. He wasn't any help.

After far too long, Hannah finally put together the best list of lumber sizes that she could.

The woman on the phone seemed dubious. "Can I just walk in at the mill?" she asked. "I want to look at it before buying it."

Hannah stifled a groan. "Sure, you can come in. We don't have dedicated salespeople in the office, but someone can show you around the lumber yard."

"Fine, then, I'll come over," the woman said. "Around two."

Hannah put down the phone with a sigh. "I never know what to do with these people with the weird requests," she said in Jack's direction. "I don't know who's going to show this lady around. Somebody would have to leave their work."

Jack shrugged. "We can work it out. Whichever one of us isn't too busy can show her around. My phone will slow down eventually."

At two PM on the dot, a young woman walked into the office. She was tall, blonde, and professional. Her blazer and skirt matched. Hannah hadn't seen clothes like that since Chicago.

"Hi," she said, with her warmest smile. "I'm Hannah. I believe I spoke to you on the phone."

The young woman extended a dead-fish hand to Hannah.

"Serena," she said. "Like Serena Williams, although I don't play tennis."

Hannah, who did play tennis, ignored this. "Do you want a tour of the lumber yard? I think you'll find plenty of options."

"I would appreciate it," Serena said. "I already tried a few places in Cadillac, and nobody had quite what I was looking for."

Hannah got up just as her phone rang.

"You can get it, Hannah," Jack called. "I'll give the lumber yard tour."

Serena turned at his voice. Her face lit up. Smiling, Serena was stunning. And that burgundy suit looked fantastic with her hair.

Jack and Serena disappeared, and Hannah dived for the phone, which was on the fourth ring.

They were gone a long time. Hannah had talked to a customer, fielded complaints from Steve, and planned most of her video, when Jack and Serena returned.

Serena had made her choices but was being picky about how she wanted her lumber loaded and stacked. Jack listened patiently, although Hannah knew he would never let anybody tell him how to stack lumber.

"I guess it's settled, then." Serena's hand was on Jack's arm, and he wasn't shaking it off. In fact, he was smiling. He probably found her attractive, which was fair.

"Hannah will help you with the order," Jack told Serena, and Serena approached the desk.

"I'm glad I came to see the lumber," she said. "If you want something done right, you have to do it yourself."

That sounded like Steve. Hannah filled out Serena's order

form and printed her invoice. "All set," she said at last. "Thanks for stopping by."

"You're welcome." Serena nodded. Instead of going for the door, however, she went for Jack's desk.

Hannah should mind her own desk and not eavesdrop on her coworker's conversation. But what was that woman doing? Hannah couldn't tell what Serena was saying—she was speaking quietly—but Jack responded cheerfully to her. Hannah pulled up the office inventory spreadsheet. Maybe she should order pens or something.

She looked up to see Serena shaking Jack's hand. "It's a date," Serena said, loud enough for Hannah to hear.

A date? Jack had a date with that woman? That was quick. She had certainly pounced on him immediately. Hannah was dying to know what was going on, but she didn't want to come right out and ask.

At his desk, on the phone again—that man was always on the phone—Jack still looked cheerful. His dark green henley had the sleeves pushed up, showing muscular forearms. Steve was right—Jack would make a good football player. Hannah turned back to her desk.

A few minutes later, Hannah needed a drink of water. The water cooler happened to be by Jack's desk.

"So," Hannah said casually, stopping by Jack's desk with her water, "how'd the tour go?"

He looked up. "Fine."

"Do you know Serena?"

He shook his head. "I just met her." His face was innocent.

"Really? It seemed like you guys knew each other, talking there before she left."

Jack leaned back, looking up at Hannah. "She was thanking me for the tour."

"Uh-huh." Then what was that business about a date?

A grin came across Jack's face. "You're jealous."

"What?" Hannah exclaimed. "Jealous? No such thing. I just—" She spluttered.

"You just wondered what we were talking about, didn't you?" Jack said.

"Nonsense," Hannah said. "Why would I care what women you talk to? I came over for a drink of water." She sipped her water, keeping her eyes on Jack.

"Well, in case you're curious," Jack said, "while I was showing her around, she mentioned she's going to be working part-time at the sheriff's office. Answering phones, doing paperwork, and such. I was filling her in on what it's like to work there."

"Oh." So Serena and Jack would be coworkers, at least when he worked at the sheriff's office. That didn't explain why Jack had said "it's a date."

"I guess you'll be seeing a lot of her, then," Hannah said.

Jack looked up, the mischievous grin returning. "Yep. She's pretty, isn't she? But I don't take a lot of shifts at the sheriff's office, so you don't have to be too jealous."

Ignoring him, Hannah plunked herself at her desk. Jealous, indeed! Jack knew she wasn't interested in him. They were just friends. Although—why was she so bugged by Serena? She'd wanted Jack to find a nice girl. She shouldn't chafe at the idea of him finding somebody. But this wasn't the kind of girl Hannah had had in mind for Jack. Maybe that was it.

Why was her mind going back to that time in the treehouse, with Jack's warm brown eyes resting on her? She busied herself with reorganizing her pen cup for the seventh time that day, refusing to dwell on how it felt to be so close to Jack that time. She didn't feel that way about him. She didn't.

On Thursday evening, Hannah had nothing to do. She was tired from working, so she didn't feel like making next week's video. But spending the whole evening at home felt so boring. If only she could hang out with somebody.

She ate dinner on the couch while watching a clean romance movie set in Hawaii. The scenery was breathtaking. It would be cool to live by a beach and swim every morning. Of course, Hannah lived on the river, but it was too cold to swim this time of year.

The couple in the movie had a glorious time, when the plot wasn't in the way. They went for walks on the beach and had picnics. If only Hannah had somebody to have picnics with. Picnicking alone wasn't fun.

Jack would be fun to go to the beach with. She could imagine having a picnic with him, eating sandwiches, wading, skipping stones, and talking about life. Hannah shook her head. No, she wasn't interested in Jack. They just ate lunch together every day. Lunch at the beach wasn't that different from lunch at work, was it?

What had Serena meant by "it's a date" earlier? Were she and Jack really going on a date?

Hannah wasn't jealous. Jack could date any single woman in the world, for all she cared.

What Hannah really ought to focus on was looking harder for her Mr. Right. He had to be out there. When she found him, she'd be able to stop stressing about other people. Especially these confusing thoughts about Jack that kept popping up uninvited.

Fall Festival

The next morning was the fall festival. Hannah woke up late — all those early mornings still made her extra tired — and headed to the festival, only pausing to eat some overnight oats she had made last night.

The festival was in the center of town. The whole main street was closed off, and anybody trying to drive through Fraser's Mill had to go around. Hannah walked to the festival to avoid parking and was glad she'd decided not to wear her tallest boots. Although these ones did have enough of a heel that she had to be careful not to twist her ankle again.

The day was sunny, with an October snap in the air. The trees were brilliant in red and gold, and the sky was clear blue, almost royal. Fraser's Mill was a little hick town, but it was a pretty place. And today there was plenty going on. The festival would be a great subject for this week's video.

Near the center of town, two policemen in brown and black

were directing traffic. Extra parking had been set up in a field off a side street. One of the policemen, almost unrecognizable in dark sunglasses and a black baseball cap, was Jack. He nodded and smiled in Hannah's direction. Hannah waved back.

The festival sprawled all over the street and the park. Carnival rides rose and fell or spun in circles. Hannah smelled frying donuts, cinnamon, and popcorn. One big area had vendors—farm stands, artisans selling handmade items, food tents—and another area was designated for contests. Tables were piled with jams and jellies, pies, cakes, fruits and vegetables, and knit and crocheted handicrafts.

Hannah wandered past the booths, not getting too close. She shouldn't get loaded down with purchases before she'd seen everything. Besides, she was trying to save money. She hadn't given up on finding a place to rent in Chicago. She took video footage of the booths as she went along. Since she wasn't buying, maybe she could at least get her viewers interested in supporting small business. Maybe some of the vendors had online platforms she could mention in her video.

On the other side of the park, children ran a three-legged race with moms watching. Hannah heard her name.

"Aunt Hannah!"

It was Evelyn, waving excitedly, with Christine and baby Noah. Hannah hadn't known they would come so early.

"Evelyn." Hannah caught her niece in a hug. "Hi!"

"I'm going to do the sack race," Evelyn proclaimed. She was wearing overalls with a mini denim jacket and cowboy boots. Christine always found cute clothes for her.

"She was too little for the three-legged race." Christine shifted Noah to her other hip. "The sack race is more her speed."

The three-legged race finished, and Evelyn ran to where a number of other little boys and girls were grabbing burlap sacks. The game was organized by a mom with a blonde ponytail, who ran around helping the kids sort themselves out.

"One—two—three—go!" she announced, and the kids were off. Evelyn, on the edge of the group, started well, but after a few feet she tripped and fell on her face.

"Come on, Evelyn, you can do it," Hannah called.

Evelyn got up slowly, looking like she was about to cry.

"Evelyn, you can keep going," Christine called. "Come on! You can do it."

Evelyn took a deep breath, hitched up the sack, and hopped in the direction of the finish line.

As soon as she was across the line, she wriggled out of the sack and ran to Christine and Hannah. "I did it," she announced. Her face was streaky—some tears must have fallen—but she was smiling.

"I'm proud of you, Evie." Christine hugged her, one-armed. "You did it."

"You're a brave girl." Hannah tousled Evelyn's hair. "How about if Aunt Hannah gets you a donut?"

"I love donuts!" Evelyn hopped up and down.

"That sounds wonderful," Christine said. "That's very nice of Aunt Hannah."

"Thank you, Aunt Hannah," Evelyn said politely. She took Hannah's hand and swung it. "Can we get the donut now?"

Christine winked at Hannah. "I think that would be all right."

They strolled toward the food vendors. One area was set up for some kind of woodchopping or sawing competition. That was sponsored by the sawmill. Sarah, from the mill, and her husband were setting it up.

Beyond that was a dunk tank with a waiting line of children and teenagers. All the proceeds from the dunk tank went to the town food pantry. In the tank, wearing a wetsuit, was Sheriff Hank Liddell. Although Sheriff Hank was universally beloved, the town children couldn't resist getting to dunk the sheriff. As Hannah and her family went by, one little girl in a pink dress and pigtails threw a fast ball and hit the target squarely. The sheriff went down with a splash and climbed back on his bench, laughing.

"Tell your parents to sign you up for softball," he called to the girl who had thrown the ball.

After her small breakfast, Hannah was hungry. She might as well get a donut for herself too, and some cider.

They stopped at one of the first stands, a booth with bags of large red apples, pumpkins, jars of honey, donuts, and a huge thermal container that said "Fresh Hot Mulled Cider." A middle-aged woman, with dark hair smoothly pulled back in a clip, was handing a small girl a steaming cup. It smelled amazing.

"Christine, do you want anything?" Hannah asked.

Christine shook her head. "I had enough sugar this morning. Thanks though."

When the small girl left, Hannah approached the booth, Evelyn at her heels. "Hi."

The woman running the booth looked up. "Hi." She tilted her head to one side. "You must be Hannah."

Her cheery smile and deep brown eyes seemed familiar, but Hannah couldn't place her. "Yes, I'm Hannah."

The woman nodded. "You work with my son Jack."

That's how she seemed familiar—Jack had a family picture on his desk. Both mother and son had the same dark hair and eyes.

"Oh! It's nice to meet you, Mrs. Rogers," Hannah exclaimed.

"Call me Julia." Jack's mom shook Hannah's hand. "It's good to meet you. I've heard so much about you, I feel like I know you. I probably shouldn't have said that, but it's too late." She smiled, mischief in her eyes. "Have cider and a donut. On the house. You brought my boy soup when he was sick. He never tells me when he's sick. I have to learn everything from Barb Kowalski."

She poured Hannah a generous cup of cider and put two donuts in a bag. "Here you are. The donuts are fresh this morning. Felicity and Agnes helped make them. Agnes splashed hot oil over half the kitchen, but she didn't burn herself. Her guardian angel works overtime."

"Mom," a cheerful voice said, and Jack appeared. "How's it going? Hi, Hannah. Who's this?" He crouched down to Evelyn's height. "Hi there."

"Hi," Evelyn said. "Are you a policeman?"

"Sure am." Jack tapped the badge on his chest. "Nice to meet you, young lady."

"My niece, Evelyn," Hannah explained.

"Ah." Jack stood up. "Steve said something about bringing

his family." He turned to Julia. "Hi, Mom."

"Jack." Julia kissed him on the cheek. "What are you doing here? I thought you were on duty."

"I'm on break," Jack said. "I thought I'd get some donuts and catch some of the food judging."

"Make sure you eat more than just sugar," Julia warned him, but she started putting donuts in another bag. "They're making hamburgers over on the right."

"Don't worry, Mom, I'll get real food." Jack went behind the table and poured his own cider, pulling money from his pocket and sticking it in the cashbox while his mother's back was turned. "Where are David and the girls?"

"David's trying to dunk the poor sheriff, and the girls went to the food judging."

"Thanks. David wants to videotape the wood chopping contest. Of course, I'll fail miserably. I'm up against the cousins, and they've been practicing for weeks."

"Now, Jack, you're much better at chopping wood than those boys are," Julia said.

"Hope so, Mom. I'm gonna go get a hamburger. You want one, Hannah?"

He was being nice, but with the whole Serena business and the strange way Hannah had been feeling, Hannah thought she and Jack could use some space from each other. Hannah shook her head. "Thanks. It's a little early for me. I think I'll watch the judging."

Jack nodded. "See you there."

Hannah headed back to Christine, at a shaded bench, and

gave Evelyn her donut.

Christine smiled at Hannah. "You're getting to know some people," she said. "You seem more at home in Fraser's Mill than before."

"Huh. Maybe." Hannah sipped her hot cider. Did she seem more comfortable here? She was surviving in Fraser's Mill, but she would never say she was at home. If Christine was judging her interaction with Jack and his mom, she wasn't getting the whole picture. Hannah was always polite to people she'd just met—like Jack's mom—and her friendship with Jack was complicated.

Thankfully, Christine didn't press her on it. She changed the subject to donut-making, and when Evelyn had finished eating, she took the two kids to the restroom to wash Evelyn's sticky fingers and change Noah.

Hannah headed over to the booths with the food and crafts for judging. She was looking at some elaborate needlework when someone said, "Hi, Hannah."

She turned. It was Grace in flannel plaid, jeans, and a cowboy hat, and Doc in an orange sweater and khakis.

"Hey, Hannah," Doc said. His hand was linked with Grace's.

"Hi, guys," Hannah said.

For some reason, she didn't mind running into them. Maybe she was getting used to the idea.

"We're going to catch the pumpkin judging," Grace said. "Alex entered a massive pumpkin. They had to bring it on a trailer. Wanna come?"

"Sure, why not?"

Hannah trailed along after Grace and Doc to a booth filled

with huge pumpkins—not on a table (they would probably break it) but on the ground. People clustered around, waiting for the judges. Alex was there with Charlie, bouncing with excitement.

"That's my pumpkin." Alex pointed to a large one in the corner. "We had a time getting it here without cracking it. If it cracks, it's disqualified. Or if it has rotten spots."

"I looked it all over," Charlie assured her. "It doesn't have any rotten spots."

"I think some of those other ones might be bigger," Alex said. "We have to wait until they weigh them. And this is nothing compared to the real giant pumpkin competitions. These are just big regular pumpkins."

The two judges, middle-aged farmers in overalls, weighed the pumpkins and loudly announced the winners.

"Third place, Matthew Jorgenson; second place, Alexandra Martin; first place, Walt Daniels."

Alex squealed. Hannah, Grace, Doc, and Charlie clapped loudly.

"I'm surprised," Alex said. "A bunch of those other pumpkins looked bigger than mine. Mine must have been heavy for its size."

"That's incredible, Alex," Hannah said. "Congratulations!"

"Thanks!" Alex turned and hugged Hannah. "I'm so excited! I didn't expect to win anything!"

Alex's face was so happy, Hannah couldn't help beaming.

"Good job, Alex." Walt Daniels, the first place winner and the husband of one of the choir ladies, patted Alex on the shoulder. "Heard this was your first year growing a pumpkin. I'm impressed."

Other categories were being judged. Jack stood with a couple of his sisters by a booth with a lot of jams and jellies. Maybe Hannah shouldn't join them. With her confused feelings about Jack, it might be better to keep some distance. On the other hand, why couldn't she hang out with a friend and his little sisters at the festival? Hannah was about to head that direction when someone tapped her shoulder.

"Hey, Hannah." It was Steve.

He was with a guy who looked strangely familiar. The newcomer had curly brown hair and a stubble beard. He wore a bomber jacket over a white T-shirt with jeans.

"Hannah, this is Blake Whitaker," Steve said. "His parents are friends with Mom and Dad, and he's gonna work at the mill."

Blake smiled, showing movie-star white teeth. He extended his hand toward her. "Nice to meet you."

Hannah could only stare. It couldn't be, but it was. It was Blake from the dating website.

Blake

It seemed like Hannah had been standing there forever with Blake waiting to shake her hand. Hopefully it had only really been a few seconds.

"Hi." Hannah grasped the proffered hand like a lifeline before she remembered to loosen her grip. "Nice to meet you."

Should she mention the dating site? No point. Mentioning the site would make things awkward. Blake was even better-looking in real life than he was in his profile.

"I hear you work in the mill office." Blake's ice-blue eyes seemed like he could look right through Hannah. "We'll be seeing a lot of each other. I'm going to drive a forklift."

It was funny how different somebody could be in person than online. Online, Blake had looked at Hannah's profile and ignored her message. Here, he was warm and personable.

Steve slapped Blake on the back. "Come on, I'll show you around. Hannah, want to come with us?"

Unexpectedly, she did. Hannah hurried to keep up with the men. This was an interesting development. Maybe Blake had missed seeing her message. Maybe he'd typed a message and it hadn't sent. Those sites could be glitchy. Maybe he'd meant to respond and then forgot—after all, he'd just moved.

What was he doing here? She couldn't believe he had come all the way from Chicago to work in Fraser's Mill. People didn't do that. Eligible young men, especially, didn't do that. Weren't there plenty of jobs in Chicago? Maybe this guy was doing the Frasers a favor. Steve was always complaining he couldn't find competent workers.

Steve took his job as host seriously. After introducing Blake to Christine and the kids (Evelyn was now completely sticky), he took him to the dunk tank, the food vendors, and the games area where people could toss rings or darts or shoot guns and win a prize. The two talked loudly about assorted topics. Blake's conversation was as impressive in person as his dating profile had been. Blake had designed an investment management app, whatever that was. He had grown bored with his pursuits in Chicago and wanted something new, and Dad had mentioned the mill needed another forklift driver. So Blake was doing the mill a favor. That added to his impressiveness.

Too bad Steve was doing so much talking. Hannah would have liked to talk more with Blake herself.

Blake stuck with the Frasers until Steve had to go back to Cadillac. Then he politely excused himself. "I'm still setting up my apartment. I got here this morning, and my stuff's still in boxes."

He said goodbye to Hannah separately, saying he looked

forward to seeing her again. She was excited to see him on Monday.

It had been a memorable day—the beautiful fall weather, the excitement and bustle of the fall festival, and the new guy from Chicago.

⁂

Usually for Hannah the weekend went by like a flash and the week dragged like molasses. This weekend, however, felt unusually long. Maybe it was because Sunday was a long dull day, and Blake didn't show up at St. Anthony's. Hannah hadn't expected him to—Steve and his family lived in Cadillac too, and they always attended Mass there—but she was disappointed when the opening hymn rolled around and Blake wasn't in the pews. Oh well. She'd see him at work tomorrow.

It wasn't like she fell for any good looking guy who came along. But Blake's arrival, right when Hannah had decided to put more effort into finding Mr. Right, felt almost providential. Blake intrigued her, and it wouldn't hurt to get to know him better.

On Monday morning, Hannah decided she had gotten into a stylistic rut. She had mostly been wearing the same things—white or light jeans, fitted T-shirts or loose button-downs, and chunky white shoes she still didn't like much. Too bad Steve didn't allow heels at work.

She straightened her hair, something she hadn't done since Doc, and put on mascara. Thankfully she had gotten up early enough this morning.

What could she wear that was pretty and stylish and yet casual enough for a mill office where you had to keep running out to the yard and greeting truck drivers? Hannah finally decided to take a leaf out of Christine's book with a striped shirt and red lipstick. It was a casual outfit, but it had a little pop of something extra. She decided on boots with low heels.

Rats. She was late now, and she hadn't eaten breakfast or packed lunch. She'd have to eat out of the vending machine. Maybe Jack would have an extra sandwich. Not that she wanted to mooch off his lunch, but knowing Jack, he would probably offer.

Blake would probably eat lunch in the break room. She wasn't going to try to hang out with him there. It was so public, and she would have to deal with people like Drew and Spencer. She would eat lunch in the office, and if Blake chose to come by, she wouldn't complain.

Hannah pulled up at the sawmill five minutes late. Was Blake in the yard driving any of the forklifts? She didn't see him. Maybe Steve was showing him around.

In the office, Jack was on the phone. Steve was nowhere. Good, she wouldn't get a lecture about punctuality. Hannah clocked in, sat down, and used her phone camera to check her hair and makeup. She looked all right.

The door from the mill opened, and Blake appeared, with a hardhat and safety vest over casual clothes. Hannah wouldn't wave. That would be undignified. She wasn't going to get embarrassing about Blake, like she had about Doc.

"Hannah," Blake said. He came over to her desk, leaning on the counter.

"Your brother's been showing me around. You run an efficient operation here."

"Thanks. We do our best."

Blake smiled. "I'm glad to be on board," he said. "I've got to go drive the forklift, but I'll see you later?"

Hannah nodded. "I'll be right here."

Truth be told, Hannah didn't get much work done that morning except for answering the phone at intervals. She was daydreaming about Blake.

Lunchtime came, and Hannah was starving. A customer had kept her tied up on the phone a little into her break, so most of the guys were already in the break room. She had seen Blake go by, lunchbox in hand.

She ought to keep granola bars or something in her desk so she wasn't stuck eating vending machine food or mooching off Jack (who was currently on the phone). But she never thought of that when she was at the store. She'd slip into the break room and get a couple cookies. Those pre-packaged chocolate chip cookies were, surprisingly, growing on her.

Blake was in the break room, sitting at a table with a bunch of the guys. He was talking to Sarah's husband, the operator. It was good that Blake was fitting in with his coworkers.

Hannah had inserted her debit card in the vending machine when someone reached around her and pulled it out. That hand was familiar.

"Jack," Hannah protested, turning around.

Jack was grinning. "You forgot your lunch again."

"Can't I use my own work vending machine?" Hannah put her hands on her hips. "Those cookies are actually pretty good. What if I wanted dessert?"

Jack looked around. "What have you done with the real Hannah Fraser?" he asked. "I know what you actually eat. Come back to the office. I've got a thermos of chili, and I can dig up an extra bowl and spoon somewhere."

"Fine, all right," Hannah said. "I'll come."

As they went back into the office, Jack looked at Hannah funny. "Are you going somewhere?" he asked. "You don't usually get this dressed up for work."

Of course he would think that. "I do have a professional job here," Hannah said. "A girl can dress nicely for work once in a while if she wants."

"Don't get me wrong, you look great." Jack grabbed his lunchbox and thermos from his desk and brought them over, leaning against Hannah's desk. "We missed you at the woodchopping competition yesterday. Sarah said you and Steve were showing some new guy around."

"Yes," Hannah said. "His name's Blake. He's a new forklift driver. And get this—he's from Chicago, and his parents know my parents. Somehow my dad learned he was looking for a job, and we needed a forklift driver."

"A Chicago guy, eh?"

"Yes. And get this, too." Hannah lowered her voice. She was too embarrassed to mention this to Blake, but she had to tell somebody. "It's the weirdest thing, but I've met him before. Sort of. I've seen his online dating profile. It was so surreal seeing him turn up in real life."

"Uh-huh." Jack picked up Hannah's empty coffee mug, turning it around in his hands. He was looking down at the mug, and he spoke casually, yet with an odd carefulness. "You're awfully jittery for somebody who hasn't had her morning coffee. Want me to grab you a cup?"

"Sure, thanks, Jack, that would be great."

Hannah hadn't been thinking about coffee this morning. Jack was right—she was jittery. It was weird how much Blake affected her.

⚬⚬⚬⚬⚬

Quitting time was five PM. Hannah fixed her hair, got her things, and wrote herself a reminder to buy or make granola bars. If she kept homemade ones in an airtight container, they wouldn't attract mice or bugs.

She hadn't seen Blake since lunchtime. Maybe he would come through before he left, instead of going out the big mill door. She wanted to at least say hi to him as he came by.

Jack was ready to leave. "Walk you to your car?" he called to Hannah.

Hannah shook her head. "Thanks, Jack. I think I'll be a few more minutes."

"All right, see you tomorrow." Jack shouldered his lunchbox and disappeared.

Did she always leave her desk in a mess like this? Hannah straightened piles of papers and office supplies. She must usually run out as soon as quitting time came.

"Hi, Hannah," a voice said.

Hannah looked up, her breath catching, to see Blake. He wasn't wearing his hard hat now. "Hi, Blake," she said, smiling.

"Steve was right," Blake said. "It's a long day here. But the view isn't so bad."

Was he talking about the view of the woods, or about her? Hannah blushed. "How was your first day?"

"Not bad." Blake looked at her keenly. "It's crazy, but I have the feeling I've seen you before."

Hannah laughed. She knew why Blake thought that, but she wasn't going to tell him. It helped a woman to maintain a little mystery. "I know the feeling."

"Maybe I've seen an actress who looks like you," Blake said. "You don't eat lunch in the break room?"

So he noticed her absence at lunchtime.

"It's crowded in the break room," Hannah said, "and I don't really hang out with the guys from the mill."

"Too many men hitting on you?" Blake's expression was knowing. "You're out of their league."

She blushed again. "Thanks."

Blake looked at his watch. Was that a Rolex? "I've gotta get going. I'm still setting up my apartment, and I've got a call with a business contact in Chicago. See you tomorrow, Hannah."

"See you tomorrow," Hannah breathed.

She needed a way to get to know Blake outside of work. He seemed like he would be fun to hang out with. Maybe an opportunity would come up.

Crime Wave in Fraser's Mill

Before bed that evening, Hannah checked social media. A post caught her eye: it was a note from the sheriff on the Fraser's Mill town page. The gas station had been robbed. The suspect was on the loose. The sheriff warned everyone to lock their doors, windows, and cars.

Robbers in Fraser's Mill? Hannah had never heard of such a thing. Maybe it was an out-of-towner passing through. She made sure the house was locked before bed. She didn't check the boathouse lock, but it was dark and cold, and she didn't feel like going out there. Besides, who would steal the junk in the boathouse?

After a restless night, worrying about robbers, Hannah asked Jack if he knew anything about the robbery. Jack was full of information. As a volunteer deputy sheriff, he was always filled in on police matters.

"A guy in a black hoodie and a ski mask held up the gas

station at gunpoint," he explained when Hannah came outside to give him an invoice for an order he was supervising. "It was the end of the day, and they had a lot of cash on hand. The security cameras caught the whole thing, but it didn't do any good, because nobody can identify him. He could be anywhere."

"Is anybody going after him?"

"No leads," Jack said. "We don't know which direction he went. We've warned the police departments in the nearby towns to watch for armed robbers."

Hannah shook her head. "It's crazy that something like that would happen in Fraser's Mill."

"Not what you would expect," Jack said.

"Hey, Jack," one of the guys by the truck yelled. "Which order is this? We've got the papers mixed up."

"Oh, boy." Jack took off at a run, invoice in hand.

Hannah started back to the office. A forklift went by, and the driver waved. It was Blake. Hannah waved back.

"Hi, Hannah," Blake called. "How's it going?"

Hannah tucked her hair behind her ear. "Good!" she called back. "How are you?"

"Great!" Blake answered, but the forklift was far away now.

Smiling, Hannah went inside. The forklift drivers didn't usually call to her across the yard. Blake definitely seemed intentional about his interactions with her.

❧❧❧

On Wednesday, as Hannah was starting lunch (a pre-packaged quinoa meal, grabbed in haste when she had last gone shopping) and Jack was in the break room getting them coffee, Blake came in with his lunchbox.

"May I join you?"

Oh wow, he was leaving his buddies to eat lunch with her. Hannah smiled. "You may. You'll have to get a chair from the break room—that's Jack's."

"The dispatcher?" Blake asked. "I've met him." He whisked into the next room and came back with a chair. He sat backwards, resting his arms on the chair back, fixing Hannah with his intense blue gaze. It was disconcerting, but exciting.

"So," he said, "how long have you been working here?"

"About a month," Hannah said. "I started right after Labor Day."

"You like it?"

"It's been interesting," Hannah said. "Not quite what I had expected, but it's all right for the moment."

"I take it this isn't your dream job." Blake took a wrapped sandwich from his lunchbox.

Hannah smiled, shaking her head. "Nope."

"You wanna tell me what your dream job is?"

Hannah wrinkled her nose. "I'll give you three guesses."

"Hmm." Blake bit his sandwich and chewed meditatively. "One. Actress."

"Close, but no."

"Two. Model."

Hannah was blushing. "Thanks. No."

"Three—"

"Hey, what's this?" Jack had reappeared with two cups of coffee. "That's my spot," he told Blake. "And this isn't your office."

That was unusually brusque. Hannah looked at Jack in surprise. "Jack, I said Blake could sit here. There's your chair. There's plenty of room for you."

Jack put Hannah's coffee on her desk. "Thanks anyway, Hannah. I'm going to read my book." He grabbed his lunch, then went away.

"Touchy, isn't he?" Blake asked.

Hannah shook her head. "He's usually very friendly. It's probably that robbery that's stressed him out."

"Robbery?" Blake asked.

That's right, Blake was new to town and probably hadn't seen the update. Hannah told him about it. "I can't imagine how something like that would happen in Fraser's Mill," she said. "Chicago, sure. Here, never."

"People are the same all over," Blake said. "Even in little towns."

"I guess that makes sense," Hannah said. "You never finished guessing what my dream job was."

"My third guess is — singer."

"That's another close one. I like singing, but I don't want it as a career. Actually, I have a video channel. My dream job is to grow that channel until it's a sustainable career. Go big or go home, right?"

"Aha," Blake said. "Maybe I've seen some of your videos. That might be why you looked familiar."

"Maybe." Hannah avoided a smile. She wasn't going to mention the online dating profile.

"So what's your channel called?"

Hannah shook her head. "I don't give out my channel name

to people I've just met," she said. "It feels weird. I don't want new acquaintances to learn about me from my videos."

"Too fast? Okay, no worries," Blake said. "Not trying to make you uncomfortable. Hey, I'm going into Manistee tonight to get burgers and drinks with a couple of the operators. You ought to come."

It was the same kind of invitation Drew had given Hannah, but it felt different. Spending time with Blake and a couple of the operators wouldn't be the same as going out with Drew and Spencer's crowd. After all, Blake's parents were friends with Hannah's parents. They had the same social circle. And she wouldn't mind getting to know Blake better.

"I'd love to," Hannah said. "Where are we meeting? What time?"

"We're leaving from the parking lot right after work," Blake said. "Sarah's the D.D. if you want to carpool."

Designated driver? She hoped nobody was planning to drink too much. No, that wouldn't be it. It made sense to carpool, that was all.

"Sure, I'll ride with you," Hannah said. "It sounds like fun."

Much more fun than driving to Manistee and back by herself. Hannah had done that enough times to be sick of it.

Blake finished his sandwich and got up, crushing the sandwich wrapper in his hand. "Gotta run. I'll catch you later." He disappeared.

Jack had just returned to his own desk, working on his computer. It would be fun if he came, and Hannah wouldn't have to worry about people behaving badly.

She went over to his desk. "Hey, Jack."

He looked up. "What's up?"

"I'm going with Blake and Sarah and a couple of the operators to get burgers and drinks in Manistee after work. You should come."

Jack shook his head. "Thanks, Hannah. I'm helping Serena build a fence, and then I was planning on finishing my book and getting enough sleep for once."

Sometimes she forgot what a goody two-shoes Jack could be. "Building fences? Reading? Getting enough sleep? Jack, you should come with us. It'll be fun, and you ought to get to know your coworkers better."

He shook his head. "Have a good time."

"Thanks. I intend to." Hannah turned away.

"Hey," Jack called after her.

She stopped. "What?"

"Who's driving to this thing?"

She could see the deputy-sheriff cogs turning in his brain. He was probably worried people would be drinking and driving. "Sarah's the designated driver. And nobody's going to drink too much."

"Sarah's a sensible woman. I'll tell her to keep an eye on you."

"Jack, you sound like I'm a twenty-one-year-old going out for drinks for the first time."

"I don't know that I trust all those guys, that's all."

"I can take care of myself."

"I know."

"Good."

The car ride that evening was noisy. Sarah insisted that Hannah ride shotgun while the men (including Sarah's husband) rode in the back. "I'm not gonna make you sit back there with the boys," she told Hannah. "I don't get a lot of female conversation these days. Before I took that job at the mill, I worked at a grocery store. It was a sociable job. Driving the forklift, it's just me and my thoughts. And in the break room the guys all talk about sports and food and hunting. Sure, I can talk to Tex when we get home, but it's not like having another woman to talk to."

Through Sarah's conversation Hannah gleaned that she and her husband were a new couple, having been married less than a year; that her husband, Tex, could fix any broken object known to man; and that Sarah was thirty-nine, and she hoped they'd be having kids soon.

"Any special guys in your life?" she asked Hannah.

"Uh, not exactly," Hannah said.

"What about you and Jack?"

Hopefully Blake hadn't heard that. "No, no," Hannah said, slightly louder than Sarah had asked. "Jack and I are just friends."

"Could have fooled me," Sarah said. "I never see one of you without the other. Jack isn't coming?"

"No. He can be a real stick-in-the-mud. He wanted to stay home and read a book."

Sarah laughed. "Might have been a good choice. He'll save money. Why it costs so much to get a burger and fries and one drink, I'll never understand."

She went on about food prices, but Hannah was only half listening. Why did people always assume Hannah and Jack were romantically involved? Hannah didn't want Blake to get that impression. She didn't need anything to spoil her chance with this guy who seemed to check quite a few of her boxes for Mr. Right. She and Jack were just friends, and Jack was probably interested in Serena now.

They were pulling up outside a small bar. It was probably crowded on the weekends, but it didn't seem too bad tonight. They had a party of five: Hannah, Sarah, Tex, Blake, and Luis, the other operator. Inside, the hostess led them to a round booth.

Blake motioned to Hannah to go ahead of him and slid into the booth next to her. His leg bumped hers, and she felt herself blushing. There was no way Blake would have asked her to come along tonight unless he was interested in her, was there?

The men were still in the middle of their conversation from the car, something about investments. Hannah didn't know what a reverse stock split was, and she wasn't filled in on the relationship between the stock market and the cryptocurrency market (if there even was a relationship there). All she gleaned from the conversation was that crypto was down, and it wasn't expected to come back up any time soon.

The waiter came to take everyone's orders. Hannah got a burger and a glass of wine. She wasn't much of a beer drinker. Everyone else ordered beer, except Sarah, who wanted lemonade. Not pink lemonade. Why people needed their drinks to be an unnatural color, Sarah would never understand.

"So, Hannah," Blake said, "I promise not to ask you too many questions, but I've gotta ask this one: what made you decide to come out to Fraser's Mill instead of staying in Chicago? Don't like the city?"

"I could ask you the same thing," Hannah said. "I came here for summer vacation. Then my parents decided to do a house swap with some people from Germany. I had been living with my parents in Chicago—don't laugh, you know how expensive rent is—so I was stuck here for six months."

"I'm not laughing," Blake said. "That sounds perfectly reasonable."

Good. Hannah didn't like being judged for still living with her parents.

"Anyway," she went on, "they needed somebody to take the office administrator job at the mill—so here I am."

"What are you going to do after the six months?" Blake's eyes made this question more momentous than the words did.

"I'm going back to Chicago."

He raised his eyebrows. "Really."

"Yes. Fraser's Mill is fine—I'm glad my grandpa founded the town back in 1950-whatever-it-was—but I wouldn't want to spend my life here. And there's nothing for my video channel. I did practically all the videos I would have wanted to do, right at the beginning of the summer. Back in Chicago, there are way more things to do, and I won't run out of content."

"You still won't tell me what your channel's called?"

Hannah shook her head, smiling. "Another time, maybe."

"Aha. So if I'm persistent, I might learn? I like that."

At that point Luis asked Blake a question, and he plunged

into a conversation about fantasy football. That was another thing Hannah didn't know about. She was beginning to know what Sarah meant about missing female conversation. Across the table, Sarah winked.

Blake seemed to know about many topics. His dating profile hadn't exaggerated much—he had been all over and worked jobs in many fields. That gave him the added appeal of the well-rounded traveling man. He was good looking, too. The unshaven look only helped.

Of course, Hannah was still getting to know Blake. But so far, he'd impressed her. The traveling, the financial know-how, his ability to converse intelligently on many topics, his suave attitude—when Hannah envisioned the qualities of the kind of guy she would like, they all matched up. And just sitting next to him gave her butterflies in her stomach. So clearly there was chemistry there.

The ride back to Fraser's Mill, in the dark, was louder than the ride out. It wasn't that the guys had drunk too much, but they were still talking about sports, and apparently they cheered for different teams.

They pulled into the mill parking lot, and Hannah tucked a five-dollar bill into Sarah's cupholder. "Gas money."

"You don't have to do that," Sarah said. "It was my pleasure. I enjoyed your company, especially with all the men arguing in the back seat."

Hannah laughed. "Likewise. Keep the money, really. I know how much gas is these days." She jumped down from the vehicle. "Thanks, Sarah," she called. "Bye, guys."

She was halfway to her car when someone called. "Hey, Hannah." It was Blake, strolling in her direction.

"What?" Hannah stopped.

"You look really good in that outfit." Blake's tone was cool, but his blue eyes were admiring.

Hannah tucked her hair behind her ear. "Oh. Thanks." Good thing she had worn a cute pink shirt today instead of the white button-down she had almost worn.

Had he come over just to compliment her outfit? If so, that was flattering.

"Walk you to your car?" Blake asked.

It was only about five steps, but Hannah giggled. "Sure."

She hit the auto unlock, and Blake got her door. "Goodnight, Hannah."

"See you tomorrow," Hannah said.

It wasn't too far-fetched to think Blake was interested in her, was it?

The Polar Zone

After a lifetime in the Windy City, Hannah was used to cold temperatures. But she wasn't used to cold temperatures indoors. At work on Friday, it was just as nippy inside as outside.

"What's going on in here?" Hannah asked Jack. "Why is it so freezing?"

"The temperature dropped, and the heat's not on. I don't know who's in charge of that."

"I'll ask Steve," Hannah said.

She put on a hard hat and went into the mill, so quickly that she nearly crashed into a passing forklift. The driver—not Blake—gave her a dirty look.

Steve was out in the lot, talking to a truck driver. He was wearing a T-shirt and didn't look cold in the least, even though the temperature was frigid. Why did guys never seem to feel the cold? Hannah was freezing in a woolly sweater.

"Steve," Hannah shouted.

Steve turned. "Just a minute," he called.

Hannah waited, arms wrapped around herself. She should have taken a coat when she left the house this morning.

Steve finished his conversation, and Hannah hurried over.

"Hey, do you think we could turn the heat on?" she asked. "It's freezing in the office."

Steve's brow furrowed. "It's not cold enough in the mill for the heat," he said. "Have you seen those poor guys working? It's an oven in the summer, and they're just beginning to not feel so miserable. And it's expensive as heck to run the furnace. I don't turn it on till Thanksgiving."

"Thanksgiving? Can't we heat the office and not the rest of the place?"

Steve shook his head. "Sorry. The boiler heats the whole building. It's an old system. Blame Grandpa, not me."

"What are we supposed to do in the office?" Hannah demanded.

"Wear a coat," Steve said. "Sorry, Han. It's the best I can do."

Grumbling, Hannah went back to the office. At least it wasn't quite as cold in there as it was in the lot.

Jack was on the phone when she came in, so she couldn't complain to him. She sat down at her desk and rubbed her cold arms. Maybe at lunchtime she'd dash home and get a coat. Nobody had warned her about this.

Her phone rang. It was a guy with a small but fiddly lumber order for a shed. He was hard of hearing, too, so Hannah had to repeat everything a couple times, loudly, to make sure she was on the same page.

While she was still on the phone, a steaming cup of coffee

appeared at her elbow.

"Thanks, Jack," Hannah mouthed at him, still listening to the guy with the lumber order.

Jack waited until she was off the phone. "How'd it go with Steve?"

Hannah grimaced. "He never turns the boiler on this early because the men in the mill get too hot and it's expensive as heck to run it."

"That's tough," Jack said. "I wish I'd brought my jacket. I'd lend it to you."

He was sweet. Hannah smiled. "That's all right. The coffee will help. Thank you."

"Anytime." Jack smiled.

He was the best. In a platonic way, of course.

It was almost lunchtime when he returned to her desk. "Here, maybe this will help with the cold. I forgot I had it."

"What's this?" Hannah looked dubiously at the folded silver-colored thing he handed her.

"Emergency blanket," Jack said. "I keep it in my desk."

Hannah shook her head, smiling at him. "Were you a Boy Scout? You're always prepared."

"Eagle Scout. Before the organization changed. My brother David does Trail Life USA now."

"Ah, that makes sense. Well, thank you."

She would look silly wearing a blanket around her shoulders in the office, but it was better than freezing.

At that moment, Blake sauntered in. It must be lunchtime.

"Hi, Hannah," he said. "How's it going?"

"Great!" His smile was infectious, and Hannah smiled back. "How are you?"

"Terrific," Blake said. "Mind if I join you for lunch?"

Since she usually ate lunch with Jack, she hesitated—but when she turned, Jack had disappeared. Maybe he'd had to rush off suddenly. Maybe he didn't fancy Blake's company.

"Not at all," Hannah said. "I was just about to have mine."

Blake took Jack's chair. He started right into his lunch without praying—maybe he'd said grace in the break room. He kept looking at Hannah strangely.

Hannah made a face at him. "What are you doing?"

"I'm still trying to figure out where I've seen you before," Blake said. "It's driving me crazy. Maybe we saw each other in Chicago. Do you know the Bonners? Or the Van Camps?"

Hannah shook her head.

"Maybe I just don't recognize the name Fraser. What's your mom's maiden name?"

Hannah laughed. "She doesn't go by it, but it's Warner."

He shook his head. "Not familiar either."

Hannah bit her lip. There ought to be some way to put him at ease without mentioning the dating site. "My parents know your parents. Maybe we've seen each other when we were younger."

It could be true, after all. It seemed to be a good enough theory for now, anyway, and Blake stopped pressing the topic.

Halfway through his sandwich, Blake asked, "So what are you planning to do when you get back to Chicago?"

"Oh, lots of things," Hannah said. "Grow my video channel. And do all the activities that they don't have out here. There's nothing to do in Fraser's Mill."

"No concerts, no theatre, no restaurants, no sights to see—have I covered most of it?" Blake smiled knowingly.

Hannah laughed. "Pretty much. The only things here are town social events."

"No wonder you can't wait to get back to Chicago." Blake leaned back in his chair. "You seem like the kind of girl who likes to keep busy."

"Always," Hannah said.

"I like that," Blake said. "You're not the type to stagnate in a little do-nothing town."

If he also thought of Fraser's Mill as a little do-nothing town, what was he doing here? "That reminds me, I've been wondering what made you decide to come here. I mean, I know we needed a forklift driver and you wanted some variety in your work, but why here? Why Fraser's Mill? You could have gone anywhere with your experience—maybe even Europe."

"I was tired of my current business ventures," Blake said. "You get sick of working from home. So I thought I'd go out of state and do something completely new. A little adventure. And this place pays all right."

Hannah liked an adventurous man. "So are you planning to stay here a while, then?"

Blake crumpled his sandwich wrapper and attempted to throw it into Hannah's trash can. He missed. "My bad." Blake got to his feet to retrieve it. "I figure I'll stay here as long as it's still interesting. Then I'll go back to Chicago. I told Steve I'm only temporary here."

"How temporary?" Hannah asked.

"That depends on how long it stays interesting."

"I thought you said it wasn't interesting here at all."

"The town? No. But the work is a change from what I was doing before. And the company isn't too bad." Blake winked. "I figure I'll last maybe three months, maybe six."

So Hannah and Blake would be back in Chicago at the same time. This opened up all kinds of possibilities. Hannah wouldn't have to worry about getting to know Blake long-distance. And if she was reading Blake right, he was interested in her.

"Will you ever show me your videos?" Blake said. "I'm beginning to think you made the whole thing up."

Hannah laughed. "Fine, all right. I'll show you."

She pulled up her Fourth of July video from earlier in the summer. Fraser's Mill had had a big Independence Day celebration, with a speech from the mayor, a parade, booths with things for sale, lunch at the fire hall, and fireworks in the evening. Doc had helped Hannah get footage for it. For a while she hadn't been able to stand watching the videos Doc had helped with, but she didn't mind so much anymore.

"I have to warn you, I'm still learning videography," Hannah told Blake, as she started the video. "This won't be the best thing you ever saw."

"Who cares?" Blake asked. "The most successful people have to start somewhere. And this looks good."

He probably didn't know anything about videography, but Hannah appreciated the compliment.

"Well," she said at the end of the video, "that's it—a pretty good representation of the sort of content I've been videoing this summer. But I do a variety of things." She was on her channel's landing page now, with thumbnails and titles for her videos.

"So I see," Blake said. "It looks like you've been busy."

Hannah nodded. "It does take a while to edit everything. But I haven't had time to do anything fancy lately. I've mostly been making quick videos and throwing them together last-minute."

"This job takes all your time." Blake got up and stretched. "And I've gotta get back to the grind. See you later, Hannah."

Where was Jack? He'd left without a word at the beginning of the lunch hour, and at one PM, he still wasn't back. Maybe he'd had a family emergency. Should Hannah call him? No, that was silly. He was probably just late. But he didn't usually leave the mill during lunchtime.

"Hey, Jack," Steve's voice said, and Hannah turned to see him, hard hat on, frowning at Jack's empty chair. "Hannah, have you seen Jack?"

"No, I haven't seen him." Hannah didn't elaborate — if Steve wanted to investigate Jack's disappearance, he could, but she wouldn't rat on a coworker.

"What the heck?" Steve asked. "I'll look in the lot."

Should she save Steve the trouble of looking by telling him Jack wasn't here? Was it wrong to let him go on a wild goose chase? Maybe Jack was out there in the lot after all, though.

It was five after one when Jack came in, holding a large cardboard box.

"Jack!" Hannah exclaimed. "Where have you been? Steve's looking for you."

"I ran into him in the lot," Jack said. "Some guy called wanting to know why his lumber hadn't arrived yet, and he was looking for me so I could track the truck." He plunked the box on the counter in front of Hannah. "This is for you."

"What is it?"

Jack grinned. "Open it."

Inside the cardboard box was a small appliance that looked a little like the window fans at the log cabin. "What is it?" Hannah repeated.

"Space heater. I thought you could use it until Steve turns on the boiler."

"Wow. Jack, you spent your whole lunch getting this for me? You must be starving."

"I had lunch at my parents'," Jack said. "This is theirs. You can borrow it—they don't use it much since my dad put in a wood-burning stove last year."

"Wow," Hannah said again. "Thank you, Jack. This is great."

"I didn't want you to have to go around wearing a blanket," Jack said. "Besides, this will be good for customers too. Nobody likes to come into a freezing office. We can tell Steve that if he complains about the electricity bill."

"Jack, you're the best." Hannah found a wall outlet and plugged in the space heater, turning the switch to high. Might as well heat up the room as quickly as possible. "Please tell your parents thank you for me."

"I will." Jack smiled. "Feeling any warmer?"

"Yes, it's already starting to work," Hannah said. "I can give you that blanket back."

"Keep it as long as you need it," Jack said. "Did you eat lunch? And I mean lunch. I don't mean vending machine cookies."

She laughed. "I had a real lunch, thank you very much, and Blake kept me company."

"Uh-huh." Jack's brow furrowed. For some reason, he seemed allergic to the mention of Blake. "If you're still hungry, I brought a couple of my mom's donuts."

Hannah shook her head. "Thanks anyway, but I couldn't eat anything else," she said. "But your mom's donuts are delicious. I had them at the fall festival."

Jack looked like he was about to say something else, but his phone rang and he had to dash to answer it.

"Oh, hi, Serena," he said. "What's up?"

So Serena was calling him! Well, that was fine. Jack could talk to Serena. If he liked her, well and good. It wasn't Hannah's business, and she had her own romantic interest.

Like clockwork, whenever Hannah saw Blake, she got butterflies. Hopefully it didn't show on the outside. She wasn't about to chase Blake. If he wanted to chase her, though, she wouldn't say no.

There ought to be some other opportunities to hang out with Blake soon. Maybe Sarah and her husband would organize another group hang out. Also, Alex's Halloween dance was coming up. She'd said she was inviting the whole town. Although Blake was still a newcomer to town, so maybe he hadn't been invited. But it would be exciting if he came.

Halloween

October 31st was a Monday, and not too cold, which Hannah appreciated. She didn't want to wear a coat over her costume at Alex's barn party.

Although it was early in the day, Hannah felt more awake than usual. She was alone in the office — Jack had gone outside — and the phone wasn't ringing, which gave Hannah a chance to daydream. Half the fun of a party was planning it out in your head beforehand. What you would wear, who you would talk to and dance with —

"Are you going to the party tonight, Hannah?" It was Blake, appearing at Hannah's desk with his hard hat on.

"I am," Hannah said. "Wait, which party do you mean?" She hadn't mentioned the party to Blake, in case he wasn't invited. Hannah's parents had told their children it wasn't polite to talk about parties in front of people who might not be invited.

"The Martins'," Blake said. "They've invited the whole town.

I heard about it at the tavern on Saturday."

"Oh!" Hannah tried not to look too excited. She was finding it harder to control her expressions around Blake the more time they spent together. Hannah mustn't look too interested, in case he wasn't actually interested. She refused to repeat her experience with Doc earlier this summer.

"So are you going?" Blake asked.

"Yes, actually, I am," Hannah said. "I don't know what I'm wearing, though. Do you?"

Blake shook his head. "I'll probably grab something from Walmart."

Hannah laughed. "Then you'll be a slice of pizza or a dinosaur. Those are the kinds of costumes they always have at places like that."

Blake chuckled. "Maybe they'll have a Batman costume on sale."

He disappeared, and Hannah's phone rang. She picked up. "Hello?"

"Hi, this is Serena Sanders," a voice said. "I bought some lumber from you a while ago."

How could Hannah forget? But what was Serena calling about?

"I remember," Hannah said. "How can I help you?"

"Actually," Serena said, "I was trying to get hold of Jack, but he's not answering."

Hannah looked at Jack's empty desk. "He's out. I'll have him call you back. What's your number?"

"He's got my number. Just tell him to call me."

Hannah was dying to ask Jack what was going on with him and Serena, but if she asked, he would probably tease her.

Besides, what did she care about Jack's love life?

When Jack finally came in from the yard, Hannah called to him. "Serena Sanders wants you to call her."

"Oh, okay." He didn't look surprised. "Thanks." He pulled out his personal phone and dialed a number.

"Hey, Serena!" he said into the phone. "Sorry I missed your call. Were you calling about tonight? I get out of work at five."

Probably Jack was taking Serena to the dance tonight. Hannah made herself busy doing office supply inventory.

She couldn't help sneaking a glance at Jack on the phone. He looked cheerful and animated. She shouldn't eavesdrop. It was ridiculous to feel curious about Jack's personal business. She and Jack had a good solid friendship. Sure, she'd had some confusing feelings about him a while ago—in the treehouse, and the time they brought in the dock, and when Serena had first showed up—but that was a while ago. It was before meeting Blake. And the confusion she'd felt about Jack was nothing compared to the butterflies and excitement she felt around Blake.

She couldn't wait to see Blake at the dance.

❧❧❧❧❧

In her room, after work, Hannah still didn't know what to wear. It was too late to borrow a costume from Christine. The party was at eight. Hannah hadn't brought any costumes to Fraser's Mill. Why hadn't she planned for this? She'd been too busy planning this week's video, singing in the choir without any practice (she had forgotten choir practice again last Wednesday), and daydreaming about Blake to think of a costume.

Maybe Grace had something Hannah could borrow. She lived close, she was going to the party too, and she and Hannah were around the same size. Hannah texted her.

"Sure, come right over!" Grace replied. "I'm getting ready myself. I don't have a lot of things, but I'm sure we can come up with something."

Hannah put on her coat, threw her makeup bag and her purse into her backpack, and went over to Grace's.

The front porch light seemed to invite visitors into the cheery two-story house. Hannah knocked at the door and was answered by Grace's mom, a short blonde woman with a ponytail.

"I thought you were a tall trick-or-treater," Grace's mom said. "Come on in, Hannah. Grace is upstairs."

Grace was in front of the mirror in her room, doing something to her hair with a bristle brush. Right now her curly hair stood almost straight up in a look that couldn't possibly be a hairstyle—could it?

Hannah had never been in Grace's room. Clearly, this had been her room as a kid. A bunk bed stood in one corner. Grace must have shared with a sister. The white-painted dressers were covered with old-fashioned knickknacks. One dresser was a small shrine. Assorted posters papered the walls.

"Oh, hey, Hannah," Grace said, seeing Hannah behind her in the mirror. "Come in. Sorry I look scary. I'm trying to do 1910s hair."

She must be ratting her hair for a Gibson Girl hairstyle. Hannah wouldn't have the first idea how to do that. She had the idea it worked better with long hair, but Grace's hair wasn't much longer than Hannah's. Well, if Grace straightened her hair, it would probably be pretty long. Those curls must cause the hair to shrink.

"I don't have a lot of actual costumes, per se," Grace said, "but you can look in my closet. I have a medieval dress, and I have a lot of random pieces of fabric. And a few hats."

The medieval dress sounded the most promising. Hannah looked through Grace's closet with interest. It wasn't often she got to snoop through somebody's clothes. Grace wore a lot of bright colors, particularly yellow and red. Hannah tended toward neutrals and pastels. But bright colors worked well for costumes.

The medieval dress was at the back of the closet. It was blue, with bell sleeves and a laced bodice. Hannah pulled it out. "I think I'll try this."

There was one section of zipper Hannah couldn't reach, no matter how she twisted her arms around. Grace had to help zip it.

Hannah inspected herself in the mirror. The dress fit all right. That was the good thing about lacing — it was a quick and easy way to make a dress one size fits all. But something was off. She couldn't place it. Maybe it was her hair — just-past-shoulder-length straight hair didn't look medieval. Or maybe medieval costumes just weren't her style in general.

"I don't know." Hannah turned back and forth to see the outfit from different angles. "It's a great dress, but it doesn't feel quite like me. What do you think?"

Grace stopped fastening hairpins and surveyed Hannah, her head on one side. "Are you asking me about clothes? Aren't you the one who makes fashion videos?"

"Costumes aren't exactly fashion," Hannah said. "I'm not

sure about this."

"Then let's try something else." Grace tapped her chin. "Pirate? I've got a brown vest and a pair of striped socks."

Hannah shook her head. Maybe she was being silly. She should just wear the medieval dress. It was a costume, after all, and it was just for one night. But she didn't see herself talking to Blake in a trailing medieval costume.

"I've got an idea." Grace dived into the back of her closet and pulled out a bright red dress, knee length. "You could go as a cowgirl."

Hannah laughed. "Flouncy dress and cowboy boots?"

"Absolutely. Here. Hold this." Grace disappeared into the closet again and pulled out a denim vest with embroidered flowers on the back. "What size shoes are you?"

"Eight."

"So am I. You can wear my boots." Grace pulled out a pair of brown boots—not the cheap flimsy kind, but real leather. "My dad gave them to me a few years ago. He said they'd last half a lifetime."

"You're sure you want to lend your special boots?"

"Absolutely, you can't hurt them."

Hannah took one last look at herself in the medieval dress and shook her head at her reflection. "If you'll help me with this zipper," she said, "I'll try the red one."

Grace's red dress fit Hannah perfectly with a belt around the waist. She put on the embroidered vest, slipped on the boots, and looked at herself in the mirror. "Wow," she said. "I feel like I'm in *Annie Get Your Gun*."

Grace laughed. "You just need French braids and a cowboy hat."

"I don't know how to French braid."

"I do."

"Won't we be late?"

"We've still got time. I can braid quickly."

It was a new Hannah, a Wild West Hannah, that looked into the mirror a few minutes later. This girl looked like she'd never been to Chicago. She looked like the kind of girl who would dance all night at a barn dance and get up early the next morning to break wild horses.

"You look fabulous," Grace said, using far more hairpins than necessary in her own hair. "I'll just be a couple more minutes."

Grace had a light pink Edwardian-era skirt suit with a high neckline, puffed sleeves, and a slim-waisted skirt. She had found it at a vintage shop in California. She and Doc were going as a couple from the 1910s. "Jim didn't have much that looked like the 1910s," she said, "but we found a bowler hat, and he's wearing a fake mustache, so it ought to be good enough."

Ready at last, the girls sallied forth. It had grown dark, and Doc Johnson was waiting for Grace on the porch. He raised his eyebrows when he saw her, and his face crinkled in a smile that threatened to unseat the false mustache on his upper lip.

"Miss Murray," he said, like somebody in a stage production, "may I have the honor of escorting you?"

Grace laughed. "Thank you, sir," she said. "Would you mind if my friend Miss Fraser came with us?"

"Of course not." Doc grinned at Hannah. "I didn't think you were the cowgirl type."

"Tonight I am."

Doc gave one arm to Grace and extended the other to Hannah. "Come on, ladies," he said. "Let's go."

◦◦◦◦◦◦◦

They went to the party in Doc's classic Chevy Chevelle, a car on which he obviously spent a lot of time and care. Hannah sat in the back and listened to Doc and Grace banter.

They were almost there when Doc looked over his shoulder. "I don't think I've ever known you this quiet, Hannah. You okay?"

"Thanks. Yeah, I'm great."

Truth be told, Hannah was too excited about the evening to talk much. It was ridiculous. She had been to all kinds of dances and parties in high school and college. There was no reason to be so worked up about this one. But Blake was going to be there, and he had asked if she was going.

The field in front of the Martins' barn was filled with cars. Doc parked carefully in an empty spot and led the way by flashlight toward the big barn. Light streamed from the open barn doors, and even at this distance, music floated out.

Hannah stopped in the barn doorway as Grace and Doc went in. The barn was decorated for the dance—Christmas lights overhead, bales of straw to sit on, tables groaning with food, and a trailer at one end that served as a stage. People in costume milled around. The dancing hadn't started, but a speaker somewhere played bluegrass.

Where was everyone Hannah knew? It was hard to pick out faces in a costumed crowd.

"Hannah." It was Alex, wearing a trailing navy dress with

bell sleeves. Her dark hair was down, falling past her waist.

"I almost didn't recognize you," Alex said. "Grace said you were coming as a cowgirl."

Hannah laughed. "I'm not sure I recognize myself either."

"You should get some food," Alex said. "There's lots. Charlie's in charge of it." She motioned toward the tables, at which stood a tall guy in a hooded cloak. "He agreed to be Aragorn after all."

Alex disappeared, and Hannah made her way slowly toward the table. She wasn't hungry. She'd skipped dinner in all the fuss of getting ready for the dance, but her stomach was all butterflies and she didn't care if she ate anything.

Where was Blake? He had said he'd be here, and it wasn't early. Hannah scanned the crowd.

Maybe he'd gotten held up picking out that Walmart costume. He'd probably be here any minute.

"Hannah?" A familiar voice behind her made her turn. It was Jack, but Hannah almost didn't recognize him. He didn't have his glasses, and he was wearing—of all things—a tuxedo.

Jack surveyed Hannah, his eyebrows raised. "You look like the spirit of Fraser's Mill."

Hannah laughed. "I love how these rural areas in Michigan seem to think they're the Wild West. I totally feel like Annie Oakley."

He smiled. "I knew you had it in you."

"And look at you in a tuxedo!"

Jack laughed. "I told you I'd wear a tuxedo to the next barn dance."

It had been that afternoon up in Jack's treehouse. "I

remember," Hannah said. "And I said you'd have to warn your date, or she'd come in a flowered dress and cowboy boots."

She looked around the room. "Did you bring Serena?"

"Serena?" Jack looked confused.

"I thought—I overheard you saying something to her on the phone about tonight." It was embarrassing, admitting she'd heard his phone call. Hopefully he didn't think she was eavesdropping.

"That wasn't about the dance." Jack suddenly looked amused. "I was going to help her build a shed after work, before coming here. But she had to move it to next Thursday."

"That's it?" Hannah asked. "She wanted help building a shed?"

Jack looked surprised. "Sure. What did you think?"

So it was just business, after all. Nothing romantic. How silly could Hannah get? She'd thought there was something going on between those two for weeks. Well, it didn't make a difference now. "Never mind." Hannah shook her head.

"Aha." Jack grinned. "You thought she and I were going out, didn't you?"

"I just made a perfectly logical assumption." Hannah held her chin high.

"Still jealous, Hannah." His grin was bigger. "No, I didn't bring anybody to the dance. Did you?"

"Not exactly." Blake asking if Hannah were coming to the dance wasn't the same thing as asking her to go with him.

"Not exactly?" Jack raised an eyebrow.

"Have you seen Blake anywhere?" Hannah asked. Jack had probably been here longer than she had. He would know better who was at the party at this point. "He's supposed to be here," she said, "but I haven't bumped into him yet."

Jack shook his head, his mouth compressed. "I haven't seen him."

It was useless. Jack didn't like Blake, and that was that. Hannah could find him herself.

"I've got to say hi to some people," she said. "See you around, Jack."

He nodded, his face serious. "See you around."

Jack moved away. The dancing had started with cheery music and a caller announcing the moves. Hannah didn't know how to square dance, but it didn't look too hard. If she had a partner. But for some inexplicable reason, Blake still wasn't there. She'd been around the barn multiple times.

Hannah sat on a straw bale with a sigh. Maybe she'd send Blake a text. Then again, that might make her seem desperate. Might as well wait. Maybe he'd get there eventually.

Cards on the Table

The Christmas lights strung in the Martins' barn were cheery — a good aesthetic — and square dancers wove in and out in what was probably a fun dance, but Hannah was still sitting on a straw bale, not taking part in anything. What an evening. Hannah had gone to a lot of trouble, dressed up, rode all the way to Alex's farm — with Grace and Doc, too — just for Blake to never show up. Maybe something had come up. Maybe he'd had an important conflict.

This morning, she had been excited about the party even before she'd heard Blake was planning to go. It was ridiculous to waste the evening moping. She had come for a good time, and she was going to have a good time. Forget about Blake.

Hannah got up from the straw bale and headed toward the food table. Appetizing smells had been wafting in her direction, and if the food was sponsored by Charlie and the diner, there had to be something good.

They had homemade apple pie, almost too hot to eat. Hannah cut herself a slice of pie and ladled some Swedish meatballs from a Crock-Pot. The butterflies in her stomach had subsided with Blake's absence, and she was hungry.

She was sitting on another straw bale, finishing the pie and the meatballs, when someone tall stopped in front of her. Hannah looked up.

"Blake never showed, huh?" Jack surveyed her, head on one side.

What business was it of Jack's? "I guess something must have come up," Hannah said.

"Uh-huh." Jack sounded unconvinced. "May I?"

Hannah made room for him on the straw bale. "Sure, fine."

Jack sat down. In his tuxedo, his shoulders looked even broader than usual. "How's the food?" he asked.

"Mmm." Hannah's mouth was full. She swallowed. "Good."

"My sister Felicity made the pie." Jack motioned across the room, where a tall dark-haired girl wearing some kind of Greek or Roman costume was dancing with a guy in a dinosaur costume. He'd probably gotten it from Walmart.

"Your sister made this? Wow. It's really good." She should have expected as much, having tried Jack's food. Julia really taught her kids to cook.

As Hannah finished her last bite, the song ended. The caller prepared to announce the next one.

"Would you like to dance?" Jack stood and turned toward Hannah, holding out his hand.

"I don't know how to square dance. I can do partner dancing

or the Virginia Reel."

"I'll show you," Jack said.

It was just a casual Halloween party in somebody's barn. It didn't matter if Hannah made a fool of herself. "Sure." She took Jack's hand.

They went out onto the dance floor, where people were arranging themselves in squares of four couples. Hannah came face to face with Grace and Doc.

"Do you know how to do this?" Grace asked Hannah, over the noise.

"No," Hannah said.

"Me neither," Grace said. "We can get lost together."

Alex bustled up, dragging Charlie behind her. "We know this one," she announced.

How did they know which song it would be? Alex must be filled in on the playlist. Another couple joined the square, and the music started. Everyone began clapping to the beat, and Hannah joined in. If this was going to be utter chaos, hopefully it would still be fun. She looked up and caught Jack's eye. He smiled.

"Bow to your partner," the caller instructed.

Hannah curtsied, holding out the skirt of her dress, and Jack bowed.

"Say hi to the corner," the caller said. "Take hands, circle to the left."

Maybe this wouldn't be too bad.

They circled to the right and the left. They split into groups of "head couples" and "side couples" and took turns going to the center and circling in the middle. They went one way, then the other way, and Hannah got lost. She crashed into Jack coming the other direction.

"You okay?" Jack steadied her, hands firm on her elbows.

"Yeah," Hannah said breathlessly, turning around the way she was supposed to go. "I'm fine."

"Partners, face each other," the caller shouted. "Do-si-do."

Hannah remembered that from the Virginia Reel, and she managed to go backwards around Jack without crashing into him or anybody else.

Jack smiled at her. "Nice."

Circle around. Swing your partner. Do-si-do. This was kind of fun. Jack danced like he'd done this his entire life. For a farm boy, he was surprisingly graceful. And his confident smile, as he led Hannah through the steps, made her warm.

Why was her pulse so fast? Maybe it was the exercise. She was remembering that time in the treehouse and the strange closeness she'd felt to Jack then.

The dance ended, and everybody clapped. Doc's fake mustache was coming off, and Grace laughed at him.

"Want some punch?" Jack asked Hannah. "It's non-alcoholic."

She was thirsty now. "Sure."

They went to the corner with the punch bowl, a busy place. Jack made his way through the crush of people and came back with two cups of punch, sherbet floating on top.

The drink was fizzy and cold and refreshing. "Thanks, Jack," Hannah said. "You're the best."

"You're welcome." For some reason he looked serious. "Hannah, can I ask you something?"

"What?" It was hard to hear over the noise.

Jack looked around. "Come with me."

They went outside. The night air was cool, but not as freezing as it had been, and it felt good after the exertion of the dance.

"What is it, Jack?" Hannah asked. The intensity and warmth in his brown eyes made her apprehensive.

"Hannah," he said, "will you go out with me?"

Hannah's heart did a flip. Oh, no, she should have known this was coming when she saw him wearing the tuxedo.

"Oh, Jack."

This was exactly what she was trying to ward off when she told Jack she didn't go out with coworkers, more than a month ago. Although she couldn't say that again, because she was hoping to go out with Blake.

"Hannah." Jack took a deep breath. "I fell for you the first day you came into the office."

He still hadn't gotten over her. Maybe she should have realized that. He'd hung out with her so much—maybe it should have been obvious he was hoping for more than friendship.

"Jack, I don't know what to say," Hannah said. "I don't—Jack, you've been a friend to me. A real friend. You make working at the sawmill bearable. You're probably the person that I spend the most time with in Fraser's Mill. And I've really enjoyed all the time we've spent together."

The warm light had gone out of his eyes, and his lips were compressed. "You don't think of us as anything more than friends."

Hannah shook her head. "No. I'm sorry, Jack."

"I know you said you didn't date coworkers. But I thought—I

hoped — you might change your mind."

Hannah looked down at her feet, unfamiliar in Grace's cowboy boots. Why had she used that stupid line when Jack asked her out? It had been the first excuse that came into her head, trying to let Jack down nicely. And now, if she ever went out with Blake, she'd look like a hypocrite.

"It's not that," she said.

His broad shoulders were slumped. "I know I'm just a small-town guy. I'm not a rich Chicago professional. But I hoped that maybe you — cared."

She couldn't leave it like this. She had to explain. "I do care a lot about you, Jack. You know I do. But I have feelings for somebody else."

"I see." A muscle worked in his jaw, and he looked down. He didn't ask who it was. He probably knew, anyway. She'd been trying not to seem too interested in Blake, but she had been hanging out with him enough for Jack to guess.

"I don't want to hurt you, Jack. Please understand."

Jack swallowed. "I understand. It's all right." But the hurt in his brown eyes spoke differently. He turned away, going back into the barn.

"Jack —" Hannah started after him, then stopped. Oh, what was the use? What more was there to say?

The party carried on inside, people laughing and dancing. It was cold outside. Hannah wrapped her arms around herself and shivered.

Why had she carpooled to the party with Grace and Doc? Her car was at Grace's house, and she had no way to get home by herself. Grace and Doc were probably having a great time. She didn't want to ask them.

Well, she wasn't going to freeze out here. She went inside the barn, where another dance had started. She didn't see Jack. She didn't want to run into him again, anyway.

Hannah found a corner and sat down on a straw bale. The music and the people were a blur.

She should have known, when she refused Jack that first time, that he wouldn't be happy being just friends. He must have thought, after all the fun times they had spent together, that she had changed her mind. She could see how he'd been confused—after all, she'd had some confusing feelings about him too until Blake showed up.

"Hannah?" Someone was saying her name, as though from a long way away. A hand touched her shoulder. It was Grace.

"Are you okay?" Grace asked. "Jim said you didn't look so good."

Hannah shook her head. "I'm okay. I just—had a conversation that didn't go the way I expected it would."

"I'm sorry." Grace sat on the straw bale next to Hannah. "Do you want to talk about it?"

She didn't know Grace enough to want to talk about it. "Not right now. Thanks though."

"All right, that's fine," Grace said. "Do you want to stay longer? Or would you rather go home? Jim can run you down to my house. He won't mind."

She hated being beholden to people, but she didn't want to stay here.

"Thanks, Grace. I'd like that."

Back home at last, after a quiet ride in Doc's car — he had asked if she wanted to talk about whatever was wrong, but she politely declined — Hannah sank onto her couch, hugging a pillow.

She could still see Jack's hurt face. How would she face him at work? What would happen to their friendship? He probably wouldn't want to talk to her anymore, and she didn't know that she blamed him. It must hurt him, too, when she hung out with Blake.

But she couldn't help it. Just because you were friends with somebody, that didn't mean that you would be right for each other. Jack was good and kind and friendly, but he was part of the Fraser's Mill world. He wasn't the right man for her. He couldn't be the other half of her "power couple" — an impressive guy who would fit with Hannah's life in Chicago. He wasn't exciting and suave and all the things Hannah was looking for.

Jack was honest and wholesome and dependable. He would be a fantastic match for some nice girl. But he needed to find a girl here in Fraser's Mill, and Hannah needed to find her own Mr. Right from the city.

Blake — well, Hannah still didn't know what was happening with Blake, but her feelings about him were completely different than her feelings for Jack. There was an impressiveness and an excitement about Blake. There was a spark, an electricity, that Hannah felt when they were around each other. There was none of that between Hannah and Jack.

Around Jack, Hannah usually felt calm — no butterflies, no sparks. His friendship had been welcome at a time when Hannah needed it, but that was all it was—friendship. The couple times when Hannah imagined something more between them were probably just because he was friendly and she saw him all the time. She wasn't actually attracted to Jack.

She wanted to talk to somebody about everything. Christine would be a good person to call. Except it was late now. Christine and Steve had probably taken Evelyn trick-or-treating and would be having a quiet evening with the kids in bed. She shouldn't bother them.

Hannah hugged the couch cushion closer, and a tear slipped down her cheek.

Thief On the Loose

Hannah woke the next morning with a raging headache, not wanting to get out of bed. Good thing it was All Saints' Day and the mill workers had the day off. Steve always closed the mill on the Church's holy days of obligation. Hannah could go to Mass and come straight home.

She made herself roll out of bed. There was still time to get to the eight AM at St. Anthony's. Since the church was only two houses down from Hannah's, getting there was quick. Hannah hastily washed and brushed, put on a cream-colored sweater and skirt with tights and boots, and got herself to church.

There was no choir for this Mass. Hannah's usual choir was scheduled to sing at a seven PM High Mass, but she had missed practice. It surprised Hannah how many people attended the early Mass. There were a lot of elderly people—they must like to get up early—and a few large families with small children. Hannah could imagine how challenging it would be to wrestle all those small children into their clothes and into the car.

The kids in the pews ahead were so cute, wiggling around and waving Mass books and holy cards. It was a distraction, but probably not the worst kind to have.

Hannah settled herself at the end of a pew halfway up the church, adjusted her chapel veil, which always slipped down, and got out her missal.

Then she saw Jack.

He was a few pews ahead and to the left, wearing a suit at eight in the morning, kneeling with his head bent. As Hannah put down the kneeler in her pew, Jack's head turned. He'd seen her. But he didn't make any sign of recognition, just turning away.

Poor Jack. She hadn't wanted to hurt him. She could only imagine how he was feeling this morning—she wasn't feeling great, and she had been the one who rejected him.

The bell rang, and the priest and two altar boys began to process into the church. Hannah dragged her thoughts away from Jack and last night's party. It was time to pray, not think about one's problems. But at least one could pray about the problems.

"Lord, please don't let Jack feel too bad about yesterday," she prayed. "And please show me what to do about Blake."

oᕉᑎᕉᑎᕉ

Hannah was back home after Mass, eating an extra jar of overnight oats she had made a couple days ago and forgotten about.

Her phone rang. It was Christine.

"Hannah," Christine said. "Did you hear the grocery store in Fraser's Mill got robbed last night?"

"What?" Hannah exclaimed. "How? And how do you know?"

"I saw it on the Fraser's Mill page," Christine said. "The sheriff posted about it. The whole cash register was wiped out. Nothing else—the burglar only took cash. Whoever it was got in by cutting a hole through the glass in the front door and unlocking it from the inside. The cash register was pried open."

"Wow," Hannah said. "That's terrible."

Grace and her family worked so hard to make that grocery store a success. It had been extra difficult since a dollar store opened in Fraser's Mill this summer and took some of the store's business. Losing the contents of the cash register—probably all of Monday's take—would be a blow.

"I'm getting worried, Hannah," Christine said. "That's the second robbery in Fraser's Mill in the last couple weeks. There must be a criminal living in town somewhere."

"I guess so," Hannah said. "Unless these were totally unconnected incidents. I don't know much about robbers and their patterns."

"Be careful," Christine said. "Don't walk around at night, and make sure you have enough gas in your car."

"You sound like Mom," Hannah said. "I'll be careful."

"Good. Well, I'd better get off. I've gotta get the kids fed before noon Mass."

Hannah ate her overnight oats absently. What would the Murrays do about the theft? Wasn't there any way to trace the burglar?

It was creepy to think of a guy cutting holes in the glass and opening the door from the inside. Hannah looked at the back sliding door in her kitchen, entirely glass. Somebody with that skill could get inside, no problem. But if she wedged something in the door track at the bottom, she'd feel better. She'd better get a dowel or something and cut it to size. Or a short piece of scrap lumber. They had all kinds of things lying around at the mill.

In the meantime, Hannah took a towel and rolled it up as tightly as she could. She stuffed it into the track of the door. That should at least delay a burglar.

෧෯෧෯෧

Hannah didn't have much to do on All Saints' Day, so she went to bed early and was up in plenty of time for work on Wednesday. She came in early and found Steve in the office, staring at a piece of paper.

"What's wrong, Steve?" Hannah asked.

"What?" Steve looked up. "Hi, Hannah. Guess who turned in his two weeks? Jack, that's who."

"Jack?" Hannah's gut plummeted. Oh no, no, no. He didn't want to work with her anymore. He must be feeling a lot worse than Hannah thought.

"Oh, Steve, it's all my fault," Hannah burst out. "Jack asked me out, and I told him I didn't feel that way about him. I didn't know he'd go and turn in his two weeks so he didn't have to work with me."

Steve was staring like she was insane. "Huh? He didn't say anything about you. He's leaving to become a full-time deputy sheriff."

"Oh." Hannah's face reddened. Why had she blurted that to Steve without waiting to learn what was going on?

250

Hannah took the paper Steve held out to her. It explained Jack's reason for leaving: with the recent armed robbery and burglary in town, it had become clear that Fraser's Mill and the surrounding county needed a greater police presence. Sheriff Hank Liddell had offered Jack a full-time job as a deputy, and he was going to take it. He offered to help train someone else for the dispatching job in the two weeks he had left.

It was just like Jack to help where he was most needed. Hannah couldn't say she was too surprised about that. But it was still a shock to think about losing him as a coworker.

"I don't know where I'm supposed to find another dispatcher," Steve said. "Does he think they grow on trees? I'll have to ask Dad if he knows anybody." He shoved the letter into a drawer and went out to the mill.

A brief investigation showed Hannah that Jack was out in the lot, supervising thc loading of a truck. Well, he was still around for two weeks at least. It would give Hannah a chance to somehow restore her friendship with Jack. Even if they couldn't get back what they'd had before Jack's confession, maybe they could get along again. It still hurt Hannah to think of him being unhappy with her.

Blake had apparently shown up to work just fine, driving a forklift in the lot. He had some explaining to do, if he ever came by. He didn't seem to have gotten into an accident. Maybe he had forgotten about the party, or remembered a previous engagement. Maybe he didn't exactly owe her an explanation for why he wasn't at the dance, but she sure wanted one.

Hannah was making sure she was caught up on her

paperwork — she had left in a hurry on Monday night to get ready for the party — when Jack came in.

"Good morning, Hannah." Jack nodded in her direction, going straight to his desk.

Not a word about his two weeks. Hannah didn't blame him. But she wasn't going to sit around, knowing that he knew that she knew, and not say anything.

Hannah approached his desk. "I heard about you turning in your two weeks."

Jack nodded, his face neutral. "I figured they need me more at the sheriff's office. It'll be tough on Steve, trying to find another dispatcher. If you know anybody who could do dispatching, let us know, will you?"

Hannah nodded. "I can't think of anybody, but I'll tell you if I do."

"Thanks." Jack turned to his computer.

Hannah turned away, then stopped. "Jack."

"What?" He looked up.

"We'll miss you."

"Thanks." He didn't look particularly touched, but why should he? He probably wanted to get out of here as soon as he could. Hannah went back to her desk and relieved her frustration by shredding a large pile of old receipts.

꧁꧂

At lunchtime, Blake came in, hard hat in hand. He made a beeline for Hannah.

"So how was the party?"

He did remember it. Did he have any idea how disappointed Hannah had been when he didn't show up?

"Oh, it was good." Hannah was careful not to look at Jack. "There were lots of people there, and the food was good."

"Bummed I missed it," Blake said. "Something came up at the last minute. A couple friends and I are running a hedge fund, and we had an issue with some stocks. We spent the whole night on a video call, and the only thing I got to eat was cold leftover pizza."

If he'd texted Hannah about it, she wouldn't have waited for him and gotten so upset. But he seemed penitent, at least.

Hannah laughed. "If you reheat pizza in the oven, it's almost as good as new," she said. "Sorry you couldn't make it."

"Did you dress up?"

"I was a cowgirl."

Blake raised an eyebrow. "You? A cowgirl?"

"Yeah. It was pretty fun." It had been fun until her conversation with Jack, but Blake didn't need to hear about that.

Blake leaned forward, his elbows on the counter. "I'd like to make it up to you for missing the party."

"Oh, Blake, you don't need to do that." Butterflies had taken hold of Hannah again. Was Blake about to ask her out?

Blake shook his head. "I know I don't need to, but I want to. Would you go to dinner with me sometime this week?"

"I'd love to." Hannah hoped she wasn't smiling too broadly, like she had been waiting impatiently for this.

"Fantastic. How about tonight?"

Maybe it was a little odd to ask a girl on a date for the same evening—etiquette probably would advise men to ask at least a day or so in advance—but Hannah wasn't busy tonight, so why pretend that she was?

"Tonight would be wonderful."

"Six PM?"

"Six PM," Hannah repeated. "Where?"

"I'll find a place and text you. What's your number?"

Hannah gave him her number, and he put it in his phone.

"Thanks." He smiled. "See you later."

"You're not eating lunch?"

"Gotta talk about stocks with some of the guys. I'll see you around."

At her desk, propping her chin in her hands, Hannah fell into daydreams. What would dinner with Blake be like? What would they both wear? What would they talk about? Hopefully Blake would show up this time. After all, this was a date. One question had been settled: Blake must like Hannah.

Dinner with Blake

Blake texted halfway through the afternoon. He suggested a bar and restaurant in Manistee. Hannah looked it up online. The place had mostly steak and seafood, and it advertised local Michigan wines.

It was hard to concentrate on work. Hannah hadn't been on a real date in a long time. Doc had never asked her on a date, and Chicago felt like forever ago. At least this wasn't a first date with someone she'd never met. She had been kind of dreading that when she signed up for the dating site. Hannah didn't like one-on-ones with strangers.

Jack didn't interact with her much. She wasn't sure if he had witnessed her conversation with Blake at lunchtime. He'd been sitting at his desk, but he might not have been paying attention.

He ate lunch in the break room, and when Hannah happened to go in there for a cup of coffee, Jack was reading a book at the farthest table. Probably what he had normally done before he started eating lunch with Hannah.

They'd had good conversations over those lunches. Hannah missed Jack's easy camaraderie, his joking around, and his thoughtfulness. If only there wasn't this awkwardness between them.

At home, after work, Hannah fussed over her appearance. Should she straighten her hair? Too boring? Maybe she could figure out how to do one of those half-ups Christine had demonstrated in that video a while ago.

After twenty minutes of watching the video and fumbling with her hair—why couldn't this stupid house have a three-way mirror so she could see the back of her head?—she gave up. Hairstyling was for the talented. Or the people whose hair wasn't so slippery.

Hannah straightened her hair, put in two drops of a serum that was supposed to tame flyaways, and put on her pink dress with the black dots. It was getting cold for that dress, but she liked it.

Blake was going to meet her at the restaurant. It was a half hour drive from Fraser's Mill to Manistee, and Hannah had plenty of time to get nervous. What if she said dumb stuff? What if Blake decided he wasn't interested in her, after all? Steve had mentioned his parents were wealthy. But her parents weren't badly off. And Blake was working for her family's company. Hopefully he considered Hannah to be in his league.

At the restaurant at last, Hannah checked her hair and makeup in the car. She looked all right. She had decided against red lipstick and worn a more muted shade of mauve, and her eye shadow was subtle shades of brown. Classy, not flashy.

She shouldered her purse, made sure she had her car keys, and headed inside.

A look around showed her a long bar counter (pretty full, at this hour) and a sea of tables, lit by warm-toned Edison lightbulbs and several fireplaces scattered throughout the restaurant. Blake was nowhere.

"Table for one?" A harassed-looking blonde hostess with a sleek ponytail and large rhinestone earrings approached.

"Um, no, I'm meeting somebody," Hannah said. "His name's Blake. He might not be here yet."

"Do you want to get a table, or wait at the bar?" the hostess asked.

"Table, please."

The hostess led the way to a small table near the edge of the room, by a gas fireplace that gave off a cheery warmth. Hannah hung her coat over the chair, sat down, and perused the menu.

It was 6:05. Where was Blake? Maybe he got stuck in traffic. Hannah checked her phone, but there weren't any messages.

6:10. Maybe she had gone to the wrong place by mistake. Hannah checked Blake's last text. No, it was the right place. She had almost decided on an entrée, a fancy salad, from the dinner menu. This place seemed to have a good variety of dishes.

6:12. Hannah's leg bounced under the table. If Blake didn't show up in three minutes, Hannah was going home. What did he mean by being so late to a first date? He'd better have a good explanation.

At 6:14, Blake walked through the door.

"Hey, Hannah," he said nonchalantly, sauntering up to her

table. "Sorry I'm late. I brought you this."

He pulled out a small gift bag from behind his back. Distracted from asking why he was so late, Hannah looked in the bag. Filled chocolates, wrapped in cellophane.

"Strawberry creams," Blake said. "Made in small batches in an ice cream shop near the beach."

Maybe he wasn't so good with punctuality, but he was thoughtful. Hannah's annoyance began to evaporate.

"Wow! I love strawberry creams. Thank you."

Blake sat down opposite Hannah. "You're welcome." Those blue eyes looked intently at her. "You look gorgeous."

Hannah blushed. "Thanks."

He didn't look so bad himself. He was wearing a leather motorcycle jacket—he seemed to have a lot of jackets—a light blue button-down that matched his eyes, and jeans. Casual but classy, with an edge. Maybe he was a biker. The idea was intriguing.

A waitress came and took their drink orders: Hannah, red wine; Blake, Oberon. She asked if they were ready to order.

"Do you know what you want?" Blake asked Hannah. At her nod, he told the waitress he'd take a twelve-ounce steak, medium rare, with a baked potato and mushrooms.

Hannah ordered a steak salad.

"Women and their salads." Blake laughed. "So tell me more about the party on Monday."

Was that party only two days ago? Hannah had lived through ages since then, with all the things that had happened with Jack and Blake.

"It was a good party," Hannah said. "Practically the whole town was there. The food was good, and there was square dancing."

Blake nodded. "Sounds like a good time."

She probably sounded unenthusiastic, but there had to be better topics for her and Blake to talk about. Online, he had mentioned all kinds of interests, and although she couldn't use that information without revealing she had seen his dating profile, she could still ask him questions.

"So, Blake," Hannah asked, "besides Chicago and Fraser's Mill, are there any favorite places you've been?"

It turned out to be a good conversational choice. Blake had been everywhere, it seemed. After college, he had taken a summer to travel. He had been to the Taj Mahal in the moonlight; he had ridden camels; he had seen royal jewels in London; he had been to the Empire State Building, but preferred the Chrysler Building. Even though tourists weren't allowed at the top of the Chrysler Building, he had managed to sneak in. Boldness—Hannah liked that in a guy.

"Wow," Hannah said. "I've always wanted to travel, but I haven't had much chance to do it. How were you able to drop everything and go abroad for so long?"

Blake shrugged. "Investments," he said. "Stock market and crypto. If you know what you're doing, you can make more than a little cash."

It took more than a little cash to travel like that. Blake must be awfully good at investing. He got more impressive all the time.

"So where would you go, if you went abroad?" Blake asked.

"Ooh, that's a hard one. Maybe Paris."

"Why Paris?" Blake leaned forward, attentive.

"Well, it's got incredible food, art—like the Louvre—and fashion. I know haute couture is hideous these days, but it would be interesting to see why Paris has led the fashion world for so long."

"I could see you in Paris," Blake said. "The last time I was there, I went for a dinner cruise on the Seine."

"That sounds beautiful. Expensive, though."

Blake winked. "Everything that's really worth it is expensive."

Was that sentence meant to be more meaningful than it sounded? Was Blake talking about her? She was pretty high-maintenance, but she wasn't expecting a boyfriend to lavish money on her.

Anyway, a dinner cruise on the Seine sounded heavenly. She could imagine doing it someday, with a handsome guy opposite her in the boat—maybe somebody wearing a leather jacket, with dark hair and five o'clock shadow.

Except for being late, Blake behaved like the perfect gentleman. He said "I'll take it" so quickly when the check came that she didn't get a chance to offer to pay her share of the bill; he walked her to her car; he didn't try any funny business saying goodbye, but gave her a normal hug.

He didn't ask for a second date, but Hannah preferred that guys ask her later anyway. That way, if she was planning to end it there, it wasn't awkward having to refuse the guy at the end of the first date.

Not that she would refuse Blake if he asked for a second date. He was even more interesting and impressive than she'd thought, and he lined up with so many of the things Hannah had been looking for. Maybe—just maybe—he really was Mr. Right.

Transitions

Hannah had never dated a coworker before. It was going to be strange, she decided the next morning as she got ready for work, seeing Blake around every day. Of course, he was mostly out in the lot and she was mostly in the office. But they would probably eat lunch together.

She straightened her hair again and wore her nicest cream-colored sweater. As long as she didn't spill anything on it, she would be all right. That should be easy since lunch was pre-bagged salad again with grilled chicken. Hannah had had no inspiration lately in the way of cooking.

Blake wasn't around when she parked next to Jack's truck in the mill lot. Maybe he had the day off, although that was unusual for the mill workers.

She went into the office, which was pleasantly warm in spite of the chilly day. Jack was at his desk with an unfamiliar guy. He was pointing out something on his computer.

Jack saw her and stood up. "Hannah."

"Hi, Jack," Hannah said. "What's up?"

"This is Aaron," Jack said. "He's going to be the new dispatcher. Aaron, this is Hannah."

"Hi." Aaron nodded his platinum blond head in Hannah's direction, his expression blasé. Although it was November, he was wearing a Hawaiian shirt.

"Aaron's been working on the line, but he used to drive an Uber, so Steve thought he might be good at figuring out truck routes," Jack told Hannah.

His phone rang, and he answered it. Aaron didn't seem inclined to chat, so Hannah went back to her desk. Her space heater was on. Jack must have turned it on for her. Even though Hannah had hurt his feelings, he didn't want her to freeze in the cold office. Her heart warmed in a bittersweet way.

What would it be like, working with this new guy? He didn't seem likely to care if Hannah was eating a balanced lunch, or be willing to joke around in the office. Jack hadn't even left yet, and Hannah missed him already.

About twenty minutes later, as Hannah was updating the mill's inventory, Blake finally came in. He had his lunchbox, but wasn't wearing his hard hat or his safety vest yet.

"Hannah." He stopped at her desk. "Here's a thank you for last night. I've got to run. See you later." He winked and disappeared into the mill.

Hannah looked at the small thing Blake had left on her desk—an organic dark chocolate bar, fair trade, the expensive kind. How did Blake know she liked that? Was it a lucky guess?

Maybe she'd eaten chocolate in front of him recently. She couldn't remember.

It was a good thing Steve hadn't come in when Blake was arriving. He didn't take kindly to people being late, especially that late. Hannah had learned her lesson the first time Steve had bawled her out.

❧❧❧

For the next couple days, Blake ate lunch with Hannah. He watched videos with her, gave suggestions for upcoming videos, and came up with nicknames for their coworkers. It was casual and friendly, no pressure. He still hadn't asked her out again. But he probably hadn't been able to fit it into his schedule. After all, he had a life, and he had a lot of busy evenings. He didn't have every minute free to spend with her.

Friday evening, Hannah was about to leave, when her phone rang.

"Is this Fraser's Mill Lumber?" a guy's voice said. "My name's Roscoe Patin. I was supposed to get a load of lumber in today, and it still hasn't arrived."

"Just a minute," Hannah said. "I'll ask the dispatcher. Would you please hold?"

She went over to Jack's desk, where Aaron was on the phone and Jack was listening. She hesitated. Should she wait for Aaron to get off the phone?

Jack looked up. "What is it?"

"There's a guy on the phone who says his lumber is supposed to come today, but it didn't get there. Roscoe somebody."

"We've got a couple trucks delayed. Let me check." Jack did something on his computer. "Yeah, that's one of the delayed ones. I can talk to him, if you want."

"Would you?" Hannah hated explaining to people why their lumber was delayed.

Hannah waited at her desk while Jack explained the situation. It sounded to Hannah, who could only hear one half of the conversation, that the guy on the other end was upset and Jack was smoothing him down. She was glad Jack stepped in.

"There," Jack told Hannah as he hung up the phone. "He wasn't going to start building tonight anyway. He'll be all right until the lumber arrives."

"You're a big help, Jack. Thank you."

He smiled. "You're welcome."

Good, he was smiling at her again. He'd been so serious ever since Halloween, and it was such a relief to see him smile, Hannah couldn't help beaming back at him.

"Hey," a voice said.

They turned to see Blake.

"Can I help you?" Jack asked.

"Actually, I wanted to talk to Hannah," Blake said.

"What is it?" Hannah asked. Of course she was happy to talk to Blake, but did he have to interrupt like that, just when she and Jack were getting along again?

Blake looked at Jack. "Would you excuse us?"

It must be something personal. Jack's expression changed, his lips compressed. "Sure." He headed back to his desk.

Blake came around the counter, sitting on the edge of

Hannah's desk. "So I've been thinking. Drinks and dessert tomorrow night?"

His timing wasn't great, but his invitation was. "Totally," Hannah said.

♊︎

Blake picked a classy place for their next date. It was about forty-five minutes from Fraser's Mill, but Hannah didn't mind the distance much. It was worth it, going someplace special with Blake. Some people in Fraser's Mill—Grace and Doc among them—seemed to spend their entire dating relationships hanging out in town. It was nice to get out and go someplace where they didn't serve the food on ancient green-edged plates that had been through the dishwasher ten thousand times.

The restaurant was small and crowded. It was one of those places with exposed brick walls and no dollar signs next to the menu prices. There were a lot of places like that in Chicago. It reminded Hannah of hanging out with her girl friends. Especially since Blake hadn't arrived yet. He was late again. He must have a good reason—maybe he'd stopped to get something for Hannah, like the chocolates last time.

Hannah had waited ten minutes, trying to decide between the almond clementine cake ("Lemon curd, blood orange and raspberry gelee, honey lemon ice cream, 12") and the Mackinac Island fudge cake ("Double chocolate cake, chocolate mousse, house-made oreo crumbles, malted milk ice cream, warm chocolate fudge sauce, 14"), when Blake finally arrived. He was wearing the leather jacket, jeans, and button shirt again, and he held a small box.

"I know I'm late," he said, "but you'll forgive me when you see this." He handed Hannah a velvet box, rectangular and flat. Velvet boxes were jewelry. Blake had gotten her jewelry? Hannah held her breath as she opened it.

Inside was a gold-colored pendant, wider than it was long, on a slim golden chain. The top edge of the pendant was a city skyline with miniature buildings. One was familiar — the Eiffel Tower.

"It's the Paris skyline," Blake said. "I found it and thought of you."

"Oh, Blake," Hannah exclaimed. "It's lovely." He had remembered what she said about Paris. How thoughtful! His love language must be gift giving.

Blake smiled. "I thought you'd like it," he said. "Did you get a chance to look at the menu? I'm getting the baked Alaska."

"You don't have a lot of trouble making up your mind, do you?" Hannah asked.

Blake shook his head. "I've never had trouble figuring out what I wanted."

Hannah debated a moment longer before settling on the Mackinac Island cake. Good chocolate was always worth trying.

❧❧❧❧❧

On Sunday evening, Hannah was invited to Steve and Christine's for dinner. Christine made roast chicken, and Evelyn wanted to show Hannah a finger puppet show in a small wooden theater she had gotten for her birthday.

Steve was in good humor. "I think Aaron will be okay as

a dispatcher," he told Hannah, as he helped Christine serve cherry fluff for dessert. "He catches on quickly. It's too bad Jack's leaving, but it could be worse."

"If you make Hannah talk about work the whole evening," Christine said, "you'll hear from me later, Steven Fraser. I want to hear more about Blake."

Steve laughed. "Girl talk," he said. "I knew that was why you wanted Hannah to come over. Can I have my dessert in the living room? I want to watch the Bears game." He kissed his wife and disappeared into the next room.

"Men." Christine sat down with her cherry fluff. "So tell me about Blake. You've gone out with him twice?"

Hannah smiled. "Yes." She filled Christine in on Wednesday's dinner and Saturday's dessert-and-drinks, as well as the strawberry creams, the necklace, and the chocolate bar Blake had given her.

"Wow," Christine said. "Wow. Honestly, I think he's going a little fast."

"You mean all the gifts?" Hannah was eating her cherry fluff, light and sweet and tangy with pieces of pineapple and cherry. She had to remember to ask Christine for the recipe.

"Yes. It seems a little unusual to give so many gifts to somebody you've just met." Christine held up a hand. "Now, I'm talking off the top of my head. I know I don't know the whole situation."

"I guess if I only heard about the dates and the gifts, I might think that too. But the thing is, he's been a perfect gentleman. He hasn't tried to get physical. And his parents know my parents, so he must be all right. Maybe gift giving is his love language."

"Maybe." Christine sounded dubious. "I've only gotten to meet this guy briefly. Why don't you invite him over for dinner next Sunday? That is, if you decide to keep going out with him. I'd like to get to know him better."

Christine's voice had that big-sister tone. "You're trying to scope him out, aren't you?" Hannah asked. "I don't trust you."

Christine smiled a mischievous dimpled smile. "I just want to meet this guy my sister-in-law keeps raving about."

"You already met him. You mean you want to grill him."

"I'll only ask a few nosy questions," Christine promised. "Just invite him. He doesn't have to come if he doesn't want."

"Fine, I'll ask him right now." Hannah pulled out her phone. "I really do want you to meet him. Even if you're trying to scope him out."

She was about to leave when Blake texted back. He couldn't come to dinner the next Sunday—he had a previous engagement in Traverse City. Well, Hannah's family could get to know him better eventually.

Hannah put on her coat and hugged everybody goodbye. There was no point in mentioning Blake's text now. Christine might just think Blake was being flaky. Hannah didn't need to add any more reasons to make her sister-in-law suspicious of him.

Deputy Sheriff

Jack's last day at the office was a Monday. Hannah had almost forgotten he was leaving, and she was jolted into remembering when Jack began packing up a cardboard box after work. Aaron, the new dispatcher, had already gone home.

Jack took everything out of his desk drawers. There was the emergency blanket he had lent Hannah. There was his coffee mug with the John Wayne quote.

Hannah walked over to Jack's desk. "Do you start working full-time for the sheriff's office right away?"

"Yeah. They want more guys out patrolling. Did you hear some places in Cadillac have been getting robbed too? Sheriff Hank thinks there could be a connection."

"Wow," Hannah said. "I hope you don't have to tangle with any burglars. Especially armed burglars. Please be careful."

Jack smiled. "Thanks. Better me than the sheriff, though. He's getting on in years. It's time he got more young guys to help."

That was like Jack, looking out for others. She'd better pray for his safety. "Will you come back and visit us?" Hannah asked. "It'll be weird with you gone."

Jack nodded. "I'll look in occasionally," he said. "I'm not going to the ends of the earth. I'll still be in Fraser's Mill. You'll see me around."

"I'll have to watch my speed then, officer."

He laughed. "Don't expect me to let you out of any tickets."

"Of course not," Hannah said. "I'll drive safe. And I'll keep an eye out for those burglars."

Jack turned serious. "Hannah, if you run into any burglars, get out of there and call 911. Catching criminals is our job, not yours."

"Believe me, Jack, I'm not trying to look for burglars," Hannah protested. "I just meant I would be careful."

"All right. If I were you, I wouldn't walk around by myself in the dark."

"I never walk around by myself in the dark," Hannah said. "If I come back late from anything I always park and go straight into the house, locking the door behind me."

"Good." Jack picked up the family photos from his desk and put them into the box on top of the emergency blanket. "It always pays to be careful."

Wait a minute. The emergency blanket had reminded Hannah: she still had Jack's space heater.

"Hey, Jack, what about the space heater?" Hannah asked. "It's your parents', isn't it?"

He shook his head. "They don't need it back yet. You can go ahead and keep it until Steve turns the heat on. You know where I live."

"Thanks, Jack. That's really nice of you."

"Happy to do it." Jack put his lunchbox and his book on top of the box. "Well, I'm all packed up." He smiled. "See you around, Hannah."

It felt so final, even though he wasn't even moving away. The mill office wouldn't be the same. And Jack probably wouldn't hang out with Hannah after this. She'd friend-zoned him, and they didn't work together anymore.

"I'll miss you," Hannah said. "Aaron can't possibly take your place."

"I'll miss you too." Jack swallowed. His brown eyes, deep and thoughtful, rested on her. "Goodbye, Hannah."

It felt like an odd goodbye. Words didn't seem like a good enough farewell for a friend like Jack. Hannah didn't know if she should shake hands, hug, or—

With sudden warmth, Hannah stood on tiptoe and kissed Jack on the cheek. "Goodbye, Jack."

He looked down at her, the hint of a smile on his face.

"Hey, Hannah," a voice said. It was Blake, sticking his head in the door. Oh no, had he seen Hannah and Jack just now? Hannah didn't know what had come over her.

Blake didn't look annoyed or anything, though. "Are you ready to go?" he asked.

"Just a minute," Hannah called. Blake disappeared.

Hannah turned back to Jack. "I've got to go."

He nodded. "Dinner with Blake?"

"Yes." Hannah went to grab her purse.

She was halfway to the door when Jack's voice arrested her. "Hannah?"

He was going to address the kiss, wasn't he? She turned, her pulse quickening. "What?"

"About Blake," Jack said. "Be careful with him."

"Careful about what?" Hannah asked.

Jack hesitated. "I don't trust him."

What rash judgment! "You don't even know him." Hannah put her hands on her hips. "What are you basing that on?"

Jack shook his head. "Just be careful with him, Hannah."

"I'm always careful," Hannah retorted. "I've got to go. Goodbye, Jack."

As she and Blake drove off for their date—they were going to a nearby winery for a wine tasting—Hannah fumed inwardly. Her relationship with Blake was none of Jack's business. Why did everyone try to give her so much unsolicited input regarding her relationships? Hannah was fully capable of taking care of herself.

⁕⁕⁕

It was strange, coming into work the next day and finding Jack gone. The new guy, Aaron, kept to himself at his desk, doing his work quietly.

Hannah didn't like the thought of working with somebody for the next several months without making friends with him. Accordingly, she went over to his desk.

"Hey, Aaron." She smiled. "If there's anything I can do to help make your job easier, let me know."

"Sure." Aaron turned back to his computer.

Not a particularly friendly start, but maybe he was stressed by the new job. Maybe he didn't talk much.

But no. In the lunchroom, Aaron had a marvelous time talking with the guys—almost yelling—about football. Hannah witnessed this as she came in for a cup of coffee. So Aaron did talk—just not to her. Rude.

∽⌇∽⌇∽

Blake was busy that evening, and besides, he and Hannah had gone out yesterday. And Hannah had a video to edit.

She had been hard pressed to get things out on Tuesdays lately. There wasn't any more to videotape in Fraser's Mill than there had been before. She had gone a number of places with Blake, but going on a date wasn't the time to make a video. So Hannah had spent her Friday taking short video clips as she went about her day, titling the video "A Day In The Life of a Small-Town Mill Office Administrator." Hopefully her viewers didn't mind vlogs.

Hannah was splicing video clips together when someone knocked at the door. She hit save on her laptop and went to answer it. It was Elaine.

"Sorry to bother you," Elaine said. "I know it's late. But I've got some boxes of books for the library that need to go into my car before tomorrow morning, and I was wondering if you'd help."

"Sure." Hannah slipped on her tennis shoes, next to the door. "No problem, Elaine."

They went into Elaine's house, where six large boxes of books sat on the dining table.

273

"They're donated," Elaine explained. "Another library had them for sale for a quarter a bag. My friend Ruth lives out there, and she picked out some things she thought would be good for our library."

Ruth had done her job thoroughly. There were all kinds of titles there, from philosophy and religion to cooking and knitting.

"The problem with most libraries," Elaine said, as she followed Hannah and the first box of books to the porch, "is that they keep getting rid of things they consider out of date. They put in as many new books as they can and push out the old ones. I believe that a library ought to hold a record of human thought throughout the years."

Hannah underestimated how heavy boxes of books would be, and her arms ached under the weight. She didn't blame Elaine for not wanting to do it herself.

"Thank you so much for this," Elaine said, as Hannah picked up the last box. "If you hadn't been around, I would have had to wait until tomorrow evening and see if Charlie could do it after work. He has the early shift at the diner tomorrow. And I was hoping to get some of these books in the system before then."

"No problem," Hannah said. "I'm glad I could help."

"It's nice having a neighbor next door," Elaine said. "Living between the church and the closed-up house, I didn't have a lot of neighbors. Why my husband decided to build a house down here at the end of town, where nobody else lives, beats me. How long will you be here, anyway? Are you staying through Christmas?"

"I'll be here until March," Hannah said. "That's when my parents' house swap is over and they come back to Chicago."

"How are things going for you at the mill?"

"It's been good," Hannah said, "but there's been a lot of upheaval lately." She found herself telling Elaine about Blake, about Jack asking her out and then leaving, and about the new and unfriendly dispatcher, Aaron.

"I don't think I've seen Blake. Does he go to St. Anthony's?"

"No, but he is Catholic," Hannah said. "He goes to—actually, I don't know what church he goes to. I didn't think to ask. We've just been going out for a couple weeks."

Elaine nodded. "It takes a while to really get to know a person."

"I know," Hannah said. "I've had a few people tell me they think Blake's going too fast in this relationship. But isn't it possible to figure someone out fairly quickly? I don't know everything about Blake, but I know the important things. His parents are friends with my parents, and he came to work at the sawmill when we needed help. He's the perfect gentleman. And he's thoughtful. He remembers little things I like. For instance, I told him I'd always wanted to go to Paris, and then he got me this necklace with the Paris skyline."

Elaine examined the necklace. "That's very nice," she said. "When I was a girl, my mother always said you should see the guy you're dating in all different circumstances. You should see him doing tough jobs and being stuck in traffic and being around his family. You can tell a lot about a man from the way he treats his family members. Actions speak louder than words."

She closed the trunk of her car, the last box of books deposited inside. "There, now I can get these down to the library in the morning. Thanks a lot, Hannah. I can get one of the library helpers to transfer them from the car to the workroom."

"Anytime," Hannah said. "Thanks for the talk, Elaine."

She went back to editing her video, but now her mind was distracted by Blake and everyone's opinions.

Elaine was probably right. It would be good to see Blake in other surroundings. But there wasn't any traffic in Fraser's Mill, and she couldn't exactly see him interacting with his family when they were in Chicago.

Maybe she could see him interacting with her family instead. She was sure Steve and Christine wouldn't mind rescheduling that dinner with him. Or he could come over for Thanksgiving. He didn't have family nearby, and Christine's Thanksgiving dinner wasn't a dinner to miss. Of course, Hannah would have to check with Steve and Christine first. But she doubted they would say no.

The Big Snow

It was getting on toward Thanksgiving. The space heater in the mill office was a tremendous help, as it kept getting chillier. Any day now, Steve ought to turn on the boiler.

The atmosphere was chilly in more ways than one. As she came from the break room with a cup of coffee—she'd had to make it herself ever since Jack left—Hannah glanced at Aaron's desk, where he was on his computer. Working with Aaron was like working by herself. That man wasn't interested in interacting with her. When Hannah said hi to him in the morning, Aaron barely looked in her direction, let alone saying hi back. When she asked a question, he answered it and went right back to his work.

It wasn't like Jack had spent all his time chatting with Hannah. But he had been a friendly presence. Hannah missed looking up and seeing Jack smile in her direction. She missed him leaning on her desk, drinking a cup of coffee, telling her about a prank his youngest sisters had played on his middle sisters. She missed him keeping her from eating vending machine lunches. She'd eaten more cookies lately than she cared to admit.

Blake came by her desk often, but that wasn't the same. It wasn't just that he couldn't help her with tricky customers the way Jack had. (Hannah definitely missed Jack's input about her more difficult phone calls.) Blake was a suitor, and that was flattering, but she didn't have the same easy camaraderie with him as she did with Jack.

Hannah sighed and got up to retrieve invoices from the printer. Well, Jack was out doing important things, and Hannah appreciated that. There had been another burglary in Fraser's Mill, the hardware store this time. The sheriff and his deputies were looking for clues to the burglar's identity, but again the security cameras had only captured the image of a guy in a black hoodie and a ski mask. There wasn't anything to go on.

Steve set up extra security cameras in the mill office. The cameras were operated from Hannah's computer, and Steve walked Hannah through the system. "I want you to know how to turn the cameras on and off," he said, "and how to look at the camera feeds. Not that I think this place is likely to get burgled, but I'll feel better having the cameras on. Let me show you how it works."

"I can figure that out myself," Hannah protested, but Steve gave her the walk-through anyway.

❧❧❧❧❧

It was a Thursday when a weather warning came. Apparently

Fraser's Mill was going to get dumped with snow, even though it wasn't Thanksgiving yet. What else could one expect from Michigan?

From her desk, Hannah looked out the window. The first white flakes were falling. She hadn't seen snow yet in Fraser's Mill. If it didn't melt immediately, it would be pretty. Of course, Hannah was used to snow in Chicago. But snow in the country was bound to be different from snow in the city.

Near the end of the day, Blake popped up. "I've got an idea," he told Hannah. "Did you hear work is canceled tomorrow?"

"No," Hannah exclaimed. "How did you learn?"

"Steve told me. He just decided. The mill will be closed because of the snowstorm."

"Wow." They hadn't had any sudden days off since Hannah started at the mill. She could sleep in tomorrow and get things done that she'd been putting off. Maybe she'd even do laundry before she got down to the last few shirts she didn't like as much.

"I've got an idea," Blake said again. "What do you say to a movie marathon?"

"A movie marathon?"

"Yes. I'll come over to your place tomorrow afternoon, and we can watch something."

He was inviting himself to her house? Well, he was a gentleman—he wouldn't mean anything other than actually watching a movie.

"But how will you get there if we get dumped with snow?" Hannah asked.

Blake laughed. "I've got a lifted truck with four-wheel drive.

I can get through anything."

"You can still slide off the road," Hannah said. "And it's been getting dark early. The thought of you driving home through the woods in the dark when the roads aren't plowed makes me nervous."

"If it gets too bad, I'll get a room at the bed and breakfast," Blake said. "Come on, Hannah, it'll be fun."

His smile was charming, and Hannah was getting butterflies. How bad could the storm possibly be?

"All right," she said. "I'll make food."

It would be a change of pace. Despite the fact that Hannah and Blake had been going out for weeks, he hadn't even seen the log house. It would be a chance for Hannah to show off her cooking. Blake liked pretentious restaurants, but Hannah would show him she could cook pretentious food too. At least, she hoped she could.

❦

By Thursday evening, the snow was four inches deep on Hannah's driveway and still coming down. Probably a smart idea to shovel it before it got too thick. Hannah put on her warmest coat, found a pair of Grandpa's work gloves in the garage, and pulled a beanie over her ears.

Her parents hired their driveway plowed in Chicago, but she doubted Fraser's Mill had snowplow services. Of course, you never knew. There could be somebody with a pickup truck and a plow who did it. Hannah ought to ask around and see if anybody in the area would do her driveway. She had a hunch that shoveling the whole driveway by herself all winter would get old quickly.

The snow was heavier than she had expected. It wasn't that cold out, just cold enough to snow instead of rain. The snow shovel from the garage was heavy and kept getting snow caked on it so that subsequent shovelfuls didn't do much. By the time Hannah had cleared the driveway and the front walk, she was ready for a hot shower and a mug of cocoa.

࿊

Hannah almost couldn't believe her eyes when she looked out the next morning. The snow must have fallen all night. There had to be another six inches in the driveway, and it was still coming down.

First things first. Before she ate breakfast, she would shovel again. If she shoveled after breakfast, the vigorous exercise would cause a cramp. Hannah had always heard you shouldn't work out immediately after eating, especially swimming.

The driveway was as much of a chore as last night, except that it was light out, which boosted Hannah's spirits. This was going to be a good day. She had been able to sleep in, she didn't have to go in to the mill, and Blake was coming over.

At noon, Blake sent her a text. He'd be there at two.

She was running out of time to get ready. There was no food in the house, and she had especially wanted to impress Blake with her cooking. She'd better go to the grocery store. The Murrays lived next door to the store — they probably wouldn't close because of snow.

Getting the car down the recently-shoveled driveway was easy. Getting it into the street, floundering through unplowed snow, was another thing. Why didn't Fraser's Mill plow the streets? Maybe the plows were busy somewhere else. At least they weren't likely to have a lot of out-of-town traffic right now.

The lot at Murray's Grocery was full, mostly because somebody with a truck and trailer had inconsiderately parked sideways and taken up half the lot. Hannah had to park across the street.

She deliberated for a long while in the store. Although Murray's Grocery had started to carry more specialty items recently (thanks to Grace and her parents working hard to improve the store), it was still a small place that couldn't stock everything. Hannah wanted to make baked feta to serve with tiny baguette toasts, but the store carried neither feta nor the shallots and capers that the dish required. She'd have to settle for something else.

Hannah finally decided to make homemade margherita pizzas. She had a basil plant at home, and the store sold tomatoes, mozzarella, and olive oil. The pizza dough could rise while she and Blake watched something and ate meatless charcuterie. It was Friday, after all, and even though it wasn't a Lenten Friday, Hannah preferred to give up meat than substitute an alternate penance.

Grace was at the counter, ringing people up. "Isn't this something?" she asked Hannah. "Jim says we're supposed to get up to twenty inches of snow, total."

"It's something, all right," Hannah said. "I'm glad I don't have to drive anywhere too far."

"Want to come over this evening?" Grace asked. "Jim and I are playing board games with Alex. Charlie's got to work. Half the town goes to the diner when it snows—they can't get out of town to go anywhere else."

"Thanks," Hannah said. "That sounds like fun. But I'm hanging out with Blake, so I won't be able to make it."

"Ooh!" Grace raised her eyebrows. "I heard you were going out with somebody. Is he nice? I don't think I've met him."

"Very," Hannah said. "Maybe we can all have a game night next time."

Outside, Hannah nearly fell on her face crossing the street in the snow. This kind of weather was treacherous.

She started her car, turned on her lights, and began to pull into the road. Oh, no. The wheels were spinning and spinning and doing nothing. She was stuck. Panic made her heart race.

Reversing didn't work either. Oh, why did she have to have two-wheel drive? And why hadn't she thought to bring a shovel?

Hannah parked and got out. It wasn't like she was in the middle of a snowbank. You'd think the car could drive over that amount of snow. Apparently not.

A car pulled up next to her. "Need some help?" a voice called.

Hannah turned. It was a sheriff's patrol car, driven by Jack. How did he always show up when she was in trouble?

"Jack," Hannah said. "My car's stuck! I can't go forwards or backwards."

"I'll be right with you," Jack called. He pulled ahead, parked farther down the street, and produced a shovel from the patrol car.

"Why don't you get back in the car," Jack said. "I'll dig you out."

"Okay, thanks." It was getting colder, and the snow was still coming down. Hannah hadn't thought to wear a hat. She got in the car and hugged herself, waiting for Jack.

He circled the car with the shovel, digging around all four tires. There was a lot more snow on the street than Hannah would have thought. She must have driven into the snowbank when she parked.

In a couple minutes, he tapped at her window. Hannah rolled it down, realizing after she hit the button that that might be a bad idea if the window was frozen. To her relief, it rolled down smoothly.

"Try it now," Jack said.

Hannah started the car and cautiously tried pulling forward. The car moved.

"Hooray," Hannah exclaimed, braking. "Jack, you're a lifesaver."

"Glad to help," he said. "Where are you headed? If I were you, I might stay off the road until the snowplow gets through. Want to warm up at the police station?"

It was tempting, partly because she was cold and partly because she hadn't seen Jack in a while, but Hannah shook her head. "Thanks," she said, "but I've got to go home. Blake's coming over."

"In this weather? Doesn't he live in Cadillac?" Jack's brow furrowed.

"He's got a truck with four-wheel drive."

Jack shook his head. "I wouldn't advise it. Even a truck with four-wheel drive can go off the road. We're asking people not to drive except in an emergency. Blake sees you all the time. It's hardly an emergency for him to come out here."

There Jack went, complaining about Blake again. Hannah's brow furrowed. "It's too late to tell him not to come. I'm sure he's on his way already."

"That guy's a daredevil." Jack's eyes were deep brown and serious. "He'll get hurt someday if he isn't careful. Or worse, hurt somebody else."

It was time to face the subject head-on. "Jack," Hannah said. "You don't need to be so down on Blake. I know you don't like him. But I think it's just because he's dating me. You're just— you're just jealous, that's all."

He started back, as though from a blow, and Hannah immediately regretted her words. It was too late to take the sentence back. Well, it was true, even if it wasn't the most tactful thing to say.

"So that's what you think? I'm trying to prevent you from going out with anybody?" Jack's voice raised.

"What am I supposed to think, under the circumstances?"

"I'm only trying to warn you to be careful."

"So I'm supposed to be careful about Blake for some reason you won't tell me."

Jack shook his head. "I've heard Blake talk around the other guys, and I've seen him interacting with people. It's my job to notice things, and he doesn't seem like a good guy."

Jack hadn't known Blake any longer than Hannah had. Sure, Hannah hadn't seen Blake in a lot of stressful situations, like the ones Elaine had mentioned, but she wasn't an airhead, either. "Jack, I am a good judge of character. I sized you up almost the first conversation I had with you. I think I can figure out Blake's character without input from anybody else."

"Fine." Jack threw up his hands. "Good luck with that."

"Fine!"

Hannah drove away, leaving Jack standing there.

୭ଏ୬ଚ୬ଚ

Despite what Jack said, Hannah looked forward to Blake coming over. Having him at her house would be a lot more cozy than meeting at a restaurant. They'd eat snacks and sit together on the couch. She could just see herself now, resting her head on Blake's shoulder — cue the butterflies!

Making homemade pizza was longer and messier than Hannah had remembered. She was only halfway through making the dough when Blake arrived in his big truck, pooh-poohing the weather warning.

"It's deep out there, that's all," he said. "It's not slippery. They'll have the roads plowed soon. Honestly, Steve didn't have to cancel work today."

Maybe if everyone had huge trucks with four-wheel drive, Hannah thought from her own experience. But she didn't say anything. She didn't feel like talking about Jack and the stuck car.

"So what are we watching?" Blake asked, shucking his winter coat. He wore a navy sweater and jeans.

Hannah shrugged. "I thought maybe you had an idea, since you suggested a movie marathon."

Blake shook his head. "I thought we could stream something."

It was a good thing Hannah's parents had put in a smart TV,

because in the old days the log house couldn't stream movies. Hannah's grandparents had had a VHS player. Of course, Hannah could stream movies on her laptop, but it wasn't as fun to sit in front of a laptop screen, straining to hear the dialogue from the computer speakers.

"I'm almost done making this pizza dough," Hannah said. "The remote's by the TV. Do you want to come up with some ideas?"

"Sure."

Some five minutes later, as the pizza dough rested, Hannah came into the living room and found Blake with his head inside the cabinet under the TV. They didn't keep movies down there — what was he doing?

"Got any movie ideas?" Hannah asked.

Blake jumped, hitting his head on the cabinet. "Ow! You startled me."

"Sorry." Hannah smothered a giggle. "Are you okay?"

"Sure, sure." Blake straightened up, rubbing the back of his head. "Let's see what there is to stream."

"What were you doing down there?"

"Checking if everything was hooked up right." Blake sat on the couch, grabbing the remote. "I don't think anything good has come out lately, but let's look."

"That's all right." Hannah settled cross-legged on the other end of the couch. "I like older movies, anyway."

"Good. Then it shouldn't be too hard to find something," Blake said. "How about *The Terminator*?"

Hannah shook her head. "I think that has scenes we'd need to skip, and it's probably too intense for me."

"Okay." Blake kept looking. "What about *The Matrix*? Or *John Wick*? That's a good one."

"Uh," Hannah said. There was some kind of disconnect here. "I hate to say it, but I'm not really a big action movie person."

"You're not." Blake stopped scrolling. "What kinds of movies do you like?"

"Let me think." Hannah had a hunch Blake wouldn't be caught dead watching her Hallmark movie collection. What did she like that a guy might like? "There are a lot of good old westerns."

Blake shook his head. "Not a westerns guy."

"Okay, then, how about superheroes? Maybe Superman?"

Blake laughed. "You had to pick the most boring superhero of all time. I'd go for Batman."

Hannah shook her head. "Still too much for me."

It was increasingly evident that Blake didn't like anything Hannah would want to watch, and vice versa. They went through more ideas of Blake's — all scary — and more of Hannah's favorite things that Blake didn't like or was tired of watching.

They finally compromised on Star Wars. Blake said he was tired of the original trilogy, but he hadn't seen the prequels in a while. He looked up the first prequel while Hannah rolled out the pizza dough and put the toppings on it. She was making one large pizza in a jelly roll pan.

It was too bad she and Blake didn't have more overlapping taste in movies. She could see this happening anytime they watched anything. It was draining, having so many things you liked dismissed in one breath. She wouldn't suggest another movie day anytime soon. But at least they had something to watch now.

Hannah finished putting the toppings on the pizza, stuck it in the oven, and set the timer. She'd pause the movie to take the pizza out.

She had seen the Star Wars prequels once before, but she had forgotten how long it took the first movie to get off the ground. She just wanted to see little Anakin and the pod racing. She didn't care so much for all the traveling and politics, and she especially didn't care for Jar Jar Binks.

Blake leaned back on the couch, not saying much, looking almost asleep. Hopefully he wasn't horribly bored with the movie compromise. He couldn't be as bored as Hannah was — it had been his own idea to watch this.

When the kitchen timer dinged, Hannah got the pizza out. Outside the kitchen window, snow fell thickly. There would be a lot more to shovel tonight.

Blake roused himself when the pizza arrived, steaming hot, on Grandma's extra set of china.

"This is good," he told Hannah. "It tastes like it's made by a real chef."

Hannah smiled. "Thanks. I'm glad it turned out."

Blake set his plate on the couch, scooting closer to Hannah. "Wanna start the movie again?"

Hannah hit play.

Blake yawned and stretched, putting his arm around Hannah's shoulder. Sure, she'd kind of expected that, although it was one of the oldest ruses in the world.

"Your hair smells good," Blake said, low, in her ear.

Hannah shivered, pulling away. She didn't know why, but

she was suddenly aware that she still didn't know Blake well and that they were alone in a practically snowed-in house. "Blake, I" —

"You what?" He leaned toward her, his arm around her shoulder pulling her closer, his mouth puckering.

Hannah's stomach knotted. "No." She pulled back.

"What?" Blake let go. "What's the matter?"

She shook her head. "I'm not comfortable with that."

"Too fast for you?" Blake sat back against the couch.

"Too fast," Hannah said. "Blake, we've only gone on a few dates. We barely know each other. When I agreed to the movie marathon, I didn't have that in mind."

His eyebrows looked skeptical, like he'd expected a different reaction. "Okay, fine." He moved over to the edge of the couch. "I got it. I won't try to kiss you again."

"It's not that I'm not interested in you," Hannah said. "It's too soon for me. I mean — I've never kissed anybody. And we've only barely gone out."

"Sure." He didn't look at her.

"Are you mad?"

He shook his head, still looking straight ahead. "I understand."

"Okay, good."

A silence ensued, during which the movie, still going on in the background, continued.

Hannah got up. "I forgot the crushed red pepper. Do you put crushed red pepper on your pizza? No — well, I do." She whisked into the kitchen.

The movie kept playing while Hannah looked for the pepper.

That was all right with her. How much more of the movie was there? An hour and a half? It felt like ages.

She came back with the crushed red pepper and a box of cookies. "We have cookies." Hannah put the box on the couch next to Blake, sitting on the other side of it.

"Thanks," Blake said. "Chocolate chip. Those are my favorite."

He sounded cheerful, but it didn't feel normal. Conversation lagged, and they both sat there watching the screen.

❧

The movie over, Blake stretched and got up. "Now what?" he asked. "Episode two?"

Not another one. This wasn't turning out to be anything like the way Hannah had imagined. She was tired of Star Wars, and after Blake had tried to kiss her everything felt awkward. She hadn't expected to react that way, after all the butterflies she felt about him before. But when he tried to make a move, the only thing she wanted was for him to let go of her.

"You know what," Hannah said, "it's getting late, and I still have to shovel the driveway before tomorrow. I think I'd better not watch another movie."

Blake got up. "That's all right. I'll just get back to Cadillac."

Hannah looked out the window of the front door. "Are you sure you ought to drive in that?" she asked. "It's super deep. I think you'd better go to the bed and breakfast like you said."

"I'll be fine." Blake put on his coat. "I'll go slow. That truck wouldn't get stuck even if I drove it in Alaska."

"As long as you're sure," Hannah said. "I'd hate to think of

291

you sliding off the road in the middle of nowhere. Nobody will be out there until morning."

Blake shook his head. "I'm not gonna slide off the road."

He went out, not stopping to give Hannah so much as a handshake, and backed his truck out. It left deep wheel ruts in the driveway. That was going to be a lot to shovel. Somebody else might have volunteered to help Hannah clear the snow, but she wasn't too surprised Blake hadn't offered.

Would this afternoon with Blake put a damper on his interest in her? Weirdly, she almost hoped it would. Earlier today, Hannah had only been thinking of how to pique Blake's interest in her further. Now her feelings about him were muddled. Why, when Blake tried to kiss her, had she only wanted to get away?

Maybe it was just too soon. It was probably normal to be hesitant about your first kiss, right? Right?

Over the River and Through the Woods

Apparently, Blake's interest in Hannah hadn't been dampened. On Monday, when the mill was open again, he came by Hannah's desk with a small bag. "I acted like an idiot the other day. Here, I brought you this."

"This" was three bars of something called ruby chocolate.

"I haven't tried it, but I heard it was good," Blake said.

"Wow. Thanks, Blake," Hannah exclaimed. "That's really nice of you."

He smiled. "I wanted to do something to make up."

"Thank you." Hannah smiled back. Her feelings about him still weren't clear, but he'd apologized, and she might as well give him the benefit of the doubt. Maybe their conversation at the log house, awkward as it was, would help pave the way for better communication in the future.

It was a good thing Jack wasn't there to hear Blake's apology. He might wonder what Blake was making up for. Hannah didn't want Jack to be even more suspicious of Blake.

In any case, Hannah might as well extend an olive branch. "Have lunch with me?" she asked Blake.

"Actually, why don't we go out for lunch?" Blake asked. "We've got time to hop over to the tavern and back."

"Well—" She had a lot of work to do this afternoon, and it might be better to stay here. On the other hand, all she had in her lunchbox was a sandwich made with two thin slices of ham and a slice of cheese. She had run herself out of groceries over the weekend.

"Sure, that would be nice," Hannah said.

☙◗⬖◖◗⬖◖❧

Hannah was helping a walk-in customer before lunch when Blake came in, waiting right in her peripheral vision. Hannah was almost running over into her lunch time, but a customer was a customer. There would still be time to grab something at the tavern.

As soon as the customer went out the door, Hannah sprang into action. "I'll be ready in a second," she told Blake. "I have to count the cash in my drawer and put it in the safe. Steve doesn't want me leaving it in the drawer during lunch. It's one of his robbery prevention tactics."

Blake nodded. "You've got time. The tavern's never full at this time of day." He pulled out his phone, leaning against a file cabinet behind Hannah's desk.

Still, Hannah didn't want to make herself late for work after lunch. She hurried to count the money in the drawer. Steve had changed the safe combination recently, and Hannah could never remember it, so she had it on her computer. It was in a password protected document for safekeeping, and her computer was also password protected, so there wasn't any danger of someone finding out the combination.

It seemed a little like overkill, but she wasn't about to give out the numbers to anybody. Blake didn't count—he was a trusted employee. Besides, he was on his phone, and he wasn't paying attention.

The mill ought to be safe enough, anyway. There were always people around when the place was open, and it was secure when it was closed. Hannah was honestly more worried about somebody breaking into her house—there were a bunch of ground-floor windows in both front and back, and the property had enough trees for burglars to hide behind. Maybe Hannah ought to look into home security systems. They were probably expensive.

"You ready?" Blake asked from behind her. "You've taken long enough to put away the money three times."

The money was in the safe. Hannah grabbed her purse and turned to Blake.

"Okay, I'm ready."

❧❧❧❧❧

Hannah had been waiting for a good time to invite Blake to Thanksgiving dinner. Over the weekend, Steve and Christine had agreed that Thanksgiving would be a good time to reschedule with him. Christine was still curious to actually get to know Blake in person, and Hannah was secretly hoping that seeing Blake around her family, in a casual setting, would bring out more of Blake's normal personality.

Since the movie afternoon, she had been nagged by a feeling that she didn't know Blake as well as she had thought. But she wanted the chance to see him in other settings, like Elaine suggested.

Having lunch with Blake at the tavern, laughing and talking about old college stories from when he was in undergrad, it seemed like a good time to extend the invite.

"Hey," Hannah said during a gap in the conversation, "do you already have plans for Thanksgiving dinner? If you'd be interested, Steve and his wife, Christine, have invited you to come with me to their house."

Blake smirked. "Who's going fast in this relationship now?" he asked. "Family Thanksgiving dinner? I haven't even met your parents yet."

He was teasing. "That's because my parents are in Germany." Hannah sipped her smoothie. "You know Steve. And he and Christine are going to have a wonderful Thanksgiving dinner."

Blake nodded. "Sure, I'll come. I haven't been to a real Thanksgiving dinner in a couple years. Last Thanksgiving I was in the Bahamas, and I had steak and lobster at a restaurant."

Hannah made a face. "Steak and lobster in the Bahamas is all very well, but I think Thanksgiving is a time for family and friends."

He laughed. "All right, all right, I get it," he said. "I'll be there on Thanksgiving. Tell Steve and his wife I'll bring dessert."

On the morning of Thanksgiving Day, Hannah slept until nine. It was nice to have a weekday when she didn't have to get up early. After morning prayer and picking out an outfit for the day—jeans and a cream-colored sweater—she checked her phone. There was a text from Blake.

"Hey, Hannah," the text read, "sorry, but I can't make it tonight after all. Believe it or not, I'm flying to Chicago to have dinner with my parents. Your talk about seeing family for Thanksgiving inspired me."

That was great that Blake was going to see his parents for Thanksgiving, but it was disappointing for Hannah. She replied. "Wow! Have a great time with your parents!"

If Blake wasn't going to be there, there was no one to bring dessert. Better go down and see if there was anything at the grocery store that Hannah could bring instead. She was out of desserts at home, and the store had been selling fresh homemade baked goods lately.

Wait, was that place even open on Thanksgiving? Hannah had forgotten to check until she got there. Oh good, there were cars in the lot. Hannah parked and went into the store.

Grace was behind the counter. "Hey, Hannah," she called. "Happy Thanksgiving!"

"Happy Thanksgiving!" Hannah replied. "You don't have to work here all day, do you? That seems like a pretty miserable way to spend the holiday."

Grace shook her head. "We're closing at two. Mom and Dad figured that people might need last-minute Thanksgiving ingredients, so they decided to open the store for half the day.

Then I can go home and help cook. My sister Katie and her family are coming. Are you spending Thanksgiving with any of your family?"

Hannah nodded. "My brother and his family out in Cadillac. I'm trying to find some kind of dessert to bring to them. Blake—the guy I'm seeing—said he was bringing a dessert, but then he ended up going back to Chicago to see his parents, so I thought I'd better bring something myself."

"I keep hearing about Blake, and I still haven't met him," Grace said. "What does he look like? Nobody's been able to point him out to me yet."

"He doesn't live in town," Hannah explained as she looked at the baked goods display. Homemade cherry pie—the very thing. "He lives in Cadillac. Wait a minute, who's been telling you about him?"

Grace got an odd look on her face, but she laughed. "Fraser's Mill has a pretty good town grapevine."

While Grace checked out the cherry pie and whipped cream (pie, in Hannah's opinion, was not nearly as good without whipped cream), Hannah told her about Blake and about the times they had gone out together. "I wish he could have come for Thanksgiving," she said. "I wanted to get to know him better in a non-date, non-work setting."

Grace nodded. "That makes sense. You know, when Jim and I were getting to know each other, we weren't out on dates. Actually, I couldn't stand him."

"What? Really?"

Grace laughed. "Let's say my first impression of him wasn't

great. I thought he was trying to steal my mom's car, and he was actually noticing it had a flat tire. And I found this out after I'd already run outside and yelled at him."

"Wow." It had been so obvious that Doc was interested in Grace as soon as she arrived in Fraser's Mill. Hannah had long felt that Grace came in and swooped Doc up. It had never occurred to her that maybe Grace hadn't chased Doc at all.

"So what happened?" Hannah asked. "How did you get to know him?"

"He lives next door," Grace said. "He was always around, whether I wanted him to be or not. So we had to interact a lot. And then, right before the Fourth of July, my car broke down, and he drove out to rescue me. That's when we really started to get to know each other. But it wasn't a date."

"You started dating after you came back from California, right?" Hannah asked.

"Yeah," Grace said. "I know now that I had actually liked him before that. But I'd been ignoring it and telling myself we were wrong for each other."

"And I told him you were dating somebody else." Hannah clapped a hand to her head. "Sorry about that."

Grace laughed. "That was because Lucas told you he and I were dating. Don't worry about it. Anyway, Jim and I cleared up our misunderstandings, and we're good now."

"Wow," Hannah said again.

"The whole thing snuck up on me," Grace said. "I wasn't looking for him. And I'm really glad we got to know each other as friends before we ever started going out. Of course," she added hastily, "it works differently for different people. But—this is what I was going to say in the first place—I think you're right, that it's good to get to know people better in a non-dating setting."

"Totally," Hannah said. "You're absolutely right."

They'd been talking about Blake, but the picture that flashed across Hannah's mind wasn't Blake. It was Jack, sitting across from her in the rowboat, relaxed and cheerful as he propelled the boat upstream. They'd gotten to know each other pretty well, Hannah and Jack. Just as friends. And it was really too bad that the friendship seemed to be spoiled now.

❧❧❧

The world had transformed since Hannah's last drive to Cadillac. Deep snowdrifts blanketed the ground and the trees. The pines looked like they had been dipped in frosting. The roads had been plowed out by now, and cars were more frequent—probably because of Thanksgiving.

At Steve and Christine's house, Evelyn opened the door for Hannah, struggling with its weight and bracing her heels against the floor to pull it open. "Aunt Hannah."

"Evelyn." Hannah hugged her niece with her free arm. Her other arm had the bag with the dessert. "Happy Thanksgiving!"

"Happy Thanksgiving, Hannah." Steve came out of the kitchen, Noah toddling behind him. "How do you feel about having dinner with us instead of Mom and Dad?"

"Oh, it'll be good." Hannah wasn't about to disparage Steve and Christine's company and their no-doubt excellent dinner. "You guys are family too. And I wasn't about to go all the way to Germany."

"I wish I could go to Germany," Steve said. "Take Christine and the kids. A real family trip. Ha! As if. Nobody's got money for that. I'd do a house swap like Dad, but I can't leave the mill."

Hannah nodded. "I'm happy for Mom and Dad, though."

"Me too," Steve said. "They worked hard all these years. They deserve to go to Europe. Something to look forward to, when we're all old and successful as they are."

He talked as if it were a certainty. Hannah still hadn't made a lot of strides toward that success. Her mill job wasn't exactly a ladder to an important position.

"So Blake ditched you for his parents?" Steve raised an eyebrow.

Hannah made a face. "He didn't exactly ditch me. Parents are higher priority than somebody you've been going out with for a few weeks."

"I'm not so sure about that guy," Steve said. "He's not been pulling his weight around the lot. Sarah says she has to keep finishing things he was supposed to do."

This was news. "Blake is leaving stuff for Sarah to do?"

"Uh-huh."

"You're sure there isn't some kind of miscommunication?" Now that she thought about it, Hannah hadn't heard about Blake hanging out with Sarah and her husband lately.

Steve shook his head. "You can ask her yourself. She'd been at the mill a while, and she's not a complainer. I think Blake's slacking."

"What are you telling her, Steve?" Christine came out of the kitchen, drying her hands on a dish towel. "That thing Sarah told you? I think maybe Blake is still learning how to do his job.

But I wish he had come to dinner, so I could size him up for myself. I'm beginning to think he's avoiding us." She laughed. "Happy Thanksgiving, Hannah. What's that? A pie? Good, Evelyn's been asking all day if we were having pie."

Hannah laughed and hugged Christine. "Yes. And it's homemade. Not by me."

It was odd, hearing this new opinion about Blake from Steve. When he'd first met him at the fall festival, he'd seemed to like him just fine, and Hannah hadn't thought to wonder how the boss and employee relationship could affect things. Well, Christine didn't seem to share Steve's opinion. Hannah should probably give Blake the benefit of the doubt unless she learned differently for herself.

Darkness, My Old Friend

After a delicious—and enormous—meal at Steve and Christine's, an episode of a show from the 90s called *Road to Avonlea,* and a long dishwashing session during which the three adults washed practically every dish on planet earth, Hannah went back to Fraser's Mill. Other than some deer that ran across the road in the dark, and a couple slippery patches, the drive went fine.

Hannah was almost home, passing the sawmill, when she noticed something unusual—inside the office, a light was on. Oh, no. She must have left one of the lights on when she closed up yesterday. It was probably her desk lamp. It would waste electricity if the light was left on all weekend, and Steve would be mad if he learned about it. Better stop and turn the light off.

Hannah parked in the lot and walked toward the building, her muscles tensing against the brisk air. Why did Thanksgiving have to be so cold in Michigan? She had been assured that winters in Michigan weren't all like this, that this snowstorm was a fluke and the earliest and deepest in about ten years, but as far as she was concerned, Michigan winter started way too early.

A shadow through the window made her stop in her tracks. What was that moving inside the office?

There was definitely something moving. Somebody was inside the building. Maybe it was a burglar.

She couldn't see the person clearly. Better verify before doing anything drastic. Hannah crept closer to the window, walking as quietly as she could so the person inside wouldn't hear her.

It was a guy dressed in black, facing away from Hannah. And he was turning the lock on the office safe. It had to be a burglar.

Heart pounding, Hannah pulled out her phone. Better call the police.

The man straightened up and opened the safe door, and at that moment, Hannah caught a glimpse of his face. It was Blake. Blake was robbing the office safe.

Anger hit Hannah like a freight train. The guy she had been going out with was robbing her parents' business. She shoved her phone into her pocket and pulled out her keys to unlock the door.

Hannah opened the door and stepped inside. "Blake Whitaker." Her voice was quiet, edged with steel. "What do you think you're doing?"

Blake turned from the open safe, his face shadowed but unmistakable in the glow of the desk lamp. He wore all black and gloves. "Hannah?"

Something twisted in Hannah's gut. "I can't believe it," she said. "We trusted you. What are you doing here, in the mill office, with the safe open?"

"Go home, Hannah." Blake stepped toward her.

"Stay back." Hannah held out her hand toward him. "Dad hired you because he knew your parents. I went out with you. For weeks. And this is how you repay us?" Her voice was rising beyond her control.

"Get out of here, Hannah." His tone was menacing, and he was hulking in the lamplight. "Go home."

"No, you get out of here. Close that safe back up and go."

"Or what?" Blake pulled the cashbox out of the safe, holding it under his arm. That thing had thousands of dollars in it. One customer in particular had made a large cash purchase on Wednesday, Hannah knew, and there had been no one to take it to the bank before closing time.

"I'll call the police."

"So what? They won't get here before I'm gone. And you're gonna call the police whether I take this or not. I know girls like you."

"Yes, I am gonna call the police whether you take it or not," Hannah exclaimed. "But you'll be in a lot less trouble if you put it back and come along quietly."

He started toward the door, but Hannah stood in the way.

"You're on the security cameras," she said. "They'll find you."

"Nope." His expression was scornful. "I turned the security cameras off yesterday, when you went out for a cup of coffee and left your computer unlocked."

Her stomach plummeted. She'd played right into his hands. He had been hanging out with her and acting friendly while all the while he had been planning to rob her family.

"You're horrible," Hannah said. "You jerk. You absolute sicko. You pretended to like me."

"I did like you. Who wouldn't? You're kinda cute." His taunting expression made Hannah even angrier.

"Blake Whitaker, I'll have the law on you if it's the last thing I do."

"I'll be long gone. Get out of my way."

Hannah remained in front of the doorway.

"I'm armed. Move." Blake elbowed past her roughly, rushing into the parking lot.

She hurried out after him. He had broken into a run, going down toward Hannah's house. Hannah started after him, but her boots had high heels and she couldn't keep up. It was dark, too.

Blake had to have a car somewhere around. If she caught up with him before he reached it, she could get the license plate number.

Hannah raced back to her own car. She shot out of the parking lot and down the street.

In front of her, near her house, a truck was pulling onto the road from the shoulder. It had to be Blake. Hannah sped up, trying to see the license plate. It was an Illinois plate, and the number was BC 44956.

She had to remember that. BC 44956. BC 44956. Better stop and write it down. There was no point in chasing Blake any farther. Her little car couldn't compete with his truck with the four-wheel drive. Besides, it wasn't safe to go on a high-speed chase in snowy weather like this. She could go off the road and hit a tree and get killed.

Hannah pulled over, entered Blake's license plate number

into her phone notes, and called 911.

"Hi. I'd like to report a robbery."

Now that the encounter with Blake was over, she had trouble keeping her voice from shaking.

⚬⚭⚬⚮⚭⚭⚮⚭

Hannah was asked to come down to the police station to talk to the sheriff. It was just as well. She had to talk to someone. She didn't want to be all alone in that big log house after what had happened. Going to the police station would make her feel safer.

It was hard to wrap her mind around the whole story. Blake—whose parents knew hers, who had seemed so friendly and regular, whom Hannah had thought was intriguing and cool—was a robber. How much of his friendliness to her had been real? Why had Dad taken to him and hired him to work at the mill? Had Blake been planning to rob the mill before taking the job, or was it something he decided to do later on? And was he the guy who had robbed the gas station and the grocery store? That guy had worn a mask, whereas tonight Blake had no mask. Maybe he had forgotten it, or maybe he had thought there was no way someone would notice him in the office window.

It was humiliating to have been so impressed with someone who turned out to be a criminal. She should have listened to Christine when she said Blake was going kind of fast. She should have listened to Jack when he warned her about Blake. Maybe Jack was out there right now, going after him.

If they caught him and there was some kind of trial, she would have to testify against him in court. What would Blake's parents think about their son being a burglar? What would Dad say when he learned about all this?

It was around ten PM when she walked into the sheriff's office. Sheriff Hank Liddell was at his desk. He got up when he saw Hannah.

"Hannah. Glad you could come in. Are you all right?"

"I think so," Hannah said. "Is somebody going after Blake?"

"I've got two of my deputies out there after him. Why don't you sit down and tell me what happened from the beginning. Want a cup of coffee?"

Sheriff Hank was kind and collected and put Hannah at ease. She filled him in on the whole situation, from seeing the light to chasing Blake's car down the street.

"I don't know how he got into the office," she said. "Maybe he jimmied the lock. Or maybe he got a key somewhere. I know he'd disabled the security cameras, because he told me that as he was about to get away with the money. I don't know how he got into the safe, unless he saw me opening it."

She swallowed hard. "I did open it one time when he was in the room. It never occurred to me he could be watching. He was wearing gloves, so there won't be any fingerprints."

The sheriff nodded and took notes. "And how did you say you know Blake?"

Hannah sighed. "He works with me at the mill. But we were also seeing each other. I went out with him on a bunch of dates. I had no idea he was doing this kind of thing." She dropped her face into her hands. How had she been such an idiot?

Wait a minute—if the police caught Blake, wouldn't they

suspect the girl he was going out with to be a robber too?

She raised her head and faced the sheriff. "Am I a suspect? I mean, as far as you guys know, I could have been an accomplice who changed my mind and decided to get Blake in trouble."

"Where were you on the night of October 25th?" the sheriff asked, then grinned. "I'm kidding. I have an idea that the chances of you being an accomplice to rob your family's own lumber company are pretty small."

Hannah smiled. "I'm glad to hear that. I don't know what my mom would say if I ended up in jail. Although it would make an interesting story for my video channel."

The sheriff chuckled. "We're not planning to make any more interesting stories for that channel tonight," he said. "Don't worry, Hannah, nobody's thinking you ought to be in jail." His expression turned sober. "But you should have called the police right away when you saw there was someone in the building. I know you meant well, and you know the guy, but it isn't safe to confront people like that."

"Yes, sir. I'm sorry, sir. I didn't think about him getting away before the police could get there if I confronted him."

"It's easy to lose your head in a crisis," the sheriff said. "But the important thing in situations like that is to keep yourself safe and notify the police when you can. We'll take care of it. There's no need for you to confront criminals."

"Yes, sir."

Hannah was leaving when a call came for the sheriff over the radio.

She didn't know police codes, but it was clear the person on the other end of the call was in distress. Something about a car accident. Wait a minute. That voice was familiar. Was it—oh no, was it Jack? Had he been in the accident? Hannah's chest clenched.

"Hang in there, Jack," Sheriff Liddell said into the radio. "What happened? Are you all right? What's your location?"

Oh, no. Jack. From the way Jack's voice was slow and garbled, barely getting the words out, he must be hurt badly. Somebody had run a stop sign and smashed into his car while he was chasing Blake.

Everything seemed to be moving in slow motion. Hannah's heart raced, and she felt like she couldn't breathe.

Jack needed medical help right away. In these parts, if you called an ambulance, it took forever to get there. Doc was probably the closest person to call.

The sheriff told Jack to hold on, that help was coming. He called Doc, who said he'd be right over to Jack's location.

Hannah waited, her arms wrapped around her, a sick feeling of helplessness in her gut.

"I've gotta go out there," the sheriff told Hannah. "You go home and stay safe."

"Can't I go with you?" Hannah asked. "Please. Jack's a friend of mine."

At least, he had been a friend of hers. She didn't know what he thought of her now, but if there was anything she could do to help him, she would.

The sheriff shook his head and put on his coat. "We'll take care of everything," he promised. "Doc will probably get there before I do. You can either sit tight here or go home. Be careful either way."

The sheriff hurried off, leaving Hannah in the police station by herself.

What should she do? She should go home. There was no point in staying here. She didn't know when the sheriff would get back. But how horrible, that Jack had gotten injured chasing Blake, and she couldn't help. She didn't even know how badly he was injured.

Poor Jack

Hannah's car was cold. It was only half a mile from the police station to her house, and she spent the half-mile shivering. The heater would only blast cold air, so she kept it off.

Jack was out there in the cold somewhere, injured and miserable. He was probably in the middle of nowhere when the accident happened, judging by the time elapsed between Blake's departure and the accident. What kind of idiot would run through a stop sign and hit a police car?

At her house, Hannah made sure her doors were all locked. Blake was still on the loose. This was probably one of the last places he would come, but she didn't want to take any chances. She kicked her shoes off, flung her coat onto the kitchen table, and sat on the couch curled in a ball, hugging a pillow to herself.

If Hannah had called the police when she saw Blake instead of confronting him, they might have caught him red-handed and there wouldn't have been a chase. If Jack hadn't been out chasing Blake, he wouldn't have gotten into an accident. If Hannah had done what Jack told her, and not interfered with a robber, Jack would be safe and sound right now. This whole thing was her fault.

Before her eyes flashed images of Jack, sitting in a patrol car, trying to stanch some bleeding injury, waiting for Doc and the sheriff to arrive. Maybe he had broken bones. His voice had sounded awful.

Jack had warned Hannah to be cautious about Blake, and Hannah had been so irritated that he was meddling. She had spent more than a month going around with Blake, daydreaming about her and Blake as a couple, talking about Blake. And maybe the whole time, he was planning to rob her family.

Angry tears slipped down her face. She remembered herself at that Halloween dance, waiting and waiting for Blake to show up. Of course he hadn't shown up. He was probably doing nefarious things elsewhere. Wait a minute, wasn't that the same night Murray's Grocery had been robbed? Maybe Blake had been involved with that too. And Hannah had trusted him.

She was actually wearing the necklace Blake had given her, with the Paris skyline on it. She'd wanted to look special for Thanksgiving. With a hard yank, Hannah broke the chain and hurled the necklace across the room. Her neck hurt. She deserved it.

Her phone dinged. It was a message from Grace.

"Please pray for Jack Rogers," it read. "He was in a bad car accident. Doc's on his way to take him to the hospital."

Of course Grace knew what was going on — Doc must have

texted her.

"I was at the sheriff's office when he heard," Hannah replied to Grace's message. "Do you know what happened? How bad is Jack hurt?"

"I don't know," Grace replied. "He was in too much pain to talk on the phone. Something about his arm, I think, but maybe he's hurt elsewhere too."

Poor Jack! Jack didn't deserve to have this happen to him. Especially as the result of something Hannah had done.

Hannah dropped to her knees in front of the couch. "Please, God," she prayed, "let Jack be all right!"

More pictures played in front of Hannah's eyes. The time she had brought Jack soup when he was sick. The time he had carried her because her ankle was sprained. The time he had shown her his treehouse in the woods. The time he had taken in the dock and come in for cocoa afterwards, and unlike Blake, hadn't tried any funny business.

None of the times she had gone out with Blake—with her pride flattered by his attention and his gifts—could compare to being with Jack, working and helping each other and having so much fun together. She felt at peace with Jack. She felt safe and listened to and cared for. And she cared for him too, so much more than she had thought she cared for Blake. Why had she been so stupid as to run around after Blake when Jack was right there?

She could still see Jack's dejected face when she told him she was interested in someone else.

How had she thought Jack wasn't the impressive man she was looking for? He was kind and smart and hard-working and honest—everything that mattered, that was, far more impressive than wealth and travels. And even after Hannah had looked down on him, even after he'd seen how shallow she was, he'd stuck around. He'd become her best friend. Jack was the man she wanted to be with. Why had she been so stupid, not to see that?

And it was her stupid fault that now he was on his way to the hospital. She had to talk to somebody. Maybe she'd better call Christine and Steve and tell them what had happened. Steve wouldn't be happy to learn that Blake had stolen all the money out of the safe. Come to think about it, Dad wouldn't be happy about that either.

She was picking up the phone to call Christine when she got another message from Grace. "Are you all right?" Grace asked. "You said you were in the sheriff's office?"

Right, Grace wouldn't have heard about Hannah's part in the situation. "Yes, I was," she replied. "I caught Blake robbing the mill office!"

"WHAT?" Grace replied in all caps. "Blake? The guy you were going out with?"

"Yes," Hannah replied. "Hey, could we talk on the phone? I have to talk to somebody, or I'll go crazy."

"Oh boy, you're home alone, aren't you?" Grace replied. "I've got a better idea. Why don't I come over? I'll bring coffee."

"Grace, you're a godsend," Hannah replied. "That would be wonderful. Thank you."

Grace came over in record time, bringing two travel mugs of hot coffee.

Hannah met her at the door. "Come in, come in," she said. "I'm so glad you're here."

"Hannah, you look like you've seen a ghost," Grace said. "You're not okay. You oughtta sit down. Here, have some coffee."

Hannah took the travel mug, cool on the outside but steaming when she opened the lid. "Where did you get hot coffee at this time of night?"

"French press," Grace said. "I just made it. I was going to settle down and read a book I've been meaning to finish."

"Night owl?" Hannah asked absently.

"No, I was trying to sleep in the living room because my nephews have my bedroom. But I couldn't fall asleep on the couch. So I figured I might as well forget the whole thing and stay up. I don't have to work until the afternoon tomorrow." Grace walked into Hannah's living room. "Wow. I didn't know the ceiling in here was this high. Do you ever light a fire in that fireplace?"

"Jack did once."

"We should light one," Grace said. "Want me to?"

"Sure, thanks. I don't know how. Although I know Jack started it with newspaper." Hannah's eyes were brimming over unexpectedly. "Grace, it's my fault. Jack could have gotten killed, and now he's going to the hospital, and it's all my fault."

"Hey, hey." Grace turned to Hannah, looking her straight in the eye. "Jim will take care of Jack. He's gonna be all right. You've gotta believe that. And it can't possibly be your fault. Why don't you tell me all about it, and I'll light the fire."

"All right." Hannah sat on the couch, wiping her eyes. "See, I caught Blake robbing the mill, and I should have called the police, but instead I went in and confronted him."

While Grace went back and forth, getting together kindling and logs and starting the fire, Hannah filled her in on what had happened with Blake.

"I can't believe it," Grace said. "He got your father to give him a job at the mill. He hung out with you for weeks. He pretended to be such a nice guy. And all the time he was a robber. Maybe he was the same guy who robbed our store."

"Maybe he was." Hannah told Grace about Blake missing the barn dance right around the time the store was robbed. "We'd better tell the sheriff. Maybe he can do something about the money that was stolen from you."

"I hope so." Grace shook her head. "I still can't believe it. Right here in Fraser's Mill."

"And I don't even know why he would do it," Hannah exclaimed. "He always seemed like he had plenty of money. I guess now I know where it came from."

"You always seem like you have plenty of money, too, and I assume you don't spend your weekends robbing banks."

Hannah laughed shakily. "Thanks," she said. "Blake told me he invested well, and like an idiot, I believed that. Because his parents know my parents, I assumed he was a normal well-behaved guy. And I wasn't suspicious of him, even when I ought to have been. Steve told me he was slacking on the job, Jack told me he didn't trust him, and I was getting some funny feelings about him too, but I ignored all of it."

"He sounds pretty sneaky," Grace said. "I never met him, but I bet he'd have fooled me too. Nobody expects a newcomer to Fraser's Mill to be a bank robber."

"I know. But I feel so awful about it. And now poor Jack got hurt chasing him. That's the really awful thing. Jack asked me out at the Halloween party, and I told him I wasn't interested in him that way because I was interested in somebody else."

"So that's what happened on Halloween," Grace said. "I wondered, but I didn't think I should ask."

Hannah nodded. "I didn't want to talk about it then. I felt awful."

The fire was going well now. Grace joined Hannah on the couch.

"Do you mind if I say something nosy?" she asked.

"Go ahead."

"Usually when a girl turns a guy down, she doesn't spend the rest of the evening looking completely miserable," Grace said. "Jim and I saw you and Jack dancing before that happened, and I told Jim that I thought there was something going on between you two. And to me, it didn't seem totally one-sided. I'd have sworn you liked him."

Hannah shook her head. "I didn't think I did. I thought I was upset about rejecting him because I didn't want to hurt him and our friendship. But I know now that I do like him. I think I have for a while, but I didn't realize it."

Grace smiled. "That's what happened with me and Jim. I realized I'd liked him for a long time, but all that time I'd kept telling myself I didn't."

Someone's phone started ringing. Grace dashed across to the entryway and rummaged through her purse, which she had left on the entry table.

"Jim," she said into the phone. "What's going on? Are you at the hospital? How's Jack? Can you tell me without breaking some kind of doctor-patient confidentiality?"

Doc must be filling her in, because there were a lot of "yeah"s and "uh-huh"s from Grace's end of the conversation. Hannah listened, ears strained. From the tone of Grace's voice, at least it didn't sound like Jack was at death's door.

Finally she was off the phone.

"What's going on?" Hannah asked.

"Jack's at the hospital in Cadillac," Grace said. "He has a pretty badly dislocated shoulder. He's gonna need surgery. He was in a lot of pain, but he's on pain meds now, which are helping."

"Poor Jack!"

"Jim called Jack's parents, and they're on their way over. The sheriff stayed at the scene of the accident to ask questions. The driver of the truck was driving drunk. He wasn't too badly hurt, but he hit Jack's car right in the driver side door. It's a wonder Jack wasn't killed."

Just like that, Jack could have been gone. Hannah would never have seen him again. And he never would have learned how she actually felt about him.

Tears fell again.

"Hey, it's all right," Grace said. "It's not your fault, Hannah. You weren't the one driving the truck. That could have happened to anybody, anytime. Jack could have been on his way to the grocery store and had the same thing happen."

Hannah shook her head. "I was the one who got Jack sent

on a chase on Thanksgiving night. That's one of the biggest drinking holidays of the year. He could have been safe in the sheriff's office if it weren't for me."

Grace placed her hand on Hannah's arm. "Jack wouldn't want you to blame yourself."

He probably wouldn't. Hannah could hear him now, telling her not to think like that. She wiped her eyes again.

"He has surgery tomorrow," Grace said. "Well, today, now. It's after midnight. I don't know what his family is planning to do. They'll probably drive home, unless somebody stays with him all night."

A lightbulb went off in Hannah's head. The hospital was a public place, wasn't it? Anybody could go there.

"I want to go out there." Hannah sat up straighter. "To the hospital."

"Hannah, it's the middle of the night. They wouldn't let you see Jack. He's probably trying to sleep."

"I don't care if they won't let me see him. I want to be there. I've spent the last few weeks not being there for him, and I caused this whole problem, even if I wasn't the one who drove the car that hit him." Hannah got up from the couch.

Grace shook her head. "Why don't you get some sleep and go to the hospital in the morning?"

Hannah picked up her phone and stuffed it in her purse. "I really want to do this. The roads are clear now. I couldn't sleep if I tried."

Grace sighed. "It sounds like a crazy idea," she said, "but I know where you're coming from. If Jim was in the hospital, I'd be doing the same thing."

"Thanks. I'm getting my coat. Would you put out the fire? I'm sorry, you went to a lot of trouble to make that fire for nothing."

"No problem. It was good while it lasted." Grace got up to put out the fire. "But I'm coming with you to the hospital. I can't sleep either, and Jim's out there. He can drive me back. Let me give him a call."

From what she could glean from Grace's end of the phone call, Hannah pieced together that Doc thought it was pointless for them to go to the hospital in the middle of the night, but he wouldn't mind Grace's company on the way back to Fraser's Mill.

"All right." Grace was off the phone. "You still want to go? Jim says visiting hours were over at eight."

Hannah nodded. "I still want to go."

The Visit

"We'd better take my car," Hannah said, "if Doc's driving you back." She and Grace were dressed warmly for driving, and Grace had remembered to bring the two travel coffees they hadn't finished yet.

"Do you want me to drive?" Grace asked. "I don't think you're in a good state to drive."

"You're probably right." This night had been so wild that Hannah was beginning to feel as if she had imagined the whole thing. "Are you fine driving?"

"Sure," Grace said. "As long as we don't break down, I'm fine. Jim teases me that I can't look at a car without it breaking down." She took Hannah's keys and got in the driver's seat.

Hannah hadn't given up on the idea that she might be able to see Jack after all. There ought to be a way to get in if you knew a family member. Or maybe Doc could get her permission to see Jack. Then again, maybe Jack didn't want any visitors. Maybe he was trying to sleep. And maybe Hannah was the last person he wanted to see right now, after she caused him to go after Blake and get hurt.

But even if Jack didn't want to see her, she wanted to be on hand. Maybe she could stay at Steve and Christine's house after she went to the hospital. Looking at her phone, she had a barrage of missed messages from Christine. She'd better call them.

Christine answered the phone. "Hannah, are you all right?" she asked. "Steve's been on the phone with the sheriff. I can't believe you found Blake robbing the mill! You must be in shock."

"I'm all right," Hannah said, "but poor Jack went out to chase Blake, and his car got hit. He's badly hurt in the hospital."

"What? Oh, that's terrible! Steve, come here. I'm putting this on speakerphone."

Hannah told Steve and Christine a condensed version of what had happened.

"Poor Jack!" Christine said. "That's awful. We'll pray for him."

"Thanks," Hannah said. "I wish I hadn't confronted Blake. I should have called the sheriff's office and let them surprise him in the act of robbing the place."

"In all the time we've had the mill," Steve said, "we've never had a robbery. How did Blake get into the safe, anyway? Did you leave the combination lying around where he could see it?"

Thankfully, Steve didn't sound mad—just curious.

"No, I didn't leave the combination around. But I know he got into my computer at least once, because he used it to turn off the security cameras. He told me that tonight, when I caught him. Although the file with the combination on my computer was a password-protected file. I really don't know."

"Anyway, we know who he is," Steve said. "He can't go far. Somebody will find him."

"And we know his license plate number and who his parents are," Hannah said. "I know we'll find him. I'm more worried about Jack."

Hannah asked about crashing at their house after going to the hospital.

"As long as you don't make a ton of noise and wake Noah up," Christine said, "we don't mind. I'm gonna make a big day-off breakfast in the morning. Egg, tomato, spinach, and feta casserole."

Steve yawned loudly. "Can't we eat Thanksgiving leftovers?"

"Nonsense," Christine said. "You don't have to go to work tomorrow, and I don't have to get up early. So I'll make something nice."

"It sounds wonderful," Hannah said. "Thanks, guys. I'll be around eventually. Don't be alarmed when I knock."

❧❧

Grace had apparently been to this hospital before. She confidently led the way through an entry area, down a hallway, and past a gift shop to a windowed waiting area with chairs. A few people, mostly hospital workers, ambled around. The place was quiet. Hannah had never been to a hospital in the middle of the night before.

A guy sitting in the waiting area got up when he saw Grace and Hannah. It was Doc, wearing an orange sweater and khakis.

"Grace. Hannah. There you are." Doc strode over to them. He didn't look tired, although it was so late. He must do this sort of thing a lot.

"Doc, how is he?" Hannah asked.

"Resting," Doc said. "He was in a lot of pain before he got here, but he's had some pain meds now. His parents are with him."

Nothing must have changed since Grace called then. Hannah nodded. "That's good."

"I don't know if you can see him," Doc said. "It's not visiting hours. And he's probably trying to sleep."

"I know," Hannah said.

Doc shook his head. "I still don't understand why you wanted to come out here in the middle of the night."

"Jim." Grace put her arm through his. "She cares about him. If you were in the hospital, I know I'd come and sit there, even if I wasn't allowed to see you."

Doc looked at her, recognition dawning on his face. "I see." He turned to Hannah, grinning. "The last I heard, you said Jack wasn't your boyfriend."

Hannah found herself blushing.

"Jim." Grace thwacked Doc lightly on the chest. "You don't have to tease her."

"He isn't my boyfriend," Hannah said.

"Huh?" Doc asked.

"It's a long story. He asked me out, and I turned him down, and now I know I shouldn't have."

"Ah." Doc nodded. "So that's what you're doing here in the middle of the night."

"Yeah."

That was all fine and good, but now that she was here, she

felt a little silly. Grace and Doc were right—there was nothing she could do, so there was no point coming in at this hour. She should have waited and come tomorrow after Jack's surgery. Now she would be exhausted tomorrow for no purpose.

"Either of you want a cup of coffee?" Doc asked. "There's a café downstairs. I don't have anything else to do here."

"We've already had enough coffee to last us the next twenty-four hours or so," Grace said. "Thanks, Jim. Why don't we keep Hannah company for a while before we head back? It's not any fun waiting in the hospital alone."

Doc nodded. "I'll pop in and tell Jack's parents I'm heading out soon."

He was going to Jack's room? "Wait," Hannah said. "If Jack's awake, would you tell him I'm here? I'm not trying to bother him. I know he's resting. But I want him to know."

Doc nodded. "Sure."

Grace and Hannah found a place to sit near a window. It was pitch dark outside, except for streetlights and car headlights.

"Thanks a lot for coming with me, Grace," Hannah said. "I know this was a crazy idea. But I had to be here."

Grace nodded. "No problem. I might have stayed up this late anyway, trying to sleep on the couch at home."

"Hey, do you want to stay over at my house?" Hannah asked. "I can give you my house key."

Grace shook her head. "No, no, that's all right. Thanks, Hannah. That's nice of you. But I should probably be at my house in the morning anyway."

"If you change your mind, let me know," Hannah said. "I'm

going to Steve and Christine's in any case."

"All right." Grace yawned. "I'm not tired, I promise. I yawned for no reason."

"Uh-huh. I don't believe you," Hannah said. "You probably got up at the crack of dawn, working in the store this morning. Doc had better drive on the way back."

***

Hannah didn't notice Doc had come back until he was standing right beside her. "Hannah. He wants to see you."

"Huh?" Maybe she had dozed off, because this wasn't making sense. "What?"

"Jack's awake, and he wants to see you."

"Oh," Hannah said. "I thought that wasn't allowed. I mean, it's not visiting hours, and I'm not family."

Doc laughed. "It's all right. Come with me."

"I'll walk with you," Grace said.

The three of them went down a hallway and around a corner. Doc tapped gently on one of the doors and opened it slowly, peering in. "She's here," he said.

Voices inside the room said something Hannah didn't catch, and Doc opened the door wider, motioning Hannah in.

Jack's parents sat next to each other on chairs by the hospital bed. And there was Jack, lying in the bed propped up with pillows. He had Band-Aids on the left side of his face, and his left arm was in a sling and supported with a pillow.

"Hey, Hannah." Jack's voice was tired, but it was his voice, and Hannah's eyes began to water unexpectedly.

"Jack," Hannah said, and didn't know what else to say.

Jack's mother got up and came to meet Hannah, pressing Hannah's hand in both of hers. "We heard what happened with the mill getting robbed. That must have been so scary for you."

"Thank you, Julia," Hannah said. "I'm all right. But Jack was going out after the robber when the accident happened. I feel just terrible."

Julia shook her head. "Oh, honey, it's not your fault. It was that drunk driver." She turned to her husband, who looked like he was half asleep on his chair. "Come on, Pete, let's go get some coffee downstairs. Let Hannah talk to Jack."

"All right, dear." Pete rubbed his eyes, getting up. He patted Hannah on the shoulder as he went by. "Good to see you, Hannah."

The door shut, and Hannah was alone with Jack.

"Thanks for coming." Jack spoke haltingly.

"Oh, Jack." Hannah sat down next to his bed. "How are you feeling?"

He smiled. "Better, now that you're here. Sorry—pretty loopy. They gave me a lot of pain meds."

This wasn't the time to talk about Hannah's feelings. But she did want to apologize.

"Are you all right?" Jack asked. "Blake—he didn't hurt you, did he?"

She shook her head. "I'm all right." She took a deep breath. "Jack, I'm so sorry about all of this. If I hadn't confronted Blake, maybe you guys would have gotten there in time instead of having to drive around chasing him. You told me not to confront burglars, and I didn't listen." A big tear rolled down her face.

"Don't cry," Jack said. "Hey. I'm gonna be fine."

"I could have lost you." Hannah wiped her eyes.

"Nobody's lost anything, Hannah. I'm right here. It's all right."

Hannah took his non-injured hand and pressed it to her cheek. "I'm so glad you're going to be okay."

Jack smiled.

She would have liked to stay a while, but she knew Jack needed his rest. When his parents returned with their coffee, Hannah got up.

"I should probably go," she said. "How long will you be here?"

"I don't know." Jack shook his head.

"Surgery's tomorrow," Pete said. "Then they'll probably send him home when he's recovered enough to travel."

"Maybe I could come back tomorrow."

"Aw, honey, you don't need to do that." Julia patted Hannah's arm. "He'll be in surgery and then recovering. But if you'd pray for him from home, we'd all appreciate that."

That was a bummer, but she understood. "Of course." Hannah laid her hand on Jack's. "Bye, Jack. Feel better."

"You're not driving all the way home, are you?" he asked. Of course he would be worrying about her. If her car broke down, he wouldn't be around to stop and rescue her again.

"No, no, I'm staying at Steve and Christine's," Hannah said. "It's not far."

"Good," he said. "Goodnight, Hannah."

She wanted to hug him, but that might injure his shoulder. She squeezed his hand and turned away.

Julia gave her a hug. "Thank you so much for coming,

Hannah. It means a lot to have you looking out for our boy."

That felt completely undeserved after all that had happened. "Thank you, Julia, Pete," Hannah said. "You raised a good son."

Pete shook her hand. "Thanks for coming, Hannah."

She walked through the hospital hallways. The panicked sensation that had stuck with her most of the evening had dissipated while she sat with Jack. Now there was just a peaceful warmth. Jack was going to be okay. And somehow, soon, Hannah needed to find a way to show him how she felt about him.

⚬⚬⚬⚬⚬

Hannah couldn't remember much of what happened between leaving Jack's room and crashing at Steve and Christine's house. She must have made the drive safely, though, because she woke up the next morning on her brother's living room couch with Evelyn patting her on the shoulder.

"Aunt Hannah, I didn't know you were here."

"I got here in the middle of the night." Hannah yawned and sat up, pushing her hair out of her face.

"Wow." Evelyn's brown eyes were wide. "Mommy and Daddy never go places in the middle of the night. When I'm a grownup, can I stay up all night like you?"

Hannah laughed. "Probably not such a good idea, Ev."

Christine appeared in the doorway. "Oh, you're up," she said. "I'm making egg casserole. Want some coffee? Steve wants to hear the whole story of the robbery. The police are still looking for Blake."

Over strong coffee at the kitchen table (she'd had a lot of

coffee in the last day), Hannah filled Steve and Christine in on the whole robbery story and her visit to Jack in the hospital.

"I told you she liked him." Christine nudged Steve's shoulder.

Hannah blushed. "I didn't know I did until last night."

"You said he was having surgery today?" Christine asked. "We can say our family Rosary for him. Poor guy, just becomes a deputy sheriff and this has to happen to him. I bet it'll take him a while to get back into his job. Maybe they'll give him a desk job or something while he recuperates."

"Maybe," Hannah said. "I don't know how that works when you get injured on the job. Maybe he'll get some kind of workers' compensation."

The kitchen timer rang, and Christine peered at the casserole in the oven. "Five more minutes, I think."

Hannah stretched her legs under the table. She'd been tense for so long over the last day.

"If the police catch Blake, they may be able to relax," Steve said. "If he turns out to be the guy who robbed those other places, that is. He didn't say anything about that?"

Hannah shook her head. "Nothing. Not that most robbers go around giving a list of all the places they've robbed."

Steve poured himself another cup of coffee. "All the robberies were cash, right? So it's not like there are stolen goods to trace. We don't know if he was working alone or with somebody else. There could be a crime ring around here for all we know."

"I certainly hope not!" Christine was setting the table around them. "If Blake thinks he's going to hide, he'll have to do a lot of work. The police know his name, his parents, and his license plate. I can't imagine what he thinks he'll do now. Give himself up? Flee to another country?"

"I hope he confesses the whole thing," Hannah said. "What I really want to know is, why did he do it? He always seemed to have lots of money, and he had a good job. He was always talking about investments and cryptocurrency. I don't know why he would feel like he needed to steal."

Steve shook his head. "Mystery to me." He took a sip of steaming coffee, his brow furrowed. "Wait a minute. Did you say cryptocurrency?"

Hannah nodded. "Yeah. I don't know much about it, but he mentioned it a number of times."

"Ah." Steve leaned forward, stroking his chin. "We've had a few big crypto crashes this year. If Blake had a lot of money in crypto, he could have lost it all. I'm gonna look more into that. It might not be a clue—but it could provide a motive."

Down on the Farm

Hannah spent most of Friday in a groggy state after all of the excitement and staying awake so long the day before. Her parents called—Steve had told them about the confrontation with Blake—and she filled them in, but the whole thing felt like a blur. She finally drove home from Steve and Christine's house around dinnertime and crashed at the log house.

On Saturday morning, Hannah opened bleary eyes and stared up at the log ceiling. She felt as if she had been having the wildest dreams, although she couldn't remember anything clearly. Had everything with Blake and the accident and Jack been a dream? No, it couldn't have. She reached for her phone, and opened her text conversation with Grace, finding the messages about being at the police station. It had really happened, then.

Hannah rubbed her forehead. She didn't usually confuse dreams and reality, but the whole thing had been so crazy. It was going to take some time to process everything, especially with all these new feelings that wouldn't stop running through her head. Why did it take something like this to realize what Jack meant to her? How had she not appreciated the time they spent together?

She'd hurt him by her refusal, and then she'd gone out with Blake right under his nose. She wouldn't blame Jack if he never wanted to see her again, much less give her another chance at going out together.

But she had to see him. Even if he rejected her this time, she had to show him how she felt.

But somehow, deep down, she had faith he wouldn't reject her. He'd been so kind when Hannah showed up at the hospital. He'd even said he was better now that she was there. Remembering gave her a warm fuzzy feeling inside. Of course, he'd been pretty groggy and out of it, but didn't people reveal their true feelings more when they were groggy?

She didn't know if Jack was home from the hospital yet, or when she'd have a chance to see him next. She didn't want to bother him by texting, and she didn't have the number of any of his parents or siblings. Instead, she texted Grace to see if she'd heard anything.

"I don't know," Grace replied. "Let me ask Jim."

A few minutes later, she replied again. "Jim says Jack went home yesterday after his surgery."

Was Jack all alone in that apartment by himself? At least he had Barb to keep an eye on him, but a landlady probably didn't have unlimited time to keep an eye on a tenant who just had shoulder surgery. It might be a friendly gesture to bring something over.

Accordingly, when Hannah had washed and dressed, she went downstairs to look in the pantry. Unfortunately, there wasn't much food in the house. She hadn't been shopping since before Thanksgiving. She had forgotten to make her usual overnight oats, too.

Hannah ended up making regular oatmeal for breakfast, with celery sticks and peanut butter on the side. It was unconventional, but she was getting all the major food groups.

Now, what to bring for Jack? If she were recovering from shoulder surgery, she would go for comfort food of some kind. Something substantial that didn't require using both hands to eat.

The first thing that came to mind was lasagna. Her mom's family had a little Italian in them, and they always made lasagna for gatherings. They didn't have it often otherwise. Today would be a great day to bring back that tradition.

Should she text Jack she was coming? Then he might feel obligated to invite her in, and maybe he'd run around cleaning his apartment and go to a bunch of trouble. Better to just show up on his doorstep.

❧❦❧

Lasagna carefully held in both hands, Hannah went up the steps of the house where Jack lived and hit the doorbell with her elbow.

Barb came to the door, an apron on over a button shirt and jeans. "Hannah. How are you? How can I help you?"

"Actually, I was hoping I could give this to Jack," Hannah said. "Is he up for visitors?"

"Huh?" Barb looked at her oddly. "He's not back yet. He's staying down on the farm for a few days while his shoulder gets better. I told his mom I'd take good care of him, but she wanted to do it. She said his siblings would help cheer him up."

"Oh." Deflated, Hannah rested the lasagna on the porch railing. She should have texted Jack instead of just showing up. It was good that he was on the farm with people taking care of him, but he wouldn't need her lasagna—she'd seen examples of his mom's fabulous cooking—and if she brought it, there wouldn't be enough for Jack's whole family.

"Barb," Hannah asked, "would you like some lasagna?"

"I'd love some." Barb opened the door wider. "Why don't you come in? I've been eating Thanksgiving leftovers all day, and Jack's not around to help me finish them up, so I'm sick to death of them."

Hannah laughed. "Thanks."

Over lasagna—which was good, and it was too bad Jack had to miss it—Barb sang Jack's praises. He was the best tenant she'd ever had. Always asking how he could help. Always fixing things around the house. He wasn't a tenant, really—he was family. Hannah believed it.

She found herself spilling the story of Jack and Blake and the robbery, along with her newfound feelings for Jack. Barb listened sympathetically, clucking at poor Jack's woes and coming up with several inventive names to call Blake.

"I told you." Barb shook her head at Hannah. "I thought you and Jack would be good together. Now what are you going to do about it?"

"I've got to talk to him," Hannah said. "That was why I got the idea to bring him lasagna. Now I've got to come up with something else."

Barb smiled. "Just talk to him. If he still likes you—and I'm sure he does—you don't have to make it fancy. Just tell him."

Hopefully Barb was right. Hannah just needed to find the right time.

❧

On Sunday, Hannah decided to sing in the choir for Mass even though she hadn't been at practice on Wednesday. She had missed a lot of choir practices lately, what with going out with Blake and having other conflicts and forgetting practice existed. But it would help restore some sense of normalcy to her life. Besides, she already knew most of the music, and Grace and Doc would be there.

It was hard not being distracted by Jack and his family, down below in the church. It was a relief to see Jack up and around after last seeing him in the hospital. His arm was in a sling, which would be the case for several weeks, Hannah understood.

She still had to show him how she felt about him. Unfortunately, she had no idea how to get into that conversation. How did one admit they had friend-zoned someone out of stupidity and a lack of understanding one's own feelings?

After Mass, she went down to the vestibule, hoping to say hi to Jack. She found him mobbed with people asking about his injury. Jack was patiently telling the same story over and over. Hannah didn't want to break into the circle.

Someone nudged her. "You can go talk to him," Grace said in an undertone, her brown eyes mischievous.

Hannah laughed. "I know," she told Grace, also in an undertone. "I don't want to interrupt."

Besides, she was already a little shy about talking to Jack, now that she knew her feelings—she didn't want to try to talk to him in the middle of a crowd.

Before the crowd parted, though, Julia made her way through the vestibule to Hannah.

"Hannah," she said, "that was kind of you to come to the hospital when Jack got hurt. Thank you. It really cheered him up."

"Oh." Hannah flushed. Why did Julia keep thanking her for that? "I'm glad. Jack has done a lot more than that for me."

Julia smiled. "I have an invitation for you," she said. "And this is really last-minute, so I apologize, and it's completely all right if you can't make it. Would you like to come to Sunday dinner on the farm? It'll be around three-thirty or so, but you can come any time before that. We always eat early because everyone's starving after missing lunch. This noon Mass really cuts the day in half."

Dinner on the farm? There was no question whether Hannah wanted to go. She hoped Jack wanted to see her, too, and this wasn't just his mom's idea. "I'd love to. I know you're up the road a ways, but would you give me your address?"

After Hannah typed the address in her phone, one of the younger Rogers girls came along to ask her mom about something.

"I guess I'd better hurry home and change," Hannah said. "I'll see you around three-thirty."

People were still talking to Jack about his accident. As Hannah looked over, Jack caught her eye with a smile. She smiled back, her heartbeat quickening.

She'd had feelings like this around him before—like the time in the treehouse—but she'd been quick to ascribe her elevated heart rate to something else. Now there was no reason to hide from her feelings. And today, she'd tell Jack.

◉◉◉◉◉

What did one wear for Sunday dinner on the farm? In case the family showed her around, maybe it would be best to wear casual clothes. If she wore Mass clothes and they decided to walk around the property or hang out in the barn, the clothes might not hold up. Hannah settled on blue jeans and a light-blue-and-cream striped sweater.

It wasn't far up the road to the Rogerses' farm. Their farm seemed to be mostly fruit trees, stretching a long ways on both sides of the house. Hannah remembered Jack's family grew apples, maybe other fruits too. The house, a large light-blue two-story with a wraparound porch, stood far back from the road at the end of a long gravel driveway. Beyond the house, at the top of a rise, stood a red barn. Still beyond that rose woods going down to what Hannah knew must be the river. Jack's treehouse was somewhere back there.

It was a beautiful day for the end of November. The sun was bright, and the snow all but melted. It still felt like winter, but that was Michigan for you.

Hannah went up on the porch and knocked on the door.

A tall girl, probably one of Jack's sisters, answered it. "You must be Hannah." She smiled, dimples appearing on either side of her mouth. "I'm Felicity. Come on in."

"Thanks." Hannah came in, wiping her boots carefully on the mat.

The house smelled like roast meat and baking bread. Julia must do a lot of cooking. Hannah hung her coat in a capacious closet that Felicity pointed out and followed her into a large and well-lit living room with big windows.

Around a low table, Jack, two of his sisters, and his younger brother (probably around ten years old) were all playing a board game. A tall blond guy — he must be a cousin — had his feet up on the couch reading a book. Hannah walked closer and recognized the board game as Risk.

"Hi," she said.

Jack looked up. "Hannah," he said. "Hey, you guys go on without me. David, are you all right playing our team by yourself?"

"Sure," David, Jack's brother, said staunchly. "I've got a whole strategy worked out. The girls are gonna fight over Australia anyway."

Jack laughed. "As always." He got to his feet, bracing himself against the table with his good arm, and came over to Hannah. "Hi."

"Hi," Hannah said.

She looked down, shy to meet his eyes. The last time she had talked to him — apart from the conversation in the hospital — they had been arguing about Blake.

"I went over to your apartment yesterday," Hannah told Jack. "I didn't know you were staying on the farm until Mrs.

Kowalski told me."

"Oh, yeah," Jack said. "My mom insisted I stay here for a couple days until I'm more used to doing things with one arm. Sheriff Hank says he won't let me set foot inside the sheriff's office yet, so I figured I'd take a weekend at the farm."

"I tried to bring you lasagna," Hannah said. "But you weren't there, so—I'm sorry to say Mrs. Kowalski and I ate it."

She felt sheepish, but Jack burst out laughing. "That's all right. You know what they say—it's the thought that counts."

Julia appeared in the doorway. "Dinner's ready," she called.

The farmhouse kitchen was large, which was a good thing, since there were so many people there. Besides Jack's immediate family—his parents and all seven of their children—Jack's three tall blond cousins, who worked on the farm, were there. Hannah learned that their names were Will, Joe, and Nick. She thought she'd seen them around town before. There was also a young guy with a buzz cut that she assumed was another cousin before learning he was Felicity's boyfriend. The boyfriend, Adam, also worked on the farm.

The food was laid out buffet-style on the kitchen island— homemade bread, a beef roast, carrots and potatoes, pickled beets, and two kinds of pie. The pie looked homemade. Julia must have put a lot of work into this dinner.

"Wow," Hannah said. "Julia, how do you have the time to go to noon Mass and still make all this?"

"Oh, honey, it's just Crock-Pot roast and bread-maker bread," Julia said. "And the girls made the pies last night. I thought we'd better make a lot because we're all out of Thanksgiving leftovers. The cousins eat a lot of leftovers."

"Hey, I object," one of the cousins said. "Adam was the one who finished the turkey. And David helped out."

"I sure did." David piled pot roast onto an already heaped plate. "What can I say? I'm a growing boy."

Everyone laughed.

"All right, let's say grace," Pete announced from the head of the table.

It was a new experience, sitting around the crowded table with Jack's family. Hannah could hardly remember the last non-holiday when her family had all been together for a meal. Maybe it was because she was at the tail end of the family and her siblings had moved out of the house so long ago. Even though she lived with her parents, Hannah's schedule often didn't match theirs. They ate dinner together when they could. But it was nothing like this.

Jack sat next to Hannah, and everyone was jammed so close together that Hannah was right up against his side. She'd only been this close to him once or twice before, and a shiver ran through her. How had she not realized before how attractive he was?

The table conversation was lively enough that Hannah forgot about her previous nervousness. The older girls and the cousins were debating the relative merits of two different kinds of cherries. Apparently some of those fruit trees Hannah had seen driving in were cherry trees.

"Somebody's got to fix the eavestrough at the end of the house," Adam said. "That snowstorm put too much weight on it, and it's coming down. I'll do it, if you give me the time."

"Sure, Adam, thanks," Pete said. "I don't have any wish to stand around on a ladder at this time of year."

"Thank goodness," Julia said from the end of the table. "We don't need you getting hurt too. One person in the hospital per month is my maximum."

"I've never fallen off a ladder in my life, Julia," Pete said. "Now, Will here almost fell off the roof last month replacing shingles."

"I did not either, Uncle Pete," Will said. "I slipped a little."

"From what I hear, you slid all the way to the edge and grabbed hold in the nick of time."

"Sounds like one of Zita's tall tales," Will said.

"I don't tell tall tales," Zita protested.

Jack leaned toward Hannah. "Believe it or not, it gets louder than this," he said in her ear.

Hannah laughed. "That's okay. I feel like I'm in a scene from *Seven Brides for Seven Brothers*."

"Good. It can be overwhelming." Jack's eyes twinkled behind his glasses.

Hannah was, in fact, overwhelmed. But it wasn't because of the talking. She was keenly aware of Jack's nearness to her, of the sound of his voice, of how glad she was that he was here and not killed or critically injured in a hospital somewhere.

"How are you holding up?" Hannah asked him. "Are you in a lot of pain still?"

"It's all right," Jack said. "I'm still on pain meds, which are helping. And Mom's been running around trying to wait on me hand and foot. I'm going back to my apartment tomorrow."

"Where Mrs. Kowalski will try to do the same thing."

He chuckled. "Probably."

"I'm bringing you dinner one of these days," Hannah said. "I'll make you a lasagna, and don't you dare say no. There's no way you can cook with your arm in a sling."

Jack laughed. "All right, all right. Thank you, Hannah."

"You're welcome, Jack."

So many things she wanted to say to him, and no way to say them. Under the level of the table, Hannah slipped her hand into Jack's.

He looked at her, surprise in his eyes, followed by a look of understanding that made Hannah catch her breath. His hand tightened around hers.

And they were still at the crowded dinner table.

"Hannah," Jack said, "why don't I give you a tour of the farm?"

Hannah got up. "I'd love one. I'll get my coat."

❧❦❧

The siblings and cousins were all eating pie when Hannah and Jack slipped out, although Hannah had an idea Julia had noticed them leaving. They strolled toward the nearest orchard, a grove of apple trees.

"Your parents' farm is lovely," Hannah said. "It must have been really cool growing up here."

He nodded. "You ought to see it in the summer, when everything is green and the cherries are ripe. Of course, I say that now. Back when I used to help with the cherry harvest, the only thing cherries meant was hard work."

Hannah laughed. "That work sounds kind of interesting. It

would be a good subject for a video."

Jack nodded. "A lot of farm life would make a good subject for a video. It's funny how many people in America don't know a thing about where their food comes from. Around World War II, one in three Americans lived on a farm. Now it's more like one in twenty-eight families."

"I hadn't ever thought of that," Hannah said. "Wow. Everybody depends on the farmers, and most people don't even know what they do." A video series on farm life could be really educational.

"Including you, I bet," Jack said. "Why don't I show you the animals? I can point out the difference between a cow and a goat."

Hannah laughed. "I think I've got that one down, thanks."

They went up the rise to the barnyard, which had one big barn and a number of other outbuildings. Hannah was glad she wore boots with sturdy heels, because although it was November, the ground still had some give to it. Cows stood around in the yard.

"Do you keep them outside?" Hannah asked.

Jack nodded. "They live in the pasture in the summertime. We put them in the barnyard in the winter — they can go in there if they want." He motioned to a smaller barn, left open, on one side of the yard.

"Wow," Hannah said. "I didn't know cows could live outside year-round. Are they milk cows?"

"Beef," Jack said. "Dairy cattle are different and require more work. With these, pretty much all you have to do is feed them. They get a container of grain every day — which is cracked corn — and every so often they get a new bale of hay in their feeder."

They went into the big barn by a large side door. Unlike

Alex's family's barn, which was completely open and could be cleared out for events, this barn had stalls on each side for animals. Jack's family had several goats, two sheep, and a pinto horse named Little Joe. Little Joe, Jack explained, belonged to the girls. They had all pooled their money to buy him at an auction last year.

"In the spring, we'll have a few more animals," Jack said. "The girls and David do 4-H. They raise animals and show them at the county fair, where people buy them."

"That must be hard," Hannah said. "Selling the animals after they've worked with them, I mean."

Jack nodded. "It is. They always cry. It's one of the tough things about being a farm kid. But I think the whole thing is a good experience to have."

Hannah couldn't imagine having responsibility for something so big as a farm animal when she was as young as Jack's brother David. Growing up in the country must be a whole different experience. Maybe that was why Jack was the way he was.

"Did you ever raise animals for 4-H?" she asked.

Jack nodded. "Cattle, mostly. My dad thought about switching over to just raising beef. He decided to stick with a variety of things."

"And then you decided to leave the farm and become a police officer," Hannah said. "Do you ever regret it?" They were standing by the open door, the golden evening light streaming into the barn.

Jack shook his head. "If we were all farmers, who'd go out

and chase the bad guys?"

Right. Bad guys like Blake.

"Jack," Hannah said, "I can't tell you how grateful I am for what you did, chasing Blake. And I still feel terrible that you got hurt doing it."

He shook his head. "Don't feel bad. That wasn't your fault. I'm just glad that drunk driver didn't kill anybody."

"I feel bad anyway." Hannah gently touched Jack's injured arm. "It must be a real pain going around like that."

"It won't be for long. Just a few weeks. The doctor said I might have the sling off before Christmas." Jack's expression was thoughtful. "I've got a question for you. My memory from the night of the accident is pretty hazy, so I don't remember everything too well. But when I was in the hospital, in the middle of the night, you were there."

Hannah nodded. "I drove out with Grace."

"You had just been through a traumatic experience yourself," Jack said. "Most people don't rush out to the hospital in the middle of the night on the off chance the doctors will let them in. Why did you?"

Hannah took his good hand, lacing her fingers through his.

"I know it seems silly," she said, looking down at their linked hands, "but I felt so horrible that you had gotten hurt on my account, and I needed to be there with you."

He smiled, his hand tightening around hers. His presence, safe and comforting, gave her strength.

"Jack." Hannah's voice was almost a whisper. "You're my best friend. But I've realized—you're more than that to me. I didn't know how much I cared about you until I was afraid I'd lost you."

A warm light had come into Jack's eyes, and he spoke slowly. "You know how I feel about you. But I won't try to push you into anything, Hannah. You told me once that you only thought of me as a friend. I don't want you thinking you have to be more than that because of the thing with Blake and the car accident."

She shook her head. "That's not why. I know now that I never even really liked Blake. He was from the big city, and he flattered me—and I let myself get carried away by my pride. But all along, deep down, I should have known that wasn't what I wanted. I want a good, kind man—the sort who rescues me when I'm in trouble and makes sure I eat a real lunch. The sort who's still kind to me, even when I pushed him away. I'm so sorry for that, and for everything."

"Hannah."

Jack's voice was gentle, and she found the courage to meet his eyes. She'd seen that expression in them before, once or twice, and suddenly her heart raced fast enough to get a speeding ticket.

Hannah raised her face to his, drawing closer to him. Jack leaned toward her, his eyes dropping to her lips, and Hannah's own eyes fluttered closed as she leaned toward him.

"Jack? Hannah? Are you in here?"

Startled, Hannah turned, letting go of Jack's hand, her heart still pounding.

Zita, Jack's youngest sister, peeked into the barn entrance.

"There you are," Zita announced. "Will you two come and play charades with us? It's way more fun when the older ones play."

Jack burst out laughing, and Hannah couldn't help laughing too.

"Sure, sure, Zita," Jack said. "If Hannah wants to play."

"Sure, I'll play." Charades with Jack's family had to be entertaining.

"Yay," Zita said.

She skipped ahead of them, and behind her back, as they followed her out of the barn, Jack took Hannah's hand.

The Dinner

Monday hit like a freight train. Hannah could hardly believe the long weekend was over and she was back at work. Blake was gone—Steve was looking for a new forklift driver—and the safe was still empty of cash. The mill office still felt boring without Jack, but Hannah had a job to do. It was all right that the new dispatcher wasn't a chatty guy. He was doing what Steve had hired him to do, and that was the important thing.

Halfway through the morning, a voice spoke above Hannah's head. "Morning, Hannah."

She looked up. Jack leaned against her desk.

It couldn't be him. He didn't work here anymore. He was recuperating from an injury. Maybe she had fallen asleep at her desk, and this was a dream.

"Jack." Hannah blinked. "What are you doing here?"

"My dad dropped me off," Jack said. "I know how you feel about Mondays. Want some coffee, or something?"

He was smiling, and Hannah's Monday morning blues were replaced by a happy fuzzy feeling. Jack had stopped in just to make her Monday better?

"Aw, Jack. Thank you. I'd love a cup of coffee. I started the coffeemaker and then completely forgot about it."

He disappeared into the break room. Hannah's eyes lingered on the doorway.

How had she ever refused Jack when he asked her out? Hadn't she noticed how warm his eyes were behind his glasses and how handsome he looked with the front strand of his hair flopping into his face?

Well, maybe she could make up for her refusal somehow. She knew how Jack felt about her. She'd been trying to let him know how she felt about him yesterday in the barn, before Zita had interrupted. What she and Jack really needed was some one-on-one time to talk about things. Specifically, a date. And since she had turned Jack down the last two times he asked, it only seemed fair that it was her turn.

By the time Jack returned with the coffee — liberally doctored with cream and sugar, just the way Hannah liked it — she had figured out what she wanted to say. For some reason, her pulse fluttered. It was ridiculous to be nervous. But she got herself to smile at him as he leaned against the desk next to her.

"Jack," Hannah said. "I've been thinking. Unless you have other plans tomorrow night — will you take me out to dinner?"

Jack smiled, and the dimple to the left of his mouth appeared. "On a date?"

Hannah nodded. "On a date."

His eyes shone. "Great," he said. "Where do you want to go? I'm not supposed to drive with my arm in a sling, so if you're okay with driving we could go someplace fancy in Cadillac. Or we could go to the diner here in town. Whatever you'd rather do."

She had been to a bunch of fancy places with pretentious menus with Blake. She was tired of fancy places. "Let's go to the diner," Hannah said. "Give those Fraser's Mill gossips something to talk about."

Jack laughed. "Want me to drop by your house at six?"

"You're going to pick me up? You can't drive with your arm—you mean you're going to walk to my house?"

Jack nodded. "I'm old-fashioned."

So different from Blake, meeting at restaurants and being late. Hannah smiled. "All right then. Six o'clock tomorrow."

෧෨෨෬෧

Tuesday evening, at six o'clock on the dot, Jack showed up on Hannah's doorstep, and they went down to the diner.

Hannah had had a day and a half to anticipate this date— playing all the possibilities in her head, wondering how things would go, imagining what she would talk about. It was different being friends with somebody and going on a date with him. What if it didn't go well?

But when Jack actually arrived, Hannah forgot about all the things that could go wrong. He was good looking in a suit and a long wool coat. (The left sleeve of the coat hung loosely, as his arm was in a sling underneath.) Hannah was glad she had dressed nicely herself, wearing a cream-colored Fair Isle sweater dress, tights, and boots.

A few weeks ago, Hannah would never have considered rush hour at the Fraser's Mill diner to be a romantic date. The place was full of customers, and they learned upon coming in the door that they would have to wait some time to be seated.

Jack looked at Hannah. "Would you rather go somewhere else?" he asked. "I'm sorry. I forgot how busy this place gets."

Hannah shook her head. "Let's stay here. I don't mind it being a little loud."

Jack chuckled. "Still quieter than Sunday dinner at the farm."

One of the great things about Jack was how easy it was to talk to him. They had a long wait for their food, even after they were seated, but Hannah wouldn't have cared if it had been ten hours. Any nervousness she had felt before Jack picked her up had melted away. She was just there with her best friend.

"I mentioned to Barb that I was going on a date," Jack said. "Now half the town's probably talking about us."

Hannah laughed. "Let them talk."

"I still don't know why there are so many people here on a Tuesday." Jack surveyed the packed restaurant. "Maybe they all ran out of Thanksgiving leftovers at the same time."

A Tuesday?

"You know something, Jack?" Hannah asked.

"What?"

"It's Tuesday. I always put out a video on Tuesdays, and usually I spend half the week worrying about what I'm posting. Now it's Tuesday night and I completely forgot. And you know what?" Hannah smiled. "I don't even care."

He looked concerned. "Gee, Hannah, I know how much that channel means to you. Do you want me to help you film something tonight?"

Hannah shook her head. "No. I'll make a video tomorrow. The viewers can deal with it."

"Are you sure?" He looked ready to spring up and do her bidding, even if she asked him to film a full movie from scratch tonight.

"Totally," Hannah said. "There are some things that are more important than putting a video out on time."

"Hold up," Jack said. "Dinner with me is more important than getting a video out? Who are you, and what have you done with Hannah Fraser?"

Hannah laughed. "Let's say I've had a change in priorities."

When their dinner finally came—Hannah got meatloaf and Jack got chili and cornbread—it was worth the wait. They split a piece of chocolate cake for dessert, lingering over it, talking about anything and everything.

"Excuse me." Charlie stood by their table. "I hate to rush you guys, but I've got the morning shift tomorrow, and I should really get home and get some sleep."

"Oh, I'm so sorry, Charlie." Hannah hadn't realized they were the only ones in the restaurant. "Sure, we can go." She got up.

The clock on the wall said ten PM. Had they really been there for almost four hours?

"No problem." Charlie waved a hand. "Come to the front, and we'll settle up. I probably don't need to ask this, but is the check separate or together?"

"Together," Jack said, and Hannah had never heard him sound so proud.

At the log house, Jack walked Hannah to the front porch. She had offered to drop him at his apartment on the way back, but he said he liked to see a lady home and didn't mind walking back.

They stood in front of the door, under the porch light. "Well," Jack said, and seemed at a loss for words.

They both laughed.

"Well," Hannah said, "thank you, Jack. I had a wonderful time."

"Me too." Jack hesitated. "Hannah, I know you've been through a lot this weekend. After all that, I imagine you don't want to jump into anything new right now."

"What are you saying?"

Jack reached up, cupping Hannah's cheek in his hand, his touch feather-light.

"You told me I was more than just a friend to you. But things have been so crazy this last week. With Blake, and the accident. And that kind of thing can be confusing."

He thought she wasn't really interested in him. Well, Hannah had been doing some soul-searching herself. She could put that worry to rest.

She shook her head. "It wasn't just the last week. Jack, I should have seen a long time ago that I liked you as more than a friend. That time you took in my dock, and we had cocoa. I didn't want you to leave. And that time we sat together in the treehouse." Just thinking about it made her blush. "I don't know how I could have been so blind not to see that I liked you."

A little smile crossed Jack's face. "I've got some glasses if you need them."

Hannah laughed. "I think I would have needed a stronger prescription than that." Jack's coat lapel was turned up on one side, and she reached up and fixed it, her hand lingering. "You were the one I really cared about, all along, and I didn't see it."

He smiled for real now. "How about when you called me a goody two-shoes farm kid in a Canadian tuxedo?"

"Did I say that? I guess I like goody two-shoes farm kids in Canadian tuxedos."

Jack chuckled. "Hannah," he said, and looked as if he were about to say something else, but changed his mind. "Hannah—"

"Jack," she said, "you can say my name all night if you want—I love hearing you say it—but I'm tired of waiting. Are you going to kiss me, or should I say goodnight and go in?"

He laughed. "You have to get up for work, is that it?"

"Your sister interrupted us the last time." Hannah made her tone sound as aggrieved as possible.

"Then it's a good thing my siblings aren't here." Jack stroked her face again, gently drawing her closer.

"Yeah," Hannah breathed, raising her face to his.

Jack bent his head and kissed her—slowly, gently—and she leaned into him, kissing him back.

News from the Sheriff's Office

On Thursday morning, Hannah texted Jack. "Would tonight be a good night for me to make you lasagna?"

"That sounds wonderful," Jack replied. "If you want, you could make it at my place. I can help one-handed."

"That sounds great."

Accordingly, after work, Hannah went to the store and picked up the ingredients. The only lasagna noodles Murray's Grocery sold were the no-boil kind, but Hannah always boiled them anyway. She'd never been successful with the no-boil kind on its own—the lasagna always turned out crunchy.

Jack was a good help in the kitchen, even though he could only do things with one hand. He got things out for Hannah, set timers, and helped layer the lasagna in the pan. He set a table for two.

Jack had news about his job. Sheriff Hank said he could work in the sheriff's office again, helping with whatever he could there, starting on Friday.

"There's one thing I know about you," Hannah told Jack. She put the pan of lasagna into the oven to brown. "You're not a slacker."

Jack grinned. "I've got to do something, or I'll go crazy. If the sheriff hadn't let me come back to work, I'd have had to go home and help my mom around the kitchen."

They were sitting on the couch, waiting for the lasagna to bake and talking about politics (Jack seemed to know a good deal about politics) when Jack's phone rang, and he got up to answer it.

"Hello, Sheriff," he said. "What's going on?"

Hannah tried not to listen. It was probably important police business, and she wasn't a police officer and didn't need to know. Still, it was tempting. She went to Jack's bookcase and looked through his books.

He must read a lot. He had books on topics ranging from philosophy and theology to westerns and King Arthur. He had a lot of books on politics and the current situation in America.

"Thanks, Sheriff, I'll let Hannah know," Hannah heard Jack say as he ended the call.

"Let me know what?" Hannah demanded, putting back the book she'd been examining.

"Blake's been arrested," Jack said. "He was trying to rob a gas station in a small town up north near Traverse City."

"Oh, wow." The thought of Blake in handcuffs, heading to jail, was weird. "Do they need me to come in and identify him or anything?"

"There's no need," Jack said. "He had his ID in his pocket,

and the license plate number on the car was the same one you gave the sheriff. You will have to appear in court eventually, but that'll probably be a while."

"Did they find the money he stole?"

"I don't know. I don't think anybody knows where he was hiding out, yet. He wasn't at his apartment in Cadillac—the police checked that out a while ago. But he must have been somewhere in the area."

Hannah shook her head. "I can't believe he would keep going around with the same car and his ID in his pocket, even after I identified him robbing the mill. And then he tried to rob another place? I thought he would have fled the state, or even the country. He was always talking about all these far-off places he used to go. The Taj Mahal and stuff like that."

Jack shrugged. "I don't know. Sometimes criminals stay in the area because they know most people expect them to flee. Blake must have been lying low someplace around here. The sheriff says he hadn't heard anything about his possible whereabouts before that."

"Wow," Hannah said. "What a dumb thing to do—robbing a gas station while he was trying to hide."

Jack nodded. "I'm guessing Blake hasn't been at this robbery business that long."

"I don't know how he got into it in the first place." Hannah sank down on the couch. "His parents know my parents. He went to some Ivy League college—I don't remember which one, but he ought to have gotten a degree that could get him some kind of good job. Why would he start stealing—and why would he steal from people that know his parents? Steve thinks he might have lost money trading cryptocurrency, but that's just a hunch."

Jack sat down next to her. "Maybe we'll find out," he said. "He was in Chicago for a while. They've got crime in Chicago. Maybe he was involved in something back there before he ever came out here." He shook his head, a twinkle in his eye. "You're from Chicago, Hannah. Are you secretly a gang member, planning to rob the Fraser's Mill community of everything we possess?"

Hannah laughed. "Of course. I'm the great-great-granddaughter of Al Capone, and I'm gonna be the crime boss for the entire Midwest."

"Hope you like Alcatraz, then," Jack said. "They still give tours—I'm sure they could fix up a place for you."

ᕲᓂᓇᓀᓇᓂᕲ

The preliminary hearing for Blake's trial was on December 14th, and Hannah was called in as a witness.

She had never been in a courtroom before, let alone been a witness to a crime. The summons informed her that she would need to present her testimony before the court and possibly be cross-examined by the counsel for the defense. She would greatly have preferred not being involved, but her family was still missing money that Blake had stolen, so she also had a personal stake in the matter. The night before the hearing, she practiced her testimony to Jack, trying to make it as clear as possible. She had to get off work for the hearing, which was in the morning. Steve would take over her office duties while she was gone.

360

Jack came with her — she drove, because he still had his arm in a sling — and they went to the nearest district court, where the preliminary hearing was. Jack wore his police uniform. He was on duty for this.

It was a cold day, and Hannah shivered as they walked up to the courthouse.

"Are you all right?" Jack asked. "You don't have anything to be nervous about. Just tell your story the way you told it to the sheriff."

"I know," Hannah said. "I feel dumber and dumber about not calling the police right away. The whole thing got so much worse after I confronted him. I'll have to explain what a dummy I was, in front of everybody."

It was an opportunity for Jack to say "I told you so," but he didn't say it. "It's all right," he said instead. "We've all taken risks that worked out badly. If I'd been in your place, I probably would have been tempted to confront Blake too."

That was comforting, even if it didn't completely solve the problem.

Blake was sitting in the front of the courtroom. Hannah recognized the back of his head.

She and Jack found seats. Hannah looked around. There were familiar faces. Grace waved to Hannah from across the room. Her family probably wanted to know if any information had come out about their store getting robbed.

The gas station owner, Ed, was there as well. Probably interested to find out if Blake was the guy who had robbed his gas station.

The prosecution and the defense were there, and the judge

came into the room. "All rise," someone said, and Hannah rose.

Blake looked over his shoulder and caught Hannah's eye. His expression was hard. Hannah looked away. How could she ever have thought that man was attractive? Good thing she had caught him robbing the mill — what if she'd gone on dating him and then been suspected as an accomplice in his robberies?

The lawyer for the prosecution began to lay out the case against Blake. She called her first witness, the man who had caught Blake trying to rob his gas station near Traverse City. The man was a tall, thin guy in jeans and a plaid shirt.

"It was the middle of the afternoon on Wednesday," he said, "and a man in a black hoodie, with a black ski mask on, came into the gas station. I was over on one side of the store, restocking things, and Shawna over there" — he motioned to a fifty-something woman with gray hair in a ponytail — "was at the counter. There wasn't anybody else in the place. It was a slow afternoon. This guy came up to the counter and pulled a gun on Shawna. And he said, 'Give me all the money in the cash register.' I came up behind him and pulled out my own gun — I got a concealed carry permit — and told him to drop it and put his hands in the air. Then I told Shawna to call the police."

"And that's why we have concealed carry," Jack said in Hannah's ear.

She nodded. "Maybe I ought to get my own permit. I could learn how to shoot."

Jack grinned at her. "Good thing you know a police officer. I can teach you."

The prosecution was speaking to the witness. "Do you

identify the defendant as the same man who was trying to rob the gas station?"

"Yes," the gas station owner said. "I made him take off the ski mask. It's the same guy."

Shawna, the other gas station worker, came up to testify next. She corroborated the story of the first witness.

It was Hannah's turn.

"Good luck," Jack whispered to her as she got out of her seat. She threw him a grateful look. The walk up to the witness stand seemed long.

Under oath, Hannah laid out the whole story of Thanksgiving night as she had witnessed it. Blake sat glaring at her from his seat, and she did her best not to look in his direction.

When she had finished, she expected to go down to her seat, but instead the lawyer for the defense — a young man with slicked-back blond hair — asked to cross-examine her.

This was the part she had been most nervous about. Jack told her that the cross-examination could include leading questions, and since she had been going out with Blake before the robbery, she didn't know how the defense might use that information.

"Miss Fraser," the defense attorney said, "you were going out with the defendant in the weeks prior to Thanksgiving, weren't you?"

"Yes."

"And within the week leading up to Thanksgiving, you had quarreled with the defendant?"

That wasn't really a yes-no question, and Hannah stopped to mull it over before answering. Blake must have told the lawyer to bring that up for purposes of his own. If she said yes, that wouldn't be a fair representation—they had argued during the movie afternoon, but had parted amicably. If she said no, that wouldn't be completely accurate either.

"I wouldn't call it a quarrel. The defendant and I were on good terms the week of Thanksgiving after a slight disagreement a few days before," Hannah said at last.

The defense attorney's shoulders slumped. "No more questions, Your Honor."

Phew. Hopefully nobody would try to drag Hannah into this any further, not with all the evidence against Blake. Hannah returned to her seat.

"Good job," Jack said in her ear.

"Thanks," she whispered back.

The rest of the hearing went quickly, and at the end the judge announced that Blake would have to stand trial.

"There," Jack told Hannah, as they filed out of the building with the other people. "If Blake takes a plea deal—which would probably be the smart thing to do, because I don't think you could possibly convince a whole jury that he isn't guilty—we're all done. Except for getting the money back."

"I wonder where he's keeping it," Hannah said. "Dad and Steve won't be happy until it's found."

Christmas in Fraser's Mill

On December 20th, Blake took a plea deal. He confessed to the attempted armed robbery at the gas station and the burglary at the mill. Hannah learned this when the sheriff called her and asked her to come into the sheriff's office. The police had recovered the missing cashbox from the mill safe.

"Did you ever find out whether Blake robbed the Fraser's Mill gas station or the grocery store?" Hannah asked the sheriff, when she had come in to fetch the cashbox.

Sheriff Hank nodded. "He confessed to those too. He had a lot of money stashed away. Hadn't spent it yet. He owed a lot of money to a guy back in Chicago. Seems he was trading cryptocurrency for somebody else when the crypto market crashed."

"Wow," Hannah said. "I guess that explains why he was desperate. I hope he can go straight now."

The sheriff nodded. "Hope so. He's still young. He can become a productive member of society yet."

"Thanks a lot, Sheriff," Hannah said. "Steve and my dad are gonna be really happy we have the money back."

"I'm relieved this whole thing is over," Jack called from the other side of the room, where he was going through paperwork one-handed. "Now we can all get back to normal."

"I know, right?" Hannah said. "All those robberies—Fraser's Mill was beginning to feel like it wasn't such a safe little town anymore."

The sheriff chuckled. "Now we can go back to warning people to watch for deer."

It was probably time for Hannah to go. They were done talking about Blake, and she didn't want to get Jack in trouble by hanging around his work.

"Well," she said, "I'd better get back to the mill."

"Wait a second," Jack said. "Hannah, come look at this." He held up a red-and-green flyer.

"Save the date for the Fraser's Mill Christmas Dance!" the flyer said. "December 30th at the fire hall. Fancy dress. See you there!"

A Christmas dance sounded special. It would be an opportunity to dress up, too.

"Will you go with me?" Jack's eyes smiled behind his glasses.

"I'd love to." Hannah beamed at him.

"It's fancy dress," Jack said. "Just like Chicago, eh?"

Hannah laughed. "Let's give Chicago a run for their money. Do you still have that tuxedo?"

"I'm pretty sure I can come up with something."

It was December 23rd, and Hannah was closing up the mill office after work. The place would be closed until after New Year's. Tomorrow was Christmas Eve, but it didn't feel like it.

Hannah had never been out in the country for Christmas before. All the special things her family would do around the holidays — visiting relatives, driving around to look at Christmas lights, watching the Nutcracker onstage, Christmas shopping in the city, listening to a gorgeous Festival of Lessons and Carols at St. John Cantius — were things she couldn't do in Fraser's Mill. As much as she had come to appreciate the people in the little community here, she wasn't sure how a Christmas in Fraser's Mill would be. At least she would spend Christmas morning with Steve and Christine's family.

Thinking of Chicago — she had to figure out what to do. Before everything with Jack, there hadn't even been a question about it. She'd planned on going back there as soon as her parents returned from their house swap. But now she wasn't sure what she wanted. The thought of leaving Jack and going long-distance wasn't appealing. But did she really want to stay here in little Fraser's Mill?

Hannah buttoned her coat and went out the office door, locking it carefully. Behind her, car tires crunched on the gravel. If somebody was trying to buy lumber at this hour, it was too late.

She turned around to see a police car in the lot.

What was this? Was she in some kind of trouble? Had something new happened with Blake? She squinted toward the police car, blinded by the headlights.

The passenger door opened, and a tall, familiar silhouette

stepped out. Thank goodness, she probably wasn't in trouble. It was Jack. Just the person she wanted to see.

"Jack." Hannah hurried over to him, catching her boot heel on an icy patch and falling into him.

He caught her one-armed, laughing as he steadied her. "Trying to sprain your ankle again right before Christmas, Hannah?"

She laughed, hugging him. "What are you doing here?"

"I got done with my shift, and the sheriff offered to drop me off." Jack nodded toward the police car, now pulling out of the lot. "I have a question for you. I know you probably have Christmas plans with your family. But my mom asked me to invite you to Christmas dinner at the farm. If you want to come, of course."

It sounded like something straight out of *Little House on the Prairie*. "Totally," Hannah said. "I'd love to. I'll be at Steve and Christine's on Christmas morning, and my whole family's doing a video call, but I didn't have anything planned for the evening."

Jack smiled. "Wonderful. I'll tell my mom. Just to warn you, the house will be full and loud."

"I don't mind. It'll be fun."

Snow had begun to fall, illuminated by the lights in the parking lot and dusting Jack's dark hair. He looked up, snowflakes landing on his glasses. "Looks like we're having a white Christmas this year."

"The best kind," Hannah said. "Although it doesn't feel much like Christmas to me."

"Why's that?" Jack looked down at her.

"I've never not been in Chicago for Christmas," Hannah

said. "Everything is so exciting, with the lights and the holiday activities and the people. It isn't the same here."

"Hmm," Jack said. "That won't do. What you need is a little Fraser's Mill holiday cheer. Got any time this evening?"

"Time to do what?"

"Why don't we make Christmas cookies at my apartment?" Jack asked. "I didn't have a lot of time to go Christmas shopping for my family this year, and a few cookies will help to round out the presents."

"I'd love to," Hannah said. "Right now? Have you had dinner? Do you have the ingredients?"

"I've got dinner in the Crock-Pot back home," Jack said. "Do you like clam chowder? And sourdough bread? We'd just have to stop by the store for cookie ingredients."

"Clam chowder sounds amazing."

Hannah drove with Jack to Murray's Grocery, falling snow dancing across her car's windshield. Main Street of Fraser's Mill had transformed in the last few days. Twinkling Christmas lights decorated almost every house and store, and wreaths hung on the street lights.

In the grocery store, Hannah and Jack filled a cart with cookie-making supplies. Flour. Sugar. Butter. Baking soda. Molasses. Mini marshmallows. Red and green sugar. Chow mein noodles.

"Good thing we got here now," Jack said. "They'll probably be out of most of these things by tomorrow morning. Everybody does their Christmas baking at the last minute."

The store's front counter was wreathed in greenery, and behind the counter, Grace was cheery in a red sweater and green apron. "Merry Christmas," she told Hannah and Jack. "Am I going to see you two at Midnight Mass?"

Jack looked at Hannah. "Want to go?" he asked. "Unless you're planning to go with Steve and Christine."

She shook her head. "They go to a four PM vigil with the kids," she said. "I'd love to go to Midnight Mass."

"Great," Grace said. "We've got carols starting at eleven-thirty. Mary Jane picked out some really pretty ones this year."

"I feel bad I haven't been at choir in a while," Hannah said. "There were so many things going on—with Jack—and the robbery business—"

"Don't worry about it," Grace said. "We miss you, but everybody understands."

"Well, I'm excited for tomorrow night," Hannah said. "Thanks, Grace."

❧❧❧❧❧

Barb Kowalski's house smelled deliciously of clam chowder as soon as they walked in the door.

"I'm gonna bring Barb some soup and bread." Jack dashed down the basement stairs with the groceries at an alarming speed. Hannah followed more slowly.

Jack's apartment looked like it was in the middle of Christmas preparations. A bushy green Christmas tree, bare of ornaments, stood by one wall. Near the tree sat an assortment of Christmas wrapping supplies and some things to be wrapped, most of them books. It would be tough for Jack to wrap gifts with his arm in a sling. Maybe he'd let Hannah help.

"Want to start up some Christmas music?" Jack asked. "I've got some records."

Hannah hadn't noticed the record player next to Jack's couch before. While Jack bustled around setting the table and getting Barb her soup and bread, Hannah perused his record collection. He seemed to listen to a lot of old music. Hannah picked out a Bing Crosby Christmas record and put it in the player.

In a few minutes, Jack had taken up Barb's food and returned to eat dinner with Hannah. He had changed out of his police uniform. Now he was wearing jeans and a cozy dark blue sweater that made Hannah want to hug him.

The clam chowder was rich and tangy, pairing perfectly with the sourdough. It was so good, Hannah had to close her eyes to enjoy it.

"Good?" Jack's voice asked.

Hannah opened her eyes. Jack was watching her, his face amused.

"So good," Hannah said. "I could just melt."

He laughed. "Don't melt yet. We've still got to make cookies. I'm gonna show you the best Christmas Fraser's Mill has ever had."

The soup cleared away, Jack pulled out cookbooks from a cupboard. He brought out two aprons.

"What's this?" Hannah looked suspiciously at the frilly red-and-white checked apron that Jack handed to her. "You have women's aprons in your apartment?"

Jack laughed. "It's Barb's. I borrowed it when I brought her the soup."

Hannah laughed. "Good."

"Jealous again, Hannah?" Jack leaned against the kitchen counter, his smile a challenge.

"Of course not," Hannah said. "Wait a minute. You're implying I was jealous before, when that girl kept coming to the mill office and calling you."

Jack raised an eyebrow. "Well?"

Hannah threw up her hands. "Okay, I was totally jealous. I guess I didn't want to admit it—even to myself."

His smile grew broader. "Look at that. Hannah Fraser owning up to her true feelings."

"Oh, shut up." She swatted at him. "Are we going to bake those cookies or what?"

They measured and mixed, starting out with a sugar cookie recipe that was a tradition in Hannah's family.

"My mom has all these fantastic cookie cutters," Hannah said. "But if you don't have cookie cutters, we can make cardboard cutouts and trace around them instead."

"I've got cardboard," Jack said. "What shapes do you want?"

"Well, let's not try anything too crazy. How about bells—and stars—and Christmas trees?"

"Anything you want," Jack said. "Unless you want a full-size model of Fraser's Historic Water-Powered Sawmill."

Hannah laughed. "That old thing? Not very Christmassy."

She rolled out the dough as Jack rummaged in a drawer for cardboard. The dough was stiff—good, because it would take a lot of handling—but it made it hard to roll out.

"Jack, do you think this is thin enough?"

He came up behind her, one arm going around her waist, his

cheek resting against her hair. "It looks good to me."

She laughed, relaxing into his hold. "Don't blame me if these cookies end up half an inch thick."

How had she not realized long ago that while being anywhere close to Blake made her nervous and jittery, being close to Jack was calming and secure—like coming home? How had she not seen that the perfect person for her was the man who had quietly become her best friend?

They made sugar cookies, gingerbread men, and haystacks (a Rogers Christmas staple) all while Christmas records sounded cheerfully from the player and the snow fell outside.

"Jack, are you going to put any ornaments on that tree?" Hannah asked, testing a melt-in-your-mouth sugar cookie during a lull in the baking.

"Sure," Jack said. "Actually, why don't we decorate it together? Unless you have to go."

Hannah shook her head, smiling. "I can't think of one single thing I have to do. I'd love to decorate your tree with you."

In Chicago, Hannah's mom had always put up two different Christmas trees. She would do themes for the ornaments, like all gold or all snowmen. She wanted her tree to look classy—no little-kid art project ornaments in the Fraser household.

Jack's tree was different. He pulled out a box of ornaments from a closet under the stairs—leftover ornaments from his family, he said—and told Hannah the history of some of the delightful, brightly-colored, mostly vintage decorations. That little shepherd boy was his favorite growing up. Those striped glass balls had belonged to his grandparents. Those pipe cleaner candy canes he had made when he was little.

Jack hung the higher ornaments. Hannah hung the lower ones. Working together, they wrapped strings of white and multi-colored Christmas lights around the tree. Jack brought out a glazed ceramic angel for the top of the tree — the angel from his Nativity scene, he said — and put it on top.

"Come on, let's turn the lights on," Hannah said. "It already looks so pretty, and it isn't even lit yet!"

"Wait a second," Jack said. "Here. You get ready to plug them in. I'll turn off the overhead light."

In darkness, the Christmas tree bloomed with sudden light. Hannah stood to appreciate it, letting out a long breath. "It's beautiful."

Jack took her hand. "It might be the nicest one I've ever had."

"It's just so quaint and old-fashioned and sweet." Hannah leaned her head on Jack's shoulder as she admired the handmade and vintage ornaments nestled in the branches. "I love it."

People weren't decorating trees like that in Chicago — at least, not anybody Hannah knew — but Chicago could take some pointers from Jack's family.

Chicago. Hannah's parents would be back there in March, and Hannah could go back home if she wanted to. She'd been so excited about that before. But now, with Jack's hand in hers, Chicago didn't seem so interesting anymore.

◦◦◦◦◦◦

On Christmas Eve, right before eleven-thirty, Jack showed up at Hannah's house to walk her to Midnight Mass. They didn't have far to go — the church was only a couple houses down. Snow squished underfoot, and the stars twinkled above, looking higher and brighter than usual in the crisp air. The town was quiet, most of the windows dark.

Inside the church was ablaze with candles and decorated with trees and greenery and poinsettias. Hannah and Jack sat in a pew as the choir sang above them — old hymns and new, English, Latin, and even German and Spanish, the high and low voices blending seamlessly.

You didn't have to have a big church with an elite choir to have special music for Christmas. You just needed random people who loved singing for the glory of God and a good director to pull them together. Hannah ought to sing with the choir more, now that things had settled down with the mill.

Altar boys served Midnight Mass in red cassocks and surplices. Father John preached on the Incarnation, quoting Venerable Fulton Sheen: "If man is ever to be lifted up, God, in some way, must come down to man."

Christmas wasn't about the exterior trappings, the decorations, the activities — as special as those were. All of those things were supposed to point to the One who came to save the world.

In the vestibule after Mass, people crowded around, wishing each other a merry Christmas. Grace and Doc, Alex and Charlie, Elaine, Jack's family — everyone beamed with happy excitement, despite the late hour.

At two-thirty, Hannah tore herself away. After all, she had Christmas morning with Steve and Christine's family.

"Well, what do you think of Fraser's Mill Christmases now?"

Jack asked as he and Hannah walked back in the snow, their footsteps loud in the quiet night.

Hannah drew a deep breath, throwing her head back to watch the stars glitter. "Just wonderful."

"Good." Jack squeezed her gloved hand. "Missing Chicago?"

"Not at all."

❧

Christmas morning at Steve and Christine's house, with the adults sleepily drinking coffee in their pajamas and Evelyn squealing over her presents, was beautiful chaos—as was the family video call with Hannah's parents in Germany and all her siblings scattered around the U.S.

In the afternoon, Hannah drove down to Jack's family's farm. She parked in the circle driveway in front of the house, appreciating the big Nativity scene in the yard, and went up to the front door, which bore an enormous wreath.

Jack opened it, handsome in a cream-colored sweater (his arm still in the sling) and jeans. "Hannah." He smiled. "Come on in!" He folded her into a hug. "I'm so glad you could come."

"I wouldn't have missed it." Hannah smiled up at him.

The entryway was strung with Christmas greenery and full of boots and coats. Various Rogers relatives were bustling through. Hannah didn't recognize some of them. They must be visiting for Christmas.

"Let me take your coat." Jack helped her with it, one-armed. "Wow." He appraised her, eyebrows raised, admiration written all over his face. "You look fantastic."

Hannah smiled. She'd hoped Jack would like her red sweater dress, worn with tights and boots. "Thanks, Jack."

"Let me introduce you to some people," Jack said. "You've met my siblings and some cousins, but you don't know my cousin Claire—she just moved to Fraser's Mill—and do you know Grace's brother Thomas?"

Hannah shook her head. "I still don't know a lot of the people here."

"Come with me." Jack took her hand, bringing her to the living room. They stopped in the doorway, looking in. The room was almost completely full. People—mostly kids and young adults—sat around on couches and chairs and the piano bench and even the floor.

"Hey, Jack!" a curly-haired young man—probably one of Jack's cousins—called. "Look above your head!"

Hannah looked up. A sprig of greenery with smooth leaves and waxy white berries hung above the doorway. Mistletoe.

"Come on, Jack, you know what you have to do," the curly-haired cousin called.

Caught under the mistletoe. In front of at least a dozen Rogers relatives and friends. Well…Hannah didn't know that she exactly minded.

Hannah looked up at Jack and found him blushing. "I swear, I didn't put that there," he said, just loudly enough for her to hear.

Hannah's smile broadened. "Well, since somebody clearly went to a lot of trouble—"

Jack's mouth quirked. "Wouldn't want all that trouble to go to waste."

He bent his head and kissed her. Hannah threw her arms around his neck, kissing him back, ignoring some ooh-ing and whistles from the peanut gallery.

"Well," Jack said, as they broke apart, "now we've given the small fry something to talk about for a week — why don't we go in the kitchen and say hi to my mom?"

Hannah laughed. "I'd love that."

Apart from the teasing, Jack's extended family was cheerful and friendly. Hannah met aunts and uncles and cousins; struck up an immediate friendship with Jack's newcomer cousin Claire; sat down to eat at a crowded table loaded with ham, kielbasa, sweet potatoes, and cranberries; and sang Christmas carols around the piano.

Sitting on the living room floor by the Christmas tree (they were out of chairs), leaning against Jack as he told the story of the car chase and his separated shoulder to yet another interested person, Hannah didn't want the night to end. Christmas in Fraser's Mill wasn't boring. It was totally perfect.

❧❧❧

Even after the excitement of Christmas Day was over, there was still the Christmas dance to look forward to. Hannah was excited about it. Since it was a fancy occasion, the dress she'd picked out was a long formal one, burgundy, with a sash and lace sleeves. She had worn it years ago to a friend's winter wedding and had always hoped for a reason to wear it again. It seemed silly asking her mom to mail it with her other warm clothes, earlier in the fall, but now she was glad she did.

378

It was the day of the dance, and Hannah was wondering if she should try one of Christine's half-up hairstyles that evening, when her phone rang. It was Mom.

"Hannah," she said. "Our friends, the Campbells, in Chicago, are having their daughter move out in the next couple weeks. They'd be happy to have you live with them—and only pay minimal rent—for a while. It would be a way for you to get back to Chicago before we get back to the U.S. What do you think?"

"Wow," Hannah said. Back in September, she would have been ecstatic to hear this. Now it was interesting, but it didn't really matter.

"I know," Mom said. "It's not the same thing as being at home, but your father and I know the Campbells really well, and they're nice people. And they have a really nice house. You'd like staying there."

"Thanks, Mom," Hannah said. "But things are actually good in Fraser's Mill right now."

"Really?" Mom sounded intrigued, but not surprised.

"Yes. I've gotten a lot better at my mill job. Jack is here, and I've made some friends. Plus Steve and Christine aren't too far away. Please tell Mrs. Campbell thank you for me, but I'm staying here for the rest of the six months."

Mom laughed. "I won the bet. I told your father that if you stayed long enough in Fraser's Mill, you would decide it wasn't so bad after all."

Hannah laughed too. "I guess you were right. I didn't like it here at first. But the people—and even the town—have really grown on me." She bit her lip. "It's something I've been thinking about a lot lately. I feel awful about the idea of leaving. Especially because of Jack, but also, I think I'm gonna miss it here."

"Wow." Mom hesitated. "You know you can stay in Fraser's Mill as long as you want, don't you? I mean, your father and I would miss you, but most of all, we want you to be in a place where you're happy."

That was true. Hannah had been considering the pros and cons of Chicago and Fraser's Mill, but she hadn't put it to herself like that.

She rubbed her neck. "That—wow. Thanks, Mom. I know what I want to say, but I'd better think about it first. I've made a lot of big decisions lately, and I want to make sure I choose the right thing."

"Take your time," Mom said. "After all, we're still in Europe. You've got at least three more months in Fraser's Mill before you have to decide anything for sure."

She hung up, and Hannah sat on the couch to think. It was good she had time to decide what to do. Now she needed to go through her options.

Let's say she went back to Chicago in March. Then she would be back in the city making her videos, and the people of Fraser's Mill would be singing in the choir, putting together dances, and getting ready to plant their gardens without her. And she and Jack would be in a long-distance relationship, which didn't sound easy to Hannah. In the end, if they stayed together, one of them would eventually have to move. And Hannah didn't like the idea of Jack being a Chicago policeman. He had already almost gotten killed on the job, right here in Fraser's Mill.

That settled it. She knew what she wanted to do. Now she just had to tell the people who were important to her—especially Jack.

Well, she'd better start getting ready for tonight's dance.

At six PM on the dot, as Hannah was finishing her hair and makeup, there was a knock at the log house door. Jack must be here.

She whisked downstairs and opened the door. "Jack."

He was standing there, tall under the porch light, wearing his long coat. He had gotten his sling off the day before. "Hannah. You look beautiful."

"Thanks," Hannah said. "Come in? I just have to do a couple more things."

Jack stepped inside. "This is for you." He reached inside his coat, pulling out a single red rose. His smile was sheepish, but his eyes shone.

"Oh, Jack. Thank you." Hannah smiled up at him. "I'll put it in water. I'll be right back."

He must have brought it all the way from Cadillac to surprise her—there wasn't anywhere to buy fresh flowers in Fraser's Mill at this time of year.

Hannah had a surprise of her own for him later.

❧❧❧

Hannah caught her breath as she and Jack walked into the dance and were greeted by a glittering fairyland of Christmas lights, holly, and tinsel. She would hardly have recognized the place as the fire hall. Whoever had decorated had done a beautiful job.

Grace came rushing up to them, resplendent in a red dress and pearls. "Hannah, Jack. I'm glad you could make it."

381

"We wouldn't have missed it," Hannah said. "Did you guys do all this?"

"We had some help," Grace said. "Jim came up with the idea for the dance, and we planned the decorations together. Then a bunch of people volunteered to help set up and decorate. I'm really happy with the way it turned out. Want to hang up your coats? There's a coat rack in the lobby."

In the lobby, Jack helped Hannah out of her coat and hung up his own. He was wearing a tuxedo, and Hannah was thrown back to the Halloween dance, when he'd confessed his feelings for her. Hopefully tonight they could make a new, happier memory together.

Hannah smiled up at him, brushing lint off his shoulder. "You clean up well, Jack."

Jack smiled. "So do you." He offered his arm. "May I have this dance?"

"Are you sure it won't hurt your shoulder? You just got out of the sling."

"I'll be careful," Jack promised. "No fancy stuff. I don't know any fancy stuff, anyway."

Hannah laughed. "When your shoulder's better, we ought to learn together."

Out in the hall, a Frank Sinatra song was playing. Jack swung Hannah onto the dance floor. He clearly hadn't done this a lot, but he had a good sense of rhythm.

Besides, with Jack's arm around her waist and his other hand holding hers as he smiled down at her, what did Hannah care about the exact dance steps they were doing?

They narrowly avoided bumping into another couple, and Hannah laughed. "We should do this more often."

Jack nodded. "There's probably a barn dance coming up." His eyes were serious. "We have some time before you go back to Chicago."

"Jack," Hannah said, but he hadn't finished.

"We ought to talk about what we're going to do when you go back," Jack said. "Long distance relationships aren't easy, but I think they can work if the two people really care about each other. It's not that far from here to Chicago. I can drive down and visit."

He was so earnest, and Hannah couldn't help smiling. "I have something to show you."

"What?" He looked mystified.

"It's on my video channel. After this dance, I'll get my phone and show you. I promise, it's relevant."

In the lobby, with Jack looking over her shoulder, Hannah pulled up the new video she had just made that afternoon.

Jack read the title out loud. "Why I've Decided to Stay in Fraser's Mill." He grasped Hannah's shoulders gently, turning her to face him. "You're staying here?"

Hannah nodded. "That's what I was trying to tell you."

Jack shook his head. "Hannah, you love Chicago. You don't want to be stuck here in a tiny little town."

"Yes, I do." Hannah set her chin firmly. "I've been thinking a lot about it, and I've come to the conclusion that Chicago isn't what I want anymore. I don't care about art and theatre and fancy galas and being around a million people. I guess Fraser's

Mill has kind of grown on me."

He was smiling. "Really."

"I like watching the sunset over the river. And racing around with Grace and Alex and the other people in town, organizing events where everybody already knows each other. I like knowing who my neighbors are and singing with them in the choir. I like the fresh air and the big sky. And I like how a certain cute deputy sheriff will stop and dig my car out of the snow and pick me up when I break down by the side of the road, like he's my own personal Superman."

Jack grinned. "This guy you're talking about seems pretty great. Should I be jealous?"

Hannah thwacked him lightly on his non-injured shoulder. "Very funny, Jack."

He was serious again. "Are you sure, Hannah? What's going to happen to your video channel? You've said many times that there was nothing to videotape here in Fraser's Mill."

"I have an idea for that," Hannah said. "I always wanted my video channel to raise awareness for a good cause. And I've found one. What you guys have in Fraser's Mill — what we have in Fraser's Mill — is special. I used to think nothing important could happen in a tiny little town, and I was so wrong."

Jack took her hand, lacing his fingers through hers. "I'm glad we made a good impression on you."

"Mm-hmm." Hannah smiled up at him. "I want more people to know about the way of life you have out here in the rural Midwest. The friendly community. The hard work. It's so wholesome, and I think it's disappearing, and that's a shame.

I think I'll do a series shadowing different people and their occupations. You think maybe some of your family would be interested in showing the Internet what farm life is like?"

"They'd love it," Jack said. "Especially my cousins. Those guys are all single. They'll jump at the chance to have the young ladies online see videos of them lifting hay bales and driving farm equipment."

Hannah laughed. "All right. And maybe if it wouldn't bother the sheriff's department too much, I could do some videos shadowing a sheriff's deputy in his work around town?"

"I think the sheriff will be all right with that," Jack said. "And I know one deputy who'd be happy to show you around."

"Thank you, Jack." Hannah smiled at him.

"Anytime, Hannah." Jack smiled back.

A new song was playing in the hall, and Jack held out his hand. "May I have this dance?"

She took his hand. "Absolutely."

The night was still young, and as they danced, the Christmas lights around them shone like stars.

If you enjoyed this story, please leave a review on Amazon and Goodreads!

Coming Soon...
Maria and the Montana Rider
Releasing 2026

Acknowledgements

In the nearly three years since I began writing this book, so many incredible people have helped and encouraged me along the way. To all of these people, thank you!

A huge thank you to my parents, who first modeled storytelling for me and who have been a constant support; to Cili, for being so enthusiastic about Hannah and Jack; and to Michael and Peter, for their encouragement.

Thank you to my editor, Amber, for helping and cheerleading me through the whole story revision process (and especially for helping straighten out the multi-chapter mess of moving the Serena plotline). You're the best!

Thanks to Alt19 Creative for the beautiful book cover—you've outdone yourselves again!

A big thank you to Danny, for filling me in on the care and keeping of beef cattle; to Cynthia, who unknowingly saved Draft 4 from being deleted when my computer crashed; to my ARC readers and cover reveal team; and to Rachel, Olivia, Madelyn, and the clean book community on Instagram.

And another big thank you to Grandma, Uncle Rich, and all the cousins, relatives, and friends who have been so kind and enthusiastic about this project. Many thanks, especially, to the kind people of St. Mary's, whose warm little community is my real-life Fraser's Mill.

Above all, thanks be to God Who makes every good thing possible. To Him be all glory, now and forever!

About the Author

Ursi Engebretsen has always loved a good love story with a happy ending. So she decided to write her own—cozy clean romances with sparks flying, strong family themes, and picturesque settings, with the light and joy of the Gospel shining through. Although her characters have their struggles and problems, she wants her readers to walk away happy and uplifted at the end of every book.

Ursi grew up in Michigan and received her BA in liberal arts from Thomas Aquinas College in California. She's a Catholic Christian, a writer, a musician, a voracious reader, and a country girl at heart. Her day job is directing music and playing the pipe organ at her church. She likes bubble tea, a good sunrise, and using too many exclamation points. (She's working on that last one.)

https://ursiengebretsen.com
https://www.instagram.com/ursiengebretsenauthor